The Magic Redeemer

Books by Clayton Taylor Wood:

The Runic Series

Runic Awakening

Runic Revelation

Runic Vengeance

Runic Revolt

The Fate of Legends Series

Hunter of Legends

Seeker of Legends

Destroyer of Legends

Avenger of Legends

Magic of Havenwood Series

The Magic Collector

The Lost Gemini

The Magic Redeemer

The Magic of Magic Series

Inappropriate Magic

Ridiculously Inappropriate Magic

The Magic Redeemer

Book III in the Magic of Havenwood Series

Clayton Taylor Wood

This is a work of fiction. Names, characters, businesses, places, events and incidents are either the products of the author's imagination or used in a fictitious manner. Any resemblance to actual persons, living or dead, or actual events is purely coincidental.

Published by Clayton T. Wood.

ISBN: 978-1-948497-08-4

Cover designed by James T. Egan, Bookfly Design, LLC

Printed in the United States of America.

Special thanks to my brothers for their invaluable advice…and to my wife for inspiring so much of this book. And to my daughter Bella, for whom this series was written.

Table of Contents

The Magic Redeemer

Prologue

For Craven, Torpor was the little death, its end a kind of rebirth.

He could not quite see while in its clutches. Nor could he quite hear, or feel, or smell. There was only a vague sense of things, as when waking slowly from a dream. An eternity could seem like a second while in its numb embrace…and a second could seem like an eternity.

For some, Torpor *was* death, or rather the last thing Craven's kind experienced before it. But for him, there would be no death.

For him, death was impossible.

As his awareness rested in the inky black waters of his self-imposed sleep, Craven felt a *tugging* on his psyche. A soundless voice beckoning him.

A woman's voice.

Craven obeyed, emerging from Torpor like a man rising from the depths of a lake, breaking through the surface of his subconsciousness. He came alive, first in his head, bright light accosting his eyes, then in a spreading wave down his neck and shoulders, his chest, his belly, and finally his legs.

He found himself reborn in the usual place. Standing on a great gold and crimson pedestal in the Locus Legis, the great chamber that served as his home in the heart of the Palatium, the palace of Queen Eldora. And as usual, he was facing the great shimmering circular portal that led to the throne room of Queen Eldora herself, the first and only ruler of the Pentad.

His eyes were always drawn to the queen, even in Torpor.

For the queen was Craven's sole master, the great woman for whom he had been created. Carved out of a single block of indestructible Invictium, a metal so rare and powerful only a single statue had ever been sculpted from it. In his left hand, he carried Aganon, a legendary golden shield so powerful that it could – and had – defeated entire armies. His right hand was clad in Dextro, a magic gauntlet of formidable power.

And Craven himself was the right hand of the queen, bringing justice to the world by enforcing the great monarch's laws.

On his body he wore the red and gold plate armor called Invictus, and while it was not made of Invictium, it could withstand nearly any attack. Its inner surface was painted in places, making it impossible to trap Craven within a canvas while wearing it.

He was a juggernaut, Craven. The mighty champion of the Pentad, the Queen's protector for eternity…and bringer of justice to anyone who dared oppose her.

He felt the call of Queen Eldora again, not so much a word as a silent compulsion. Craven stepped down from his pedestal, his huge feet *thumping* on the stone floor below. Two pale guards holding white swords stood before the shimmering portal to the throne room, and Craven towered three-and-a-half feet over them, a giant among men. Without a word, they parted for him.

Craven *thumped* past them, striding through the portal to answer the call.

He found himself in a long cylindrical hallway, one with stairs climbing upward toward a large chamber ahead. The stairs were golden, the walls and ceiling blood-red…and everything but the stairs seemed to pulse faintly, the walls and ceiling rippling with subtle waves that traveled up the tunnel.

Craven began the long journey up those stairs, wondering as he often did if he was still within the palace in the capitol…or whether he'd been transported to another place in the world. Or even another plane of existence.

There were no windows here. No natural light. Only the magical light from the walls. For Queen Eldora did not suffer the light of the sun.

Onward Craven climbed, until at last he reached the great chamber of the queen. The Heart of the Pentad.

Which, quite literally, was shaped like a human heart.

It was perhaps the largest room in the palace, with a ceiling well over a hundred feet tall. The tip of the heart – the Apex Cor – was opposite Craven, and the location of the gold and ruby-red throne of the queen. And while a human heart had four chambers, this room had only one.

But the queen was not on her throne, as Craven had expected her to be. She was standing beside a small wooden stool at the far right of the chamber, gazing through a golden monocle up at a huge globe levitating above the floor there. A perfect replication of the world.

She was tall and slender, clad in a simple but elegant crimson robe. Two long red ribbons extended from the back of her robe behind her shoulders, spiraling tightly around her arms all the way to her wrists. Her skin was as pale as any he'd seen, her long red hair falling in perfectly straight strands to the backs of her knees. She wore nothing else. No adornments. No crown. No jewels of any kind.

Queen Eldora was complete in and of herself. Perfection could not be enhanced.

He hesitated, then stomped dutifully to her side, stopping there.

She gazed up at the globe, her crimson irises seeming to glow.

"What do you require?" Craven asked. The queen lowered her gaze – and her monocle – turning sidelong to look at him. He could not read her expression, but then again, he'd never been able to.

"The law requires you," she corrected.

"What does the law require?"

Queen Eldora returned her gaze to the globe, and Craven followed it. They were looking at a land mass south of a great ocean. She handed Craven the monocle, and he lifted it to his right eye. His vision zoomed in rapidly, the land mass expanding as if he were falling toward it at great speed.

Then it slowed, focusing on a mountain with a white castle atop it. At the foot of the mountain was a large lake, beyond which was a grassy plain leading to a mushroom forest that surrounded the base of the mountain and the lake. And beyond that, encircling the entire forest and mountain, was a massive white dragon.

Still the monocle zoomed in, to an area near the base of the mountain. A street spiraling up the mountain came into view, with buildings clustered to one side of it. The monocle focused on one building in particular…or rather a set of tables set outside of it.

Sitting at that table was a man and a woman…but the monocle focused on the man.

Somehow, through the monocle's magic, the view shifted, now as if facing the man from the side rather than from a bird's-eye-view. He was in his forties, it appeared. A man with chocolate-colored skin and short, curly dark hair. The man wore gold-rimmed glasses, and was smiling as he talked to the woman seated opposite him. Craven of course could not hear what they were saying, but that was beside the point. He recognized this man.

Thaddeus Birch, author of The Magic of Havenwood.

Craven lowered the monocle, handing it back to Queen Eldora.

"You wish me to apprehend him?" he asked. She said nothing at first, staring up at the globe. Then she sighed.

"Tragedy is a prolific lover, isn't it?" she mused.

Craven said nothing, knowing the question did not require his answer. His answers could never be sufficient. His actions, however, always were.

"Tragedy begets tragedy begets tragedy," she continued.

Still he waited, and she turned to face him.

"Do you ever feel remorse, Craven?"

"Only in failure," he answered. "So no."

"Mmm," she murmured. "You are as I had you made. The law feels nothing. It only executes its function."

"As you say."

"But what is law without temperance?" she inquired, putting a pale hand on his chest, over where his heart would be. If he'd had one.

"Temperance invites manipulation," Craven answered. "Abuse."

"And mercy, and context," she countered.

"You order, I obey," he replied, inclining his head.

"Yes," she agreed, withdrawing her hand. She turned back to the globe, lifting the monocle to her eye and peering through it. Nearly a minute passed, and Craven did not stir. He would wait for her for hours if she wished it. For an eternity. There was nothing else for him to attend to. No bodily function, no urge other than to serve her. This was how he'd been made. This was his life.

At long last, she lowered the monocle.

"Tragedy is a prolific lover," she repeated. "Do I follow the letter of the law and allow it to multiply? Or do I practice temperance and neuter it?"

Craven did not answer.

"Who wrote the laws, Craven?"

"You."

"And therein lies the problem," she mused. "For in authoring them and demanding that all be subject to them, I've become as much a prisoner to them as my subjects have."

"You are prisoner to no one," he countered. "You are queen."

"We are all prisoners to our past," Queen Eldora countered. "Our pasts author our futures, unless we have the courage to defy them."

"You do," Craven replied. She nodded.

"I do," she agreed. "The question is not could I, but *should* I."

"I cannot answer."

"I know," she replied with a smile. "I would merely have you know my mind."

"I cannot."

"Not entirely," she agreed. "But Queen Eldora cannot be seen as indecisive by her subjects."

"Am I not your subject?"

"No," she replied. "You are my right hand, Craven. And as a part of my body, you are me."

"As you say."

She stared at the globe for a long while, then sighed, lowering her gaze to the wooden stool beside her. A small golden ring had been set there, carved to resemble a tiny snake biting its tail. Craven recognized it immediately. For he himself had given it to her after he'd returned from Blackthorne. A gift from Gideon Myles.

Extinctio, the Painter's legendary weapon.

Queen Eldora picked it up, then slid it onto her right ring finger, staring at it for a long, silent moment.

Then she turned away from him, gliding across the floor to her throne. She sat upon it, resting her pale arms on its oversized armrests, and regarded him with cold eyes.

"Lucia Birch lives," she announced, her tone suddenly hard. "Gideon fathered a child with her. Thaddeus published a book illegally on the black market. Havenwood gives amnesty to hundreds of artists creating without licenses within the sovereign borders of the Pentad."

Craven stared back at her impassively, watching as she took a deep breath in.

"You are my right hand, Craven. Execute the law."

Craven inclined his head.

"It will be as you demand," he vowed.

"Leave me," she ordered.

He did so at once, turning about crisply, then stomping back toward the stairs leading down to the portal that would take him back to Locus Legis.

"And Craven?" he heard Queen Eldora add. He stopped, twisting around to look at her.

"Yes my queen."

"Gideon and Thaddeus and Lucia," she stated. "I want them alive."

"As you wish."

He turned about, continuing to the stairs. He took them three at a time, so tall was he. And he would not rest until he had carried out his task. For he was the law, an unstoppable juggernaut. Once set in motion, he could not be denied. There was no reasoning with him, no pleading. No way to bribe him or corrupt him. He was pure, absolute. Invincible. The right hand of the queen.

As Craven reached the mid-point of the long stairwell, he heard a faint sound echoing through the long tunnel. A sound he had heard countless times before, but never here.

A woman weeping.

Chapter 1

Bella Birch stood in the darkness of the Water Dragon tunnel, squinting at the light shining beyond the mouth of the cave. Water gushed in a steady stream to Bella's right, the sound reverberating off the rough stone walls of the tunnel. It was the Everstream, a continuous flow of water created in the heart of the magic Water Dragon tunnel. It somehow flowed *up* to the mouth of the cave, continuing beyond it to the cliffside beyond. Then it dropped thousands of feet to Lake Fenestra far below, at the base of a great mountain called Dragon's Peak.

It was the mountain upon which the great Castle Havenwood stood, a shining beacon of hope for artists all over the world. For while the world was unkind to artists, fearing and controlling their formidable magic, Havenwood welcomed them and set them free.

As it had set Bella free.

Three weeks had passed since the great kingdom had been attacked by the Gemini, an army of glittering soldiers whose bodies had been composed of mirrored facets. Since Miss Savage had been defeated and peace had once again been restored to Havenwood. And two weeks since Mom had been resurrected from the dead – a second time – and Bella's family had been made whole. During that time, Bella had spent roughly half of her time in Havenwood, and the other half in the Plane of Death, studying Necromancy with her mother in the Guild of Necromancers. Half of her time in the light, the other half in darkness.

And today, she planned on doing both at the same time.

Bella smiled at the bright sunlight ahead, brushing a few strands of curly dark hair from her face. Then she continued up to the mouth of the cave, stopping where darkness met the light. She looked down at that sharp divide, then knelt, tracing it with her fingertip.

"Where dark meets light," she murmured. Then she stood, taking a deep breath in. "Okay," she told herself. "I can do this."

"Do what?" a voice asked from her right hip. Bella glanced down, seeing a human skull hanging there. Or rather, levitating there. It was Cain the cane, her right-hand man…literally. Able to extend his spine from the base of his skull, he served as a formidable weapon…and a formidably chatty one at that.

"I'm going to cut myself in half," Bella answered.

"Oh," Cain replied, clearly taken aback. "I do hate it when you die," he added with as best a shudder as he could manage. "Makes me feel like I've failed you every time."

"I'm going to try to do it without dying this time."

"Ah, good," Cain replied. "But still, do be careful."

"Don't worry," she reassured him, patting the top of his head affectionately. "I'll be fine."

"Yes, well, I can protect you from others," Cain reminded her. "But not from yourself."

And then she focused inward.

Bella felt two forces within her, split by a magical dagger she'd painted about a month ago. The twin sides of her nature, the dark and the light. Luna was the darkness, the side of her that loved death and decay. And Lux was the light, thriving in sun and cheer.

Luna she'd inherited from her mother Lucia, a great Necromancer. And Lux from her father Gideon Myles, perhaps the greatest Painter alive. Her parents had come together to make Bella.

And now Bella was going to try to split herself apart.

Normally she had to die to separate Lux and Luna, a rather unpleasant way to do so. But Bella had become convinced she could do it without dying.

"You can do it," Cain declared with his customary confidence.

"Shh," Bella replied, and Cain's bony jaw snapped shut with a *click*.

She focused, trying to find Lux and Luna within her. She could almost feel them, and imagined herself peeling them apart from each other, like pieces of Velcro.

Nothing happened.

Bella grit her teeth, trying harder. She imagined ripping herself quite literally in two, visualizing Lux and Luna pulling apart from each other within her. Looking down at her hand, she could swear that she saw it outlined in bright light on one side, and inky black shadow on the other.

Come on…

Bella concentrated on making the opposing outlines wider, trying as hard as she could…but they stayed as they were.

With a grunt, she gave up, and the light and shadow snapped back into her hand, vanishing from sight.

"Well shoot," she swore.

That's not a swear, a voice in her head said.

She felt a presence above and behind her, and saw a dragon swooping through the air toward the mouth of the Water Dragon cave. A skeletal dragon with eye sockets that glowed deep red, wearing epic-looking black metal armor. It landed before Bella, magnificent in the morning sun, folding its wings on its back.

"Hey Nemesis," Bella greeted.

Hey yourself.

"Still no flesh?" she inquired. After all, Nemesis could breathe out a red light that sucked flesh out of living things, making herself into a fully fleshed-out dragon with black scales. But the flesh slowly left the Familiar, going back to those she'd stolen it from.

This way people don't expect me to talk to them, Nemesis replied. For without vocal cords, the only person the irritable dragon could speak to was Bella, through their psychic bond.

"Probably for the best," Bella said.

She focused inward again, trying to split herself a second time. Again she saw the shadow and the light outlining her hand…but that was about it. She glanced at Nemesis, who laid down on the rocky ground, curling her tail around her body and watching Bella.

"What're you doing?" Bella asked.

Watching you fail, Nemesis answered. *Very entertaining.*

Bella rolled her eyes, pointedly ignoring the dragon. Again and again she tried to separate Luna from Lux, and each time she got a little closer, the dark and light outlines growing a hair's width wider. But in the end, they remained stubbornly together.

What's the point?

"I want to see if I can do it," Bella answered.

Just kill yourself, Nemesis counseled. *I'll do it if you want.*

"Ha ha," Bella grumbled. Then she sighed. She really was getting nowhere, and she did want to experiment with Lux and Luna. She'd been struck with an idea last night while tossing and turning in her comfy bed, waiting for sleep to come. And now she was impatient to try it.

"Fine," she decided. "Kill me then."

Thought you'd never ask, Nemesis replied, standing up on all fours. She felt the dragon smirking, though of course without flesh, it was only a thought. The dragon grabbed Bella's throat with one clawed hand.

"Oh dear," Cain stated, rotating to bury his glowing green eye-sockets in Bella's hip. "I can't watch."

"Make it qui-" Bella began…and then Nemesis squeezed.

Hard.

Pressure built up in Bella's head, her eyes feeling like they were bulging out of their sockets. She resisted the urge to resist Nemesis, forcing herself to keep her arms at her sides. It wasn't the first time she'd been strangled to death, after all.

"You vile serpent!" Cain moaned.

Bella's vision darkened, the distraught cane's voice seeming far away. She felt oblivion reach for her, and only then did her instincts take over. Bella reached up for Nemesis's hand, trying to pry the bony fingers from her throat. She gasped for air, struggling in vain to breathe. To live. But Nemesis's grip was impossible to break. The world faded away, and the urge to fight death faded with it. Bella relaxed into her fate, giving herself to the inevitable.

Thus came death, an eternity in a moment…and a moment lasting an eternity. A state of utter surrender.

And in that surrender one became two.

They opened their eyes, these twins of Bella's soul, the dark and the light. Luna and Lux staring at each other across an impenetrable wall: where the darkness met the light. Luna stood in the shadows just before the light streaming into the Water Dragon cave, staring at Lux, who stood in the light.

She was a being of light, Lux. Standing in the sun as if a mirror-image of Luna. She looked like Bella, but as if light had been concentrated in Bella's form. And at the same time, Lux stared at Luna, seeing a being of concentrated shadow, darker than night itself. Each seemed a mere silhouette, features barely visible. For they were pure light and dark, and as such, there could be no shades of gray without combining once again.

They were Bella, Lux and Luna. But each missing each other, combining to reform her if they drew close enough to each other. The first time they'd been split, during the battle with Simon and Miss Savage, they'd shared a single consciousness, always aware of each other, as if sharing minds. And the closer they drew to each other, the more powerful the urge to recombine. Despite weeks of practice, every time they split, they combined again rapidly, unable to resist the pull of each other.

But this time they had a plan.

Luna tore herself from the edge of the light, throwing herself into the blackness of the rock wall to her left. But instead of striking it, she tried to *meld* with it, to become one with it. She was shadow, after all; the darkness should be her ally. And when she'd been a part of Bella, the girl had theorized that anything that threw a shadow could throw Luna.

But instead of melding with the shadow on the wall and being able to move within it, Luna *became* the shadow.

Suddenly she was huge, a massive creature of darkness that spiraled down into the earth, throughout the whole length of the Water Dragon tunnel and beyond. She could see anything within it, hear anything. And she knew without a shadow of a doubt that, with a thought, she could tear herself free from the rest of the darkness, appearing wherever she liked within it.

Luna did just that, and found herself rising from the floor of a narrow tunnel…the one at the very bottom of the Water Dragon tunnel, leading to the cavern containing her mother's mansion. A garden of glowing white and blue mushrooms near either side-wall of the cavern illuminated the way ahead in a gentle glow.

"Well I'll be," she murmured, breaking out into a grin. "It worked, sister."

This was the first time Luna had ever been so far from Lux. The urge to combine with her sister was weaker now than it'd been moments ago, a desire that still burned within her, but could be resisted…for the moment. She could still feel Lux far above, but at this distance something very curious happened; their shared consciousness seemed to split, their minds no longer one, but two.

And without the light, Luna was free to be herself.

Luna stood there, safe within the utter darkness of the narrow tunnel, staring at the mansion far ahead within the cavern beyond. A giddiness came over her, and she laughed, the sound echoing off the rock walls. It startled her, this sound…deeper than Bella's, but still feminine.

"Time to see what the darkness can do," she purred.

Luna stood, striding into the large chamber.

But as soon as she reached the soft glow of the bioluminescent mushrooms, it was like hitting a plush wall. She seemed to sink into it, her stride slowing, then stopping. Luna pressed against it, trying to push through the faint light, but it pushed back. Not a hard, immovable wall like the light above had been, but still impassable.

Luna felt a flash of irritation, taking a step back and crossing her arms over her chest. She grit her teeth, glaring at the glowing mushrooms that dared bar her way.

"Fine," she muttered. "Be that way."

She looked around, spotting a few rocks beside the tunnel wall. She picked the largest one up – about the size of her fist – and walked as far as she could into the cavern. Then she leaned over to place the rock on the cavern floor. It cast a slim shadow…not utterly dark, but dark enough. She slid her hand under it, beyond where she'd been able to go a moment before.

It worked.

Luna broke out into another smile, retrieving her hand and standing up straight again. She melded with the shadows once more, stepping out of the rock wall of the Water Dragon cave an instant later, at the mouth of the cave once more. Lux was still there, waiting for her like the good little girl she was.

"Good news, dearest sister," Luna said as she was inevitably drawn to her twin, their hands touching the invisible wall where darkness met light. "Death just got a *lot* more interesting."

* * *

Bella gasped, blinking in the sunlight streaming down from the blue sky far above. She realized she was standing where she'd been moments before, when Nemesis had killed her. She looked down at herself, seeing her familiar Painter's uniform, black leather with canvas sewn in on her chest, belly, arms, and legs.

"Whew," she blurted out, rubbing her neck gingerly. It wasn't even sore, of course. After she was killed, Lux healed in the light, and Luna in the darkness. When they'd healed her enough for Bella to live with her wounds, they could combine with each other to form Bella again…and she would have healed as much as they had.

"Is it over?" Cain asked hopefully, still at her side. For some strange reason, he vanished when she split into Lux and Luna, reappearing when they recombined.

"Yes," Bella reassured him, patting the top of his head. "I'm fine."

"Oh thank goodness," Cain replied.

How'd it go, Nemesis asked. For while the dragon was her Familiar, Nemesis couldn't really hear Lux or Luna's thoughts very well. Bella broke out into a smile.

"It worked," she answered. "But not like I thought. Luna *can* combine with shadows…but when she does, she *becomes* them. Like the whole shadow. And she can come out of any part of that shadow."

Ooo, Nemesis replied, clearly impressed. *That's…*

"Incredible," Bella agreed. The implications weren't lost on her, of course. If it were nighttime, Luna might technically be able to go anywhere she wanted in the darkness.

Darkness that covered about half of the world at a time.

Makes Lux look like a wimp, Nemesis noted. Bella grimaced, but she had to agree. As far as she knew – at least so far – Lux had the power to bounce off of reflective things like light could, and move rapidly afterward as a sort of beam of light until she stopped herself or struck something non-reflective. A paltry power compared to her twin's.

"I want to see if I can go to the Plane of Death as Luna while keeping Lux here," Bella said. If she could do that, she could train with Mom while spending time with Grandpa and Gideon at the same time. After all, she remembered everything Lux and Luna remembered. Doing two things at once would be very efficient.

"Later, please," Cain begged. "I can't bear to see you die twice in one day!"

"Okay," Bella agreed. Nemesis rolled her eyes psychically.

Spoilsport, she grumbled.

"Let's go back to the mansion," Bella prompted.

Nah, I'm out, Nemesis replied. And with that, the skeletal dragon took off, running to the edge of the cliff and jumping off. She soared through the air, eventually vanishing from sight. Bella could still sense her Familiar's location though. She usually could, unless they were in different planes of existence from each other…or if Nemesis shut her out.

And so Bella began the long trek back to her mother's mansion, deep within the bowels of Dragon's Peak. It took her considerably longer than it'd taken Luna, of course. Bella could remember everything her two halves did, which was quite odd. For when Luna had been separated from Lux, their consciousness had diverged, and they'd truly become two different minds. But to Bella, her memories of their experience happened at the same time.

It was all a bit confusing.

"I really don't think that winged serpent has your best interests at heart," Cain warned, seeming quite vexed by the idea. "I swear it seems to actually enjoy harming you."

"That's Nemesis," Bella replied.

"Well it isn't right," Cain insisted. Bella smiled.

"Love you too Cain," she told the disembodied head, rubbing his bony dome affectionately. This mollified him, and they made the rest of the trip in silence. Eventually they reached their destination: a large mansion in an even larger cavern deep within the earth. Blue and white bioluminescent mushrooms lined the walls on either side, just as Luna had seen earlier. Bella walked through the front gate of the black wrought iron fence surrounding the property, continuing to the closed portcullis that marked the entrance to the estate. A swirling mist greeted her there, on the other side of the portcullis. It was Mom's Familiar.

"Hey Animus," Bella greeted. "Is Mom back yet?"

The portcullis opened, and Animus swirled about excitedly, flowing into the foyer beyond. Which meant that Mom probably *was* back…from the Plane of Death. A powerful Necromancer, Mom could travel from the living world to the Plane of Death at will, through the magic coffin on the second floor of the mansion. As could Bella…on a probationary basis.

For Mom was training Bella to become a Necromancer like her, a member of the Dark Circle.

Bella followed Animus into the grand foyer, watching as the mist went leftward toward a long hallway beyond. Bella followed, smiling and waving at the half-decayed boar standing guard in the middle of it. His name was Terrible, or more accurately, Terrible Boar. Mom admitted that it'd been Bella herself – at the tender age of five – that had named him. After fighting the Gemini – the mirrored soldiers that had cast Terrible into the Plane of Reflection – Gideon had been forced to retrieve the poor thing.

"Hey Terrible," Bella greeted, patting the boar as she walked past. The soft, furry, not-decayed part of the boar, anyway. Terrible sniffed the air, then turned to lick her hand. She blew him a kiss, then continued past him, following Animus.

There was a set of narrow stairs leading up at the other end of the hallway…stairs that would lead her to a small room with her mother's magic coffin. Animus went right up them, and Bella followed the Familiar up those stairs into the room beyond.

Bella found herself in a small room, a closed black coffin in the center of it the only furniture within. A painting hung on each wall, and a lighting fixture on the ceiling, casting a pale light on the coffin below. Animus swirled around the base of the coffin, waiting for her.

"Oh, she's not back then," Bella realized. She paused, eyeing Animus. "She's waiting for me?"

Animus swirled eagerly around the coffin.

Bella undid the metal latches on the side of the coffin, then pulled the lid of the coffin open.

And saw a woman lying in it.

"Oh!" Bella blurted out, taking a step back. It was a rather beautiful woman with dark brown skin, her curly dark brown hair not even an inch long. She was dressed from neck to toe in a form-fitting black leather uniform, with silver skulls and spikes adorning it. And at her hips were twin silver daggers, instruments of death.

Animus surged into the coffin, flowing into the woman's mouth and nostrils, until no more mist could be seen. The woman got out of the coffin, smiling at Bella.

"Hey pumpkin," she greeted.

"Hey Mom," Bella replied. Her eyes went to Mom's daggers…and what appeared to be fresh blood coating the blades. "Uh…what've you been up to?"

"Murder of course," Mom answered with a smirk. "What else?"

Chapter 2

It was a rare treat for Mom to venture out of the Plane of Death, and even rarer for her to leave the dark confines of her mansion to travel to the surface. But Grandpa had insisted on a family luncheon at The Painted Feast, his favorite restaurant. Not just for some family time, but because he'd finally decided to introduce everyone to the woman he'd been spending an inordinate amount of time with over the last few weeks. A Sculptor named Kanja.

"It's about time you introduced us," Gideon told Grandpa as they all made the journey down the spiraling cobblestone street leading to Downtown, near the base of the mountain. The sun shone in full force overhead, and its rays felt marvelous on Bella's skin. She walked beside Mom and Gideon, with Grandpa taking the lead. Myko trotted beside Gideon as usual, the giant silver wolf taller than his master. Nemesis, in contrast, was nowhere to be seen.

"I wanted to be sure it wasn't merely a dalliance," Grandpa explained. Mom nudged Bella.

"Dalliance," Mom repeated, waggling her eyebrows suggestively. Bella made a face.

"Ew Grandpa," she complained. "I really don't want to know."

"No no," Grandpa replied rather quickly. "I assure you our relationship has been platonic so far."

"So far," Mom repeated, nudging Bella again, this time with a wicked grin. She turned forward then. "It's about time," she added. "I've been telling you to find someone for forever."

"Ever since you found Gideon," Grandpa corrected. "Yes. I suppose I was still wrapped up in my guilt about what happened to your mother."

Mom's mother – Grandpa's wife – had been murdered by an assassin from a rival country decades ago, when Mom had been just a girl. In a botched attempt to kill Grandpa…a fact that Grandpa had never been able to forgive himself for.

"It wasn't your fault Dad," Lucia told him.

"Yes, well, you didn't always feel that way," he reminded her gently. She grimaced.

"I was a dumb kid," Lucia admitted. "I was angry, and you were the closest target."

"I know," Grandpa replied, giving her a reassuring smile. He linked arms with her, and they walked side-by-side down the spiraling street.

"I'm still sorry," she pressed.

"I don't want you to be," he replied. "All I want is for you to be happy. And safe." He gazed out over the side of the mountain, at the landscape spread out before them. "That's why I created this place."

"You made it out of guilt," Lucia retorted. Grandpa smiled ruefully.

"That too," he confessed.

They walked in silence for a while, until Grandpa stirred.

"So you're not upset that I've started seeing someone?" he asked her. Lucia gave him a look.

"Hell no," she answered. "You gave Mom what, almost forty years?" He nodded. "I want you to be happy too," she continued. "If this chick does that for you, I'm okay with it."

"Chick?"

"Just don't expect me to call her 'Mom' if you guys get all serious," Lucia grumbled. "I'm older than she is. Which is creepy, by the way."

"Creepy?"

"You're what, thirty times her age?" Lucia asked.

"To be fair, finding someone my own age would be quite difficult," he pointed out. He was, after all, nearly a thousand years old.

Gideon chuckled at that, and Lucia grinned.

"You used to use that as an excuse to not move on," she reminded him.

"Guilty as charged," he agreed. "I was still mourning."

"You mean you were afraid," Mom translated.

"Terrified," Grandpa confessed. "Still am."

"I know how you feel," Gideon admitted. Mom shot him a glance.

"You mean when you went on your dates with that woman?" she inquired. Gideon grimaced.

"Ah, well," he stammered. "They weren't precisely dates…" he began. Then he grimaced again. "I suppose the second one was."

Bella smiled. While she'd been undergoing her trial with Mom to see if she had what it took to be a Necromancer, Gideon had been left all alone in his hotel suite in the Twin Spires. Bella didn't know much in the way of details, but apparently her father had met a nice woman in the city, and had gone on a couple of dates with her. Gideon insisted that nothing had happened between them, which was just as well. For while Gideon had assumed Mom was dead – and that he was single and available – she'd come back to life.

"You still haven't told me her name," Mom noted, leaning in so her and Gideon's shoulders were touching. She gave him a cute smile.

"There's still blood on your daggers," he noted.

"Its owner was very naughty."

"I don't want *her* blood on them," he pressed.

"I wouldn't kill her," Mom insisted. "I just want to…see what your taste in women is."

"Uh huh."

"Can't a girl be curious?"

"If she's not a cold-blooded assassin, yes," he replied.

"Aww."

Bella listened to them banter, a smile on her lips. She felt a great sense of peace, knowing their family was whole once again. A few months ago, never in her wildest dreams would she have imagined that she'd be here, walking with her mother and father and Grandpa in a magical land. Yet here they were.

Life, it turned out, had turned out just fine.

They reached Downtown at last, which was bustling with activity. Artists of all kinds – Writers, Painters, Sculptors, Actors, and Musicians – milled about, going in and out of various studios, shops, and restaurants. As usual, The Painted Feast was the busiest of them all. For the chef was quite literally an artist, and had dedicated his life to painting delicious meals. Every order was painted on the spot, then drawn out to be served as fresh as fresh could be.

In fact, the restaurant was so busy that they wouldn't have gotten a table…if Grandpa hadn't been among them. For he was perhaps the most beloved Writer alive, and just so happened to be the one who created Havenwood. As such, he enjoyed the perks of his celebrity…while trying to avoid all the requisite suffering.

Grandpa led them to one of the large circular tables in front of the restaurant, one that looked over the edge of the mountain to provide a spectacular view of the scenery below. A woman was already seated at the table, and stood when they arrived. She looked to be as old as Mom, perhaps in her early to mid-thirties, and wore a plain but pretty white dress. This contrasted with her skin, which was darker than even Grandpa's…so black that it was almost blue. She had short black hair, almost as short as Mom's, but with much tighter curls. And a rather lovely smile.

"Hello everyone," she greeted as they reached the table. She leaned in, kissing Grandpa on the cheek. This earned a rather sheepish smile, and they both sat down next to each other. Everyone else followed suit, except of course for Myko, who settled for curling on the floor next to Gideon. In optimal scraps-catching position, Bella observed.

"Everyone, this is Kanja," Grandpa introduced. "She's a Sculptor, originally from Epirus."

"But don't hold it against me," Kanja added with a smile. Everyone chuckled, except for Bella, who took a moment to get the joke. Then she remembered that the Pentad had recently won a war with Epirus, just before she'd escaped the Chronicles of Collins Dansworth with Grandpa.

"Really?" Mom inquired, arching an eyebrow. "You're dating a woman from the country that assassinated Mom?"

"Ah…" Grandpa replied sheepishly, glancing at Kanja.

"Yes he is," Kanja confirmed, wrapping an arm around his shoulder. Mom shrugged.

"Just checking."

"I also worked for the Collector," Kanja confessed. Both of Mom's eyebrows went up.

"The man who murdered me," she pointed out. "And made me miss my daughter's entire childhood."

Grandpa grimaced, lowering his gaze to the tabletop.

"Not quite the first impression I was hoping for," Kanja admitted. Mom smirked.

"Oh no, this is *perfect*," she countered. Kanja gave her a questioning look. "We're a screwed-up family," Mom added. "You'll fit right in."

"We're all criminals," Bella piped in. "Technically speaking."

"I'm an assassin," Mom offered. "Wanted by the Pentad. Probably be executed if they caught me."

"I'm guilty of helping her escape the Pentad," Gideon confessed. "And illegally teaching my daughter to paint."

"I've painted without a license," Bella stated. "They'd cut off my hands or execute me if *I* was caught."

Kanja gave a rueful smile.

"Well then," she declared. "I suppose I do fit in."

"Right then," Grandpa interjected, rubbing his hands together. "Who's hungry?

* * *

Introductions having been made, everyone ordered their meals, and in a testament to the chef's incredible speed and skill, no one had to wait long to enjoy them. By the time everyone finished eating – including Myko, who'd gotten an entire roasted pig for himself – they leaned back in their chairs, enjoying the pleasure of conversation. And when it came to conversation, Bella could see why Grandpa had taken to Kanja. For she was simply lovely to talk to…and a good listener.

At length, Mom and Dad left to get some ice cream, and Grandpa had decided to go with them. That left Bella alone with Kanja.

"I've never really talked with a Sculptor before," Bella admitted to her. "I wish I knew more about it."

"What would you like to know?" Kanja inquired.

"Everything," Bella replied. Kanja laughed.

"That'll take a while."

"Okay, well, the Flow loves stories, right? And I get how to tell a story with paint, or music, or even acting. But how do you do it with sculpture?"

"Sculpture is a little different," Kanja admitted. "The other arts start with nothing and you build a story from scratch. But with sculpture – at least the way *I* do it – I imagine that I'm *uncovering* a story."

Bella frowned.

"How?"

"Well, say I start with a block of stone," Kanja began. "I'll look at it, and all of a sudden I'll imagine that there's something trapped inside. Maybe a person, or an animal, or something else. I'll come up with a story of who or what it is, how it got there. And as I'm chipping away, more and more details will emerge. How it looks. The way it's positioned. What it was caught in the middle of doing. That kind of thing."

"So that's how the Flow works for you?" Bella asked.

"That's right," Kanja agreed. "In the process of revealing, we have revelation."

"Huh," Bella murmured. "That's really interesting."

"I think so," Kanja replied with a smile.

"But when does it come alive?" Bella pressed.

"Usually during the process," Kanja answered. "Would you like to watch me sculpt sometime? It'll be easier to show you than to tell you."

"I'd love that," Bella admitted.

Grandpa, Gideon, and Lucia returned from inside the restaurant with ice creams in hand, sitting back down at the table. Gideon dropped a scoop's worth on the floor near Myko, who ate it up in one gulp.

"What'd I miss?" Grandpa inquired, eyeing Bella and Kanja with mock suspicion.

Then the table quivered, silverware and cups rattling on its surface.

"What in the…" Grandpa began.

The ground itself seemed to rumble, the table shaking again. A deep *boom* echoed through the air, followed by a powerful wind that whipped through Bella's hair.

Gideon stood bolt-upright from his chair, gazing off the side of the mountain. Bella stood as well, following his gaze. Past the rippling waters of Lake Fenestra and over the giant mushroom forest, to what lay beyond: the massive head of the White Dragon.

Its eyes were open, its head rising from the earth to gaze down at something. What that was, Bella couldn't see. But the White Dragon only awoke in times of danger…and the last two times it had, Havenwood had been nearly destroyed.

"Thaddeus, take Kanja and initiate the evacuation protocol," Gideon ordered. "Every artist without a military background goes to the castle vault."

Grandpa grabbed Kanja's hand, rushing away without a word.

Nemesis, Bella prompted. *Make sure Grandpa's safe!*

On my way, Nemesis replied.

She reached for the right thigh-holster of her Painter's uniform, pulling out a rolled-up canvas.

"Apertus," she incanted…and the painting unrolled itself. She shoved her hand into the canvas, feeling a warm pulsing as she did so. Her hand met soft blubber, and she drew it out. A huge mass of green goo spilled out of the painting, nearly as large as the restaurant itself.

"Trouble's coming Goo," she warned. Goo's surface rippled, and he flowed to form a "U" around her.

"Let's go," Gideon prompted. And with that, he mounted Myko, who burst forward as a ray of pure silver light, moon-dashing right off the edge of the mountain. They soared over Lake Fenestra, moon-dashing a few more times before clearing the lake and landing on the shore beyond. Myko galloped across the clearing toward the mushroom forest.

"And now my ice cream is going to melt," Mom grumbled. "Someone *definitely* has to die."

She ran across the street to the edge of the mountain, leaping off as Gideon had…and turning immediately into a cloud of mist, through Animus's unique power. She zoomed over the Lake after Gideon, and Bella turned to Goo.

"Let's do this," she said.

"To battle!" Cain cried zestily.

Reaching into her chest-painting, Bella retrieved a skull-shaped mask, putting it on. She felt a chill run through her as she transitioned into a spirit form, all sound ceasing. For while in this form, she could not hear…a defense against Miss Savage's terrible songs. Bella willed herself forward, flying through the air after her mother and father. Below, Goo flowed quickly over the cliff, falling to a *plop* below and moving across the shore of the lake.

Grandpa's safe, Nemesis announced. *Coming to you.*

Bella caught up with her parents at the edge of the mushroom forest, passing through the huge mushroom stalks with ease. For in her ghostly form, she could pass through anything…except another spirit. As they neared the White Dragon, however, they saw it lowering its enormous head down to rest on the ground once again. Dust shot upward with the impact, a blast of wind striking Mom and Gideon. In her mist form, Mom was blown backward, but Bella of course felt nothing at all.

She landed on the narrow path through the forest ahead of them, taking her mask off and putting her hand on Cain the cane.

"Unleash me!" he cried.

"Hold on," Bella told him. For there, walking past the White Dragon's massive snout, was a lone figure. A man, she realized...and a familiar one at that. He was quite tall and slender, his skin as black as night, and had no hair at all. Not even eyebrows or eyelashes. He wore a Painter's uniform accented by a red and gold cape, the colors of the Pentad. And floating at his side was a huge sword over six feet long, with a blade as black as night and a gleaming golden hilt and crossguard.

The man walked right up to Bella, his sword following beside him. She felt a chill in the air suddenly, and knew it was from the sword, not the man.

"We meet again," the man stated in a deep, powerful voice. He inclined his head at Bella, then shifted his gaze to Gideon and Lucia, who stopped at Bella's side. Gideon dismounted Myko, pulling his cane from his chest-painting and leaning on it.

"Yero," Gideon greeted coolly.

"Gideon," Yero replied.

"It seems you've upset the White Dragon," Gideon noted. "I take it you didn't come to catch up with an old friend?"

"No," Yero confirmed.

"Business then," Gideon concluded. Yero nodded.

"Business."

"What does the Pentad want?" Gideon inquired.

"Confirmation," Yero replied, shifting his gaze to Bella, then to Lucia. And then Nemesis, who swooped up to them, landing at Bella's side. His eyes returned to Gideon. "And now they have it."

"Confirmation of what?" Gideon pressed.

"Treason," Yero answered.

Gideon raised an eyebrow.

"Oh really."

"Is this not Lucia Birch?" Yero inquired, gesturing at Mom.

Gideon said nothing.

"I believed in you, Gideon," Yero confessed. "You who vowed to me that you did not aid this criminal in evading the Pentad's justice. I believed in you when you promised to come home after ensuring the safety of the girl," he added, gesturing at Bella.

"Yero..." Gideon began.

"I *believed* in you as a man of honor. Integrity. Honesty."

"Yero, I can..."

"I was wrong," Yero concluded sharply, crossing his arms over his chest.

Yero's sword – Temper, Bella recalled – seemed to pulse, the air growing even cooler around it.

"How?" Gideon asked. "How did you know Lucia was alive?"

"The Pentad appreciated your apprehending the woman who called herself 'Miss Savage,'" Yero replied. "She, however, was not so appreciative.

While we took away the use of her mouth, she was eager to write a great deal about you."

Gideon grimaced.

"I see."

"You have evaded the warrant for your arrest for twenty years," Yero proclaimed. "The evidence against you was circumstantial. Now it is not."

Gideon lowered his gaze for a moment, his jawline rippling. Then he raised it, staring at Yero with an intensity Bella had never seen before.

"If I were you, I would be *extremely* careful in how you proceed," he warned, his voice deadly calm. "I still think of you as a friend, even if you do not. But I will protect my family."

"Will you?" Yero inquired.

"I will," Gideon answered. "As will Thaddeus Birch. Do you care to test the most powerful Writer in the world?"

"A Writer is not powerful if he is not published," Yero retorted.

"Hi," Lucia interrupted, walking right up to Yero and putting her hands on the hilts of her daggers. Temper flew between them, poised to strike. Lucia ignored it. "Walk away or die, Zero."

"That's Yero," Yero corrected. Lucia smirked.

"Not for long."

The White Dragon's eyes opened, a blast of air shooting out of its nostrils. A low rumble came from deep within its throat. Yero stood there, staring down at Lucia impassively.

"Your dragon does not approve," he noted. "I have not attacked you. Attack me and it will deal with you accordingly."

"He's right," Gideon warned. Lucia grimaced, taking a step back…and the White Dragon closed its eyes once again.

"You threaten murder of a ranking military officer of the Pentad," Yero noted. "Another crime to add to your extensive list."

"Wouldn't be the first 'officer of the Pentad' I've murdered," Lucia shot back.

"Your confession is appreciated," Yero replied evenly.

"Lucia…" Gideon began, but Lucia held up one hand.

"We both know they have enough on me to execute me thirty times over," she interrupted. "Your little threats don't scare me, errand boy."

"My threats should not," Yero agreed. "Queen Eldora's should."

Lucia just stared at him, as did Gideon. Yero gave them a tight smile.

"I see I have your attention."

"Just get it over with," Gideon snapped.

"Queen Eldora demands your surrender," Yero proclaimed. "And that of what appears to be your wife. And daughter. And Thaddeus Birch."

"I'm afraid she'll have to live with disappointment," Gideon replied.

"It has come to Queen Eldora's attention that there have been two attacks on Havenwood of late," Yero stated. "And that on both occasions, your dragon was barely up to the task of defending it."

Gideon just stared at him.

"A boy Painter was able to challenge the White Dragon and nearly succeed," Yero continued. "Imagine what the full might of Craven's armies might accomplish if so ordered?"

The blood drained from Gideon's face, and even Mom looked uncharacteristically subdued. A chill ran down Bella's spine…and this time, it wasn't from Temper's aura.

"You're threatening to attack Havenwood if my family and I don't volunteer to come to our executions?" Gideon asked.

"I offer a peaceful path," Yero replied, then gestured at Temper. "And its alternative."

"You wouldn't," Gideon pressed.

"Correct," Yero agreed. "Queen Eldora would."

"You're bluffing," Lucia stated. Yero turned to her.

"Unlike you, I do not live a life that requires deception."

They all stood there, no one saying anything.

"I will have your answer," Yero declared. "If you say nothing, that too is an answer."

Gideon glanced at Lucia, who shook her head ever-so-slightly. He glanced at Bella, then returned his gaze to Yero.

"Please tell Queen Eldora that I politely decline her request," he stated.

Yero stood there for a long, silent moment. Then he inclined his head.

"You have made your decision," he stated. "And you have decided for every citizen of Havenwood. They have all composed art without a license, and will be brought to justice accordingly."

And with that, Yero turned away from them, and left. Gideon watched him go, then sighed, putting his cane back in his left forearm-painting.

"We," he proclaimed grimly, "…are in deep trouble."

Chapter 3

For Simon, the dream came as it always did. Every night the same.

A tall, gorgeous woman in a form-fitting silver dress stood at the edge of a tall cliff, staring down at a town far below. Men, women, and children walked the streets, talking, laughing. Going about their lives as they usually did, enjoying the sunlight streaming from the flawless blue sky.

And Simon stood beside her.

The woman began to sing, her voice screeching like a banshee, howling like a terrible wind. And the sky turned dark, angry clouds rushing in to block out the sun. Rain fell from the heavens, bolts of lightning smashing down on the rooftops of the village, leaving purple afterimages in Simon's vision.

No!

The woman grabbed his arm, leaping from the cliff…and flying them down to the village far below. They landed in the town square, villagers all around them. Guards rushed at them, swords glinting as lightning arced in the sky behind them.

Don't!

But Simon could not stop this. He could not move. He was frozen, standing there beside the woman. She stopped singing, turning to him. Her eyes glowed bright red, blood dripping from her sockets.

"You're weak, Simon," she sneered.

She shoved him forward in front of her, and the first of the guards reached Simon, raising their sword to slash at his throat. The blade struck Simon's neck…and the guard's head separated from his shoulders in a spray of blood.

Stop!

Simon stood there as the next guard reached him, slashing at his shoulder. The guard's arm lopped itself off, and the man screamed, falling to the ground.

Please stop!

Guard after guard attacked him, and every cut, thrust, and slice was reflected upon them. Simon could only watch, frozen in place, as they each committed suicide on him. Dozens of them.

Hundreds of them.

The woman in the silver dress stared at Simon with those burning red eyes.

"The women too, Simon. And don't forget the children."

She began to sing again, and the women and children turned to face Simon, their eyes glassy, their expressions like stone. One-by-one they grabbed a fallen guard's weapon, walking up to Simon and attacking him with it.

And one-by-one they fell, their blood flowing on the cobblestones below.

"Don't be weak, Simon," the woman whispered in his ear, her hot hand on his shoulder. Caressing him. "Kill them all."

She continued her song, and more villagers stepped up to him. A pretty little girl. A young woman. A toddler. They all lined up, attacked him, and died.

Then a boy approached, kneeling down to pick up a sword. He was tall and lanky, with short blond hair and pale skin. He had kind brown eyes, his skin perfect. Unmarred by scars of any kind. It was like looking into a mirror. Into his past.

It was *him.*

Simon felt his blood run cold.

Don't do it, he urged silently. *Just walk away.*

The boy strode up to Simon, eyes glassy. Following the woman's song. Following orders.

Walk away!

But the boy didn't walk away. He lifted the sword, planting his feet and winding up to strike.

Walk…!

And then the boy swung, and Simon felt a sudden burst of pain in his own neck. He felt his head separate from his shoulders, and then he was falling, falling…

Into blackness.

* * *

Simon gasped, bolting upright in bed.

He reached for his neck instinctively…and felt nothing but smooth skin there. Looking around, he found himself in a small, single-room log cabin, lying on blankets strewn across the floor. Sunlight streamed through small windows, lighting on an easel standing in one corner of the room. A blank canvas sat upon it, seeming to glow pure white in the light of the sun.

Simon took deep breaths in and out, waiting for his heart to stop hammering in his chest.

Just a dream, he told himself.

Eventually his heart did slow, and he stood up, stretching his arms up above his head. Then he got dressed, pulling on a simple gray shirt and pants. No socks, no shoes. He straightened his makeshift bed, then went to the door, opening it and stepping outside. A circular grassy clearing greeted him, perhaps two acres or so in area. And beyond that, a dark forest in all directions. The sun blazed in a cheerful blue sky, not a cloud to be seen.

He took a deep breath in, feeling the warmth of the sun's rays on his skin…and the last of the echoes from his nightmare seeping away. As if the light were banishing the darkness within him.

Simon turned, walking around the perimeter of the cabin until he spotted a tall mirror set against the wall. He stepped up to it, looking at himself for a moment. Blond hair, growing longer than he'd had it in years. Brown eyes, the dark circles that had been under them mostly gone now. His face had filled out a bit, as had the rest of him, but he was still a bit too thin. And his gray shirt and pants were stained with a rainbow of colored paints.

He forced himself to relax his shoulders, then stepped into the mirror…and went right through it.

Beyond, he found himself stepping *out* of a mirror…and emerging into a mirror-image of the world he'd been in. For the cabin he'd slept in was in the Plane of Reflection, and *this* cabin was in the original world.

A lush garden greeted him, a firepit with two chairs placed before it. And sitting in one of those chairs was a bald, middle-aged man with a long, luxurious red beard, wearing a gray shirt and pants, his pot-belly held up by a struggling brown belt.

"Ah, good morning Simon," the man greeted, gesturing at a cup of steaming tea sitting on the armrest of the chair beside him. Simon walked up to the chair, sitting down.

"Morning Percy," he replied with a smile of his own. Percy eyed Simon, taking a sip of his own cup of tea.

"Same dream?" he inquired. Simon nodded.

"Same."

Percy sipped his tea, then set it down, gazing across the firepit to the tree line ahead. The Festering Wood, a dark forest of twisted trees growing out of a thick mat of rotted fruit. It was an apt a name as any. It extended for miles in every direction, and traveling through it was so detestable that few ever attempted the journey. But for those who had the courage to brave its challenges – and the luck to find Percy's cabin deep within – the reward was well worth the suffering.

And, nearly a month after abandoning Miss Savage – and his quest for revenge – Simon was infinitely glad he'd made that journey.

For while the man sitting next to him preferred to be called Percy, his real name was Persnickity Gibbons. A man so ancient that few remembered his name. Creator of the Underground, and of the Castle Under. Of the magical land of Anywhere, and of Memory Lane…and so many other wondrous and amazing places and things.

"From your dreams to the canvas," Percy mused. "Things that were, things that are, and things that might be."

Simon said nothing, knowing that with Percy, he could do so. Percy smiled at him.

"There's no hope for the past, Simon," he lectured. "Only for the future."

"I know," Simon replied, warming his hands on his cup of tea. He sipped, tasting sweetness with a slight bitter aftertaste. Intentional, of course. Everything with Percy seemed to be.

"Introspection, then expression," Percy recited. He stood then. "Shall we?"

Simon nodded, and they both stood, stepping through the mirror into Simon's cabin in the Plane of Reflection. Percy gestured at the fresh canvas on the easel there, then made a gesture as if pulling a chair to sit on it. And lo and behold, a stool appeared beneath him out of thin air…and he did sit on it.

Percy had performed this trick many times in front of Simon, though how Percy did it was beyond him. He'd come to expect the unexpected around the man…and every day, Percy showed him something new.

"Don't mind me," Percy told him.

Simon sighed, still not used to having someone watch him while he painted. It made the Flow much harder to feel…but Percy wanted to see *how* Simon painted, not just *what* he painted.

And so he mixed his colors, and got to work.

He started with the sky, a vast field of gray. Then he painted dark underbellies of thunderclouds. He used a painting knife to make jagged bolts of lightning that lit the clouds from below, then…

"Are we looking down on something?" Percy inquired. Simon stopped with a grimace.

"Yes."

"Then make sure the horizon is higher," he advised. "The horizon should be at five-eighths of the canvas for a straight view, more for looking up, less for looking down. Unless you're playing with the viewer's eye intentionally."

Simon nodded, continuing to paint. Percy was extraordinarily rule-oriented one moment…then cast the rules aside with zeal the next.

"Know the rules before you break them," Percy recited, for the umpteenth time.

Simon continued to paint, starting the landscape. The village in his nightmare, rooftops glowing in the flashes of lightning from the heavens. Rain falling to the street, making the cobblestones slippery and reflective. People congregated below, some staring up at him in terror, others fleeing for their lives.

At length, he finished; a painting fresh from his dream, a snapshot in time.

He stood back from it, then glanced at Percy.

"Hmm," Percy murmured, standing up and pushing his stool aside. It vanished instantly. He stepped up to the painting, leaning over to peer at it intently. Simon felt a familiar unease gnaw at his guts, and waited nervously.

Percy missed nothing.

After a while, Percy turned to Simon, eyeing him for a long, silent moment.

"What?" Simon asked at last.

"Do you realize that you only paint the past?" he inquired.

Simon blinked.

"This," Percy continued, gesturing at the painting. "And every other painting I've seen for the last twenty-six days. Always the past."

"That's not…"

"Isn't it?" Percy pressed, raising an eyebrow. He broke out into a kindly smile. "Do you know *why* you do it?"

Simon hesitated, then shook his head.

"Because you're stuck," Percy declared, jabbing a finger at his chest. "How are you going to move forward when you're tied up in the past?"

"I…" Simon began. Then he shrugged helplessly. Percy chuckled, patting Simon on the shoulder.

"Instead of painting what was," he said, "…try painting what ought to be."

Simon just stared at him blankly.

"Go on," Percy urged. "Get a fresh canvas."

Simon obeyed, putting his current painting aside and grabbing a new canvas. He glanced back at Percy, who gestured for him to get to work. Simon turned back to the canvas, staring at it for a long while.

"Well?" Percy said.

"I…I don't know what to paint."

"What ought to be," Percy replied.

"But I don't know what that is," Simon protested.

"Whatever you think it ought to be."

Simon sighed, turning back to the canvas. But his mind, like the canvas before him, remained blank. He felt a sudden irritation; he was a good Painter. No, an excellent one, according to the Collector. He could come up with amazing paintings…the Doppelganger, the Gemini. Legion. Creatures of darkness and glass and blood and porcelain. Creations so powerful they could rival the great White Dragon of Havenwood, and help kill a lord of the Pentad.

"I don't want to paint what ought to be," Simon decided, turning back to Percy defiantly. "I want to paint what *I* want to paint."

"And why do you think it is that you *don't* want to paint what you want life to be for you?" Percy shot back.

"I don't know. I don't care," Simon replied, crossing his arms over his chest.

"Oh, you care very much," Percy retorted gently. "After all, if you didn't care, you wouldn't mind painting it."

Simon stared at the man, trying in vain to come up with a response. But of course he could not.

"You're scared," Percy declared. "Because you're afraid of getting what you want. Because you don't think you deserve it," he added, grabbing Simon's wrist. He pulled it toward himself, tracing the scars on Simon's forearm with one finger. Then he glanced up at Simon, his expression suddenly quite serious. "You've never been allowed to be *you*, Simon."

Simon felt a sudden surge of emotion, and his lower lip began to quiver. He grit his teeth, forcing it down. Pushing it back in.

"Introspection, then expression," Percy chided. "There's no harm in being vulnerable with me, Simon. You have my permission to be utterly yourself."

And with that, the dam burst.

Simon sobbed, burying his face in Percy's broad shoulder. Percy embraced him, patting him on the back gently. Tears poured down Simon's cheeks, wetting Percy's shirt. His shoulders heaved with each sob, and though he instantly wanted to stop, to withdraw into himself yet again, he could not.

So he cried. And cried.

And with each minute that passed, Simon expected Percy to pull away. To leave him. To have had enough. But Percy didn't leave. He didn't pull away…not even after Simon was finally done.

He held Simon not until *he'd* had enough, but until Simon had.

Simon pulled away, wiping tears from his eyes and cheeks. He found Percy smiling at him.

"See?" he said. "Nothing to fear."

Simon smiled back, taking a deep, shuddering breath in. He let it out, then turned to the canvas.

"Nothing to fear," he murmured. "*That's* what ought to be."

And with that, he painted.

Chapter 4

An emergency meeting in Castle Havenwood was organized for seven o'clock that night, with every citizen invited to attend. In the meantime, Gideon, Lucia, and Bella retrieved Grandpa from the vault's huge mural-painting, escorting him back to Lucia's mansion deep underground. There, they convened around the dining room table, with Nemesis, Myko, and Animus.

"After thinking it through, I think we have no choice but to surrender," Gideon told them.

"Excuse me?" Mom blurted out incredulously.

"If we don't, we'll be risking the lives of every soul in this kingdom," Gideon argued. "I for one cannot have that on my conscience.

"Well I can," Mom retorted, crossing her arms over her chest.

"You're assuming we'd lose, of course," Grandpa chimed in. "And I'm afraid I don't disagree with that assumption."

"You really think they'll attack?" Bella asked. Gideon sighed, then nodded.

"I do," he confirmed. "Queen Eldora is many things, but a bluffer is not one of them. What she says she will do, she will do."

"We could fight back," Bella proposed. "We beat the Collector, after all. And Miss Savage."

"Two powerful enemies," Gideon conceded. "But nothing compared to the full might of the Pentad, I'm afraid."

"Well then," Mom declared. "I always did enjoy a challenge."

"Honey…" Gideon began.

"Don't honey me," Mom retorted. "I'm fighting. End of story." She smirked. "Besides, dying isn't the end of the world. I'm sure Petrusa would love to have all of us in Arx Mortus."

"I for one would prefer *not* dying," Grandpa countered.

"As would I," Gideon agreed. "But it appears we don't have much of a choice."

"So you're just going to sacrifice yourself and all of us for what?" Mom inquired, pointing up at the ceiling. "Those helpless idiots up there?"

"Lucia…"

"If it weren't for you, they'd be dead twice already," Mom pressed. "They can't even wipe their own…"

Grandpa cleared his throat, glancing at Bella.

"…butts without our help. If I were the Pentad, I'd accept your generous offer to sacrifice yourself, then attack Havenwood anyway and make an example out of anyone who ever tries to do art without my blessing…and anyone who dares create a place where people *can* do that."

Gideon lowered his gaze to the counter. His jawline rippled, but he said nothing. Grandpa leaned back in his chair, sighing heavily.

"She's right," he admitted. "That's exactly what they'd do."

"So we shouldn't sacrifice ourselves," Bella concluded. "That's settled then." She paused, glancing at Gideon. "Right?"

He sat there silently for a long moment, then nodded.

"Right," he muttered.

"Very well then," Grandpa stated. "We're assuming the only other alternative is to battle the Pentad. Perhaps there is another way forward?"

"If there is," Gideon replied, "…I don't know of one. Queen Eldora prefers a spectacular show of force against those who defy her. And that's exactly what we've done."

"So we fight," Mom declared. "This is going to be *interesting*."

"What about Petrusa?" Bella asked, struck with a burst of hope. "Can't she help us?"

"No hon," Mom answered. "She won't lift a finger for Havenwood. Just for me, and maybe you. And that just means she'll keep us in the Plane of Death for a while, until things cool down."

"What about Dad and Grandpa?" Bella pressed. Mom shook her head grimly.

"Sorry pumpkin."

"So we'll convene the emergency meeting, and tell the citizens that the Pentad plans on attacking us," Grandpa decided. "I think it's best if we leave the fact that we refused to surrender out of it."

"Agreed," Gideon replied. "If they think there's a way out, they'll demand it."

"They're going to panic," Mom grumbled. "Cowards always do."

"Maybe," Gideon replied. "But then again, maybe not. Not if we give them a way out."

"What are you thinking?" Grandpa inquired.

"Do tell," Mom piped in.

Gideon smiled, leaning forward and propping his elbows on the table. He gave them all a conspiratorial look.

"I think I might just have an idea," he replied.

* * *

The emergency meeting started at seven o'clock sharp, the citizens of Havenwood congregating in a large meeting hall in Castle Havenwood. Gideon debriefed everyone with shocking bluntness, and when the citizens heard the news of the impending attack by the Pentad's armies, they did exactly as Mom had foretold.

They panicked.

It took Gideon retrieving his magic lantern and threatening to active it's explosive power to get the crowd to be quiet.

"Don't panic," Gideon ordered. "I have a plan."

Everyone's eyes were on him.

"The Pentad will attack, that is certain," he stated. "But those of you who don't wish to fight don't have to be here when they arrive."

"What do you mean?" one of the artists – an older Sculptor named Griggins – asked. Short and quite round, with a long, curly white beard, he was a sort of leader among the artists of Havenwood, though he deferred to Grandpa.

"Those who wish to leave can go through Lake Fenestra to the Plane of Reflection," Gideon answered. "King Draco of the Dragonkin will have his men escort you to the Underground, which you can use to travel anywhere in the world. You'll be safe from the Pentad…and if we succeed in defeating the Pentad's armies, you can return to Havenwood afterward if you choose."

"That's actually quite reasonable," Griggins admitted.

"Those who wish to stay and fight, however," Gideon continued, "…should prepare themselves for a heated battle."

"Wait," another citizen piped in. "Why don't we *all* just run away? Why protect Havenwood at all?"

"An excellent question," Griggins agreed.

"If we don't, the White Dragon will die," Gideon replied. "And Havenwood will be destroyed. Even the Dragonkin may be annihilated."

"They can just flee too," another citizen argued.

"They won't," Grandpa interjected grimly. "I know my creations, and they are loyal to Havenwood with a singular conviction. They will stay and fight. To the death."

"Okay," Griggins stated. "But you do realize they're just characters in a book."

There was a collective gasp among some of the citizens.

"Characters that have been given life," Gideon countered. "They're as alive as you are, Griggins."

"Come on," Griggins retorted. "That's not true and you know it."

"Careful Griggins," Gideon warned. Myko – standing at his side – growled at the man.

"I'm just saying that, while it would be tragic if they died, that they only lived because Thaddeus wrote about them," Griggins argued. "If I had to choose between my own life – and the life of my family – I'd choose them over words on a page!"

Bella glanced at Nemesis, who was standing at her side.

Ass, the dragon grumbled. *He could use a lot less flesh,* she added. *Can I take it?*

"Be nice," Bella whispered.

Might save his life.

"Pay attention," she hissed.

"I think that most of us can agree that life, regardless of its origin, is sacrosanct," Gideon declared, glaring down at Griggins. Who backed down, thankfully. "Regardless, if you feel more inclined to save your own life than that of another, feel free to take advantage of the Dragonkin's kindness and let them help you to the Underground."

To that, Griggins had no reply.

"Those wishing to stay should tell myself or Thaddeus as soon as you come to that decision," Gideon continued. "We will begin preparations for the defense of Havenwood starting tomorrow morning."

He paused, gazing over the crowd.

"Any questions?" he inquired.

There were none.

"Good," he stated. "Then this meeting is-"

The floor shook under their feet.

"What…?" Griggins blurted out. "What was…"

The floor shook again, and then an ear-splitting roar echoed through the castle. A chill ran down Bella's spine, goosebumps rising on her arms. The sound was unmistakable, one burned into her memory.

The roar of the White Dragon.

Chapter 5

General Craven strode through the forest, his massive boots leaving deep footprints in the forest floor with each step. He ignored the branches in his way, walking right through them. They snapped clean off, big branches and small, unable to withstand his massive weight…and his flesh, made of pure Invictium. He was invincible, unstoppable.

The right hand of Queen Eldora. The hand of justice.

An army marched behind him, every last one of them members of the Royal Elite Guard, statues clad in magic armor wielding swords of the four elements. One thousand troops clad in the red and gold of the Pentad.

And at Craven's side, Yero the Painter, and two dozen of the Pentad's Battle-Musicians, members of an elite orchestra.

Craven spotted the end of the forest ahead, and a grassy field beyond. He stomped his way toward it, his massive golden shield Aganon clutched in his left hand.

He strode all the way to the end of the tree line, emerging into the grassy field. The sun had already set, stars twinkling in the sky. The moon was in its full power, shining brightly like a second sun. Its light cast the field ahead in soft silver…and revealed what lie beyond.

Dragon's Peak, and encircling it, the massive form of the White Dragon.

Craven stopped just beyond the tree line, studying the great serpent, its body miles long, easily the largest creature he'd ever faced. A guardian that inspired fear in any who dared face it, whose mere presence would deter almost any would-be-attacker.

He stared at it, and was not afraid.

Craven raised his right hand in the air, then made a fist…and strode forward toward Havenwood. His army followed behind him, feet *thumping* in perfect unison.

In the distance, the White Dragon stirred.

Its eyes opened, and it lifted its gargantuan head slowly from the earth, turning to face Craven. He met its gaze, his pace never faltering.

Stomp, stomp.

For he was the juggernaut, and feared nothing but the queen.

"Rise, dragon," he shouted, his voice booming across the land. "Your death approaches."

He made a signal with his right hand, and his orchestra began to play.

Drums beat in a powerful rhythm, notes low and deep. Craven felt each drumbeat rumble through his body, but the music had no effect on him. Not with his armor protecting him. But the humans in his army would draw power from it, as would the Royal Elite Guard. For they were lesser statues, vulnerable to the magical forces around them.

Craven was not.

The White Dragon of Havenwood rose to his challenge, unwrapping itself from the perimeter of the mushroom forest and lifting itself onto all fours. A creature that rivaled the mountain itself, glowing white in the moonlight. It snorted, wind blasting across the grass and flattening it.

Then it opened its great maw, and roared.

The sound *smashed* into Craven and his army, overwhelming the orchestra. They cried out, dropping their instruments and clutching at their ears. Even Yero dropped to a knee, his sword Temper floating at his side.

But Craven did not stop. He did not grimace. He stomped ever-forward, his boots drumming on the earth in a constant rhythm.

The orchestra recovered, as did Yero.

"Cut out its eyes," Craven ordered the Painter.

Yero inclined his head…and Temper burst into action, flying toward the White Dragon far in the distance.

The dragon lifted its head higher, opening its mouth wide. White light grew within its throat, a thousand times brighter than the moon.

Still Craven marched, and his troops marched behind him. He lifted Aganon before him, the golden shield flashing with its own light. The glow within the White Dragon's throat intensified…and then a ray of white-hot light shot outward, right at Craven.

Craven triggered Aganon with a thought, a massive shield of golden light bursting into existence, thousands of times the size of Aganon itself. A barrier of pure energy, large enough to cover the entire army behind him.

The White Dragon's light smashed into that golden barrier…and proved no match for Aganon. The legendary shield nullified the attack completely, leaving Craven – and his army – unharmed. The light that spilled beyond the borders of Craven's golden energy shield seared the grass and earth, moisture within the rocks and dirt superheating instantly, making the rocks explode.

Still Craven marched, never wavering, his feet pounding the earth with each inevitable step forward. Each step gouging the grassy terrain, his massive weight causing his boots to sink inches into the earth.

The dragon's attack ended, and it roared again, crouching down low.

"Back!" Craven shouted, his voice booming in the night air.

His army dropped backward rapidly, even as the White Dragon sprang forward at them, its gigantic body sailing impossibly high through the air. Its hind feet left gouges dozens of feet deep in the earth with the power of its leap, a tidal wave of dirt flying backward onto the mushroom forest behind it.

Craven stopped, lifting Aganon high above his head and setting a wide stance. He braced himself, watching through the golden shimmer of his energy-shield as the White Dragon arced toward him as if in slow-motion, lifting one massive paw as it fell right toward him.

And then the dragon landed, slamming its hand – as large as the army facing it – right on Craven's head.

The earth beneath Craven disintegrated, his energy shield flashing bright gold as the White Dragon struck it. Craven grunted as he was forced onto his back and driven violently into the earth. He was plunged into utter darkness, and still he felt himself sinking. But his arm, forged of pure Invictium, held strong, holding Aganon between himself and the White Dragon's paw. And the earth gave way around him, unable to harm his invincible flesh.

At length the sinking stopped, and the White Dragon's clawed hand lifted up from the huge crater it had created. Silver light poured in from around the silhouette of its paw as it continued to rise.

Earth spilled in on all sides to fill the hole, and Craven got to his feet. The White Dragon's head appeared over the edge of the crater, and it peered at him, a low growl rumbling in its throat like rolling thunder.

Craven lifted his right hand into the air…and his magical gauntlet Dextro flew off of his hand, shooting upward and forward. With a thought, he activated it…and flew right after it, as if pulled by a powerful magnet.

He sailed hundreds of feet into the air, clearing the crater and soaring far above it, until he was higher even than the White Dragon's head. He reconnected with his gauntlet in mid-air, then pointed his right hand down at the dragon, shooting his gauntlet right at it.

Then he held Aganon in front of him, activating his gauntlet a second time.

He shot downward and forward like a missile, aiming right for the White Dragon's head…and reconnected with the gauntlet right before it struck the dragon. At the same time, he swung Aganon, slamming his massive energy shield right between the dragon's eyes.

Right between its eyes.

The White Dragon's head snapped back violently with the impact, and it stumbled to the side.

Craven fell to the earth between the White Dragon's paws, slamming into the ground so violently that he made a small crater of his own. He used his gauntlet to fly out of it, then aimed Aganon up at the dragon's left wing. The dragon's breath attack – and the impacts the shield had absorbed – had only served to feed the ancient artifact's most powerful weapon.

The God Ray.

Craven gripped the shield tightly…and activated it with a thought.

The glowing energy shield contracted, sucking back in to Aganon…and making its golden metal glow impossibly bright. Brighter even than the sun. With another thought, Craven summoned the God Ray.

A beam of golden light burst out of Aganon, slicing through the night sky and striking the White Dragon's left wing at its root.

Its scales glowed instantly red-hot, then blackened, flying off and turning to dust. Its flesh burned instantly, the God Ray cutting right through it…and severing its wing.

The great appendage fell to the ground beside the White Dragon with an ear-shattering *boom*, its severed end glowing like the embers of a dying campfire.

Craven lowered Aganon, putting one foot in front of the other, marching toward his enemy. For he was the right hand of Queen Eldora, and her will guided *his* hand.

And by his hand, the White Dragon of Havenwood would meet its doom.

Chapter 6

Bella rushed out of Castle Havenwood, sprinting across the path and over the small bridge spanning the castle's moat. Myko moon-dashed above her in a beam of pure silver light, Gideon riding atop the great wolf. And Mom ran beside her, Nemesis flying high above.

"Nemesis, what's going on?" Bella shouted.

Hold on, Nemesis replied. The dragon soared past everyone else overhead, flying right off the edge of Dragon's Peak.

What is it, Bella pressed as she neared the edge of the mountain. She skid to a stop there, joining Gideon and Mom.

And froze.

For there, thousands of feet below, beyond Lake Fenestra and the mushroom forest, the White Dragon was unfurling, its eyes on something ahead. An army standing where the grassland beyond Havenwood met the forest. A lone figure strode from the front lines of that army toward the dragon, making its way across the grassy plain.

The dragon lifted itself onto all fours, facing the army…and roared.

Army of soldiers, Nemesis told Bella. *Red and gold armor…must be the Pentad.*

"Nemesis says it's the Pentad," Bella warned Mom and Dad.

The idiot walking up to the White Dragon's like nine feet tall, Nemesis noted. *Red and gold armor, real fancy. Carrying a big gold shield.*

Bella relayed this as well…and Gideon's jawline rippled.

"General Craven," he muttered. Then he swore, pulling his cane free from his left forearm-painting.

The White Dragon reared its head back, opening its mouth wide. Bright light built up within it…and then a brilliant white-hot ray shot outward at

Craven and the army behind him. Craven lifted his shield, and suddenly a massive energy shield appeared, protecting the army behind him.

The White Dragon's ray struck the energy shield…and seemed to make the energy shield glow brighter.

A group of Havenwood's artists rushed up around Bella and Mom and Gideon, staring at the scene far below. A collective gasp rose from them.

"Initiate the evacuation protocol," Gideon ordered. "Get to the vault!"

"What…" someone began, but Gideon glared at him.

"Now!" he snapped.

The artists hesitated, then ran back to the castle. And below, Craven marched ever forward, his army staying where it was near the tree line.

The White Dragon crouched low…then pounced!

Craven's soldiers dropped back quickly, and Craven lifted his shield above his head right before the White Dragon landed on top of him, smashing its right paw down on Craven's energy shield. The ground *exploded* with the blow, dirt and debris shooting outward and upward from the impact…and the White Dragon's paw buried itself dozens of feet into the earth.

"Yes!" Bella exclaimed, glancing at Gideon. But his expression was stony. She looked down…and saw the dragon's paw lifting up. Something was glowing deep within the crater it had created.

Craven's energy shield.

Moments later, Craven shot up out of the hole like a bullet, flying high above the White Dragon's head…and then flew downward and forward right *at* it. He swung his massive energy shield, slamming the White Dragon right between the eyes.

The dragon's head snapped backward, and it stumbled to the side.

Craven landed between the dragon's arms, and moments later, his huge energy shield shrank inward, sucking back into Craven's golden shield. But now it was glowing so brightly that it seared Bella's eyes, forcing her to squint.

A beam of golden light shot out of the shield, striking the White Dragon's left wing…and cutting it right off.

The massive wing fell to the earth, and the White Dragon shrieked in pain.

Bella cried out, covering her ears at the horrible sound…as did Gideon and Mom. Even Myko cowered, giving a low whine.

"We have to help him!" Bella exclaimed.

"I'll take Craven," Gideon stated. "Lucia, I'll make first strike against the army. You keep whatever survives off of me. If you can distract Craven, all the better."

"I see something flying around the White Dragon's head," Lucia warned. "Looks like…"

"Temper," Gideon muttered. "Change of plan. I'll take Craven. Myko, you take Temper."

Myko *wuffed.*

"I'll take Yero," Lucia offered.

"What do I do?" Bella asked. Gideon turned to face her.

"Stay alive," he answered. "Protect Thaddeus."

"But…"

"No buts," Gideon snapped. "This is not negotiable. These people will destroy you Bella. If you come down with us, you *will* die."

"He's right," Mom agreed. "Sorry pumpkin. We go alone. If we have to worry about keeping you alive, you'll only get in our way."

Bella felt tears welling up in her eyes, but she wiped them away, nodding once.

"Okay."

"You have to promise me," Mom insisted. "No matter what happens, you won't go down there after us. And if we fail, you need to run."

"But…"

"No buts," Mom interrupted. "Promise me Bella."

Bella lowered her gaze, then nodded.

"I promise."

Mom leaned in to hug Bella, then kissed her forehead.

"Love you," she murmured. Gideon swallowed visibly.

"Whatever happens," he stated, "…remember how proud we are of you."

"Don't talk like you're not coming back," Bella retorted. "You can't talk like that."

Gideon glanced at Mom, who sighed. She took off the amulet hanging from her neck, putting it around Bella's. Its heart-shaped ruby pulsed gently just above Bella's chest-painting.

"No matter what happens, my heart will always be with you," Mom promised.

And then they turned and jumped off the edge of the mountain.

***

Myko leapt over the edge of Dragon's Peak, falling toward Lake Fenestra far below. The wind howled in Gideon's ears as he clutched on to Myko's collar, his hair and cape rippling in the wind.

Temper first, Gideon told his trusty Familiar. He felt Myko acknowledge the command, even as they plummeted toward the lake. They reached the level of the White Dragon's head, and Gideon spotted Temper flying toward its right eye.

Now!

Myko dissolved into a beam of pure silver light, and Gideon felt himself zoom forward suddenly, the wind's howling turning to a shriek as they blasted toward the White Dragon. The moon-dash ended, and Myko repeated it, dashing again and again until they were within a dozen yards of the White Dragon's enormous head.

Get him!

Gideon threw himself off of Myko then, plummeting toward the ground hundreds of feet below. His magical cape activated automatically, slowing his fall. He spotted Craven standing between the White Dragon's huge front paws, Aganon gleaming dully in the darkness.

Gideon shifted his gaze to Yero, standing a hundred yards away at the head of the army of soldiers. He grit his teeth, gathering his courage for what had to be done.

He'd warned Yero. He'd told his old friend what he was prepared to do if his family was attacked.

Yero had made his choice.

Gideon felt a sudden calm come over him as he fell, his mind clearing. Time seemed to slow, and he saw the land below him with a crisp clarity. Every movement, every player. His mind ticked through his strategy.

And then he landed, and executed it.

General Craven turned to look at him, standing a hundred feet away, the White Dragon's huge hand between them. Gideon reached into his chest-painting, pulling out a small black sphere with a red dot on it.

He threw it up in the air, pointing at it with one finger. It shot upward, arcing through the night sky toward the army of soldiers in the distance. Gideon thrust his finger down, right at the army…and the black sphere fell right into the middle of it.

Nothing happened.

And then the sky above the army opened up, a huge black hole appearing in the clouds high above. A massive meteorite fell through it with terrifying speed.

The army didn't even have time to react.

The meteorite slammed into the earth, and Gideon reached into his chest-painting, pulling out the disc to his Conclave and throwing it on the ground.

"Anulus!" he cried…and then leapt into it, right as the earth erupted…and right before the inevitable shockwave struck.

* * *

Lucia fell through the air toward Lake Fenestra, watching as her husband moon-dashed toward the White Dragon. With a thought, she combined with Animus, becoming one with her Familiar. Her body turned to mist, expanding outward in all directions.

As a result, her fall slowed.

Lucia willed herself forward, zooming through the sky toward the army of soldiers far below. But she knew better than to hurry; Gideon wanted the first strike, and as much as she battled with her husband on who was a better painter, she couldn't deny the truth.

Gideon's first strikes were *epic.*

Sure enough, she saw the sky open up above the army in the distance…and a chill ran down her spine.

Cataclysm.

She'd only heard of the painting, of course. One of Gideon's legendary weapons, able to fell entire armies. And now she was seeing it.

A massive meteorite fell through the hole in the sky, flying into the earth so quickly that it was a blur.

The earth *exploded.*

A mushroom cloud of earth shot upward into the sky at the site of impact, instantly annihilating the army of soldiers. Trees in the forest beyond were flattened, in a wave extending over a mile backward. And the shockwave shot right for Lucia, slamming into her.

She burst backward, the incredible force of the impact sending her careening a full half-mile into the side of Dragon's Peak. She struck its rocky wall painlessly, her mist-form spreading across its surface…then coalescing once again. Ahead, the White Dragon was shoved backward, falling onto its back on the grassy plain. And Craven…

Craven flew bodily forward, slamming into the White Dragon and ricocheting off. He landed a quarter-mile away, tumbling to the ground and rolling for a hundred yards before coming to a stop.

With Aganon still clutched in his left hand.

Our turn, Lucia told Animus.

She zoomed forward, flying toward the site of the meteor's impact. It was impossible to see through the huge mushroom cloud still rising there, but it was her job to ensure that nothing had survived.

And that if anything had, she would correct the situation.

She flew right at the wall of dust ahead, then dropped to the ground before it, pulling herself together to form her body once again. Glancing back, she saw Gideon rising from his Conclave-portal. He closed the portal, putting it back in his top hat.

She lifted her gaze, spotting Myko moon-dashing above the White Dragon's head, something clutched in his jaws. A sword…Temper.

"Impressive," a deep voice called out from within the cloud of dust ahead. Lucia turned forward, spotting a tall shadow approaching from within it. A man emerged, utterly unharmed by Gideon's meteorite. Lucia's hands went to the silver daggers at her hips.

"Hello Yero," she greeted.

"Surrender or die," he commanded.

"Oh Yero," she replied. "Dying sounds like *much* more fun. Care to join me?"

* * *

Gideon watched as Craven's gauntlet shot toward him…and as the man himself flew right after it. They careened toward him with terrible speed.

A little help, he told Myko.

Myko moon-dashed right at Gideon at the last second, Temper still clutched in the wolf's jaws. Gideon grabbed on to the wolf's collar, feeling it yank his arm so hard it almost dislocated his shoulder. He held on for dear life, Craven's gauntlet – and Craven – missing him by mere yards. The wolf finished the moon-dash, and Gideon let go, stumbling back onto the ground.

Distract him, he ordered his Familiar.

Myko spun around, moon-dashing right after Craven. He slammed into Craven right as Craven landed, but the living statue was so heavy that Myko mostly just ricocheted off. Myko stumbled backward, growling at Craven, who slid to a stop in the grass.

Myko moon-dashed at him again, but Craven lifted his shield to intercept, and Myko bounced off of it harmlessly. The impact made him drop Temper, who slashed at Myko's body, making a huge gash in the wolf's flank.

Then Temper went right for Gideon, flying at him and slashing at his left arm.

Gideon's magical cape activated, wrapping itself around Temper and flinging it to the side…just as Craven charged at him, trying to ram him with Aganon.

Myko moon-dashed into the general's side…but bounced off yet again.

Gideon shot his hand out, his magic glove flying off and grabbing Aganon by its rim. He yanked the shield to the side right before Craven hit him, dodging at the same time. The general missed him by mere inches… exposing his back.

Gideon reached into his forearm-painting, retrieving his cane. A cane still vibrating powerfully with the force it'd absorbed from striking the White Dragon nearly a month ago.

He swung it at the back of Craven's head.

The cane struck the back of the general's skull, the full force of a dragon the size of a mountain focused to an area less than a square inch.

Craven's helmet *exploded.*

The general shot backward through the air like a missile, crossing the grassy plain instantly and soaring miles over the forest beyond.

At the same time, Temper detangled itself from Gideon's cape, thrusting at Gideon's chest.

Gideon didn't even block, allowing the blade to sink into his chest painting. He tried to grab its hilt to shove it all the way in, but Temper jerked backward, flinging itself out of his uniform.

Just as Myko moon-dashed at the living sword, catching it in his jaws.

Gideon turned to the forest where Craven had gone, calling for his magic glove still latched on to Craven's shield. Behind him, the White Dragon recovered from the concussive force of the meteorite. It stumbled as it got to its feet, its remaining wing pulling it off-balance. Then it lifted itself to its full height.

And *roared.*

The sound blasted Gideon's ears, and he grit his teeth against the sudden pain, his eyes watering. He focused, watching as his magic glove burst through the fading mushroom cloud, Aganon in its grasp.

The glove returned to Gideon's hand, and Gideon clutched Aganon…and promptly fell over with the sheer weight of it. He let go, rising to his feet. The legendary shield had to be over three hundred pounds.

"Well, it was a good thought," he muttered.

He felt a sudden burst of fear, and knew instantly that it wasn't his. Gideon ducked, feeling the wind of something whipping by right where his head had been.

Temper!

He turned to face the magic blade, lifting his cane to block another slash. His cane's magic instantly nullified Temper's momentum, and Gideon batted the sword to the side. The stored momentum sent Temper sailing away, and Myko moon-dashed into it, grabbing it in his jaws once again.

Gideon heard a *thump* behind him.

He spun around, but saw only the wall of dust that was the mushroom cloud. And Lucia battling with Yero near it. He resisted the urge to come to her aid, knowing that she was fully capable of handling herself.

Stick to the plan, he reminded himself.

There was a loud *thump* then, from beyond the wall of dust. Gideon gripped his cane tightly, peering into it.

Thump. Thump. Thump.

He reached into his chest painting, preparing for the inevitable.

Chapter 7

In Percy's cabin in the Plane of Reflection, Simon reflected on a life without fear. With Percy sitting nearby in a small wooden chair, Simon painted. And while he normally refused to paint with anyone watching, soon it was as if Percy wasn't there, so engrossed was Simon. The Flow moved his heart, and his heart moved his hand.

He painted a scene from Memory Lane, that strange land that Percy had shown Simon about a month ago. A narrow street with buildings on either side, sunlight splashing down on them in a cheery yellow hue. Some of the buildings were small, representing memories of little importance. Others looked old and abandoned, run-down from years of being neglected…representing memories that he'd repressed.

But in the distance, a huge, dark tower loomed, casting a shadow over the buildings beyond it.

Simon painted a phoenix then, a great fiery bird that flew right through the middle of the tower, making a huge hole in it. Then he painted flames engulfing the tower, black smoke rising into the cloudless sky.

That done, he set down his brush, stepped back to study his work.

"Hmm," he heard Percy say from behind. The man stood from the chair, walking to Simon's side and putting a hand to his chin. He stroked his luxurious red beard, his eye on the burning dark tower.

"What do you think?" Simon asked.

"Nothing to be afraid of," Percy quoted…Simon's own words before he'd started painting. "Is that what this is?"

"Yes."

"And that a phoenix – symbolizing resurrection, a second chance – can destroy your dark tower, letting the light fall on your life where once there was shadow?"

Simon smiled.

"Right."

"Ahh Simon," Percy sighed, patting Simon on the shoulder. "Come, take a walk with me."

They exited the cabin, stepping through the mirror leaning against the side of the cabin to travel back to the original world. Percy reached out as if to turn a doorknob, and a wooden door appeared out of thin air, lined with a deep purple light. He swung it open, revealing a portal of that purple light. Simon was about to step through when Percy stopped him.

"Age before beauty," he quipped…and stepped through first.

Simon hesitated, then followed after the man…and found himself in a place both instantly familiar and jarringly different.

It was Memory Lane, its narrow street flanked by buildings on either side. But instead of the single lane with buildings flanking it, Simon found himself standing next to Percy in a massive city. Buildings everywhere, with side-streets connecting parallel streets, with bridges arching over other streets. Most were painted in bright, cheery colors lit by the sun, while others were dark and gloomy, like Simon's tower. Indeed, Simon spotted not one, but many dark towers in the distance…as well as towers that were quite the opposite. Ones that towered over even the darkest of the towers, with bright lights at the top like lighthouses.

Light that cut through the rain and gloom directly over the darkest towers, turning even the blackest black to light gray.

Simon stared at the wondrous scene before him, at one street that seemed to dive into a dark tunnel below the city. At the tallest bright towers, so well-kept that their doors were shiny gold and brass, their walls spotless.

"Welcome to *my* Memory Lane," Percy declared, gesturing at everything around them.

"It's so…" Simon began.

"Confusing?" Percy asked.

"Detailed."

"Well as you know, I have an inordinate fondness for details," Percy replied with a wink. "That's why they call me Persnickity."

"But not Persnickety," Simon quoted.

"Right," Percy agreed. "The big picture is made of details, but becoming lost in the parts without considering the whole…"

He gestured at one of the dark towers, smiling at Simon…who swallowed past a sudden lump in his throat.

"That's what I did," Simon realized.

"That's what you are *doing*," Percy corrected. "Remember your painting?"

Simon hesitated, then nodded.

"I painted the dark tower."

"You did," Percy agreed. "You want a life without fear, so you paint a Memory Lane without pain. You want to destroy your memory of it so that it won't dominate your attention…" he continued, then gestured at a large swath of sun-kissed buildings in the city. "When all you have to do is turn your head."

Simon lowered his gaze to his feet, realizing that Percy was right. For the last month, he'd felt like he'd been healing. That he'd finally started to get beyond his past…his dark tower. And yet it was still front and center in his paintings.

And as with the canvas, so with his mind.

Simon felt an arm drape over his shoulders, and looked up to see Percy giving him a warm smile, his eyes twinkling.

"Far be it from me to judge you for being persnickety," the man quipped.

Simon had to smile at that.

Percy took a deep breath in, letting it out and gazing across the city.

"This is my Memory Lane," he mused. "And we're building it even now, as we speak. If you're always looking at the tower behind you," he added, "…you'll never see what wonderful things you're creating in front of you."

"So…turn away from the past?" Simon asked.

"Better to look forward to the future," Percy replied with a wink. "And build something that'll shine brightly in our memories when we look back at it."

Simon turned to gaze at one of the bright towers in the distance, casting their light on even the darkest of the towers.

"Build a lighthouse," he murmured.

"As many as you can," Percy replied. "Build them and visit them often, Simon. The more you visit your memories, the better cared for they'll be. Their doors will swing open more easily each time. So be careful which memories you nurture."

Simon thought of his dark tower.

"And if I don't visit the dark towers?"

"They'll fall into disrepair," Percy answered. "Their doors will creak and groan with rust, until you'll struggle to open them."

"Do they ever go away?" Simon pressed. Percy shook his head.

"No," he answered. "Though eventually they crumble, their ruins forever remain." He gestured at the cityscape. "But when we look back, they'll no longer be the first thing we see."

Chapter 8

General Craven had faced many foes in his long life, some weak, some supposedly strong. None had particularly impressed him, for they had all fallen easily to his might. He had never faced any real danger to his person, being made of a nearly invincible substance. For this reason, battle had long since ceased to excite him. It was a means to an end now, the simple fulfilment of a task. There was nothing that could challenge him, and nothing that had ever gotten close to harming him.

And then Gideon's cane struck the back of his head.

Craven's head snapped forward, the force of the blow unlike any he'd ever experienced. Suddenly the earth was flying beneath him, grass, then trees a blur far below. It took him a moment to realize that he was flying through the air…and another to realize that he was experiencing a feeling he'd never experienced before.

Pain.

It shot through his skull, his vision blackening with the agony of it. He barely registered his flight slowing, barely felt his body smash into the treetops. Knocking down tree after tree in a line a quarter of a mile long before slamming into the ground.

He rolled, then struck a large tree trunk, and stopped.

Craven laid there for a moment, his vision clearing. Then he grunted, lifting himself to his feet. He swayed a bit, reaching up to touch the back of his skull with his fingers. His helmet – the legendary helm he'd worn for a thousand years, his link to his queen – was gone.

And there, on the back of his head, he felt a dent.

Craven explored it with his fingers, unable to process what he was feeling. Unable to comprehend that this was real. That it was actually happening. He lowered his hand, staring off into space.

For the first time since his creation, he knew fear.

He took a moment to process this new emotion, then blinked, forcing himself to focus.

Complete your mission.

Craven turned around, staring at the half-mile of downed trees in a perfect line ahead. It took him another moment to realize that his left hand was empty.

That Aganon was gone.

The pain in his head continued to throb, and he grimaced, reaching for the dent in his skull again. Then he focused inward, willing himself to enter the little death. Torpor, the transformation to his original form…the form of a statue.

It came in the reverse order to which it left, his legs stiffening, then going numb as if dead. This spread to his hips, then his belly and chest. And finally, to his head.

Time went by, an eternity in every second.

Craven woke himself from Torpor, and when he could move again, he reached up to the back of his skull. The pain was gone…as was the dent.

He clenched his fists, then unclenched them.

Complete your mission, he repeated to himself. *You are the law. The right hand of the queen.*

He lifted his right hand, willing his gauntlet to shoot off like a missile. It burst through the path made by the downed trees, rising up above the treetops. With another thought, he flew forward and upward after it, the ground shrinking beneath him, trees whizzing by below.

Over the forest he sailed, reaching the end of the forest in moments. He flew over the grassland then, flying into the large mushroom cloud rising from the meteorite's impact. It was pitch black inside…and light accosted him again when he burst through the other side.

Then he dropped, landing with a *thump* on the ruined earth a few dozen yards from where Gideon stood.

Craven stopped there, staring at the man. Gideon was short for a human male, and past his prime. But looks could be deceiving, and Gideon's reputation preceded him. Craven had thought the man a fool the last time he'd seen him, at the military camp at the base of the mountain past Devil's Pass. A fool for daring to threaten Craven, for even imagining that he'd stand a chance against Queen Eldora's champion.

He stomped forward, closing the distance between them, his eyes dropping to Aganon lying on the ground before Gideon.

Gideon took off his top hat, reaching in to pull out a small black disc. He tossed this on the ground beside Aganon.

"Anulus," the man incanted.

The disc expanded, making a hole in the earth…and Aganon fell through it.

"Anulus," he incanted…and the disc shrank. Gideon picked it up, depositing it not in his hat, but in his chest-painting. Then he withdrew his cane from his forearm-painting, eyeing Craven calmly. "Shall we?" he inquired.

Craven lifted his right hand…and shot his gauntlet right at the man's face.

Gideon intercepted it with his cane, and the gauntlet stopped instantly in mid-air, dropping to the ground. At the same time, Craven charged, ramming Gideon with his shoulder.

Or at least he tried to.

Gideon dodged to the side, his cape wrapping around Craven's head. Craven tore at it blindly, flinging it away…just in time to see Gideon's cane striking him right between the eyes.

But this time, he barely felt the blow.

Craven swung one massive fist at Gideon, but Gideon struck it with his cane, stopping Craven's momentum instantly. Craven kicked at the man's legs, but Gideon tapped him with the cane twice…the first strike doing nothing, the second stopping him again. Craven rushed to grab Gideon, but Gideon struck him again and again, every other strike stopping his entire body in its tracks.

Craven paused, glaring at the man…and Gideon just stood there.

"I warned you," the man had the gall to say. "Brute force isn't everything, Craven."

"Spare me the lecture," Craven shot back. He swung at Gideon again, then again, but Gideon nullified every attack effortlessly.

Then the White Dragon attacked.

It lifted its massive tail in the air, then brought it smashing down on Craven and Gideon.

Gideon didn't even try to dodge it.

Instead, the Painter swung his cane up above his head right before the tail struck…and the White Dragon froze, its attack neutralized instantly.

Then Gideon thrust the butt of his cane right into Craven's chest.

Moments later, Craven lifted himself off the forest floor, some two miles from where he'd stood. He saw another line of downed trees in the trajectory he'd been sent…and when he looked down at himself, his chestplate was demolished.

Another part of his near-invincible armor destroyed.

He grunted, putting a hand to his chest, feeling a dull pain there. Frustration mounted, another emotion he'd rarely experienced.

He entered into Torpor, and was reborn healed. But his armor remained as it was…destroyed.

You are the right hand of the queen, he told himself. *You cannot be stopped.*

But for the first time in his life, Craven knew doubt.

* * *

Lucia eyed Yero. The man was much taller than she was, and a skilled Painter with considerable combat experience. In short, he was an exceedingly dangerous man.

"I'm going to enjoy this," she promised him, unsheathing her dual daggers. She threw them at Yero, who dodged out of the way, reaching into his chest-painting and throwing out something of his own.

A fireball.

It zoomed right at her…then passed *through* her as she turned to mist. She reformed rapidly, positioning herself between him and her daggers, which were still flying through the air toward the wall of dust.

She flicked her wrist.

One of her silver daggers stopped in midair, flying right back at her…and not coincidentally, at Yero's back.

He anticipated the attack, dodging to the side at the last minute. His gold and red cape acted just like Gideon's, unfurling from him and smacking the dagger out of the way.

It righted itself, going right back into Lucia's hand. She retrieved the other dagger in the same way, then feigned relief.

"Think of how unsatisfying that would've been if it'd worked," she quipped. Yero did not seem amused.

"I have no desire to kill you," he stated.

"The Pentad does," she retorted.

"We seek justice."

"Through murder," she shot back, spreading her arms out wide. "See? We have something in common."

"I have nothing in common with you," he retorted in disgust.

"Keep telling yourself that," she replied…and before she was even done saying it, she thrust her palm outward. A huge mist-palm flew out of her, slamming into Yero. His cape tried to intervene, but the mist-palm was too large, and it struck Yero full-on.

He flew backward into the wall of dust, vanishing from sight.

Danger, she felt Animus warn, more of a feeling than a word. Her Familiar could see in all directions, even when merged with Lucia. Which meant…

She dissolved into mist, right before a big black sword slashed through her from behind.

Lucia re-formed, watching as the flying sword stopped in midair. The air turned chilly with its aura.

"Hello Temper," she greeted. "Missed me?"

Temper slashed at her again, but she dissolved, re-forming and willing a huge mist-hand to bat the sword away. Then she threw both of her daggers into the mist where Yero had vanished.

Just as Yero flew out of the mist *over* the daggers, grabbing Temper's hilt in mid-air and chopping down at her head!

Lucia went into mist-form, flowing to the side. Temper slashed through her harmlessly, and she re-formed, kicking Yero in the temple. Or at least she tried to; his red and gold cape wrapped around her ankle, yanking her to the side.

Yero slashed at her leg, but Temper bounced off the silver spikes running down the side of her thigh, sparks flying with the impact.

Lucia yanked her foot back from Yero's cape, backpedaling away from another slash by Temper. She touched the silver skull on her right breast…and its eyes glowed green.

"Playtime's over," she announced…and transformed into Animus. But this time, she wasn't white fog…she was green.

Acid.

She flew right at Yero, engulfing him…and his skin blistered, his clothes starting to blacken and smoke.

He *screamed.*

Yero swung Temper blindly at her, but the sword passed through her harmlessly. He backpedaled, letting go of Temper and reaching into his chest-painting, drawing something out of it.

A golden mask with a large, grotesque mouth.

He put it on his face, and his body transformed, his flesh turning to solid gold…a metal impervious to her acid. His mouth opened…and opened, and opened, expanding impossibly until it was nearly as big as she was. Suddenly he breathed in, and a powerful vacuum began sucking her mist-body into that mouth.

Crap!

She re-formed as she was sucked in, barely managing to stop herself from falling into that horrible mouth by gripping its edges with both hands. The suction intensified, and she grit her teeth, her arms burning as she fought against it.

Then the vacuum weakened, fading away completely…and Lucia threw a dagger into it right before the mouth closed. She reached for Yero's mask then, tearing it from his face and tossing it aside.

Yero transformed back into himself, his skin burned and blistering.

"You know what else sucks?" she asked.

Then she flicked her wrist, summoning her dagger.

It burst through Yero's belly, between his chest and belly paintings, flying back into her hand in a spray of blood.

Yero gasped, his eyes widening. He looked down at the hole in his belly, hardly believing his eyes.

"Beaten by a girl," she mused, shaking her head. "Honestly Yero, I expected more from you."

His expression hardened, the veins at his temples bulging with rage…and his Temper flared.

The great black sword glowed bright red, its chilly aura shifting to red-hot. It burst into flames…and dozens of tiny flame-swords flew outward from it, surrounding Temper in a perfect circle.

They shot forward at her.

"Holy…" Lucia blurted out, willing Animus to shift her into their mist form. The swords passed through her…and darted in and out of her over and over again in a constant stream of attacks.

And there was no way she could re-form without getting sliced – and burned – to ribbons by them.

Well crap.

Yero went right for his golden mask, putting it back on. He turned gold once again, the bleeding from the gaping wound in his belly stopping instantly. His mouth began to open wide.

Lucia burst backward, flying away from him as quickly as she could.

A howling wind threatened to suck her backward as Yero breathed in, and Lucia's escape slowed…then stopped. She fought against the powerful vacuum, but it was too great for her to resist. She felt herself being pulled backward, even as the dozens of flaming daggers whirled around and through her.

Crap!

She pushed herself to the limit, willing herself to fly away. But there was no fighting it. Lucia slid ever-backward, only a few feet from Yero's grotesque, gaping mouth now. And if she was caught inside, he'd trap her…and take her back to the Pentad. And when he finally released her, she'd be in the capitol, surrounded by the kingdom's guards.

This is it, she realized. A sudden calm came over her, as she accepted her fate. As she accepted what was to be.

And then she *pulled* herself into her true form, slamming the palm of her hand into the skull at her left breast.

Its eyes glowed black, and her suit activated, dark tendrils rooting Lucia's feet to the ground.

Just as dozens of flaming daggers plunged into her body…and Temper's fiery blade sliced through her neck.

Chapter 9

Gideon watched as General Craven flew backward, zooming into the slowly fading mushroom cloud and punching a hole through it. The hole filled in rapidly, and Craven vanished from sight.

But he knew full well that it was only a matter of time before the living statue would be back.

The White Dragon roared behind Gideon, rearing its huge head back, then breathing its deadly white beam in the direction Craven had flown. The beam burned through the wall of dust ahead, illuminating it with a holy light. The beam faded, and the White Dragon stomped forward, charging right over Gideon and plunging into the mushroom cloud after Craven.

Slow the good general down, he told Myko.

The trusty wolf moon-dashed after Craven, and Gideon sighed, taking off his top hat and reaching inside. He felt countless rolled-up canvases within, each with a border that had a slightly different texture. He'd made a painting decades ago, after he'd promised Thaddeus to help Lucia escape the Pentad's bounty hunters. After he'd fallen in love with her.

A painting for Craven, the man he'd feared would come for them one day.

But before he could find it, he heard a blood-curdling scream to his left.

Gideon followed the sound…and saw Yero standing near the mushroom cloud over a hundred feet away. The Painter was wearing his golden mask, his Temper glowing red-hot. And falling to her knees before him was Lucia, dozens of miniature fire-swords jutting out her body like pins in a pin cushion.

Her head separated from her shoulders as Temper decapitated her…and the other flaming swords hacked her to pieces.

"No!" Gideon screamed.

He sprinted toward Yero, closing the distance between them in seconds. Yero's vacuum threatened to suck him in…and Temper flew right at Gideon.

Gideon thrust his magic glove at the flying sword, grabbing it by the hilt…and swinging it right at Yero's neck. He felt Temper try to resist, but his glove was more powerful. The red-hot blade struck Yero's neck, biting partway into his golden skin. But the metal managed to deflect Temper, and the living sword ricocheted off, leaving a deep dent in Yero's metallic flesh.

Gideon chopped again and again, but Yero raised his left arm to block the blows. Temper cut into his forearm, deeper and deeper with each blow.

Until it severed the Painter's arm altogether.

Yero howled, his metallic voice roaring out of his huge mouth.

Temper managed to jerk itself out of Gideon's glove, flying right at him and thrusting at his head. Gideon batted Temper with his cane, stopping the Familiar instantly…then took his top hat off, whipping it at the sword.

It vanished within.

Then he shoved his hat into his chest-painting, trapping Temper. And while the hat also technically contained many of Gideon's paintings – and paintings could not be stored in paintings – it served only as a portal to its own realm, and portals *could* be stored in paintings.

A primal scream shattered his eardrums.

Gideon fell to his knees, clutching his ears in his hands. Tears streamed down his cheeks…and the earth quaked beneath him. He fell onto all fours, seeing the wall of dust ahead burst forward in a swirling maelstrom, a huge shadow falling to the earth just beyond.

The White Dragon's head.

Thump, thump, thump.

A figure strode out of the swirling dust then. General Craven, his helmet gone, the chestplate of his armor caved in. He stopped just beyond what remained of the mushroom cloud, standing by the White Dragon's motionless head. Yero walked stiffly to his side, his left arm missing.

"Take him," Craven ordered Yero.

Yero strode toward Gideon, his golden skin shimmering dully in the moonlight. Gideon felt Myko coming back to him through their bond.

Stay back Myko, Gideon ordered, rising to his feet. *Wait for my command.* He faced Yero then, who stopped a few yards before him.

"Come quietly or face the same fate as your wife," Yero ordered. Gideon reached into his chest-painting, retrieving his magical lantern.

"You've lost your Temper," Gideon noted, a cold rage building within him. A vision of Lucia being hacked apart by Temper's fiery daggers came to him then, and his anger fed on it, building within him. "Now it's my turn."

Yero reached into his own chest-painting…and Myko moon-dashed into his back from behind, shoving him toward Gideon…who threw his lantern into Yero's oversized mouth. It vanished within.

"Eruptus!" Gideon cried, leaping away.

Yero *exploded.*

Gideon's cape swung around him, protecting him from hunks of flying golden metal that shot outward in all directions. Then his cape relaxed, and he gazed at where Yero had been, seeing his lantern lying there on its side on the ground. He strode forward, picking it up and placing it back in his chest-painting.

But to his surprise, despite killing Yero, Lucia did not reappear.

She's supposed to resurrect!

The heart-shaped amulet should have reabsorbed Lucia's soul from Yero, the man who'd killed her. Yet it had not.

His guts twisted, his heart hammering in his chest. Suddenly he felt sick.

"Lucia!" he shouted.

"She is dead," Craven stated. Gideon shook his head in disbelief, panic rising within him.

"No," he protested.

"She is dead," Craven repeated.

Gideon turned to Craven as if seeing him for the first time. Then he stood up straight, his jawline rippling. He pointed a finger at the man.

"Then you're next," he promised.

"You cannot win," Craven growled. "The Pentad will bring you to justice, as it did your wife. She brought her death upon her when she attacked us."

"You're right. If my wife is dead, I can't win," he agreed. He smiled grimly. "But I can make sure the Pentad doesn't hurt anyone. Ever again."

"You dare threaten the Pentad?"

"I spent my life protecting it," Gideon replied. "Serving it. Serving my queen. The same queen that ordered the death of my wife and child."

"She did not," Craven retorted. "Lucia's death was Yero's failure."

"The Pentad would have had her executed anyway," Gideon argued. "Just as they would execute me. And my daughter. And Thaddeus."

"You violated the law. You knew the consequences."

"The law?" Gideon inquired, his lips curling in a sneer. "Rules the powerful use to control the weak. Rules the few make to control the many." He shook his head. "Your laws mean nothing to me, not after this."

"They will have meaning to you soon," Craven promised.

"The Pentad destroyed my life," Gideon replied. "And now I'm going to repay the favor."

He withdrew his cane from his Painter's uniform, pointing it at Craven.

"Come to me and die."

Craven stood there for a moment longer, then strode toward Gideon, his armored feet *thumping* on the earth. Then he pointed his right gauntlet at Gideon, and it shot toward Gideon with blinding speed!

Gideon struck the gauntlet with his cane, stopping it instantly. He tried plunging it into his chest-painting, but it wouldn't go in. It had to be lined with a live canvas.

He felt the gauntlet vibrate…and then Craven flew toward him, his right hand extended.

Gideon tossed the gauntlet aside, dodging to the side and striking Craven with his cane. The attack didn't even slow him down, and Craven rejoined his gauntlet, spinning around to face Gideon.

Who tossed his cane at Craven as the general lunged at him again.

The cane struck Craven between the eyes, stopping him instantly…and the cane ricocheted off. Gideon caught it, then reached into his chest-painting for the painting he'd created just for Craven.

The general thrust his palm out at Gideon, his gauntlet glowing bright gold.

A shockwave burst outward from his palm, striking Gideon and sending him flying backward. His cape billowed outward, slowing his flight and landing him gently on the ground a few yards from Craven.

You're up Myko.

Myko moon-dashed right through the cloud of dust nearby, sailing over Gideon's head and slamming into Craven.

Who caught the wolf by the neck with one hand, snapping Myko's spine with a flick of his wrist.

He tossed the Familiar aside…and Myko moon-dashed right into Craven's flank, knocking him off-balance…and healing the wolf instantly.

Myko moon-dashed into Craven again and again, ricocheting off each time, then dashing again immediately afterward in rapid-fire. Craven kept stumbling to the side, then finally managed to plant his feet in a wide, low stance. When Myko ricocheted off of him, rematerializing after his moon-dash, Craven shot his gauntlet out at the wolf, grasping Myko by the neck. He shot forward to reconnect with his gauntlet.

And then brought his left hand up high, swinging it down on Myko's skull.

Gideon threw his cane at Craven just in time, striking the general's shoulder. The cane bounced off harmlessly…but Craven's momentum was stopped, just before his giant fist obliterated Myko's skull.

Gideon rushed forward, catching his cane and reaching into his chest-painting. He threw his Conclave-disc at Craven's feet.

"Anulus!" he incanted.

The disc grew…and Craven fell into it, vanishing from sight.

Gideon incanted again to close the portal to the Conclave, trapping Craven within. Craven's gauntlet fell from Myko's throat, and Gideon batted it away with his cane. The gauntlet rolled across the ground, coming to a stop a dozen feet away. Gideon sighed then, turning to Myko and putting a hand on the wolf's furry head.

"You okay boy?" he asked.

Myko *wuffed.*

Gideon turned to the blasted ground where Yero had been, feeling a sudden exhaustion come over him. A vision of Lucia standing before Yero came to him. Of her head falling from her shoulders, tumbling to the ground.

He shook his head, willing the memory away.

"She'll come back," he told himself. "She has to."

Myko whined, and Gideon sighed, turning away from the blasted earth to look back at Havenwood. At the castle atop Dragon's Peak…and the waterfall cascading down to Lake Fenestra far below.

Bella, he thought. *She has Lucia's amulet!*

Having the amulet close enough to Lucia's remains would bring her back to life, Gideon knew.

It *had* to.

Chapter 10

After Simon and Percy's trip down Memory Lane, they returned to the cabin in the Festering Wood. Simon went to the Plane of Reflection, discarding his painting of the phoenix and his dark tower. He got a fresh canvas, then spent a great deal of time staring at it. Waiting for the Flow to strike him like it always did.

But nothing happened.

At length Simon gave up, leaving the Plane of Reflection to find Percy just outside the cabin, sitting before the unlit firepit. He was writing furiously in a notebook, his brow furrowed with concentration. But as lightly as Simon treaded, Percy still heard him, looking up as Simon approached.

"No luck eh?" he stated, patting the chair next to him. Simon sat down on it with a sigh, shaking his head. "Why so frustrated?" Percy inquired.

"I don't usually have this problem," Simon admitted. "I can always paint."

Percy closed his notebook.

"Well of course you can," he replied. "But why do you need to?"

Simon frowned.

"What's the rush, hmm?" Percy pressed, raising an eyebrow. "Do you have someplace to be? Is there a deadline?"

Simon shook his head.

"I guess not," he replied.

"You guess correctly," Percy agreed with a smile. "Have you painted anything at all?"

"No."

"Well, no one ever finished by not starting," Percy advised. Then he paused. "Actually, the vast majority of people finish there," he corrected.

Simon sighed again, feeling suddenly exhausted, even though it was only around noontime. Percy chuckled, patting his knee.

"Tell me what's wrong," the man requested.

"I've always painted darkness," Simon confessed. "Every painting I've ever painted, it came from…my dad."

"From your dark tower," Percy murmured.

"Right."

"So pain and suffering is all that inspires you?" Percy pressed. Simon grimaced, and Percy laughed. "Oh, don't be embarrassed. So many artists think their muse lives on suffering. That it will die without it!"

"It won't?"

"Of course not," Percy scoffed. "Utter nonsense. The Flow loves all stories, Simon. Tragedies, comedies, love stories, and so on and so forth. We humans judge tragedy to be the worthiest of our attention, because it's so dreadfully *serious*."

Simon had to smile at that.

"You only see yourself as a tragedy, Simon," Percy pressed. "But what else are you?"

Simon said nothing.

Percy grabbed Simon's sleeve then, pulling it up his forearm…and exposing his scars there. Simon shrank back on reflex, pulling the sleeve back down.

"Roll them up," Percy commanded.

"Why?"

"The usual reasons," Percy answered. "Because I'm older and I said so."

Simon hesitated, then did as he was told, rolling up his sleeve.

"The other one too," Percy prompted.

Simon sighed, rolling up the other sleeve. He felt exposed, naked despite still being clothed. He stared at his scars, disgusted by them. They were raised and ugly, and not for the first time, he wished that he'd never started cutting himself. It was a constant reminder of what he'd done to himself…and what had been done to him.

"There you go," Percy stated with a satisfied smile. "That's better."

Simon was struck by a sudden idea.

"Can you paint them away?" he asked. Percy's brow furrowed.

"Why?"

"Because…I don't want them anymore," Simon answered.

"But they're you," Percy pointed out.

"I hate them."

"And now you've found your true problem," Percy replied triumphantly. Simon frowned.

"What?" he asked.

"You hate yourself."

Simon felt a chill run down his spine. His mind went blank, and suddenly he couldn't even remember what Percy had just said. He just stared at the man, feeling dazed.

Percy smiled, patting Simon's knee again.

"It's not your fault," he continued. "You were *taught* to hate yourself. You were infatuated with Vin, and he hated you for being honest about your feelings. Your father hated you for being something he didn't understand. And Ferra hated you for not being who *she* wanted you to be…her perfect weapon against the Pentad."

Still, Simon could not speak. But Percy didn't either, merely gazing at Simon with his kind eyes, a warm smile on his lips. The man sat there patiently, as if there was nothing in the world he'd rather be doing. Until Simon felt that he had to fill the silence between them with something. Anything.

"Why?" was all he could manage.

"Why what?"

"Why are you helping me?" Simon asked.

"Because you're worth helping," Percy answered.

"Am I?" Simon pressed.

"Well I certainly think so," Percy replied. "Do you?"

Simon sat there, unable to answer. He turned away from Percy's gaze, looking off into the Festering Wood in the distance. A foul land, one no person in their right mind would wish to live in. A place of darkness and rot and stink. Trees with soft, pungent wood, no good for lumber or much of anything else for that matter.

Worthless.

And yet the great Persnickity Gibbons had seen this forest and chosen to make it his home.

"Has anyone else seen your worth, Simon?" Percy pressed.

"The Collector," Simon answered.

"Who else?"

Simon gazed at the tree line far ahead, recalling the day he'd come here, after turning on Miss Savage. After helping his supposed enemy trap her within a painting. He remembered the girl who'd not only let him live, but had embraced him, even after everything he'd done to her and her family.

Beauty in the darkest dark, he thought.

Miss Savage had used him, pretending to care about him. She'd used his love for the Collector to manipulate him, playing him like just another one of her musical instruments. Even the Collector had used him at first, before he'd opened up to Simon. Before he'd let Simon in.

But one person had seen the beauty in him without any conditions at all. And had embraced him, even after he'd attacked her.

I'm not made of porcelain you know, she'd said, insisting that he embrace her back.

"Everyone deserves a second chance," he murmured, remembering her words to him.

"Pardon?" Percy asked.

Simon smiled, turning to face Percy.

"I know what to paint," he declared…and stood up from his chair to do just that.

* * *

The Flow returned to Simon with a vengeance, and he worked like a man possessed, painting until he could paint no more. For hours and hours, until his work was done.

Then he went to his bed and collapsed, falling asleep instantly.

When he awoke, he got up from his bed, turning to face the easel in the corner of his cabin. His painting was there as he'd left it, and he stepped up to it.

And stared.

It was just as he remembered, a painting unlike any he'd painted. For there was not a hint of glass, or blood, or porcelain. None of what had graced every other painting he'd ever created.

It was entirely new, this painting. Something beyond his experience. A revelation.

He stared at it, looking for something to change. A mistake to correct. But he found none.

To him, it was perfect.

He heard a knock on the door, and he turned, walking to the door to open it. Percy was there, of course.

"Well well," Percy stated, his eyes going immediately to the painting. "What have we here?"

"A second chance," Simon answered. Percy's eyebrows rose, and he walked up to the painting, stroking his red beard as he studied it. Then he began to laugh. And not just any laugh, but great belly-laughs, ones that went on and on.

Simon frowned.

"What?" he demanded.

Percy turned to Simon, a big smile on his lips.

"You did it!" he cried exuberantly…and promptly embraced Simon. Simon blinked, taken aback by this. Percy held him at arms' length then, beaming at him. "Oh Simon, I'm so proud of you!"

"Oh," Simon mumbled. "Um…thanks."

Percy turned to look at the painting again, then pulled Simon up to it.

"Well come on now," he urged. "Sign it and pull that thing out!"

Simon complied, signing the bottom-right of the painting with black paint. A breeze caressed him from behind, ruffling Percy's beard. Simon reached into the painting, feeling a warm pulsing in his fingers as he did so. It spread to his wrist as he plunged it through, and his fingertips brushed up against something soft. He thought of Bella's words to him, and smiled.

A second chance indeed.

He took a deep breath in, then drew it out.

Chapter 11

Bella stood at the edge of the cliff overlooking Lake Fenestra, the Everstream to her right and Nemesis to her left. They watched as the sky opened up high above the approaching army far beyond Havenwood's mushroom forest, a gaping hole into the heavens appearing there. Her eyes widened as a great big meteorite shot through that hole, slamming into the army and annihilating it instantly.

The very earth exploded, a mushroom-cloud blasting upward from the impact.

Seconds later, an ear-splitting *BOOM* brought Bella to her knees, a burst of wind blasting her and Nemesis backward. She landed flat on her back, her ears ringing.

She grunted, struggling to her feet. There was a trickling sensation down the left ear, and she put a hand to it, finding blood there.

Damn, she heard Nemesis swear as the dragon got to her own feet. *Your dad's been holding back on us.*

Bella ignored her Familiar, walking back to the edge of the cliff and peering down. The mushroom cloud far below was rising and expanding, three tiny figures barely visible before it…and the White Dragon of course. From this far away, she couldn't figure out who they were.

Already on it, Nemesis stated…and promptly leapt off the edge of the cliff, soaring over Havenwood toward the battleground below.

"Hey!" Bella protested. "We're not supposed to go after them!"

You're not supposed to, Nemesis corrected. *I can do whatever the hell I want.*

Bella watched as Nemesis flew over Lake Fenestra, passing it to continue on high above the mushroom forest. The dragon remained high above even the White Dragon, safely out of harm's reach.

What do you see, Bella asked.

Gideon just walloped Craven, Nemesis answered.

The White Dragon breathed its deadly white beam of light into the mushroom cloud, burning a hole through it. Then the huge dragon charged right into the cloud, vanishing within it.

What about Mom, Bella pressed.

One moment, Nemesis answered. There was a pause. *Your mom…*

Bella felt terror grip her…and then disbelief.

Then all she felt was numbness through their bond, and a sudden shutting out, as if Nemesis had slammed a psychic door between them. But despite the undead dragon's efforts, a single image had gotten through. Of her mom, dozens of miniature flaming swords jutting out of her body.

Decapitated.

Bella gasped, her heart leaping in her throat.

She'll come back, Nemesis reminded her. Mom always came back to life whenever the person who'd killed her was killed in turn. Bella put a hand to the heart-shaped amulet Mom had given her, looking down at it.

The ruby in its center pulsed no more.

Bella clutched it, her jawline rippling. With Mom dead, Gideon was the only one left fighting Yero and Craven. If he failed, Yero would live…and Mom would stay dead.

But if Bella went down there after Yero, the amulet would suck out his life force, ensuring that Mom would come back to life.

You promised not to, she reminded herself.

Gideon's fighting Yero now, Nemesis notified her. There was a long pause. *Wow, that was gruesome.*

"What?"

Your daddy just exploded Yero, Nemesis answered.

"Exploded?"

Boom. Splatter. Guts all over the place.

"Got it," Bella muttered, feeling squeamish. She pictured Yero as she'd first met him, standing tall and proud. One of Gideon's friends, a man who'd treated her decently…until he'd threatened her family and killed her mother. Despite that, she felt no joy at his death.

Just emptiness.

"Did Mom come back?" she asked.

Um…no.

"What?" Bella blurted out. "She's supposed to come back!"

I know.

"Are you sure?" she pressed, feeling sick to her stomach. "Nemesis, she…"

Didn't come back, Nemesis interjected. *She's not here.*

"But…" Bella began, then stopped herself. Her heart was pounding in her chest, and she realized she was hyperventilating. "Maybe I have to bring the amulet close to where she died."

Maybe.

"I'm coming down," Bella decided. She reached into her chest-painting, pulling out her skull mask.

You can't do that, Nemesis argued.

"I'm coming," Bella shot back.

You promised your…

And then Bella put the skull-mask on, turning into her spirit-form.

She willed herself off the cliff, flying forward and downward toward the battlefield far below. As she passed over Lake Fenestra and the mushroom forest beyond, she spotted two tiny figures in the distance, standing near the mushroom-cloud created by the meteorite. It was Gideon and Craven, battling each other.

Bella drew closer, seeing Gideon throw something down at Craven's feet. A black hole appeared below the statue, and Craven fell into it, vanishing from sight…just as Bella touched down on the grassy field a few dozen feet away.

She pulled off her mask, running up to Gideon and Myko.

"Dad!" she cried, leaping into his arms. Gideon turned to her in surprise, stiffening as she embraced him. He pushed her back.

"Bella, you weren't supposed to…"

"Come down here, I know," Bella interrupted. "But you won. The fight's over."

Gideon relaxed a little, his shoulders slumping.

"It is," he agreed. "For now."

"We have to resurrect Mom," Bella urged. "Where did she die?"

Gideon pointed to a crater of blasted earth in the distance, and Bella rushed to it, holding her amulet out in front of her.

Nothing happened.

"Come on…" she urged, kneeling down and staring at the amulet's ruby. It remained utterly dark. No pulsing light, no white spirit-energy pulling into it.

Nothing.

"What's wrong?" she said, her heart pounding in her chest again. "It's supposed to work!"

She felt a wet tongue kiss her hand, and realized Myko had walked up to stand beside her. She leaned on his big, warm, furry body, feeling suddenly exhausted. Myko whined, eyeing the blasted earth where Mom had died, then gazing at Bella with his kind silver eyes. She felt a hand on her shoulder, and turned to see Gideon standing behind her. His expression was grave.

"I don't know," he confessed. "I killed Yero. She should've come back."

Keep trying, she felt Nemesis tell her from a few hundred feet overhead. *I'll go get Grandpa and his girlfriend.*

Bella ran a hand through her hair, trying to calm down. Myko's presence helped a little.

Okay, she told herself. *Think.*

Yero killed Mom, so Mom's and Yero's souls switched bodies. And when Yero died, Mom's soul should have gone back to Mom's body, reviving it. Then again, Mom's body had been decapitated…and then cut to pieces, and apparently exploded along with Yero.

What if Mom's corpse was so far gone it *couldn't* come back? Or what if her remains needed to be closer together to be revived?

Or…

She turned to Gideon, who was still standing behind her. Then she spotted something behind him. A sort of shimmering of the air just above something lying on the shattered ground a few feet away from him. A gauntlet.

Craven's gauntlet.

The light near the gauntlet seemed to warp, as if viewed through a fishbowl…and Craven himself appeared, his right hand within the gauntlet…and his shield in his left hand.

Bella's breath caught in her throat, her eyes widening with horror. She managed to cry out…just as Gideon turned to face the living statue.

* * *

Gideon sighed, placing his cane back into his forearm-painting, then running a hand through his hair. He watched as Bella stared at the blasted earth where her mother had been murdered, then at the amulet in her hand. Her mother's heart had stopped, the amulet's steady pulsing no more. Bella's jawline rippled, her eyes moist with tears. She turned to glance at him…then beyond him, at something over his left shoulder.

Her eyes widened in horror.

Bella cried out, and Gideon turned around, reaching automatically for the cane in his left forearm-painting.

And saw Craven swinging a massive fist at his head.

Gideon's cape intercepted, grabbing Craven's fist and pulling it aside harmlessly. But at the same time, Craven kicked Gideon's knee.

It bent backward with a horrible *crunch.*

Gideon howled in agony, collapsing onto his back on the ground. He reached for his left forearm-painting with his right hand, drawing out his cane…and Craven reached down to grab his wrist, squeezing it with his terrible strength.

Bones shattered, and Gideon dropped his cane to the ground.

"Dad!" Bella cried, grabbing Cain from her hip and activating the undead weapon. She swung at Craven, but Cain bounced off Craven's arm harmlessly.

"Bella, r-" Gideon began…but Craven grabbed him by the throat, lifting Gideon up until his feet were dangling above the ground. The pain this caused his broken knee was beyond description, and Gideon had the sudden urge to vomit.

Myko!

The wolf was already moon-dashing into Craven, but Craven lifted his shield, and Myko ricocheted off its golden surface, flying violently backward. He tried moon-dashing again…but Craven activated Aganon, a beam of golden light blasting out from its surface.

The beam struck Myko, vaporizing his hindquarters instantly.

Myko moon-dashed to the side, reappearing whole some fifty feet away.

Craven stood there, ignoring Gideon's cape's attempts to pry his fingers from Gideon's neck, and Bella's repeated attacks with Cain. He gazed at Gideon impassively.

"I am the right hand of Queen Eldora," he proclaimed. "And by my right hand I execute her will."

Gideon tried to speak, but Craven's grip tightened, and no words could force themselves past it. Or air, for that matter. He struggled to breathe, black spots growing like blotches of ink in his vision

Myko, save Bella!

He thrust his right hand toward his fallen cane, his glove flying off to grab it. Then his glove shot straight up, flying high into the sky.

There was a flash of silver light, then darkness took him.

* * *

Bella swung Cain at Craven's huge arm, even as the living statue held Gideon high in the air. She watched as her father's eyes reddened, his face turning swollen and purple. Gideon grasped at Craven's hand, trying desperately to pry those metal fingers from his throat.

And then his head slumped forward, his body going limp.

"Let him *go!*" Bella shouted.

Craven dropped Gideon to the ground with a *thump*. He turned to Bella then, his stony eyes meeting hers. Without a word, he intercepted her swing, grabbing Cain's mid-shaft and squeezing. There was a horrid *crunch*, and Craven opened his hand, Cain's vertebrae had been reduced to dust.

Myko moon-dashed at Craven, ricocheting off again…and then leapt at Bella, shoving her backward away from Craven.

"No!" Bella cried.

She reached into her chest-painting, putting on her skull-mask…and felt a chill as she transformed into her spirit-form. She willed herself to fly at Craven, reaching out to touch him with her left hand. She *pulled* at his life-force…

But nothing happened.

Craven swung Aganon at Bella, and she felt it slam into her, throwing her bodily backward.

What the…!

He lifted his right arm then, his gauntlet shooting out at Bella. It struck her in the throat, somehow interacting with her spirit form, its fingers wrapping around her neck.

It *squeezed.*

Bella's windpipe closed, and she yanked her skull-mask off, letting it tumble to the ground. Craven lifted one armored foot, slamming it down on the mask.

Crushing it.

Dark spots grew in Bella's vision, and she clawed at his gauntlet futilely.

Nemesis, help!

She could already feel her Familiar diving through the air toward her, a hundred feet away and closing in fast.

I can't kill him Bella, Nemesis warned.

Save Gideon, she urged. *Leave me.*

I can't do that, Nemesis retorted. *I can't let him take you. They'll kill you.*

Bella's vision blackened completely, and she felt the world starting to fade away.

Kill me first, she ordered.

And then she felt Nemesis reach her, a horrible pain lancing through her back and into her chest as the dragon's armored tail went right through her heart.

Then one became two.

Bella felt herself split, the shadow and the light pulling free from each other. Luna stayed in the darkness of night, held in Craven's grasp as Bella had been. But Lux could not exist in the darkness…and so she shot backward, flying at impossible speed to the nearest light that could be seen.

The streetlights of downtown Havenwood.

Meanwhile, Luna found herself staring at Craven, her shadowy fingers clutching his giant gauntleted hand.

Myko moon-dashed at Craven, bouncing off the general once again. But the wolf's bright silver light struck Luna like a brick wall, and even Craven's iron grip wasn't powerful enough to withstand it. Luna burst out of his grasp, flying backward from Myko's light until she was safely within shadow.

Craven stomped after her…and she became one with the night, feeling herself expanding. Suddenly she *was* the night, a shadow extending across a half-mile of grassland…and Craven was merely an ant standing upon her.

She watched as he scanned the ground futilely, trying to find her. Gideon began to stir, and Luna willed herself to step out of the shadow as herself next to him. But at the same time, Craven strode toward Gideon, lowering his massive shield onto Gideon's chest…and pinning him helplessly to the ground.

Myko moon-dashed into him to try to stop him…and Luna was thrust a hundred feet backward.

Damn it!

Myko moon-dashed again, but this time Craven caught the wolf in mid-air, grabbing him by the neck with both hands. Myko tried to moon-dash out of the man's grasp, bursting to the side in a ray of light, but Craven slid across the ground with the wolf, holding on with a powerful grip.

Then he squeezed.

Myko moon-dashed again, this time straight up. Craven flew into the air with the wolf, bursting nearly a hundred feet upward. When his moon-dash ended, Myko dashed again and again, zipping through the air in streaks of silver light. Over and over, without a second's pause between. Craven didn't have a moment between dashes to attack, and even trying to strangle the wolf was pointless. For Myko healed completely between each dash, and with the full moon high in the sky, his ability to moon-dash was unlimited.

Go Myko!

The wolf was high enough in the sky now that little of his light reached the ground, and Luna sprinted up to Gideon, who was gasping for air, Craven's shield still on his chest. Nemesis was already there beside him, trying in vain to lift one edge of the shield off of him.

"Gideon!" Luna cried, leaning down to grab the edge of the shield. She heaved upward, but the thing was so heavy that she couldn't lift it…not even with Nemesis and Gideon helping.

Gideon gasped, his forehead slick with sweat. His breath came in quick gasps, the weight of the shield making it nearly impossible for him to breathe. If Nemesis hadn't intervened so quickly, relieving the pressure a bit, he probably would've already been dead.

There was a *thump* behind her.

Luna whirled around, seeing Craven rising to his feet not a yard away from her. Myko landed right behind the man, leaping at him and biting his armored arm. Craven ignored the wolf, studying Luna.

"What are you?" he demanded.

He reached out to grab her, and Luna backpedaled, tripping over Gideon and the shield.

"Moon-dash!" Luna cried as Craven's fingers wrapped around her inky black ankle.

Myko did so, the silver light emanating from his body slamming into her…and sending her flying backward. She tore free from Craven's grasp, instantly thrown over thirty yards away. Luna ran back toward them, shoved backward every time Myko moon-dashed into Craven. Over and over again. But this time Craven didn't bother fighting Myko. He ignored the wolf – and Nemesis – reaching down to retrieve his shield. Then he picked up Gideon by the throat again, holding him at his side, feet dangling above the ground.

Gideon gasped, clutching at Craven's hand. He started to reach into his chest-painting.

"Move another inch and you die," Craven promised. "And I will hunt your daughter to the ends of the earth. Forever."

Gideon froze.

"Tell them to surrender," Craven commanded.

Gideon stared at Luna, his mouth working soundlessly. Craven let up on his grip, and Gideon coughed, spittle dripping down his chin. Tears streamed down his cheeks, his face terribly swollen.

"Go," he croaked.

Luna stared at him, feeling numb.

"Go," he pressed.

"No," Luna protested. "I'm not leaving you."

He smiled sadly.

"I've…lived long…enough," he gasped. Then he took a few deep breaths. "Your…turn now."

"No!" Luna cried.

"Go!" Gideon commanded. "Myko, I…order you. Take…her and…go!"

Myko whined, shaking his head at his master.

"Love her…like you loved…me."

Still Myko hesitated, whining again.

"Go boy!" Gideon cried.

And then Myko turned from Gideon, moon-dashing right at Luna, separating her from her father. Again and again he moon-dashed at her, shoving her backward helplessly each time. Luna cried out, begging for Myko to stop. And eventually he did…but not before they were all the way through the mushroom forest and over Lake Fenestra, in downtown Havenwood.

She found Lux waiting for her there, huddled under a streetlamp. Luna recombined with her, forming Bella once again…and Bella turned back to gaze down at the battlefield in the distance, peering beyond the mushroom tops in the mushroom forest.

The dust from the mushroom clouds was settling…and a huge black shadow leapt out of it, bursting through the dust and sailing over Craven to land between him and Havenwood. It spun around, facing its enemy.

It was the White Dragon…but something was wrong.

Both of its wings were gone, and a long angry gash extended down its left flank, the scales and flesh burnt away there.

The dragon roared, swiping at Craven.

"Gideon!" Bella gasped in horror. For Gideon was still in Craven's grasp.

But Craven lifted his shield at the White Dragon, a beam of pure golden light shooting out of it.

The beam struck the dragon and burned through, cutting through the mushroom tops beyond, destroying them instantly. It passed over Lake Fenestra, the heat of its passage boiling the water directly below. Then it slammed into the mountainside just below where Bella was standing, turning the stone red-hot. The stone melted, lava drooling down the mountainside into the lake. Clouds of steam shot upward, obscuring Bella's view of what lay beyond.

"Down!" she cried, crouching low.

The beam winked out, and she hesitated, then stood.

She spotted a dark shape flying toward her, soaring over Lake Fenestra. It was Nemesis, she knew. The dragon landed beside Bella and Myko, twisting her head around to face her. Bella could sense that Nemesis was hiding something.

"What's wrong?" Bella pressed.

We need to run, the dragon answered. *Now.*

"Nemesis, tell..."

Nemesis leapt at Bella, grabbing her by the shoulders and hauling her up into the air...just as another beam of golden light shot outward from Craven's shield. It slammed into Dragon's Peak, missing Bella by mere yards. Then it swept across, tearing through the buildings spiraling up the mountain. Black smoke rose from the ruins, rising up the mountainside like a dark, thick wall.

Bella's gaze was drawn to the battlefield in the distance.

The White Dragon stood before Craven on the blasted plains beyond what remained of the mushroom forest. As the golden beam from Craven's shield winked out, a glowing red line cutting through the dragon's neck shone red-hot against the darkness of the night.

And as Bella watched, the dragons' head separated from its neck, and the kingdom's great protector fell at the feet of its enemy.

Nemesis flew Bella upward, and Myko moon-dashed after them, rising above even the great white towers of the castle. Craven's shield activated again, its golden beam cutting into Castle Havenwood, severing its tallest tower. It fell, smashing into the castle and collapsing a full third of the massive structure.

"Grandpa!" Bella cried in horror. "We have to save him!"

But Nemesis ignored her, continuing to rise far above Dragon's Peak.

Sorry Bella, the dragon told her. *It's too late.*

"No!" Bella cried, tears streaming down her cheeks. "Bring us back! We can still save him! We *have* to save him!"

She struggled against Nemesis's grip, trying to pry herself free. The fall would certainly kill her, at least temporarily. But she could still...

Another beam of light sliced through the castle, severing three more towers. They fell, obliterating more of the castle. Sky-bridges were severed, the huge sections of the castle each bridge led to falling down the mountainside and shattering to rubble far below.

Bella stared in mute horror, her breath catching in her throat. For as she watched, Craven's beam struck again and again, until the castle was no more.

Onward and upward Nemesis flew, Myko right behind them, a streak of silver light against the blackness of night. Far below, the ruins of Grandpa's finest creation smoldered, a dark cloud rising from the ashes of the place Bella had come to call home.

And lying at the feet of the man who'd destroyed the magical kingdom, the great White Dragon lay motionless, its guardian no more.

So it was that a dragon circle – white and good – died that day for Havenwood.

Chapter 12

Nemesis brought Bella and Myko to the only place they had any chance at escaping the Pentad's unstoppable champion: to the Underground. And within its dark, rocky tunnels, glowing softly with deep purple light from around each of its magical doors, Bella stopped, leaning against the wall. Then she slid down to her knees.

And wept.

Great, horrible sobs escaped her, tears streaming down her cheeks and dripping from her nose. She knelt there, unable to stop. Not caring if she ever did. She just cried and cried and cried, until she could cry no more.

Then she rested her back against the wall, sitting on the floor, her legs stretched out before her. Staring at nothing at all.

Empty.

Myko and Nemesis stood nearby, each trying frantically to comfort her in their own way. But she felt none of it. It was as if psychic walls surrounded her. Walls of ice, allowing no warmth to pass through.

She lowered her gaze, seeing the heart-shaped ruby amulet resting on her chest. Its gentle pulse was gone, its light no more. And so too, Bella's heart was destroyed. While once it had been filled with love and hope, now it was merely a pump, sending blood to her organs. A thing of beauty reduced to something purely mechanical.

Bella, Nemesis urged, putting a clawed hand on her shoulder. *We need to keep moving.*

She didn't respond. She didn't move.

Bella, Nemesis insisted, shaking her shoulder.

Bella stared at the amulet, ignoring her Familiar. She felt the dragon's urgency, but she didn't care. Without Gideon and Mom…without Grandpa…her life meant nothing at all.

Bella!

She took a deep, shuddering breath in, grabbing Nemesis's armored wrist and shoving it away from her.

"Leave me," she ordered.

No.

"Leave!" she shouted.

Nemesis didn't move.

Bella lifted her gaze to glare at the dragon, fixing her in a cold, heartless glare.

"I never liked you," she spat. "I wish I'd never painted you."

She felt a chill run through Nemesis, felt the dragon's sudden pain. Still, Nemesis didn't move. Cain stirred at her right hip.

"Bella, you…" he began.

"Shut *up* Cain!" she snapped.

His jaw snapped closed with a *click*.

"You let Grandpa die," Bella accused, standing up and shoving the dragon backward.

Wrong.

"You let him die," she insisted. "You let *everyone* die."

She felt a hot flash of anger from the Familiar, and Nemesis glared at her with those red, glowing eyes.

Yeah?

"Yeah," Bella shot back. "Deny it."

If I'd let you go down there to the castle, you'd be dead too.

"You don't know that," Bella shot back. "You didn't even give me a chance!"

So this is all my fault?

"Yes!"

Nemesis lunged forward, shoving Bella's shoulders backward. Her back slammed into the wall, and Nemesis pinned her there.

Yeah? Well if you'd kept your promise to Gideon and Lucia, Gideon wouldn't have been distracted, Nemesis argued.

Bella's eyes widened, a chill running through her.

You wanna know whose fault this is? Look in the mirror.

"I…"

The only reason Havenwood fell was because you *didn't listen,* Nemesis declared. *You did this Bella. Not me. You.*

Bella glared back at her Familiar, but her lower lip quivered. More tears flowed down her cheeks, and she swallowed past a lump in her throat. She tried to speak, but there was nothing to say.

Nemesis was right.

"Leave," she whispered at last. "I never want to see you again."

She meant it…and Nemesis knew it.

The dragon turned away from Bella, moving quickly down the tunnel. Within moments, she was gone. Bella felt Nemesis close down, as if a door had been shut on their connection.

And then she was alone with Myko.

He whined, nudging her shoulder with his wet nose.

"Leave me alone," she muttered.

Myko licked her cheek, and she shrank away from him.

"Go away," she mumbled. But Myko didn't. She slumped against the wall, sliding down onto her butt and hugging her knees to her chest. Myko laid down next to her, and she draped herself over his soft, warm body.

Myko, her constant companion. Always there for her and Gideon, through good and bad. Nemesis had never been so loyal. The dragon had wanted little to do with Bella since being pulled out of her canvas.

"I should've painted someone more like you," she told Myko in a whisper.

Myko didn't respond.

"I'm sorry Myko," she said.

Then she closed her eyes, burying her face in his fur.

And wept.

* * *

Bella had no desire to get up from the floor of the Underground, but her body forced the issue. The call of nature eventually grew too powerful to ignore, and she had to have some way to relieve it. She had half a mind to just squat in the tunnel, but she decided it'd be better to go someplace more sanitary. So she opened a random door, stepping into the purple glowing portal beyond.

She found herself plunged into utter darkness.

Bella froze…then felt something bump into her from behind. She flinched, then saw pale silver light illuminate the way ahead. It was Myko, and his big silver body was glowing with stored moonlight.

They were standing in a long, narrow tunnel made of pale stone, the door to the Underground open behind them. It closed of its own accord, and Bella took a deep breath in, starting down the tunnel. Eventually it led them to a dead-end…and an ornate stone platform. Above, four walls led upward like a chimney, disappearing into darkness. She felt a slight draft…and then saw a flash of blue light at her feet.

The inscriptions on the platform were glowing.

It began to rise, and Bella's stomach flip-flopped as it picked up speed. She braced herself, the walls around her speeding by rapidly. The platform slowed, eventually coming to a stop.

Bella found herself outside.

Orange-red sand extended for as far as the eye could see in all directions, fading into the darkness of night. Only the platform she was standing on broke the monotony. The sky was inky black, stars shining down brilliantly on the land to cast it in pale silver.

Bella glanced at Myko, who was standing beside her.

"I need to go to the bathroom," she told him. "I'll be back."

He *wuffed*, and she strode forward onto the sand. It sunk slightly, much as she imagined sand on a beach would. She'd seen pictures of the ocean, of course, but had never experienced it. After all, she'd lived most of her life in a book. Behind her, the platform descended, returning to its original position far below.

Onward she went, until Myko was far away. Far enough for her to feel just comfortable enough to do her business. When she was done, she stood, striding back toward him.

Then she hesitated, twisting around to face the endless terrain. Wind whipped through the desert ahead, sending a cloud of sand blowing over the land. Like the wall of dust kicked up from Gideon's meteorite.

She closed her eyes, picturing Gideon's knee caving in as Craven kicked it, his wrist crumpling under the general's horrible grip.

All because she distracted him. Because she broke her promise.

Bella, he'd said. *You weren't supposed to…*

She crouched down, burying her head in her hands. She felt sick to her stomach, and retched. But nothing came out. Her stomach was empty.

Bella crouched there, her eyes watering. She pictured the White Dragon, lying dead on the battlefield.

You did this, she told herself.

An image of Havenwood's towers falling came to her, of the castle crumbling. Killing everyone inside. Including…

She shot to her feet, her eyes widening. A bolt of terror shot through her.

"Grandpa!" she gasped.

He'd been in the castle when it'd been destroyed.

Oh god.

She put her hands over her mouth, tears blurring her vision. Her knees wobbled, and she fell onto her butt on the sand, not even feeling the impact.

Oh god!

Bella stared off into the desert wasteland, seeing but not seeing. She pictured Grandpa as she'd last seen him, in the meeting with the other artists. Pictured his warm smile. His eyes twinkling as he stared up at the ceiling in her bed every night, spinning fantastic tales.

Grandpa, her rock. Always there for her in the old apartment, sitting at his desk in the living room. She remembered the way he'd smiled so happily at her on her sixteenth birthday, when he'd gotten her her first easel and a stack of canvases that went all the way up to the ceiling.

Happy birthday sweetheart.

Tears streamed down her cheeks, her shoulders heaving as she sobbed.

You always said you wanted to be a painter like your mother, he'd said. *And if you want to* be *something…*

She shook her head, the full weight of what she'd done crashing down upon her.

"I killed him," she realized.

And as soon as she'd said it, she pictured Grandpa's painted copy back in the apartment, when Stanwitz and Reynolds had forced their way through. She pictured Stanwitz kicking Grandpa's chair over, and Grandpa falling to the floor with a *thump*.

She flinched as she heard the three shots firing, Stanwitz putting three bullets into Grandpa's chest.

And Grandpa, staring lifelessly at the ceiling, the police officer doing chest compressions. Grandpa's ribs crunching under the futile attempts to save him. But he couldn't be saved.

He was already gone.

Bella stared off into the lifeless land, picturing lying dead amidst the rubble of Castle Havenwood, like Piper and Kendra. Gone.

Forever.

Oh god oh god…

She looked down at her hands, realizing she was digging her fingernails of her right hand into the knuckles of her left. The skin there opened up, blood oozing from the wounds. She stared at them, then kept digging, ignoring the pain.

You deserve it.

Bella scraped her fingernails over her knuckles, again and again, the gouges growing larger. Her hands shook as she did so, a grim determination coming over her. She had the sudden urge to keep digging until she hit bone. To scrape her flesh away until she could scrape no more.

You don't deserve to live, she told herself. *Not after what you did.*

And she knew with utter certainty that the only way to escape this feeling was to end her life. That she would never be able to run away from what she'd done.

Bella stopped scraping, the fingernails of her right hand stained with blood. She took a deep breath, then got to her feet, her legs shaky. Looking down, she saw the various weapons in her chest-painting.

There was a flash of silver light to her right, and Bella flinched, seeing Myko materialize beside her. He *wuffed,* nudging her shoulder with his nose. She ignored him, reaching into her chest-painting.

He opened his mouth and bit her shoulder.

"Ow!" Bella blurted out, flinching away from him. "What're you doing?"

Myko whined, nudging her with his nose again. He licked the side of her cheek then, and she grimaced, pushing his head away.

"Go away," she ordered. "Leave me alone."

Myko stepped closer, assaulting her face with his tongue.

"Hey!" she protested, backing away from him. But he didn't let up. "Okay!" she stated.

This time he listened, staring at her with his silver eyes.

"What?" she asked.

He snorted, turning to look back at the hole where the platform they'd come from had been, then returning his gaze to her.

"What?" she repeated. He pawed her hand, then pawed his collar. Just like he'd done way back when they'd been in the Misty Marsh. When he'd guided her through the darkness…to meet Gideon.

She saw his face, bloated and red, Craven's hand gripping his throat. His final words echoed in her mind.

Love her like you loved me, he'd told Myko.

"You shouldn't love me," she muttered, lowering her gaze. "I don't deserve it."

Myko licked the tip of her nose, and she jerked away.

"I got them all killed," she insisted. "Nemesis was right. It's all my fault."

Myko pawed her hand again, then his collar.

"No," she told him, crossing her arms over her chest. "I'm not going back." She turned to the desolate wasteland in the distance, at the endless sand stretching out as far as the eye could see. She sighed, looking down at the rolled-up canvases in the thigh-holsters of her Painter's uniform. Then she retrieved one.

"Apertus," she incanted.

The canvas unrolled itself, revealing a painting of a bleak, war-torn battlefield. Dead soldiers littered the field, one soldier's skull in the foreground, half-hidden within a helmet. And in the center of the painting was Goo.

She had the sudden urge to draw Goo out. To sink into him and have her pain taken away from her. All of her negative emotions would go away instantly, that wonderful calm draping over her like a warm blanket.

You don't deserve it, she told herself.

Bella glanced at Myko, who was still standing there, watching her. She hesitated, then reached into the canvas, drawing Goo out. Which was a considerable task, given how truly large he'd grown. The huge blob sat on the sand, quivering at the sight of Bella. She forced herself to smile at Goo.

"Hi Goo," she greeted. "I'm tired. Can you carry me and Myko back to the platform there?"

Goo sent a head-sized proboscis upward from his flesh, nodding it once. Then he wrapped around Myko, and started flowing toward Bella. She stepped back then.

"On second thought, go back in the painting," she requested. "Bring Myko with you."

Myko whined, then barked, struggling to free himself from Goo's flesh.

"Do it," Bella ordered. "Go!"

Goo obeyed, flowing back toward the canvas. Myko continued to struggle, trying to wiggle free from Goo.

"Don't let him out Goo," Bella ordered. "It's for his own good."

Goo wrapped tendrils of flesh around Myko's back and neck, pulling Myko in until only the wolf's head was free of him. Myko barked again, then dissolved into pure silver light. But Goo anticipated this, sending a wall of flesh to block Myko's path…and even though Myko managed to free himself from his gooey prison, he slammed right into that wall, burying himself within it.

"Goodbye Myko," she whispered.

Right as Goo pulled the loyal wolf into the canvas with him.

Bella stared at the canvas, seeing Goo and Myko trapped within its static world. She took a deep, shuddering breath in, then squared her shoulders.

"Clausus," she incanted…and the canvas rolled itself back up. She stuffed it in her thigh-holster, then turned to the desert ahead, staring at the horizon.

And with that, alone at last, she started forward into the emptiness, knowing that it wouldn't be long before it – like the painting – swallowed her whole.

Chapter 13

Centrum was the shining jewel of the Pentad, the capitol city of the great kingdom. Shaped as a great circle five miles in diameter, its wide streets lay in concentric circles throughout the city. Other streets cut perpendicular to these, extending from the palace in the center of the city to the outer edges like rays of the sun.

The city's outer edges were populated by the city's lower-level workers, housed in worn-looking apartment buildings of brick and stone. The closer one got toward the center of Centrum, the wealthier its citizens – and the buildings they lived in. Great mansions of sculpted white stone, like miniature castles with tiny lawns, alongside skyscrapers of sleek steel. And in the very heart of the city stood the seat of government itself: the Palatium, palace of Queen Eldora.

The Palatium was a grand, blood-red tower made of gleaming metal that shot up into the air, easily three times as tall as any other building in the city. It came to a sharp peak, and had no windows or adornments of any kind. Surrounding the Palatium were five Golden Towers, each a third the height of the Palatium. A tower for each magical discipline, its workers dedicated to the processing and regulation of each art. Red and gold, the colors of the Pentad…blood and riches. Power and prosperity.

A quarter-mile from the Palatium and the Golden Towers, a great black statue of a demon's head could be seen. Carved from a single block of obsidian eighty feet tall, its mouth gaped impossibly wide, revealing vicious fangs and a long, forking obsidian tongue. This was surrounded by a tall fence, guarded by dozens of living statues.

A wide golden street led from the Palatium to the demon's head. And the demon's great, gaping mouth serving as the entrance to Tartarus, the largest maximum-security prison in the known world. A great subterranean fortress built in the bowels of a truly ancient alternate plane of existence.

Tartarus was, literally translated, Hell itself.

Those entering its mouth were doomed to descend into the fringes of Hell, where they would serve their sentences without hope of escape. And each prisoner would spend their time gazing out into Hell itself, knowing that – should they die while in that horrid plane of existence – that they would find themselves a spirit, transported out of Tartarus and into Hell's dreadful kingdom…to suffer for all eternity.

Tartarus existed on the very edges of Hell, one of the few links between the two worlds that still existed. Only the twin Demon Gates served as a portal there, and those had been lost to time.

The entrance to the prison was surrounded by a tall, wrought-iron fence, its gate guarded by a line of living statues. A dense crowd of citizens stood on either side of the path before the fence, held back by lines of royal guards clad in red and gold armor.

All looking at something to Craven's right, waiting.

For two guards were holding a framed painting as tall as a man there, with a Painter standing before it. And a Painter standing *within* the painting: one Gideon Myles. Dressed in the red shirt and pants of a prisoner, his hands having been painted off, leaving only stumps at his wrists.

The Queen had requested that Gideon's path to justice be a public one. To shame the Painter…and to show the Pentad's citizens that not even the great Gideon Myles stood a chance against the might and glory of the Pentad. That no one was above the law.

"Release the prisoner," Craven ordered, his powerful voice carrying easily over the crowd.

The Painter reached into the painting, drawing Gideon out.

Gideon stumbled out of the canvas, squeezing his eyes shut at the sudden harsh sunlight. He blinked rapidly, putting an arm in front of his face to shield it. And then quickly realized that there was no hand attached to it.

The crowd roared.

Craven stared at Gideon, feeling naked without his helmet. It had been destroyed, as had his chestplate, though he'd had it repaired – at least superficially – by the same Painter who'd drawn Gideon out. Still, he felt…exposed without his helm. As if everyone in the crowd knew what had happened.

That his legendary invincibility was a myth.

You defeated him, he reminded himself, stepping toward Gideon and shoving the Painter down the street toward Tartarus.

"Tartarus awaits, prisoner," Craven declared.

The crowd cheered.

Gideon glanced at Craven, meeting his gaze for a split second before striding barefoot down the street. People jeered at the Painter from either side of the street, but Gideon ignored them, walking with his shoulders back and head held high. As if he were taking a stroll between crowds of admirers instead of a righteous, indignant mob.

Craven strode after the Painter, his feet *thumping* on the stone with every step.

The crowd continued to boo and jeer, and though Craven knew the crowd's vitriol was directed at Gideon, he couldn't help but imagine that they were booing at him. That they knew what he really was.

A lie. A man pretending to be something he was not.

For he was supposed to be the law, an unstoppable juggernaut. He was pure, absolute. The right hand of the queen.

You defeated him, Craven repeated to himself.

But still, the doubt remained. Gideon had fought him with an ease Craven had never experienced. Had neutralized every attack and been the first to ever injure Craven. And had he not been so distracted by the presence of his daughter, Gideon might not have fallen so readily.

Or at all.

For Craven knew that Gideon was a master Painter, and yet had only used four paintings against him. The cane, his cloak, his Conclave portal, and the Familiar. He couldn't help but wonder what might have happened had Gideon decided to use his full arsenal against him.

He grit his teeth, stomping after Gideon, following the man toward Tartarus. Trying to ignore the booing of the crowd. Their eyes upon him.

I am the right hand of the queen!

But even after Craven had left the jeering of the crowd, as he followed Gideon to the gate of the fence surrounding the great demon's head that served as the entrance into Tartarus, so too did his doubt follow him. And he realized with sudden, awful clarity that there was nowhere he could go where it wouldn't find him. That wherever he was, it would be there.

He had the sudden urge to enter into Torpor, that little death that promised a reprieve from himself. But he knew that such a reprieve would only be temporary. For when he submerged himself into the depths of Torpor, his doubt would yet be there, just above the surface.

Waiting.

* * *

Gideon stopped before the gate of the fence surrounding the great obsidian demon's head that marked the portal between this world and his soon-to-be prison. The guards standing vigilantly before it unlocked the gate, swinging it open. Then they parted to allow himself and General Craven through.

Gideon found his gaze drawn upward, past the thirty-foot-tall gaping mouth with its long, pointed fangs and forked tongue, to the cruel eyes of the obsidian demon itself.

The entrance to Tartarus had been created to strike fear into the hearts of any that gazed upon it, and terror in those destined to enter its mouth and descend into the prison itself. A fitting metaphor, to enter Tartarus through the demon's mouth. To be swallowed whole by the devil, and be transported into the bowels of Hell.

To be digested. Absorbed. Processed, then incorporated into its system.

He glanced back, seeing the blood-red spire of the Palatium in the distance.

"Step forward, prisoner," Craven commanded from behind. "And enter into Tartarus."

Gideon turned forward again, lowering his gaze to the demon's mouth, its forked tongue serving as the floor. Then he strode forward through the open gate, stepping up onto that tongue, and followed it into the demon's mouth.

As he did so, he found himself plunged into shadow, for the sun would not dare enter the demon's cavernous mouth. Ahead, its great big tonsils stood on either side of the back of its throat, orange-red flames flickering from deep within their crevices and pits. Its long uvula – the fleshy bulb hanging from the very back of its throat – glowed bright red, casting the chamber in a hellish glow.

And beyond it, Gideon knew, was the great obsidian staircase that led down into the prison.

Into Hell.

He thought back to the Collector's castle, the man's office guarded by the twin Demon Gates. Great stone doors borne out of Hell itself, with the power to send anyone passing through them *to* Hell if they carried thoughts of harming the Demon Gates' owner.

How Xander – how the *Collector* – had managed to get the Demon Gates was beyond him.

One of the guards – a living statue – stepped ahead of Gideon, while another prodded him from behind. He strode forward obediently, making his way past the tonsils, the heat of their flames burning his skin. He ignored the pain, knowing it to be temporary.

And as the guard ahead of him descended down the steep obsidian stairs beyond, Gideon followed, content in the knowledge that the pain of his incarceration would be the same.

For, even as he was swallowed by Tartarus, and descended into the bowels of Hell, he felt no fear. He knew Hell, after all. And while here it was a literal place, in truth, the truest hell was within.

He knew it well.

Hell had been losing Xander. Hell had been his first wife leaving him. Hell had been creating the Collector, then lying to him.

And having to live with the Collector murdering his wife…and then spending a decade in Blackthorne waiting for the Collector to hunt down and murder his daughter.

Hell was not following his conscience. The end of his body – if the queen chose to execute him – was nothing. It was the end of suffering, not the beginning. And following his conscience, as he had done ever since defeating the Collector, had set him free.

So it was that, even as he made his way into Hell, continuing down that long, dark staircase lit by flames burning from within its pitted walls on either side, he felt no fear whatsoever.

For like Bella, he was light within the darkness. An island of peace in an ocean of suffering.

Heaven in Hell.

* * *

Gideon sat cross-legged on the uncomfortably warm black stone floor of his prison cell, an eight-by-eight-foot room of rough-hewn igneous rock. There was a small hole in the floor serving as a toilet, leading straight down to a pool of glowing lava hundreds of feet below. Irregular pits and small holes in the walls on three sides gave a view of the hellish landscape beyond, all lava, smoke, and fire.

And in the corner of his cramped cell stood a raised stone slab serving as a cot.

He felt beads of sweat trickle down his forehead, and ignored them. The cell had to be close to one hundred degrees, a dry heat necessitating regular shipments of water to each prisoner through the fourth wall of the cell, a set of standard vertical metal bars with a small port near the floor for water and meals to be shoved through.

And beyond those bars, a long hallway of the same stone ran perpendicular to his cell…such that his cell faced the hallway's wall.

He was sitting at the far-right corner of his cell, facing it…and facing away from the prison bars. He focused on his connection with Myko, as much to distract himself from his discomfort as to keep tabs on his Familiar. For he should have been able to still feel the wolf as if he were not in Hell…as if he were not in another plane of existence.

Placing prisoners in alternate planes of existence was useful, particularly when dealing with Painters. For Painters had Familiars…and being in a different plane of existence made communication with Familiars more difficult. Only vague communication could cross planes, after all.

Typically.

But Gideon's connection with Myko was pure emotion, and occasionally images and smells, for Myko did not think in words. So Gideon should have been able to sense his Familiar's feelings quite well through their bond…especially because, when he'd painted the wolf, he'd made sure to specify that their bond *could* cross planes of existence without issue. Creation was an act of problem-solving, after all…and he strove to solve as many as possible with each of his paintings.

But to his consternation, he could not sense Myko's thoughts. There was nothing at all. It was as if Myko wasn't there…which meant one of two things.

Either Myko was in a painting, or Myko was dead.

Gideon's gut squirmed at the thought, and he took deep, steadying breaths, redirecting his thoughts to something he could control. A trick that had proved very effective in the past. Focusing on things out of one's control would only add oil to the flames of his anxiety.

He was imprisoned, in a locked room in an alternative plane of existence, surrounded by the Pentad's countless guards, in the highest-security prison in the known world. And he was without his cane, his paintings, his hat, his cape, and his Painter's uniform. Not to mention that the Pentad had an extensive catalogue of Gideon's work. Each painting required prior approval, review, and a detailed explanation of its purpose and power. This served two functions: to control what Painters painted, and to keep tabs on what the extent of a Painter's powers were in case they went rogue.

Thaddeus's genius when writing had been to hide aspects of his magic within the story, so that the significantly less brilliant editors of the Pentad wouldn't catch them.

And, not coincidentally, Gideon had learned the art of storytelling from Thaddeus himself.

The more creative I am, the more powerful my magic will be.

He refocused, shifting the spotlight of his conscious attention to something else. Something apart from himself, but a part of himself. A weapon that could yet save him.

Now was not the time to act, he knew. It remained to be seen what Queen Eldora would do with him. There was still a chance – however slim – that she would forgive him for his crimes, or at least provide a path for him to redeem himself.

But if she didn't, then the Pentad – and the queen – would discover just how creative Gideon could be.

Chapter 14

The sun began its rise over the dunes at the horizon behind Bella, casting long shadows across the desert, and lighting the cloudless sky in a steadily brightening blue. Bella trudged ever forward, hours having passed since she'd left the platform in the desert – and the door to the Underground – far behind. A stiff wind blew across the sand, sending ghostly wisps of dust flowing over its surface.

It reminded her of Animus.

As the sun rose, so did the temperature. The chill of the desert night gave way to oppressive heat, and it wasn't long before the sun's rays went from giving her energy to sapping it from her. The light near the horizon rippled with the heat, and the temperature continued to rise until it had to be well over a hundred degrees. Still, she forged ever onward, the horizon her destination.

An impossible goal, a destination that she could never reach…and that was the point. She was doomed to fail, just as she'd doomed Gideon to fail.

So she kept walking, one step in front of the other, waiting for her failure to claim her.

Dust blew in her hair. Her eyes. Her mouth. It dried her tongue and stung her nostrils. Crept in the crevices of her clothes, rubbing the skin at her joints and thighs raw as she walked. The sand went everywhere it could, and it could go everywhere.

And everywhere it went, it hurt.

The sun continued its rise behind her, the shadows it threw shortening steadily. Hundreds upon hundreds of crude sundials marking the passage of time. But to Bella, the passage of time no longer mattered. She had no destination other than the end of *her* time, and so all she had to do now was wait for time to pass.

But time also worked on her mind, conspiring as it often did to change it.

You can still go back, her mind told her.

She ignored the thought, gritting her teeth. There was no going back, and she knew it. She didn't deserve a second chance. What was done was done, and there was no way she could fix it.

Still, she slowed, glancing back. Only more horizon greeted her, the hole to the Underground no longer visible in the distance. She'd been walking for miles, after all. But her footsteps in the sand marked the path back. She slowed further, staring at the footprints.

You could follow them back.

She hesitated, turning forward again. Only eternal emptiness lay ahead. And behind…

Bella took a deep breath, steeling herself. Onward she went, one step in front of the other.

The sun's rays became so hot that they scalded her scalp and shoulders. The air so dry that her tongue stuck to the roof of her mouth. She found herself fantasizing about a tall, cold glass of water, ice cubes floating at the top. And clinking against her teeth as she tipped the glass back, marvelous wetness pouring into her mouth and down her throat.

Eventually the fantasy faded, as did everything else. Time passed in a sort of haze, until only the position of the sun in the sky gave any indication for how much of it had gone by. The thought of turning back faded as well, replaced by numb resignation.

Her decision had been made. The die was cast.

There was no way back.

The numbness extended to Bella's psychic pain. It was like being trapped in Goo, and she welcomed its relief.

She walked, making her way toward the horizon. And with every step, the horizon stepped in equal measure away from her.

Cain stirred at her hip, rotating to look up at her with his glowing green eye-sockets.

"What?" she snapped.

"May I speak?" he asked.

She hesitated, then nodded, regretting having snapped at him. But she couldn't admit that. Not now.

"To what destination are we headed?" he inquired.

"Nowhere," she answered. He considered this.

"It is my duty to protect you," he reminded her.

"You don't have to anymore."

"We're family," he insisted. She opened her mouth to reply, almost telling him that they *weren't* family. That he was just another painting. But she'd created him to think they were family. His very purpose in life – or rather, un-life – was to protect his family to make up for having failed to do so in the past.

Something she herself had failed to do as well.

"I failed my family once," he confessed. "I vowed to never do it again."

She didn't reply.

"If I could go back in time and save them, I would," he continued. "But alas, it is my fate to live with that regret for the rest of my days." He paused. "Protecting you is my duty and my pleasure. And my redemption."

Bella sighed, lowering her gaze to her feet and stopping in her tracks. She took a deep breath in, then gazed off at the horizon. An image of Gideon being shattered by Craven came to her. Of her mother being murdered.

Her home – her *sanctuary* – destroyed.

And then she pictured Grandpa. Sweet Grandpa, lying dead amongst the ruins of the very castle he'd created. Never to smile again.

His story at an end.

She lifted her gaze, her jawline rippling…and continued forward.

"Bella?" Cain pressed.

But she ignored him, and every statement he uttered thereafter, until he stopped talking altogether. Time passed, the sun slowly making its way across the sky. The heat grew so oppressive that it felt like it was baking her alive. Eventually she found her eyelids drifting shut, and she stumbled to the side, nearly falling over. She hadn't slept since the previous morning, after all. And though she struggled to keep going, her body refused to obey. Her eyes drifted closed once again, and this time when she stumbled, she fell, landing on her side on the sand.

Bella laid there for a while, then rolled onto her back, closing her eyes against the glaring sun.

Sleep claimed her.

* * *

"Bella?"

Bella woke to light, and to pain.

She squinted against the harsh sunlight, turning her head to the side. She found herself lying on her back on the baking sand, her Painter's uniform so hot it felt like it might melt into her skin. She grit her teeth against the pain, rolling onto her left side.

"Bella!" the voice that'd said her name earlier cried. It was Cain, she realized. Sand caked her face and body, sucking into her mouth when she took a breath in.

Bella coughed, then spat. Or at least she tried to. For her mouth was so dry that no saliva came up at all. The sudden, desperate urge to drink gripped her, and she struggled to get to her feet, swaying as she did so. Her head felt as if it were floating above her body, her limbs like jelly.

She took a step forward, and her legs gave out underneath her, making her fall onto her left side in the sand.

"Bella," Cain repeated.

"Enough," she mumbled.

Bella laid there for a while, trying to collect herself.

Then she got up again, and this time she managed to stay standing. Still, she felt numb, as if she wasn't really here. As if this was all some kind of bizarre dream. She looked around, seeing endless desert all around her, every direction the same. The wind sent dusty gusts across the dunes, casting everything in the distance in a yellowish haze.

An image of Gideon came to her, as she'd last seen him.

I've lived long enough. Your turn now.

A pang of guilt struck her. The knowledge that if Gideon could see her now, that he would be horrified. That he would never want this for her. He'd slaved away for ten years to save her from Blackthorne, even suffering having his hand amputated. He'd risked his life for her…as had Grandpa, living in crippling depression for a decade. Living only for her, so that *she* might live.

She gazed across the desert.

"This was really stupid," she realized. Cain looked up at her.

"I attempted to warn you," he told her. She sighed, putting a hand atop his skull.

"I know," she replied. "I should've listened. I'm sorry, Cain."

He sighed.

"Yes, well, I can protect you from others," Cain reminded her sadly. "But not from yourself."

Bella stared at him for a long moment, then nodded mutely.

She searched the area around her for her footprints, prints that would guide her back to the Underground. But there were none whatsoever. The wind had swept them away.

And she had no idea which way to go.

Panic struck her, and she resisted the urge to give in to it, forcing herself to focus. To think.

The sun, she told herself, looking up. She'd been walking toward it the whole time. Now the sun was directly overhead, which meant it was high noon.

And that she'd have no idea which way to go until it started to fall.

She stood there, swaying a little. She felt suddenly lightheaded, and steeled herself against the sensation. Her heart began to flutter in her chest, dark spots growing before her eyes. She took a step forward, and fell.

Bella landed on her belly on the sand, and sand went right into her lungs when she took a breath in. She coughed weakly, trying to clear her lungs of the gritty stuff. Then she breathed in again, and was wracked with another round of coughing.

She rolled onto her side, hacking until her lungs were clear. Then she got up.

And her vision blackened again, and she fell to her hands and knees.

"Bella!" Cain exclaimed.

Bella stayed there, her head swimming. She felt suddenly nauseous, and dry-heaved.

Come on…

She tried to get up, but her legs wobbled and she fell onto her belly again. It was all she could do to roll onto her back before exhaustion overwhelmed her. She lay there, staring up at the blue sky, the heat so powerful that she felt as if she were in an oven. She tried to focus, but her thoughts scattered, going this way and that. Strange images swirled in her mind's eye, randomly coming and going.

And suddenly she didn't care anymore.

There was no backward or forward. No past or future. Only the present, and it was a slippery thing. Gone even as it came. Bella had the sudden, profound realization that none of it mattered. She could die now or ten years from now. Or a hundred.

It didn't matter.

"Bella!" she heard Cain's voice cry, frantic now.

She stopped trying to move. Stopped trying to try.

And then, in the merciful embrace of sleep, Bella died.

Chapter 15

Simon stood in front of the full-length mirror resting against the outer wall of the cabin in the Plane of Reflection, reflecting on his reflection. Percy was at his side, doing the same. For Simon was wearing a crisp new suit of the purest white…so white that it seemed to glow in the sun's rays. In fact, it *was* glowing, casting its light on everything around it. A white suit, white pants, and white undershirt. Even white dress shoes. A casual observer would believe that these were all separate items, but they would be wrong.

For they were all pieces of a whole, like organs in a body.

"What do you call it?" Percy inquired, admiring the suit.

"Redeemer," Simon answered.

Percy's eyes twinkled, and he put a hand on Simon's shoulder.

"Well done," he congratulated. "It seems I've chosen well."

Simon frowned, glancing at Percy questioningly.

"So what's next for my young protégé?" Percy inquired, ignoring Simon's quizzical expression. Simon turned away from the mirror, gazing off at the Festering Wood in the distance. He remembered the day he'd come here, cold and alone. His guts empty after vomiting from the forest's vile stench. How he'd traveled here after being on the mountainside where Miss Savage had attacked Bella and Gideon and the Necromancer.

Bella had given him a second chance, despite having every reason not to. She'd seen something in him that he – until now – hadn't been able to see in himself.

Beauty in the darkest dark, she'd said.

Suddenly Simon was struck with the overwhelming urge to see her again.

"I want to see her," he blurted out. Percy took his hand off Simon's shoulder, shrugging his own.

"Then do it!" he exclaimed.

"Really?" Simon asked. Suddenly he wasn't so sure. He'd expected Percy to say no. They hadn't really left the cabin for the last month, except to go to Memory Lane. To be honest, Simon was comfortable here...more comfortable than he'd been anywhere else in his life. With Percy, there was no danger. No walking on eggshells. No dramatics or demands.

Percy had absolutely no need of anything from Simon. There was nothing Simon could offer the man that Percy couldn't just make or take for himself...other than Simon's friendship, and the joy of helping someone.

Perhaps, one day, Simon could be like that.

"Well why not?" Percy replied. "If you want to do something, do it. Come on, let's go!"

And with that, he extended his hand as if grabbing a doorknob. Sure enough, a door appeared there – similar to the ones from the Underground. This one was much larger, with an ornate stone doorframe surrounding it. And, also unlike the other doors, it had a golden keyhole just above the knob.

A very familiar door.

Percy recited the following:

"Painted places stuck in time,
One world they share,
For a single person's frame of mind
A place called Anywhere."

The door *clicked*, and Percy opened it, gesturing for Simon to go through.

"Go on," he prompted. "I'll wait here."

Simon hesitated, then stepped through the doorway...and found himself in a painting. Or rather, a painted place stuck in time. A painting of a dark forest, undead ghouls frozen amidst the trees, their decaying flesh blue-green in the eerie light from a swarm of fireflies suspended motionlessly in the air around them.

One of the Necromancer's paintings. Bella's mother.

He felt an immediate kinship with her, a stirring in his soul as he regarded her work. For while the ghouls were ghastly creatures, half-consumed by rot, the light of the fireflies cast them in a honey-gold glow, and they'd been painted in such a way as to seem almost noble. As if the fact that they were horrible creatures to be feared was completely unknown to them.

That they were beautiful in and of themselves, as natural as the forest and fireflies around them.

This of course had been the last painting Simon had been in with Miss Savage, a painting hung in the office of Thaddeus Birch himself. They used it to look out through the rectangular frame suspended in the air within the painting, a window into the real world.

Beyond the frame, Thaddeus's office was empty.

Simon made his way through the painted forest, spotting another scene ahead…one of a gloomy city lit by a blood-red moon, with dark towers looming over the other buildings. He made his way to it, peering out of its magical frame, suspended in the air in the center of the scene.

And saw a small room with a lone coffin within.

Simon continued onward, traveling from painting to painting, until he made his way out of the mansion, to the paintings that he knew from experience hung on the walls of Castle Havenwood. These of course were far less gloomy, the more standard fare of bright meadows and fields and lake scenes and such.

But when he reached the first of these, stepping up to its frame, he stopped.

For instead of the hallways and rooms of the Castle Havenwood, all Simon saw was darkness beyond the frame.

He frowned, walking up to the frame and putting a hand on its surface. To his surprise, his palm did not stop there as it should have, rather plunging through a little before striking something hard and uneven beyond. Something that felt like stone.

He frowned.

The paintings within Havenwood were protected by special magic, not allowing any new portal to be created into the kingdom. And since every painting made within Havenwood had been created after Havenwood's creation, no painting within its borders could act as a portal from Anywhere into the magical kingdom.

Simon's hand should have stopped at the level of the frame, not slightly beyond it.

Which meant that something was wrong.

Simon felt a chill run through him, and withdrew his hand. He strode toward the next painted scene in the distance, finding its magical frame…and found it framing the same utter blackness.

Something was *definitely* wrong.

Simon's heart began to pound in his chest, and he whirled around.

"Painted places stuck in time,
One world they share,
For a single person's frame of mind
A place called Anywhere."

A door appeared, swinging open. Simon stepped through it…and found himself back outside of the cabin. Percy wasn't there…which meant that the man had returned to the original world. Simon stepped through the full-length mirror, finding Percy seated in his chair by the unlit fire-pit. Both of their mugs of tea were set upon the armrests of their chairs.

"Something's wrong," Simon blurted out, rushing to Percy's side. He explained what he'd witnessed, and Percy's expression turned grave.

"If the paintings still exist in Anywhere, they haven't been destroyed," Percy reasoned. "But if the magic stopping their frames from being used as portals into Havenwood is gone…"

"Then something's happened to Havenwood," Simon realized. A chill ran down his spine. "We have to go there," he urged. "Bella might be in trouble!"

"She most certainly is," Percy agreed. "If you must go, go."

"I have to," Simon stated. "She gave me a second chance. I can't just stay here while she might need help."

"You must do what you think is right, of course," Percy replied.

"Come on," Simon urged.

"No no," Percy countered. "I'll stay here."

"But…"

"This is your journey, not mine," Percy clarified.

"But I might need your help."

"You've already had it," Percy pointed out.

"But…"

"Go Simon," Percy insisted gently. "Build your lighthouse. I'm sure it'll be something extraordinary…and I look forward to seeing it."

Simon stood there for a long while, suddenly terrified at leaving Percy. The ancient artist had been his constant companion for the last month…and before that, he'd had Miss Savage. And the Doppelganger. And as terrible as they'd been, at least he hadn't been alone.

He felt his white suit tighten around his chest and back, as if he'd been embraced.

You're not alone, a voice whispered in his mind. A woman's voice, gentle but firm.

Redeemer's voice. His new Familiar.

Wherever you go, I'll be with you, she reassured. *You'll always have a second chance with me.*

Chapter 16

For most people, death was the end. But for a Necromancer, it was just the beginning.

And at the moment of her death, Bella became not one, but two. The darkness within her split from the light, for only in death could the two halves of her be apart. And while Bella herself could go anywhere she chose, the darkness could only be with dark, and the light could only live in light.

So it was that, in the blazing desert sun, Lux was able to stay where Bella's body had once been, but Luna could not.

Luna felt herself shoot backward with impossible speed, and in an instant she found herself standing within darkness. Stone walls surrounded her on three sides, with a tunnel behind her…and a familiar platform at her feet.

She realized that she was back in the tunnel Bella had gone through earlier, the nearest dark place safe from the scorching desert sun.

Luna backpedaled quickly, not wanting to trigger the platform to rise. For there was no telling what might happen if it did, bringing her into the sunlight. If the sun acted like a ceiling, and the platform rose to it, the force could crush her…and kill her. And once the platform fell again, there was no way Lux could get to her in the darkness to revive her.

She would be dead forever.

You deserve it, Luna thought. But without the weight of her conscience upon her – for Lux was surely that – the thought had no real urgency behind it. In fact, she didn't feel badly at all. She realized she was just parroting what Bella had been thinking earlier, when she'd been all mopey.

Moping, Luna knew, was beneath her. And it wouldn't do her – or Bella – any good at all.

But getting back at the Pentad? *That* would make her feel *great.*

Luna stood there, considering her options. There was no way for Lux to get to her now to revive Bella…not without risking Luna dying in the process. They could meet as the platform rose, but would only have a split-second to combine.

Which meant that, at least for the moment, they were stuck apart.

Luna stared at the platform, then turned to look down the tunnel. The door to the Underground was there, waiting for her. She smiled, forgetting all about getting back together with Lux. Her sister would just slow her down, after all. Luna felt no guilt. No shame for what she'd done. Bella's conscience was a product of Lux, after all. Her better nature torturing her with needless pain.

Now Luna was free of it…and free to act.

The Pentad has Gideon, she thought. *And they won't stop until they have you.*

So really, there was only one option left.

"Pentad's gotta die," she told herself. And that was going to take weapons. Lots of weapons. And that meant she needed to get back to her studio in her mother's mansion, to do what she did best.

So she strode to the door to the Underground to get to work.

* * *

Lux watched as Luna burst away from her, flying across the desert and vanishing from sight. The darkness, banished by the light. She immediately felt the urge to reconnect with her sister half, and dashed across the sand after her. She could *feel* Luna in the distance, miles and miles away.

The desert sun hung high overhead, beginning its journey back to the horizon. And while for Bella its heat had been deadly, to Lux it felt lovely. For she was a being of light, and the sun was her friend. And as a being of light, she needed neither food nor water. The sun's gentle kiss was enough.

And without Luna's darkness, Lux found herself free from the misery that plagued Bella moments before. For her guilt had been the light considering the dark, and without the dark, Lux felt no sadness at all.

Only the intense need to reconnect with her sister, so that she could make Luna – and Bella – feel better again.

Lux burst into action, breaking out into a sprint across the dunes. On and on she went, never slowing, never faltering. Her thoughts were only for her sister, to be made whole once again.

But even as she ran, she felt Luna's location *shift.* From directly ahead to somewhere…different.

Lux frowned, but kept up her pace, continuing toward where she'd felt Luna a moment before.

She must have gone back to the Underground, Lux reasoned. Which meant that Luna had gone back down the long, dark shaft in the desert. The one Bella had come up through on the magical platform earlier. Perhaps Luna was merely waiting in the Underground until Lux could get to the shaft.

She continued sprinting, tireless. For she was a being of light, filled with boundless energy.

And so hours passed, the sun falling gradually toward the horizon in front of her. By the time she reached her destination, a square hole in the desert sand, the sun was hanging just above the desert far in the distance, the sky starting to change color with the coming sunset.

Lux skid to a stop at the hole, kneeling and peering down into the darkness of the tunnel below.

"Luna!" she called out, her voice echoing in the depths. "I'm here!"

No answer.

Lux felt her sister's presence, but it was still…vague. Suddenly she felt it *shift* again…to someplace far, far away. Impossibly far, and behind her now.

What…

Lux stood, twisting around to look off the way she'd come. Long shadows were being cast by the dunes in the distance, a sign of the coming night. She felt a twinge of worry, and turned to look back down into the tunnel. It was the only nearby way to get to the Underground…and to follow in her sister's footsteps. But the tunnel was underground itself.

A place the light – and Lux – could not go.

Lux thought it through. Even at high noon, the sun could only reach straight down into the shaft of the tunnel. Which meant that Luna would have to meet her there. And Luna should have known that.

"She knew it was after noon already," Lux told herself. "She knew I couldn't go there until tomorrow. And…"

And night would come.

When it did, Lux could not live in the darkness.

She stopped, staring off into the distance. It made perfect sense, of course. Luna had been wise to not make the attempt to wait. The Underground had doors to places all over the world; if Luna could find one that led to a place near Lux, they could meet where the shadow met the light. She smiled to herself.

"Good idea sis," she murmured. Luna had been wiser than her, of course.

She smiled, mentally congratulating her sister. She was proud of Luna, always so clever. And mischievous, of course. An utter rascal at times. But that was one of her many endearing qualities.

Lux felt a sudden pressure against her back, and frowned. For while it started quite gently, the force of that pressure was growing quickly.

She realized she was sliding forward, her feet leaving twin ruts in the sand. Looking ahead, she saw the sun sinking into the horizon.

Uh oh.

The pressure continued to increase, as if a wall were pressing against her, shoving her forward. And it was picking up speed.

Fast.

She was being shoved toward the sun quicker than she could run now, and she lost her balance, landing on her back on the sand. Still the wall of night pushed her, faster and faster, until she was zooming across the sand so rapidly it was a blur. She felt the heat of the friction as she flew over the dunes, tumbling madly across the desert floor. But to her surprise, she felt no pain.

Faster and faster she went, flying over a tall dune and careening through the air, the world zooming by impossibly fast beneath her. Hundreds of miles per hour…and then a thousand. Traveling as fast as the world spun.

Uh oh…

Desert gave way to a grassy hill, and Lux tumbled up to the top of it in a blink of an eye, flying into the air as if she'd been shot out of a cannon. Up and up she went, hundreds of feet in the air…and then the hilly terrain gave way to a sandy shore, and the rolling waves of the ocean far below.

She felt a surge of panic as her ascent slowed, then stopped.

Lux cried out as she began to fall toward the water, her light reflected in its silvery surface. Her stomach flip-flopped as she gained speed, the wind howling in her ears.

Then she slammed into the water…and reflected off of it, shooting upward and forward in a straight line, far faster than she had before. And this time, the wind didn't howl in her ears…there was no resistance to her flight whatsoever.

It took her a moment to figure out what had happened.

I'm light, she realized. The same thing had happened when she'd fought the Gemini, those mirrored soldiers that Simon had created. She'd reflected off them, shooting backward as a burst of light.

And the ocean's waves, silver in the dying light, reflected her.

Lux continued upward and forward, not so much as slowing. She realized that she would continue like this forever…until she'd left the world altogether, shooting off into space.

Unless…

She willed herself to become corporeal once again, and immediately felt the wind slam into her, slowing her flight. Gravity grabbed her, pulling her back toward the ocean, now thousands of feet below.

And as she fell toward it, trepidation turned to exhilaration.

"Woooo!" she cried as she careened toward the ocean, the wind screaming in her ears. She laughed as the ocean rose to meet her, then crashed into its surface…and reflected off it again, zooming forward and upward like a beam of light.

Again and again she did this, each time gaining more and more speed. Until she was moving far faster than the wall of night chasing her. Across the vast ocean she went, the world zooming by beneath her. And as she went, the sun reversed its course, rising slowly from the horizon as she outpaced the rotation of the world.

She laughed out loud as she shot across the land, reveling in the utter freedom of it.

It was glorious.

And as she went, she felt her sister Luna's presence, at first getting farther and farther away…and then getting closer. She knew immediately that she'd reached the other end of the world from her sister, and that she was now circling back toward her.

She smiled, knowing that it was only a matter of time before she'd be reunited with Luna. For as the world spun, the sun's light would move across the world. And where shadow met the light, they would be together again.

* * *

Luna opened the door from the Underground to the hills twenty miles outside of Havenwood, stepping through. The night sky greeted her, the moon glowing in the sky, countless stars dotting the infinite blackness. Their light was far too weak to stop her, but it was only a matter of time before the sun would rise again. And when it did, Luna would be ready for it.

She focused, melting into the shadow of night, becoming one with it.

Luna felt herself expand, now encompassing a swath of shadow perhaps a quarter-mile in diameter. Her growth soon stopped, however; apparently there were limits to how much shadow she could meld with. But as she had back in the Water Dragon cave, she found that she could step out of any part of that shadow…and did just that to stand amidst the hills.

Then she did it again, and again, her eyes on Dragon's Peak far in the distance.

In this way, she reached the mushroom forest in less than a minute, and was standing at the mouth of the Water Dragon cave soon after. Fallen debris from the ruins of Castle Havenwood littered the ground, and Luna stepped around it, making her way to the cave entrance.

Then she melted into the shadows.

She felt herself grow to encompass the entire Water Dragon tunnel, and willed herself to step out into the cavern in the bowels of Dragon's Peak, where her mother's mansion lay ahead amidst a glowing mushroom garden.

A garden which, unfortunately for Luna, emitted too much light for her to pass through…just as it had the last time she'd tried.

"Well damn," she swore, staring at the mansion beyond the light.

Then she noticed a rock on the cavern floor, one that threw a small shadow just beyond the wall of light. She knelt before it, sliding her hand under the shadow, remembering her previous experiment with it.

A smile curled her lips, and she eyed the glowing mushrooms with grim satisfaction.

"Can't have a shadow without the light, mmm?" she murmured. And if she could cast a shadow that would move *with* her…

Luna's smile broadened, and she melted into shadow, stepping out into the night just outside of the Water Dragon cave. Then she melded again, reappearing in Downtown. It was mostly in shambles, destroyed by Craven's shield-beam and the chunks of stone from the mountainside and debris from the castle that had fallen there. But a few of the buildings and houses were still standing…and she went into each of them, searching them carefully.

It wasn't long before she found what she was looking for: a closet in one of the intact homes, with a heavy brown fur coat hanging there. Why, it even had a hood.

"Perfect," she purred.

She put it on, pulling the hood over her head. The coat was far too big for her, dragging on the floor like coattails. Which was just what she needed.

Luna melted into the shadows…and the coat fell off of her.

Damn, she thought. She reappeared, putting the coat back on.

"Guess I gotta walk," she muttered.

So she began the long journey up Dragon's peak to the Water Dragon tunnel…and to her mother's mansion. When at last she'd returned to the entrance of her mother's mansion's cave, she stopped where the darkness met the light, pulling the cloak tighter around herself – and the hood further over her head. She stared at the mushroom-light, taking a deep breath in.

Okay, she thought. *Here goes nothing,*

With her cloak around her, Luna stepped forward, bringing shadow into the light.

And to her delight, she passed through without any problem at all.

"Oh *yes*," she exclaimed with a triumphant smile. She could exist within the shadow of her cloak…which meant that with it, she could go anywhere she liked, in the darkness and in the light. Nowhere was off-limits now.

Luna continued forward through the cavern, the mushroom-light making her uneasy. She could feel a slight pressure on her face, her hood not completely blocking the light. But it was only a little uncomfortable, as if she were wearing a mask.

And when she passed through the gate to arrive at the open portcullis of the mansion's entrance, continuing into the dark foyer beyond, that pressure vanished.

She cast off her cloak then, melting into the shadows and reappearing in her studio on the second floor. Striding up to her easel, she set a fresh canvas upon it.

Then she got to work.

Chapter 17

General Craven's footsteps rang out sharply on the granite floor as he strode around the gold and crimson pedestal in the Locus Legis, the chamber that served as his resting place…and that faced the shimmering circular portal leading to Queen Eldora's chambers. Gideon followed behind him, and behind the Painter, two armed royal guards. Craven halted before the portal, twisting around to face Gideon. The Painter appeared irritatingly calm, far more so than he had any right to be. For he was about to face Queen Eldora herself, high ruler of the Pentad, an ancient being of extraordinary power.

Craven resisted the urge to grimace, facing the portal again.

"Proceed," he grumbled, then stepped through the portal.

He continued up the long, blood-red cylindrical hallway beyond, climbing the gilded stairs up to the queen's chamber. The walls and ceiling rippled with subtle waves that traveled upward, as if he were traveling through a great vessel pulsing with blood. An apt metaphor, for it led to the Heart of the Pentad, whose chambers served as the home of Queen Eldora herself.

As Craven and Gideon reached the chamber, Craven saw that the queen sat upon her throne, as she usually did for visitors other than himself. She gazed impassively at them as they approached, stopping a full ten yards away from her. Adorned in her simple crimson robe, she still managed to look the part of a queen. Regal, cold. Her posture that of a woman who knew she was above all others. Who held the power of life and death in the palm of her hand.

Gideon knelt without being asked to, to his credit…and Craven did the same.

"Stand," she ordered, her voice echoing through the Heart of the Pentad.

Both men obeyed, and she turned her eyes to Craven.

"You may leave," she told him.

Craven hesitated, glancing at Gideon…but only for a split-second. He bowed, turning about and leaving the chamber at once. For while he feared for the queen's safety, he trusted her wisdom…and would not dare disobey her command. He made his way back down the stairs and through the shimmering portal to the Locus Legis, and stepped up onto the gold and crimson platform in the center of the great room. He hesitated then, feeling ill at ease.

For Gideon was there with Queen Eldora. Alone.

Craven of course would not normally doubt the queen's ability to defend herself, nor the wisdom to allow herself to be alone with such a dangerous man. But he'd once thought himself impervious to harm…and had been proven terribly wrong.

A vision of Gideon standing over Queen Eldora's body came unbidden to his mind's eye. Of her lying in a pool of her own blood, eyes staring at him vacantly.

Craven blinked, willing the vision away.

Trust her, he told himself.

It was as Queen Eldora herself had said: he was a part of her, her right hand. But if the right hand of the queen was fallible…

Enough!

He grit his teeth, taking a deep breath in, then letting it out. He positioned himself on the pedestal, facing the portal to the Heart of the Pentad. While his eyes were on its shimmering surface, his focus was inward. For he was to return to Torpor until the queen's next command. A welcome respite from his troubled thoughts.

But even as the familiar numbness traveled from his feet upward to the top of his head – even as his mind seemed to dip below the waters of consciousness – Craven knew full well that Torpor, the little death and eventual rebirth, would not free him from himself.

His failure would be there when he emerged.

Waiting for him.

* * *

Gideon stood before Queen Eldora in the Heart of the Pentad, trying his best not to stare. For Eldora was breathtakingly beautiful to him.

She had skin of the purest white, so pale that it shone in the artificial light of the chamber. Long, perfectly straight red hair fell over her slender shoulders, cascading over her small frame all the way to her waist. Her body was angular but soft, feminine and slight, the simple crimson robe she wore rippling at her waist as she sat cross-legged on her throne. Each ripple a symphony of shadow and light.

And her *eyes*…

Big and hypnotic, with crimson irises that seemed to glow with an inner light. A cute button nose. Full, pale lips.

She was formidably lovely. Softly firm. Gently fierce. A contradiction, Queen Eldora. For though she appeared vulnerable, Gideon knew better than most what she was capable of. He'd seldom had the opportunity to meet with her, not since…

Eldora stood from her throne in one fluid motion, moving with otherworldly grace. This sent ripples throughout her robe that shimmered in the light. He suspected the robe was magical…and wondered for the umpteenth time what sort of magic it possessed. Of course, it was also possible that it held no magic at all. That it appeared magical merely because of the woman who wore it.

"You," she stated, her gentle, musical voice cutting through his thoughts, "…are your worst enemy, Gideon."

Gideon grimaced, forcing himself not to lower his gaze. He held hers instead, saying nothing.

Eldora stared at him with those crimson eyes, like a statue standing before her throne. She didn't even seem to breathe, so still was she. He knew from experience that she was waiting…and that she could wait for a very long time.

"Perhaps," he replied at last. "But never *your* enemy."

"I know," she stated. "But the law doesn't."

Gideon said nothing.

"I was hoping you'd defeat him," she confessed.

He inclined his head, knowing she was being truthful…and that she was referring to Craven.

"Why didn't you?" she pressed.

"I had my chance," he admitted. "I thought I could trap him instead. Out of respect for our friendship."

She smiled, knowing full well that he meant *their* friendship, not his relationship with the general.

"You're too considerate, Gideon," she accused. Still, she looked pleased at this.

"I'm my own worst enemy," he reminded her.

She didn't reply, continuing to stare at him. He found himself hypnotized by those unworldly eyes, gentle but somehow predatory, pinning him in place. She moved toward him, seeming to glide over the floor instead of walking, closing the distance between them and stopping a mere foot away. From this distance he could smell her scent, a subtle sweetness that took his breath away. It was not perfume, this.

It was her.

Gideon swallowed with difficulty, his heart pounding in his chest. His eyes had never left hers. His thoughts scattered at her closeness.

Eldora gave the subtlest of smiles, leaning in and putting her lips within a hair's breadth from his right ear. She took a deep breath in through her nose, breathing him in.

Then she pulled away a little, still smiling.

"The law must be appeased," she told him. And it was clear she found this distasteful.

"I know."

"So we will appease it," she continued. She put a hand on his cheek, her touch ice-cold. It sent a shiver through him, as it always did. He noticed a flash of gold on her right ring finger, a gilded ring in the shape of a snake eating its tail.

"How?" he asked.

"By execution, of course," she answered.

His jawline rippled.

"And Thaddeus?" he pressed.

"The same."

Gideon took a deep breath in, letting it out slowly. He felt a sudden, crushing exhaustion come over him.

So be it.

Eldora was still staring at him. Watching. And he knew that she saw everything. Every twitch of every muscle in his face, every breath. Every heartbeat. He could not keep his body a secret from this woman.

Then, without a word, she turned her back to him, still only a foot away. He stared at her waves of red hair, spilling down her back like a bloody waterfall flowing down her pale skin. She stood there for a long moment, exposed.

Then she held up her right hand, displaying the ring on her finger.

"It'll remind me of you," she promised. "Always."

He said nothing, knowing that there was nothing more to say.

"Until next time," she murmured.

Gideon swallowed past a lump in his throat, inclining his head even though she couldn't see it. He turned then, making the long walk through the Heart of the Pentad, back down the long stairwell leading down the great artery to the shimmering portal far below.

And when he'd gotten far enough away from Queen Eldora, so that his thoughts were no longer scattered, her scent no longer tantalizing him, he took a deep breath in, letting it out slowly. She had made her intentions quite clear…and he knew what he had to do now.

No matter his feelings for her, or for the kingdom she ruled.

For Gideon, family came first.

Chapter 18

Luna swore, chucking her paintbrush at the canvas she'd been working on. The impact knocked the easel over, sending it – and her painting – to the floor with a clatter.

"Son of a…" she began, clenching her fists.

For despite many hours of work, waiting for the Flow to come, it had not. She'd painted and painted, waiting for her muse to take over. To guide her hand as it saw fit. And yet it had not.

She fumed, unclenching and clenching her fists.

"Bitch!" she swore, kicking the fallen easel. It slid across the floor, banging into the wall of her studio. She had the sudden urge to destroy it. To pick it up and smash it against the wall until it shattered. Until she made holes in the wall. She resisted the urge, but only barely.

It was all-too-clear why she couldn't sense the Flow. And the reason only served to infuriate her more.

Without Lux, she was incomplete. The Flow came not from darkness, or the light, but from the interplay between them. And as powerful as she was, able to meld with the shadows and travel anywhere within the cover of night, it wouldn't be nearly enough to take down the Pentad.

"Fine," she muttered.

With a thought, she melded with the darkness around her, stepping out a split-second later in the foyer downstairs. She found her cloak there, donning it quickly. Then she went back outside, braving the light of the glowing mushroom-garden. As before, she passed through without incident, and made her way back up to the mouth of the Water Dragon cave. The sun was already above the horizon, but only just so.

Come on sister, she urged, standing just before the border between the shadow and the growing light. *Come to me.*

Luna closed her eyes, feeling for her sister's presence. She sensed it, ahead and far, far away. But getting closer at a rate that seemed downright impossible.

She waited.

Then, as the sun continued to rise, she spotted something in the distance. A bright pinpoint of light soaring through the sky above the sun.

Sister!

It flew toward her, shooting over the terrain like a bullet. And then, as it neared Dragon's Peak, it slowed, transforming into the shape of a girl. Lux struck the cliff beside the Everstream, diffusing slightly with the impact, then re-forming into her usual form. She ran up to Luna, a huge smile lighting her face.

"Luna!" she cried, clearly overjoyed to see her. Luna forced herself to smile back.

"Took you long enough," she grumbled. But with her sister nearby, Luna found her irritation fading. The urge to reconnect with Lux struck her, an overwhelming desire to become one with her brighter half.

She resisted the urge for a moment – just to prove that she could – and then reached out with one hand even as Lux reached out for her. Their fingers intertwined where the shadow met the light.

And then they were one.

* * *

Bella found herself standing at the mouth of the Water Dragon cave, squinting in the morning sun. And while her last memories – as herself, at least – were of terrible thirst and unbearable heat, now she felt perfectly fine. The two halves of herself had healed in their respective environments, and so she too had been made whole.

And now she knew what she had to do.

I have to save Gideon, she realized. But if she was going to do that, she'd need all the help she could get. And if she was going to find Gideon, there was only one person that could help her.

Or rather, one Familiar.

She looked down, seeing her Painter's uniform and her rolled-up paintings in their thigh-holsters. Withdrawing the painting she'd stuck Myko in, she unrolled it with a word, and pulled Myko out of Goo.

Myko's silver eyes locked on hers, and she found her lower lip quivering.

"Sorry Myko," she whispered, her voice cracking.

Myko stepped right up to her, assaulting her face with canine kisses. Bella squealed, trying to escape, but he followed relentlessly, assailing her with love. Eventually she put up her hands in surrender.

"Okay!" she cried. "I forgive myself!"

Only then did Myko stop, stepping back and staring at her, his tongue lolling out of the side of his mouth in a doggy-smile. She couldn't help but smile back…as she wiped his drool from her face with the back of her sleeves.

"We need to save Gideon," she told him. He *wuffed* in instant agreement. Then he turned to face her painting, eyeing Goo, who was still mostly trapped within. "You're right," she realized. "We'll need all the help we can get."

She pulled Goo out as well, explaining the situation to him quickly. The blob accepted their mission as readily as Myko had…a fact that filled Bella with pride…and made her rather emotional again.

"All right," she stated, doing her best to keep her composure. "Can you…"

Myko barked, interrupting her.

"What?" she asked.

He nudged her right hip, and her eyes widened in realization.

"Cain!" she exclaimed, remembering how Craven had crushed his spine. She'd been so wrapped up in herself that she'd lost her consideration for everyone else. "Are you okay?"

"I…can't…feel my…legs!" Cain gasped in horror.

Bella just stared at him.

"Just fine, thank you," he answered. "More importantly, how are *you*?" he inquired. "I was terribly worried about you back there in the desert."

Bella had to smile at that.

"I know you hate seeing me die," she replied.

"That I do," he agreed.

"I'm sorry I put you through that," she apologized. "Are you still…broken?"

"Yes," he answered. "But I believe there may yet be a solution to my predicament. If you could breathe into my mouth," he requested.

Bella recalled that she'd made Cain originally to breathe in people's air and breathe out oxygen, so that she and Calypso – or rather Mom – could breathe indefinitely underground. She'd painted Cain to take in the breath of living creatures as his energy source; if it could rejuvenate him…

She did as he requested, breathing into his mouth, over and over again.

Eventually his eye-sockets flashed brighter green…and a vertebral column – utterly intact – shot downward from the base of his skull.

"Aha!" he cried jubilantly. "Success!"

"Whew," Bella replied with a smile. "I was worried about you."

"And I about you," he confessed.

"My father was taken," Bella stated. "We need to save him."

"I shall do whatever I can to assist you," Cain declared valiantly.

Bella smiled, feeling a bit overwhelmed. Myko, Goo, and Cain were all there for her, ready to help. The fact that she had so many friends around her, ready to support her no matter what the odds, was profoundly heartening.

"I love you," she blurted out, tears blurring her vision. "All of you."

"And we love you," Cain replied with utter conviction.

Myko *wuffed*…and Goo wrapped around her ankles, giving her a squeeze.

Bella took a deep, shuddering breath in, doing her best to compose herself.

"I don't deserve it," she confessed. "Havenwood fell because of me. People got hurt…people might have died because of me."

"Poppycock," Cain declared dismissively.

"No, it's true," Bella insisted. "And now I have to make it right. Because if I don't, more people will get hurt."

"Count me in," Cain declared at once. "I shall assist you in any way I can!"

Bella smiled, patting the magical skull-cane on the head. He hovered to his usual place at her right hip, sucking his spine back into himself.

"Okay," she stated, eyeing her friends. "I appreciate all of your help, but if we're going to face the Pentad, we'll need a lot more of it."

The Pentad was an enemy beyond powerful, after all. One with capabilities she could only dream of. There was no way to know what she was up against…she didn't have the experience or the knowledge.

But she knew someone who did.

She turned to face the mouth of the Water Dragon cave, squaring her shoulders. "I signed a contract that guaranteed my protection when I joined the Guild of Necromancers," she stated. "It's time for Petrusa to hold up her end of the bargain."

And if anyone knew how to save Gideon and Grandpa, it would be Petrusa, Queen of the Plane of Death.

* * *

Bella made her way back down the Water Dragon tunnel to her mother's mansion, passing into the foyer, then making her way down the long hallway beyond. She walked past Terrible Boar, then went up the stairs beyond. The small room it led to contained the magical coffin that would bring her to the Plane of Death. She unlatched its latches and opened it, then laid within, closing the lid and plunging herself into darkness.

The coffin rotated to the left, and then stopped.

Bella pushed the lid open, finding herself somewhere entirely different; in a familiar mausoleum in the Plane of Death.

She sat up, then stood, stepping out of the coffin.

A large, rectangular room filled with rows of golden coffins greeted her, each with a single black circle surrounding a black triangle embossed on their surfaces. The symbol of the Plane of Death. The triangle represented wealth, power, and love…and the circle represented the Dark Circle, the cycle of life and death that was never-ending.

There were stairs opposite the long rows of coffins, and Bella took them to a wide hallway leading to a stone archway, beyond which there was a single wooden door. A giant ivory human skull was embedded at the top of the arch, its head tilted down such that its eye-sockets seemed to be staring right at her. The personification of Death itself.

As Bella approached, a glimmer of light appeared in those sockets.

Blackness spread over the skull, replacing its ivory color until it was covered in a thin layer of slick black skin. Blood flowed from its eye-sockets, streaming down its cheeks.

"WELCOME, BELLA BIRCH," Death's deep voice boomed.

"Hi Death," Bella greeted. "I need to speak with Petrusa."

Death paused.

"FOLLOW THE GLOWING PATH," it declared.

Bella nodded, striding past the arch to the door beyond and opening it. She strode through, finding herself outside, in the middle of a graveyard. Dark clouds hung in the sky far above, the blood-red moon peeking between them. A tall, twisted black metal fence stood ahead, and she made her way to it. There was a small gate there, and she opened it, passing through. The ground ahead was littered with half-buried bones and countless skulls, their eye-sockets facing upward. Some of which began to glow a faint blue, illuminating a winding path that continued forward to a hill in the distance.

She followed it, eventually reaching the top of the hill.

Over a mile away, she saw the great city of Arx Mortus, the capitol of the Plane of Death. And in the very center of the city, rising up above even the tallest of the shadowy skyscrapers dominating the city's skyline, was a massive black stone pillar. It had a broad base that tapered as it rose high above the city, and broadened again as it plunged into the dark, swirling clouds in the sky far above. And halfway up the great pillar was a long, flat stone platform that extended outward from it…and upon which a huge black castle stood.

Petrusa's castle.

The earth rumbled, and Bella saw the ground open up a few yards in front of her. A huge skull rose upward from the earth, its mouth gaping open to reveal a shimmering blue portal within.

Bella stepped into it…and found herself on the stone ledge overlooking Arx Mortus, the very same ledge upon which Petrusa's castle stood.

"Hello Bella," a smooth voice greeted.

Bella turned to see Petrusa herself standing next to her. Tall and slender, with skin as pale as death, The Queen of the Dead was dressed in her usual armor: a multilayered suit made of intricately connected bones. Her blue eyes were staring at Bella, with an intensity that made Bella instantly uneasy.

"Hey," Bella greeted. She opened her mouth to continue, but Petrusa held up one hand.

"Spare me the story," she interrupted. "I know what happened."

"Then you need to help me," Bella replied. Petrusa arched an eyebrow.

"Oh *really*."

"The Pentad attacked me," Bella reasoned. "And they killed Mom."

"Hardly the first time your mother has died," Petrusa replied dismissively.

"I tried to resurrect her," Bella continued, pulling out her mother's amulet. "But it didn't work."

"Then you did it wrong."

"Gideon was taken," Bella pressed. "The Pentad has him now."

"That is none of my concern."

"But…" Bella began, but Petrusa cut her off with a look.

"I am not obligated to help your father," she stated coolly. Bella crossed her arms over her chest.

"Well you *are* obligated to protect me," she retorted. "Didn't you say that if I became an initiate of the guild that you'd protect me from the Pentad?"

"You seem just fine to me," Petrusa countered.

"No thanks to you," Bella argued.

"Consider that you had every opportunity to escape into the Plane of Death," she continued. "And you did not."

"I couldn't abandon my family," Bella retorted.

"And that was *your* choice," Petrusa replied evenly.

Bella grit her teeth, glaring at the Queen of the Dead.

"So you're just going to do nothing?" she pressed.

"I'm going to do what I'm going to do," Petrusa stated. "And I have no obligation to tell you what that might be."

Bella stared at her for a long moment, then dropped her arms to her sides.

"Fine," she muttered. "If you won't do anything, I'll save them myself."

"That," Petrusa replied, "…is also your choice."

"Damn right it is," Bella agreed. "Now if you're not going to do anything, I'd like to get back to the land of the living."

Petrusa raised an eyebrow.

"I could always jump," Bella added, gesturing at the city beyond the edge of the platform. It was a very, *very* far drop to the city below. "Turns out I'm pretty hard to kill."

"That won't be necessary," Petrusa replied…and Bella felt a presence behind her. She turned, seeing another one of Petrusa's huge skulls levitating there. Its mouth opened wide, exposing the blue portal within.

"Thanks for nothing," Bella muttered…and then she stepped through the portal. She found herself back within the graveyard she'd come from, facing the entrance to the mausoleum. With a sigh, she went inside, going down the stairs to the array of golden coffins below. She found the one she'd come from – the only one whose lid was open – and went inside, laying down and closing the lid over her. She felt herself rotate to the right, returning to the land of the living.

When she opened the lid again, she found herself back in Mom's mansion. She climbed out of the coffin, then turned to stare at it.

Then she grabbed the lid, slamming it shut with a *bang!*

Fresh tears welled up in Bella's eyes, and she blinked them away, refusing to cry again. She swallowed her tears, turning away from the coffin and making her way down the stairs to the long hallway beyond. Terrible Boar was there, standing guard as always. She walked to his side, putting a hand on his half-rotted head.

He snorted, licking her arm.

Bella burst out crying, her legs giving out under her. She sank to her knees in the long, dark hallway, burying her face in her hands. Her shoulders heaved, each sob echoing down the hallway.

At length, she collected herself, rising to her feet.

"Thanks Terrible," she murmured, patting the Boar's head. Then she strode forward, her heels *clicking* on the floor with each step. She squared her shoulders as she walked, refusing to be broken by Petrusa.

And in this way, Bella made her way slowly to the surface of the land of the living, leaving Petrusa – and the Guild of Necromancers – behind.

Chapter 19

Simon strode down the long, branching tunnels of the Underground, his crisp white suit glowing bright purple from the light shining from the slight gaps between the dark rock walls and the magical doors spaced at irregular intervals. He walked with complete confidence, having long-since memorized the way to his usual destinations.

Confidence gained at a price.

For it was with Miss Savage that he'd learned his way. Following her like an obedient dog, doing her bidding. Because he'd been too cowardly to say no. Too weak to stand up for himself…to see his own power.

You see it now, he heard Redeemer soothe. He smiled, feeling another slight squeeze from his Familiar.

It wasn't long before Simon reached his destination: a door like any other, with strange symbols carved in the rock above it. He turned the knob, opening it, and stepped through.

Simon found himself in a hilly region with sparse grass and shrubs. A few shrubs grew around the door, and he slid past them, feeling the branches scratch at his suit. But they did not snag it; everything seemed to slide off of her…and nothing could stain her.

In the distance, miles and miles away, he saw Dragon's Peak, its summit shrouded in dense clouds.

Simon took a deep breath in, the warm, crisp air a refreshing change from the putrid stench of the Festering Wood. A memory of him standing here, Miss Savage at his side, came to him. Of Dragonkin bodies strewn on the ground around them, killed by the Doppelganger and the Gemini.

The last time he'd come here, it'd been on a mission to destroy Havenwood. To murder all of its artists and to capture Thaddeus Birch. Revenge that, by that time, Simon hadn't even wanted anymore.

Don't be a victim like I was, he heard the Collector's voice say. *Be a hero.*

He squared his shoulders, then continued forward. As he came gradually closer to the mountain, he found himself staring at it. The clouds at its peak were passing by, revealing the summit. But something was wrong. Terribly wrong. For the great Castle Havenwood wasn't there. It was just…gone.

His heart leapt in his throat.

Bella!

He broke out into a run, speeding over the hilly terrain, his heart pounding in his chest. For if Havenwood was gone – if it'd been destroyed – then he might be too late. Bella might be…

Simon ran faster.

Slow down, Redeemer urged.

"But I have to…" Simon began.

There may be danger, she warned. *Your strength is in your creativity. Think this through.*

Simon hesitated, then reluctantly obeyed. Redeemer was right, of course. Rushing in wouldn't help Bella, not if whatever had destroyed Havenwood was still there. He didn't have the Collector's suit anymore – a suit that had made him nearly invincible – and Redeemer's qualities had yet to be tested. He needed to be smart about this.

Whatever destroyed Havenwood must have been powerful indeed. It would take an army to defeat the White Dragon, after all…and the Dragonkin, and the artists living there. Which meant…

He frowned, reaching into his suit pocket. There was something slick there, thin and with sharp edges. He pulled it out.

A single shard, mirrored on one side, black on the other.

It was a piece of the Gemini, his mirrored soldiers. He'd told them to shatter themselves during his battle with Bella and Gideon and Thaddeus a month ago. But he'd kept a single shard, just in case. For any part of any Gemini could hear everything, so anything he said to *this* shard would be heard by all.

They were one, the Gemini. And many.

Simon put the shard to his lips, his eyes on Dragon's Peak.

"Come to me," he murmured.

He felt the shard vibrate, and returned it to his pocket. Then he smiled, putting a hand on his chest, feeling the smooth fabric of Redeemer.

"Thank you," he told her.

She said nothing, but squeezed him gently. And that was enough.

He continued forward then, walking instead of running. For the Gemini would take some time to come to him, tireless as they were. They knew of the Underground, and would use it to their advantage.

And then, with an army of his own, he would help Bella.

* * *

When Bella emerged at last from the mouth of the Water Dragon cave, she found Myko and Goo waiting for her near the edge of the cliff, just to the left of the Everstream. She walked up to them, feeling utterly exhausted.

"Hey," she mumbled. She took a deep, steadying breath. "Petrusa refused to help us. Looks like we're on our own."

Myko and Goo nodded in their respective fashions.

"So I guess we need a plan," Bella said, running a hand through her hair.

She looked down at the devastation far below, at the rubble strewn across the kingdom further down the mountain. And at the mushroom forest beyond Lake Fenestra, cut with huge black scars from Craven's shield-beam. The sight was suddenly overwhelming, and she turned away from it, putting a hand to her mouth.

You did this, she told herself.

She grit her teeth, composing herself.

"We have to look for survivors," she realized. "Myko, can you sniff them out in the rubble?"

Myko *wuffed.*

"Okay," she replied. "And Goo, you dug Nemesis out when Castle Under fell on her. Can you help Myko dig survivors out if he finds any?"

Goo wobbled agreeably.

"We should start with the castle. That's where the artists were supposed to go in case of an emergency," she reasoned.

And so they made their way to Main Street, turning left to follow it as it spiraled up to the very top of Dragon's Peak. When they reached the top, Bella slowed, then stopped, her heart sinking.

The castle had been utterly destroyed. Reduced to rubble.

"Oh god…" Bella blurted out, putting her hands to her mouth.

"Come then," Cain urged, bumping her hip. "Tears won't save anyone. We have work to do!"

Bella nodded, then continued forward.

They reached the rubble quickly, then went about climbing over the huge hunks of stone. It was slow-going at best; only Goo, with his gelatinous body, had no trouble traversing the terrain. So Myko and Bella got inside of him, riding him through the remains of Castle Havenwood.

And, with all of her negative emotions absorbed by Goo's special power, for the first time since Gideon had been taken, she felt peace.

It was glorious, like a warm blanket had been draped over her shoulders, and suddenly she wanted nothing more than to snuggle into it. To feel this way forever. But she saw Myko doing his part, sniffing the air for survivors, and knew that she needed to do hers.

"Find anything?" she asked the wolf after they'd been at it for a while. Myko shook his head.

Bella considered this, in a rather detached sort of way. Almost as if it were just a curious problem to be solved. If there were no survivors, that meant that almost all of the artists in Havenwood were dead. They'd been instructed to go to the castle's vault in times of danger, and…

Her eyes widened.

"The vault!" she exclaimed happily. "Of course!"

"Pardon?" Cain asked.

"The vault," she repeated. "The artists all went into the mural there when the Pentad attacked. It's a painting…a live painting, one they can step into. So that even if the castle fell…"

"Then the painting would survive!" Cain concluded. He knew as well as anybody that live paintings were nearly indestructible, of course. "Bravo Bella! Excellent thinking!"

"Which means that all we have to do is find it," Bella reasoned, feeling quite pleased with herself.

She focused, thinking it through. And without the weight of her pain and fear, she found thinking quite easy to do.

The mural was a live painting, which meant anything that wasn't a painting would fall right into it. And it happened to be very large. Which meant that if it had fallen face-up, rubble would've gone right into it, and there wouldn't be much – or any – on top of it.

But if it had fallen face-down, it could be buried under a considerable amount of rubble…and it could be anywhere.

"Okay," she stated. "Myko, can you moon-dash above the rubble and look for a hole in it where debris might have fallen into the mural?"

Myko did so immediately, moon-dashing upward out of Goo, then darting about in the sky high above her head. At the same time, Goo continued to flow over the wreckage, and Bella kept her eyes peeled. The sheer size of the ruins was overwhelming…it could take days – if not weeks or months – to sort through it all.

And by that time, Gideon would be…

She heard a bark from above, and looked up, seeing Myko moon-dashing back toward them. He landed in Goo beside her, nudging her shoulder with his nose, then pointing it to the right.

"Follow Myko's nose," she instructed Goo.

Goo did so, and it wasn't long before they reached a large, rectangular hole in the rubble. Bella's heart soared.

"There it is!" she exclaimed. "Okay Goo…can you dig down to it without falling in?"

Goo deposited Bella and Myko a few yards away, then got to work excavating the rubble. And to Bella's dismay, the instant she was free from him, her feelings returned with a vengeance. Fear mixed with hope, making her heart pound in her chest.

Come on…

Goo excavated the rubble with astounding speed and efficiency. For all he had to do was suck up boulders and stones into his huge body, then deposit them a short distance away. It wasn't long before he'd excavated all the way down to the shattered granite floor of the vault.

And there, lying atop it, was the mural, positioned face-up.

Bella walked up to it, studying it carefully. There were tons of stones incorporated into it, and well over a hundred people as well. She studied their faces, and then…

"Grandpa!" she cried.

For it *was* Grandpa, standing amidst the other artists. He was alive and well!

"Success!" Cain exclaimed exuberantly.

"We have to get him out," Bella stated. Which was going to be harder than she'd imagined. For Grandpa had somehow been shoved toward the middle of the painting, and it was absolutely humongous. Lying there on the ground, there was no way for her to actually reach Grandpa to pull him out. And if she tried to walk on the painting, she'd plunge through herself…at least up to her shins, where her shin-paintings were. Live canvases couldn't go into live canvases, after all. She doubted she'd be able to keep her balance, much less pull Grandpa out successfully.

But if she somehow managed to prop it up, then use something as a ladder to reach Grandpa…or maybe if she laid a large beam across the painting, long enough to cross over it without plunging in…

Myko's ears perked up, and suddenly he moon-dashed over the rubble, landing back near Main Street and gazing over the edge of the mountain. Then he bolted back toward them, barking madly.

"What is it?" Bella asked. Myko stopped halfway, whining. "Goo, bring us to where Myko was."

Goo did so, and soon they were at Main Street, looking over the edge of Dragon's Peak. Bella saw the mushroom forest below, and the blasted grassy plain beyond. There was an army there, marching around the crater Gideon's meteorite had created. No, not marching; *riding*. For they were moving toward Havenwood with formidable speed, far faster than any man could walk or run.

Coming right for them.

"Oh dear," Cain blurted out.

"The Pentad!" Bella cried, her heart leaping into her throat. "Come on," she added. "We have to get Grandpa and get out of here!"

Goo brought her back to the mural, and Bella got to work rolling the mural up. It'd been painted on canvas, thank goodness, and not directly on the stone. When she was done, the canvas was still as wide around as a good-sized tree-trunk…and had to be about fifteen to twenty feet long. To her dismay, it was far too heavy for her to lift.

Luckily, rolled up as it was, its non-live surface wouldn't trap anything.

"Goo, can you grab the painting?"

Goo did just that, and Bella turned to look at the approaching army. It was almost to the mushroom forest, and was closing in fast. From here she could barely make out what they were: soldiers riding on horses. But the horses had wings.

And as she watched, the first few rows of horses spread their wings, leaping into the air and flying upward and forward toward her!

Crap!

Bella's mind raced. She could go back into the Water Dragon cave to her mother's mansion, but then she'd be cornered…and Petrusa certainly wasn't going to help them. Which meant there was only one place she could go.

"To the Underground!" Bella ordered.

Myko nudged her, and he knelt down, letting her vault up onto his back. She grabbed his collar, squeezing his flanks tight between her thighs.

"Go!" she cried.

Myko broke out into a run, barreling toward the rubble ahead. Then his thick fur began to glow a faint silver…and Bella felt herself lurch forward and upward in a burst of silver light.

They sailed over the rubble, Myko glowing so brightly underneath her that he might as well have been Lux, leaving a long silver trail behind him. The light faded, and Myko immediately dashed again, then again, until they'd cleared the rubble altogether.

And then they plunged right over the edge of the mountain, entering into free-fall.

Bella's stomach flip-flopped as they fell, the wind screaming in her ears as they plummeted toward the mushroom forest far below. She held on to Myko's collar for dear life, and he burst forward again, soaring just above the mushroom-tops. In a few more moon-dashes, he cleared the mushroom forest, and dashed one more time to land on the grassy plain beyond, running as fast as he could.

Bella glanced back, seeing Goo falling down the mountain after them. Then her gaze lifted to the top of Dragon's Peak. A swarm of the winged horses flew over the mountain, some of them coalescing like a flock of birds on the mountaintop. But a good number of them continued onward past the mountain.

Coming right for Bella.

"They're following us!" she yelled in Myko's ear.

She watched in horror as the flying creatures dove down the mountainside after Goo, who seemed to glow bright green in the sunlight. He stuck out like a sore thumb as he reached the bottom of the mountain, vanishing from sight behind the mushroom forest.

The mounted soldiers were gaining on him…and fast.

"They're after Goo!" Bella cried, pulling back on Myko's collar. "We have to help him!"

Myko turned around, moon-dashing back toward the mushroom forest…and the swarm of flying creatures soaring above it. Bella spotted Goo rushing out from between mushroom-stalks, making his way toward her. But the flying creatures were just too fast.

They landed between Bella and Goo, cutting them off from each other. The soldiers wore red and gold plate armor, and carried long golden lances. Red and gold, the colors of the Pentad…like Craven wore.

"Goo!" Bella cried.

Goo rose up as the mounted soldiers charged him, thrusting their lances into his flesh. The lances pierced him…and then he promptly pulled them deeper into himself, sucking some of the soldiers right off their steeds and into his body.

Myko moon-dashed once, then again, closing the distance between them rapidly.

But even as Bella approached, more of the winged soldiers landed around Goo, some of which carried red lances. Lances that glowed red-hot. These soldiers thrust their weapons into Goo…and his flesh sizzled and blackened with the heat.

Goo recoiled from the attacks, but to Bella's horror, the soldiers advanced, jabbing him again and again. She reached into her chest-painting, feeling the black sphere within. A powerful explosive that Gideon had given her long ago. She grit her teeth, pulling it free as Myko galloped toward the soldiers, now only a hundred feet away. If she threw it into the air, then pointed at it, she could send it down on the soldiers.

But Goo would get caught in the blast. Unless…

"Goo, get back!" she shouted.

Goo burst backward…but was trapped by more of the soldiers with red-hot lances from behind. They surrounded him now, forming a circle around him. Bella cursed, plunging the sphere back into her chest-painting. Myko slowed, and she leapt off of him, landing on the grass beside him.

Then Myko moon-dashed into the nearest soldiers, knocking them off their winged steeds and sending them flying into Goo's body.

"To battle!" Cain cried at Bella's hip. She grabbed him, and his spine shot outward to form a cane. She ran toward the soldiers, even as they tried to fight Myko.

Myko moon-dashed again and again, sending soldiers and steeds flying.

But even as the trusty wolf did so, Bella realized that his moon-dashes were getting shorter, his glow weaker. He was running out of moonlight…and nighttime was far, far away.

And when he ran out for good…

"Get them away from Goo!" Bella ordered. If she could do that, then she'd be able to…

One of the mounted soldiers leapt off their steed, rushing at her with their golden lance!

"En garde!" Cain cried, guiding Bella's hand expertly. He blocked the soldier's thrust with a *clang*, then struck the side of the man's helmet. But the blow ricocheted off harmlessly.

The soldier charged, ramming his shoulder into Bella.

The impact threw her onto her back, blasting the air from her lungs. The soldier thrust his lance at her forehead with terrible speed, and Cain managed to deflect it just in the nick of time. The lance struck the earth to her left, the wicked tip burying itself into the soil.

Bella kicked the soldier right between the legs, striking the metal codpiece there. But despite its presence, the blow had its intended effect.

The soldier stumbled backward, letting go of his lance.

"Have at you!" Cain cried as Bella scrambled to her feet. Two more soldiers dismounted, rushing at her.

And then burst to the left as Myko moon-dashed into them, sending them flying.

Myko stood in front of Bella protectively, but she could tell he was nearly out of power…and the soldiers – dozens of them – were circling around her. Within moments, they were surrounded.

The soldiers closed in, their lances pointed right at her, Myko, and Goo.

Bella felt the heat from a few red-hot lances as they drew near, and pressed herself against Myko and Goo, huddling closer together as the circle around them contracted.

She looked down at her chest-painting, searching for something she could use. But there was nothing that would work without blowing them all up.

"Myko, moon-dash out of here," she ordered, retrieving the black sphere. Her jawline rippled. "Goo, run…no matter how much they hurt you."

She threw the sphere straight up, then raised her hand to point at it.

And then she heard shouting from behind, and suddenly hands were gripping her shoulders, yanking her backward!

"Hey!" she shouted. But more hands grabbed her, pulling her ever-backward. And as they did, a wave of glittering humanoids slammed into the soldiers.

Humanoids with bodies composed of mirrored facets, their right forearms terminating in long black swords.

Gemini!

Bella gasped, watching as the Gemini utterly overwhelmed the Pentad's soldiers, crashing into them like a tidal wave. The soldiers fell rapidly, their screams echoing through the air. Some managed to fly away on their winged steeds, but most were toppled over and killed before they had a chance to escape.

Within moments, it was over.

Bella stared at the bodies of the soldiers and their steeds littering the ground before her, and the Gemini standing amongst them, black blades stained with blood. Then she heard footsteps approaching from behind.

"Hello Bella," a voice said.

She turned around…and gasped.

Chapter 20

Bella stared.

A boy her age was standing there, surrounded by a literal army of Gemini, their facets gleaming like diamonds in the sunlight. He had short blond hair, a bit longer since she'd last seen it. And a jagged scar on his left temple, just above deep brown eyes. But the dark circles she'd seen under his eyes before were gone, and he'd filled out quite a bit, no longer the gaunt boy he'd been. And his shoulders were set back, not slouched, and he was dressed in a suite so purely white that it seemed to glow.

"Simon!" she blurted, breaking out into a huge smile. She leaned in to embrace him, squeezing him tight. He stiffened at first, then relaxed, hugging her back.

She held him for a while, then pulled back a bit, shaking her head in disbelief.

"You're here," she exclaimed. "How…?"

"I…came to visit you," he confessed. He even spoke more confidently, no longer dropping his gaze and mumbling like he had before. "When I saw that Havenwood had been destroyed, I called for help," he added, gesturing at the Gemini.

"Thank you so much," she replied. "If you hadn't come when you did, we would've been goners."

Myko *wuffed* in agreement, and even Goo jiggled a bit. Bella glanced at the blob, grimacing at the blackened pits in his flesh from the Pentad's fiery lances.

"You're welcome," Simon replied. Then he broke their gaze, staring at something behind Bella. She turned to see what he was looking at.

The mounted soldiers that had landed atop Dragon's Peak were taking flight…and coming right for them.

Thousands of them.

"Uh oh," Bella warned. She went to retrieve her black sphere, storing it in her chest-painting.

"Don't worry," Simon reassured her. "My Gemini outnumber them ten to one."

And indeed, as Bella watched, half of the Gemini transformed their chests and bellies into flat mirrors, and the other half of the Gemini reached *into* those mirrors, pulling out their own reflections. In this way, they grew their numbers by fifty percent. And, repeating the process, they did it again…and again.

But before the Pentad's flying army had gone very far past Dragon's Peak, something rose up from behind the mountain: a huge flock of flying creatures that flew after the army. At first Bella thought they were more of the Pentad's men. But as the Pentad's soldiers and the creatures behind them drew closer, it became quite clear what they were.

Dragonkin!

Bella watched as the Dragonkin gained on the Pentad's soldiers, closing the distance between the two armies slowly but steadily. The Pentad's men didn't even notice what was behind them.

Until it was too late.

The Dragonkin army attacked, cutting the Pentad's men down in mid-air, using their superior mobility to decimate the mounted enemies. The Pentad's soldiers tried to turn around to defend themselves, but the Dragonkin had the element of surprise…and used it to devastating effect.

Within minutes, the entire army was defeated, thousands of soldiers…and only a few Dragonkin…plummeting to the ground.

Bella cheered, mounting Myko and riding him toward the approaching Dragonkin. Simon and Goo followed behind her, and it wasn't long before they'd closed the distance. Bella's heart soared at the sight of the noble creatures, the original denizens of Havenwood…at least in the Plane of Reflection. They must have come through Lake Fenestra, which served as a portal to their native realm.

Myko slowed as the Dragonkin drew near, then stopped.

One of the Dragonkin soldiers – a burly man with blue-green scales, wearing the standard blue and white armor of King Draco's army – landed before them, bowing deeply.

"Daughter of the Creator," he greeted solemnly, in the stilted language of his kind. "I am named Serpo, general of King Draco's armies. I come at the behest of our king."

"Greetings Serpo," Bella replied. "This is Goo and Myko, and this is Simon and his army of Gemini," she introduced. "It's good to see you."

Serpo grimaced.

"We are ashamed," he confessed. "Your Havenwood has fallen. We didst witness its destruction at the hands of the infidels, but alas, in the darkness of night, we were unable to traverse Lake Fenestra to come to your aid."

Bella frowned. She'd forgotten that fact. Lake Fenestra was a mirror into the Plane of Reflection. But at night-time, very little light reflected off of its surface…and therefore it could not be crossed unless someone had shined light upon its surface from her side. Mom had used that particular fact to stop the Gemini from coming through the lake during the last attack on Havenwood.

"It's not your fault," she replied, lowering her gaze. "It's mine."

"Verily this is false," Serpo proclaimed. "But what is done is done. Our failure must be redeemed, daughter of the Creator."

"Well, this is a start," Bella stated, eyeing the fallen Pentad army. "But I'm pretty sure the Pentad will be back. And with a lot worse than these guys," she warned.

"Then they shall experience the might of the Dragonkin," Serpo vowed.

"I…don't think that's a great idea," Bella countered. "A man called Craven killed the White Dragon. He…defeated Gideon. If he comes back, not even your armies will be able to beat him."

Serpo hesitated, turning to look back at the other Dragonkin around him. Then he sighed, turning back to face Bella.

"We serve the Creator," he stated solemnly. "Is he…?"

"There," Bella stated, pointing at Goo. Goo wobbled, extruding the rolled-up mural inside of him until it was resting atop his huge form. "In the painting. He's okay."

Serpo relaxed visibly.

"Then there is yet hope for Havenwood," he declared.

"The Pentad is coming," Bella warned. "If they find out that Lake Fenestra is a portal into your world…" She left the thought hanging. Serpo nodded gravely.

"Should the Dragonkin be forced to abandon Havenwood, it will be done," he declared. "But only that we might regain our strength and reclaim our lands!"

"I may be able to help you," Simon offered, gesturing at the Gemini. "My army is infinitely expandable. I can offer a contingent of them to protect your version of Havenwood."

Serpo inclined his head.

"We had heard of your change of heart," he admitted. "Though once we were mortal enemies, now we are friends. Through your kindness the Creator was saved a month prior. Verily we are in your debt."

Simon swallowed visibly, inclining his head.

"I appreciate your forgiveness," he replied. "It means more to me than you'll ever know."

"We look forward to your friendship," Serpo declared, extending a clawed hand. Simon shook it. "We shall now return to our Havenwood," Serpo stated. "And make preparations for the Pentad's return."

"The Pentad wants me and Grandpa, not you," Bella replied. "I'll escape through the Underground. We need a safe place for Grandpa and the other artists to stay before we confront the Pentad."

"I'll come with you," Simon offered. "I think I know of a place." Bella smiled.

"I'd appreciate that."

"Go, daughter of the Creator," Serpo prompted.

"Thanks," she replied.

"When you need us, we shall be in Havenwood in the Plane of Reflection, or if not there, we shall relocate to the very place of our first battle together, in the ruins of the Castle Under," he declared.

"Got it," Bella stated.

With that, Serpo bowed one last time, then took to the sky. The other Dragonkin followed suit, flying back toward Dragon's Peak. A contingent of Gemini broke off from the main army, following the Dragonkin on foot. Bella watched them go, then patted Myko on the head.

"Let's go," she prompted.

And with that, Myko, Goo, Simon, and Bella made their way toward the Underground, escorted by an army of Gemini…and leaving over a thousand dead soldiers to rot in the sun behind them. Bella refused to look back, knowing that to do so would only cause her pain. That the image of the corpses would stay with her forever.

There was another, more terrible image that kept her going. One that overrode them all: a vision of Gideon hanging by a noose, and of Grandpa lying dead in a jail cell.

Bella squared her shoulders, continuing forward resolutely. The Pentad started this. They'd destroyed Havenwood and attacked her family, all because they thought they could get away with it. It'd been the same with the Collector and Miss Savage. People with power abusing those they thought were weaker than them.

I'll show them, she thought, clenching her fists.

But she knew full well she couldn't do it alone. She was going to need all the help she could get…and as she glanced from Simon to Myko to Goo, and even Cain, she realized just how lucky she was to have such loyal friends.

But as she did so, she felt a familiar sadness come over her. For she knew full well that there was something missing. A friend she'd pushed away…and that she would have to face – and forgive – if she was going to make things right.

Still, the thought of seeing her Familiar again filled her with dread…and the thought that Nemesis might not come back, even if asked to, was even more terrifying. Bella had said some awful things to the dragon, things that she could never take back.

I wish I'd never painted you.

Bella swallowed past a lump in her throat, blinking back tears.

I never want to see you again.

She felt a sudden, overwhelming exhaustion threaten to stop her in her tracks, and she glanced at Goo moving along beside her. Suddenly she wanted nothing more than to be inside of his calming embrace, to feel her worries and fears seep out of her.

To be free of her pain.

"Goo, can you carry me?" she requested.

Goo complied happily, scooping her up in his gelatinous body so that she was riding atop him, covered from the waist down in his rubbery flesh. A dark mist seeped out of her, and suddenly Bella felt that amazing calmness that only Goo could provide. It was as if a great weight had been instantly lifted from her shoulders.

She smiled, patting Goo.

"Thanks buddy," she murmured, and Goo jiggled a bit in response.

Bella took a deep breath in, enjoying the freshness of the air and the warm sunlight on her face. The world seemed bright, the colors of the sky and the scenery wonderfully vibrant, so much so that she was surprised she hadn't noticed it before. Goo carried her along, and Bella found herself focusing on what she needed to do. She'd made her bed after all, and now she had to lay in it. She couldn't take back what she'd said; what was done was done. The best thing she could do now was do her darnedest to save Gideon, and maybe even find a way to resurrect Mom, if it was even possible anymore.

Either way, as long as she had Goo, everything was going to be okay.

* * *

After reaching the Underground, Simon led Bella and the others to his safe place. Which, it turned out, was a magical door to a truly awful-smelling forest. Filled with trees that appeared twisted and diseased, and rotting fruit that covered the forest floor, the forest was unlike any that Bella had ever seen…and she gagged shortly after they'd stepped from the Underground into it.

"Ugh," she groaned, covering her nose and mouth. "Oh my god."

"Welcome to the Festering Wood," Simon stated with the faintest of smiles. Bella gave him a look.

"*This* is your safe place?" she asked.

"This is the darkness before the light," he promised. Then he strode forward into the forest, his boots squelching on the boggy mess of rotted fruit on the ground. This sent fresh bursts of putrid odors Bella's way, and she gagged again. Even Myko pawed at his nose…and was clearly reticent to step on the fruit with his bare paws. Bella looked back, seeing the Gemini streaming through the doorway. They stayed around it rather than follow their master, however.

"Are they coming too?" she asked.

"No," Simon answered. He turned to one of them. "Shatter," he ordered.

The Gemini – to a one – fell to pieces.

Bella watched this – with lots of questions churning in her mind – but resisted the urge to pester Simon with them. She had a job to do, after all; Gideon was still in the clutches of the Pentad, and he would only have so much time before something terrible was done to him. She turned forward, eyeing the muck ahead and wrinkling her nose. Then she glanced at Goo.

"Can you carry us?" she asked him. Goo wrapped himself around them and lifted them into himself, more than happy to oblige. And as the only one present without a nose, the Festering Wood bothered him not in the least.

Bella felt herself bothered quite a bit less by it as well once she was inside Goo. Swarms of little flies carpeted the forest floor and buzzed about in great clouds all around them, pelting Bella's face and body. She lifted her cape over her nose and mouth as a makeshift mask, which mostly prevented her from swallowing any of the little things. To her surprise, Simon led them forward without any trouble at all, tolerating the smells and the flies without any obvious discomfort.

And though the rotted fruit squelched up to his ankles, spattering his legs, his crisp white suit pants remained somehow – impossibly – perfectly clean.

"Where are we going?" Bella asked.

"To see a friend," Simon answered. "Someone who might be able to help you." He paused. "Someone who helped me."

"Where are we?" she pressed. "Still in the Pentad?" For if they were, it would be too dangerous a place for Grandpa and the other artists to be drawn out into. They needed a sanctuary…someplace the Pentad wouldn't go. Someplace far, far away.

"Epirus," Simon answered.

"Huh?" Bella asked. It sounded familiar for some reason, but she couldn't place why.

"A country north of the Pentad," Simon clarified. "The Pentad won't follow us here."

"Oh, right," she replied. Gideon had told her about Epirus after their escape from Blackthorne. Apparently the Pentad and Epirus had been at war up until recently, and the Collector had taken advantage of the Pentad's distraction to conquer Blackthorne. "Didn't Epirus lose the war?" she asked.

"Percy says that depends on who you ask," Simon answered.

"Percy?"

"The man who helped me," Simon explained. "We're going to meet him."

With that, they fell into a comfortable silence. Simon made his way confidently through the forest, and Bella followed, trusting that he knew where he was going. With Goo carrying her, she found herself falling into a kind of trance, gazing at the scenery around her, then at the sky peeking between the tree branches and rust-spotted leaves overhead. The leaves grew so densely that very little sunshine managed to sneak through.

The darkness before the light, indeed.

Minutes passed into hours, until at last Bella spotted a flickering orange-red light far in the distance, peeking between the trees. Simon veered toward it, leading them to a large clearing within the forest. Rotten fruit and twisted trees gave way to short, dense grass, and as soon as they stepped out of the forest, its awful smell disappeared as if by magic.

Beyond, Bella saw a small log cabin in the middle of the clearing, flames coming from a fire pit in front of it. There were three wicker chairs around the fire pit, one of which was occupied by a middle-aged man with a bald head and a bushy red beard. He was quite stern-looking, with a brown long-sleeved shirt and black pants and boots, and had a bit of a pot-belly. The man sipped a cup of tea as they approached, staring into the fire and paying them no mind at all.

Which was something else, considering it wasn't every day a massive green blob carrying a girl and a giant glowing wolf ventured across one's yard.

Goo deposited Bella and Myko onto the grass, and Myko followed alongside her as she walked up to the red-bearded man with Simon.

"Hi Percy," Simon greeted. "I brought Bella."

"So I see," Percy replied in a gruff voice.

"Nice to meet you Percy," Bella stated, walking up to him and offering a hand. Percy stood up and shook it. His hand was calloused, his grip firm but not painfully so.

"If it wasn't, you wouldn't have," the man replied with a smile. "Tea?"

"Sure, thank you," Bella replied. Percy gestured at the seat to his left, and Bella took it, sitting down before the fire pit. Her teacup was already set upon the armrest there. She took it, observing that it was hot, but not so much so that it burned her. Simon sat down on Percy's other side, and Myko laid down next to Bella. Goo, not needing to sit or stand, plopped himself opposite them all.

Bella took a sip of the tea…and nearly spat it out.

"Oo," she blurted out, making a face. For the tea was terribly bitter. She recovered quickly, glancing at Percy apologetically. "Sorry, it's just…"

"Too bitter?" he inquired, arching an eyebrow.

"A bit."

"Makes it hard to enjoy, doesn't it?" Percy mused. Bella set the cup down on the armrest, and he frowned at her. "Aren't you going to finish it?"

"Um…"

"Then set it aside," Percy advised. Bella hesitated, then did so. He smiled at her. "That wasn't so hard, was it?"

"Uh…no," she replied. She glanced questioningly at Simon, feeling rather awkward. It was hard for her to get a read on Percy. She shifted in her seat, feeling uneasy under his gaze.

"Is this everyone?" Percy inquired, looking around.

"Yes," Simon answered. Percy, however, seemed unconvinced. "The Pentad attacked Havenwood," Simon told Percy grimly. "They destroyed the castle and arrested Gideon."

"Hmm," Percy murmured, taking a sip of his own tea.

"Bella saved Thaddeus Birch and the other artists," Simon continued. "They're in that painting," he added, pointing at Goo. The painting was still suspended in his body.

"I see," Percy replied.

"They need a safe place to stay while I go back to help my dad," Bella piped in. "Can you help us?"

"Yes," Percy replied.

"Really? Thank you," Bella stated, breaking out into a relieved smile. Percy smiled back.

"You're welcome," he replied. "Now of course you'll need more room than I have here. And I have no desire for crowds, I can assure you." He made a face. "Nasty things, crowds. People are seldom their best when there's lots of them together."

Bella nodded in agreement. She didn't much like crowds either, and neither did Grandpa. She preferred dealing with people one-on-one.

"I had a home atop a mountain once," Percy mused, taking another sip of his tea and eyeing the fire. "I'm afraid it's fallen into a bit of disrepair, but with a bit of work it will surely do."

"That would be wonderful," Bella replied. "Thank you again, Percy. We're in your debt."

Percy scoffed at that.

"There are no debts between true friends," he chided. "Friendship isn't a sport; there's no need to keep score."

"Well, I'd appreciate it anyway," Bella stated. Percy patted her arm.

"I know."

With that, he stood up from his wicker chair, stretching his arms up, then heaving a sigh.

"Well, let's get to it," he prompted…and reached out with one hand, as if grabbing something. He twisted his wrist…and a door identical to the ones in the Underground appeared out of thin air before him. He pulled it open, then stepped back, gesturing for them to walk through. "Ladies, youth, dogs, and blobs first."

Bella hesitated, then stood up. She glanced at Simon, who gave her a reassuring smile. She smiled back; if Simon trusted this Percy, then she would too.

She turned to gaze at the purple light of the doorway, then stepped through into the unknown.

Chapter 21

To Craven, the dream of Torpor was like life. There was no memory of a beginning, just a sense of always having been. And while everything happened in a certain order, most of his dreams – and his life – had faded from memory, recalled only with great difficulty, or not at all. And while he was himself in both his dreams and in life, there remained a suspicion that his feeling of control over himself was merely an illusion. That he was a spectator of his own existence, controlled by forces beyond his comprehension.

But in the great dream of Torpor, Craven found an escape from himself…whereas in life his *self* returned with a vengeance.

So it was that he found himself emerging from the inky black waters of his great sleep, compelled to break through the surface of his subconscious by the siren call of Queen Eldora.

Bright light accosted his eyes, life returning to his face, then neck, then chest and abdomen, all the way to his feet. He found himself reborn for the umpteenth time, standing on his pedestal in the Locus Legis, facing the portal of the queen. While in Torpor, the great unease that had plagued him since his battle with Gideon had been muted.

But now it returned with a vengeance.

Craven grimaced, gazing at the pedestal upon which he stood. A representation of the pedestal the citizens of the Pentad placed him on in their hearts and minds. A reminder that, as the personification of Law itself, Craven stood higher than mere mortals.

He stepped down from the pedestal, not just to answer the call of Eldora, but because he was unworthy of it.

Craven realized the queen's guards at the portal were staring at him, and he relaxed into a neutral expression, stomping toward them. Their eyes followed him as he made his way up to the shimmering portal, and he wondered – for the first time – what they were thinking.

They know.

He stepped through the portal, leaving the guards behind as he entered into the long, blood-red cylindrical tunnel leading upward and forward. He strode up its golden stairs, feeling Eldora's call in his mind, a soundless voice through his new helmet. The one she'd had made for him to replace the original he'd lost. It could never be identical to the helmet he'd had; magic did not flow into art the same way twice, and it loathed copies of existing art. Magic loved creativity, and to be creative was to be novel. It was inferior to his old helmet, he knew.

A perfect fit.

At length Craven reached the top of the stairs, and entered into the great heart-shaped chamber of the queen. She was standing where he'd last seen her, at the far right of the chamber, before the huge globe levitating above the floor there. But she was not looking at it; she was staring at the floor.

Craven stomped up to her, stopping a few feet away.

"What do you require?" he asked. She lifted her gaze, turning to face him. Her crimson eyes locked on his, seeming to peer through him. Seeming to see everything.

He forced himself to stand still, to meet her gaze impassively. But inside, he squirmed.

"Peace of mind," she answered.

"I..." Craven began.

"Can't provide that," she interjected. She gave him a weak smile, putting a small, pale hand on his arm. Then she slid it off, turning to gaze at the throne at the opposite end of the chamber. "Do you know what that is, Craven?" she asked, gesturing at it.

"Your throne," he answered.

"Of course," she agreed. "Such a strange shape for a prison cell, isn't it?"

"I do not understand."

"Why would you?" she murmured. "You were created to *be* your role. I am a woman playing mine."

She sighed, gazing at the throne.

"That chair makes me do terrible things, Craven," she confessed. She turned to him, her eyes moist. "Things I would never do. As much as I love it, I despise it." She turned, looking at the simple wooden stool nearby. "I prefer that one."

Craven just stood there, not knowing what to say.

Eldora turned to stare up at him, her eyes searching his. Again, he had the feeling that she was staring *into* him. That she could see things he didn't want her to see. That he was exposed.

He squirmed, feeling his shame resurface...and had the sudden urge to leave the chamber. To escape Queen Eldora's searching gaze. The urge terrified him, and he clenched his fists, resisting it. He could not betray his weakness to her.

I am the right hand of the queen.

And he knew that if she found her right hand to be unfit, she would cut it off.

Eldora stared at him a moment longer, then turned away, gliding toward the throne. At length she reached it, running a hand over the seat.

"When I sit here, I'm a role," she mused. "A queen is not a person, Craven. It's an act." She sighed. "But there's no magic in it for me," she confessed. "I'm not an Actor."

"I don't understand," he repeated.

"Don't you?" she retorted.

He stood there, as still as the statue he was.

"You're as trapped as I am," she mused. "Compelled to act as I am. As much as Gideon is trapped and compelled to be acted upon."

"Gideon?"

"Yes," she confirmed.

"He broke the law," Craven stated. "He is a criminal."

"Yes," she repeated. She paused. "Do you think he loves the Pentad?"

Craven hesitated.

"He did."

"I believe he still does," Eldora stated. "I believe he loves the Pentad. I believe he loves me."

Craven blinked, taken aback.

"The law says he is a traitor," she reasoned. "And my throne compels me to treat him as one. But I – Eldora, not the queen – know he is not."

To this, Craven could say nothing.

"Shall I kill a man who spent his life protecting the Pentad?" she pressed. "For the crime of falling in love?"

"He harbored a fugitive."

"A woman whose mother was murdered because we failed to protect Thaddeus Birch," she countered. "A woman who – through our failure – lost her faith in us."

"She knew the law."

"The law governs reason," Eldora argued. "The heart defies it."

"Without law there is chaos."

"Without temperance there is injustice!" she snapped, her eyes hardening.

Craven took a step back, a chill running through him. The queen had never spoken to him like this…and had never looked at him the way she was doing so now. Her red irises seemed to glow, the ever-pulsing walls of the huge heart-shaped chamber around them doing so more quickly.

But as quickly as she'd revealed her temper, it vanished. Her expression softened, becoming serene once more.

"How much injustice have we committed in the name of the law?" she asked, her voice a near-whisper.

Craven couldn't answer.

Eldora gave him a sad smile.

"For you, Craven, the law and justice are the same," she murmured. "You are the right hand of the queen, and my right hand dominates. But you are only a hand, and my heart..." she continued, putting a hand on her chest, "...is on my left."

Craven bowed his head.

"As you say, my queen."

She stared at him for a long while, then lowered her hands to her sides and turned away from him. Walking back to her throne, she sat upon it, facing him. Her expression grew instantly cold.

"The scouting party I sent to Havenwood to search for Thaddeus and Bella has been destroyed, as has their military escort," she announced.

"By whom?" he asked.

"Unknown," the queen answered. "There were no survivors. I sent scouts to find their bodies. They too were massacred."

Craven waited.

"Mobilize my bounty hunters," she ordered. "Send my best to retrieve Thaddeus and Bella, and any surviving artists of Havenwood."

"As you wish," Craven replied.

"The queen does not wish," she chided. "She commands."

"As you command," he corrected.

"Leave me," she ordered.

Craven obeyed, turning about and stomping out of the chamber. He reached the stairs leading down to the portal back to the Locus Legis, taking them three at a time. And while he felt hurt by her words, the fact that she had not sensed his inner turmoil relieved him. She cared for Gideon, and felt as trapped as the Painter was. But upon sitting on her throne, she had become Queen Eldora.

And the queen could be, he knew all too well, utterly merciless.

So it was that Craven made his way to execute her command, relieved also that he was only to assemble others to complete her task. For it would be their failure, not his, if they did not succeed.

Eldora's words echoed in his mind.

You were created to be your role.

And, being thus created, was it *his* failing that he was not invincible? Or was it the failing of his creator?

The thought made him even more uneasy, and he shoved it aside. Still, he could not shake the feeling that, like Eldora, his person and his role were no longer the same.

I am the right hand of the queen.

Or perhaps not.

Either way, Craven knew that, to remain in his role as the very personification of the law, he would have to hide his innermost thoughts from the queen. And that what he *really* was would have to suffice.

Chapter 22

There had been a few times in Bella's life when she'd suddenly been possessed by the mad notion that the universe was not in fact a jumbling whirl of chaos and happenstance, but rather a creature of divine intelligence and a fair amount of wit. And that, even as it inched her life ever-closer to its inevitable conclusion, it was desperately trying to teach her something before it did.

This was one of those times.

For as she stepped through the magical doorway Percy had created, she found herself in a place entirely familiar: at the shore of a great lake, in the center of which stood a huge, dark mountain. And in the sky far above that mountain's peak, its upside-down reflection in a giant mirror.

Mount Inversus, reflected by Chiral, the great mirror in the sky.

Bella strode slowly to the edge of the lake, staring up at the mountain's peak. She could barely make out the ruins of Castle Under there. And far above, she saw the inverted castle.

It was then that she realized that Miss Savage's song, while it had destroyed Castle Under, had not destroyed Castle Over.

She felt someone step up beside her, and turned to see Simon standing there. He stared up at the mountain, his jawline rippling.

"Ah," a voice stated from behind. Bella turned, seeing Percy stepping through the doorway – following Myko and Goo as promised. The man smiled at Bella and Simon. "Home sweet home! One of them, anyway. Or perhaps two."

"This was your home?" Bella asked, turning back to the mountaintop.

"Oh yes," Percy confirmed. "Simon tells me the Collector claimed squatting rights for a bit." He shook his head. "Terrible tenant. Left the place in shambles."

Bella and Simon turned to stare at the man.

"Well then," he declared. "Care for a hike?"

"Goo can take us," Bella offered.

"Then by all means Goo," Percy replied. "Give us a lift!"

Goo did just that, wrapping himself around all of them until they were all waist-deep within him. Bella felt that wonderful sensation of calm come over her, and relaxed into his flesh with a smile. Goo sprouted thick, leg-like appendages, then waddled into the lake, and was large enough to be able to extend his "legs" to the bottom of the surprisingly shallow body of water. It wasn't long before they reached the other side, and Goo made significantly quicker progress crawling up the steep mountain. In this way, they made it all the way to the very top.

And as Goo let them go, they all gazed at the ruins of Castle Under.

The castle had been torn apart by Miss Savage's song, reduced to dark rubble. Bella stared at it – and then back the way they'd come, at the steep mountainside going all the way down to the lake far below. A vision of Lake Fenestra came to her then…and as she turned back around to look at the black stone ruins of Castle Under, a vision of the white stone rubble of Castle Havenwood.

She swallowed past a lump in her throat, glancing at Simon.

"This was your Havenwood," she realized, a chill running through her.

Simon stood there for a long while, not answering. Then he shook his head.

"No," he answered at last. "Percy is my Havenwood."

Percy smiled, patting Simon on the shoulder. Then he sighed, shaking his head at the rubble.

"Hard to find good tenants," he mused. "Never clean up their damn messes."

"So…this is *your* castle?" Bella asked.

"Yes," Percy confirmed. "Haven't been here in a long, long while though. I suspect she missed me, and that's why she allowed herself to fall to pieces."

Bella blinked, turning a questioning glance at Simon. Percy was most definitely the strangest person she'd ever met. But Simon said nothing. They both watched as Percy strolled up to the nearest bit of rubble, stroking his beard.

"The question of course is where her ears are," he mumbled, sweeping his gaze over the wreckage. "Hmm." He glanced back, eyeing Goo. "Care to take me on a tour of the rubble?" he inquired.

Goo, being quite an agreeable sort, did just that, picking Percy up and crawling over the fallen castle.

"Stay there," Percy shouted at them. "I'll be back."

They soon vanished from sight, leaving Myko and Simon and Bella behind.

"What's he up to?" Bella asked Simon.

Simon shrugged.

"Is he…crazy?" she pressed. That got a smile out of Simon.

"In the best way," he answered.

Bella paused.

"You trust him?" she pressed. Simon nodded.

"I do."

"Then I will too," she decided. She put a hand on Simon's shoulder, and he stiffened a bit at her touch. But then he relaxed, giving her a look she couldn't read. At length, Goo came into view, carrying Percy back to them. Goo deposited Percy before them, and the man patted the blob's blubbery surface.

"Thank you Goo," he stated. "Now, let's all back up a bit."

They did so, and Percy turned to face the castle.

"Come on then," he called out. "Pull yourself together darling. Daddy's home."

And before Bella's eyes, something truly extraordinary happened.

The rubble that had been Castle Under began to move.

The very top of its highest tower appeared deep in the rubble, rising upward and shoving the hunks of stone around it aside. It continued to rise, the stone tower re-forming itself as they watched. And as it did, the rest of the castle followed suit, blocks stacking atop each other to form walls and floors, and more towers rising with the first. In very little time at all, Castle Under stood whole before them once again, as intact as if it'd never been felled.

Bella and Simon stared at it wide-eyed, their mouths hanging open.

"There we are," Percy proclaimed, beaming at the castle. "Good as new!"

Bella turned to gawk at him.

"How?" was all she could blurt out. Percy raised an eyebrow.

"How what?"

"How did you do…that?" she clarified.

"I told Under to pull herself together," Percy answered. "And I apologized for not visiting in so long. She did all the rest."

"The castle is…*alive*?"

"Oh yes," Percy confirmed. "Just like your lupine friend here," he added, gesturing at Myko. "She's a work of art."

"But she's a building," Bella protested. "She's made of stone."

"So are statues," Percy pointed out with a wink.

"But…"

"Architecture is an art form, is it not?" he inquired. "I daresay I felt the Flow nearly as powerfully building Under and Over as I did with any other artwork I've created."

Bella just stared at him, at a loss for words.

"Now, statues have to move to put their pieces back together, but since buildings don't have limbs, I painted Under's tippity-top tower to be her head, the seat of her consciousness…and gave it the ability to pull the rest of her parts back together if needed."

Bella's eyebrows went up.

"Wow," she murmured.

"Saves on maintenance," Percy explained with a wink. "Now, Castle Over is her brother," he continued, pointing up at the upside-down castle. "I made him too."

"I thought it was a reflection," Simon piped in.

"Goodness no," Percy countered. "Animate things don't have copies made in the Plane of Reflection. Otherwise there'd be two of me and two of all of you," he added.

"Wait," Bella interjected, fear gripping her. "So if Havenwood in our world was destroyed, does that mean…?"

"It means that if the destroyed castle is seen in any reflection within the Plane of Reflection, that part of the castle in the Plane of Reflection will become destroyed to mirror its original counterpart," Percy replied.

Bella's eyebrows furrowed as she tried to process this.

"In any case, here we are," Percy declared. "A home for your artists, and temporarily for you, safe from the Pentad."

"Thank you," Bella replied. "We're in your debt."

Percy gave her a sour look.

"Now what did I tell you about debts?" he chided. "I give for the pleasure of giving, and expect nothing in return," he declared. "And usually my expectations are met."

"Oh," Bella mumbled. "Right."

"You have nothing to offer me besides your presence or absence," Percy told her. "And in your particular case, I prefer the former."

He bowed then, and promptly thrust his hand out as if grabbing something, twisting his wrist. A magical door appeared before him, and he opened it up.

"Until next time," he declared…and stepped through the doorway, closing the door behind him. The door vanished, leaving Bella, Simon, Myko, and Goo alone before Castle Under.

Bella and Simon glanced at each other, then at the castle.

"Well then," Bella stated. "I guess this is home."

* * *

Castle Under was truly massive, a formidable fortress indeed. It had more than enough space for the artists of Havenwood, and Bella and Simon set about to prove it. They went into the grand foyer of the establishment, then instructed Goo to deposit the rolled-up canvas onto the floor. Bella and Simon carefully unrolled it, then got to work drawing everyone out.

Which started terribly slowly.

For each artist they withdrew was absolutely befuddled to find themselves in an entirely different castle, and had to be told the awful news of Havenwood's fall. After each of these first artists calmed down, the process went quicker and quicker. For each Painter they withdrew was capable of withdrawing more artists themselves, and so on, exponentially. And instead of Bella and Simon having to tell the tale, other artists did so for them.

The artists in the painting closer to the center of the massive mural were tougher to retrieve, of course. Simon came up with the brilliant idea to roll the painting up partially, so that they could lean over the rolled-up part to reach in and grab folks. It proved quite effective, and they managed to draw every last citizen of Havenwood out of the painting.

And the last to be thusly removed was Grandpa.

"Grandpa!" Bella cried as he stumbled out. He startled, then broke out into a warm smile, and they embraced. She hugged him tight, holding on to him for a long, long while. Then she pulled away, her eyes growing moist.

"What's wrong?" Grandpa asked. "Where are we?"

"Castle Under," Bella answered. "We…the Pentad…"

Bella found herself unable to speak, though she'd told the story many times before. She lowered her gaze, tears streaming down her cheeks. A sudden, terrible shame came over her, and she felt Grandpa's hand under her chin, lifting her gaze gently to meet his.

"Havenwood has fallen," he guessed. She nodded silently.

Grandpa considered this.

"Well, it's just a place," he decided. "That dingy old apartment was too, and yet it was home." He smiled, patting her cheek. "Home is wherever *you* are, Bella."

"Oh Grandpa," Bella murmured, burying her face in his chest. She sobbed, clutching on to him, and felt him embrace her again.

"There there," he murmured. "It'll be alright sweetheart."

"No," Bella retorted, pulling away and shaking her head miserably. "They killed Mom, Grandpa. They took Gideon."

"Well, for the first, it's only temporary, and the second, we'll just have to take him back," Grandpa declared.

"No, you don't understand," Bella pressed, her vision blurring with fresh tears. "It's all my fault, Grandpa."

He blinked, looking genuinely surprised.

"All your fault?" he asked.

"Gideon and Mom, they…told me not to go down to them when they were fighting," she confessed, staring at her feet. "They said if they had to protect me, I'd just get in their way." She grit her teeth. "I promised Mom, but I didn't listen. I went down to Gideon, and distracted him. And then Craven…"

She shook her head a vision of Craven kicking Gideon's knee coming to her. Of her father's leg bending backward with that horrible crunching sound. Of Craven crushing Gideon's wrist.

All because of her.

She felt Grandpa hold her by the shoulders, and she stood there, refusing to meet his gaze. Tears dripped from her nose and chin, falling to the floor.

"Bella…" he began.

"Craven killed the White Dragon," she continued, her voice cracking. "He destroyed Havenwood. And it's all my fault."

Grandpa sighed, pulling Bella into him and wrapping his arms around her. A great sob burst out of her, and she buried her face in his chest again, her shoulders heaving. Wave after wave of sobs came over her, and try as she might, she couldn't stop them.

She cried and cried, until there were no tears left.

And through it all, Grandpa held her gently but firmly. Never speaking, never pulling away. He rocked her side-to-side ever-so-slightly, just embracing her.

Just *being* there.

At long last, Bella pulled away, taking a deep, shuddering breath in, then letting it out. She lifted her gaze to his, almost defiantly, half-expecting him to yell at her. Or reject her. To be disappointed.

But all she saw was him smiling sadly, his eyes as warm and loving as ever.

"I love you sweetheart," he declared, grabbing her hand and bringing it up to his lips to kiss the back of it. "More than anything in this world."

Bella swallowed past a lump in her throat.

"Even Mom?" she asked. Grandpa grimaced.

"Well, she's not alive right now," he pointed out. "And besides, she's…difficult."

"She didn't get everything you made destroyed," Bella countered.

"Havenwood may be gone from here," Grandpa countered, gesturing at the world in general, "…but it's still in here," he added, putting a hand to his heart. "Where it came from."

"I'm sorry Grandpa."

"And I wish you weren't," Grandpa replied. But he did so with a smile. "Your guilt comes from the best part of you, Bella. But far better to use the good in you to *do* good rather than to harm yourself."

She frowned at him.

"You're speaking in riddles again," she accused. He shrugged innocently.

"I'm a Writer," he replied. "It's what we do."

"That's your excuse for everything you do," she pointed out. Grandpa winked at her.

"Would you have it any other way?"

"Mmm…no," she replied. "Love you Grandpa," she added, leaning in to give him a hug.

“Love you too, sweetheart,” he replied. Then he pushed her away gently. “Now, how long has it been since Gideon was taken?” he asked. Bella grimaced.

“A day.”

“Well then, let’s get to it,” Grandpa replied zestily, clapping his hands and rubbing them together. “Gideon saved us once. It’s about time we repaid the favor!”

Chapter 23

The artists formerly of Havenwood congregated in the grand foyer of Castle Under for a meeting, with the sole purpose of discussing how to save Gideon from the clutches of the Pentad. Bella and Grandpa stood on a grand staircase while the other artists stood before them, and Grandpa submitted his request for their help. But to Bella's dismay, the purpose of the meeting soon shifted to self-preservation. For the vast majority of the artists wanted nothing to do with acting against the Pentad.

"The damn White Dragon couldn't save Havenwood, and neither could Gideon," one of the older Painters complained. "Now you want us to help you infiltrate the damn capitol of the Pentad? The most well-defended city in the kingdom?" He crossed his arms over his chest, glaring at Grandpa and Bella. "You're insane!"

"No offense," Griggins, the eldest of them – other than Grandpa of course – piped in. "But he's right. Gideon was most likely taken to the capitol, and is being held in Tartarus. We don't stand a chance against the Pentad, Thaddeus."

"I agree that we can't expect to win a war with the Pentad," Grandpa replied evenly. "But that's not what I'm proposing. I'm merely suggesting that we work together to find a way to infiltrate wherever Gideon is being held and save him."

"Again, that's most likely Tartarus," Griggins argued. "And you know damn well that Tartarus was specifically designed to prevent infiltration. It's the most well-guarded prison in the Pentad…perhaps even the world."

"That may be so," Thaddeus conceded. "But nothing is impossible. It'll just take a bit of creativity. And if we work together…"

"I'm out," a short, rotund woman with an owl on her shoulder stated. It was Ula, another Painter. "I'm done being hunted down like a dog. I say we stay here where it's safe."

"It might *not* be safe here," a tall, lanky man piped in. It was Connor, one of the younger artists. He gave Bella an apologetic look. "The Pentad might know of this place now, especially after the Collector was beaten."

"The Pentad will assume Castle Under was destroyed," Griggins pointed out.

"And they might come to take back all the paintings and books they think the Collector stole from Blackthorne," another artist said.

"True," Griggins conceded, looking troubled. "I hadn't thought of that."

"So none of us are safe here," Ula concluded. "I say we make a run for Epirus. They'd be more than happy to stick it to the Pentad."

"This meeting is about Gideon," Grandpa reminded them. "We…"

"We have to make sure *we're* safe," Griggins interrupted. "We all love Gideon, but helping him is a suicide mission and you know it, Thaddeus. I'm out…and I suggest a show of hands to see who else agrees with me."

Hands went up…and for each one that did, two more followed, until almost everyone in the foyer was raising their hand. Only Kanja, Bella, and Grandpa remained with their hands at their sides.

"Well then, that settles it," Griggins declared. "Sorry Thaddeus, Bella…but we have to focus on doing the most good for the most people. I suggest we redirect the focus of this meeting to planning *our* futures."

"You already have," Grandpa replied coolly.

"Thaddeus…" Griggins began.

"I've heard quite enough," Grandpa snapped. "Twice Havenwood was attacked, and most of you did nothing but try to save yourselves. If it weren't for Gideon and Bella and myself, you'd all be dead."

"If it weren't for Gideon and Bella and yourself, the Pentad never would have attacked us," Griggins retorted.

Grandpa's expression hardened, and he squared his shoulders, glaring down at them all.

"Run then," he declared. "You might just escape with your lives. But know that wherever you go, fear and shame will be one step behind you. Always."

"Thaddeus…"

"I have no desire to associate with cowards any longer," Grandpa interjected. "You're nothing but adult children, depending on the kindness of others to save you from your own inaction. From this moment forward, I will no longer do anything for those who can't be bothered to return the favor."

He turned away from them, walking up the stairs and pulling Bella with him. Kanja pushed through the crowd, following them up the staircase.

"This is goodbye," Thaddeus declared.

So, on their own, with time for Gideon running out, Grandpa, Bella, and Kanja got to work.

***

Grandpa was a man of many sayings, a master with words both written and spoken. And of all his sayings, perhaps his favorite was his oft-repeated advice to Bella when they'd lived together in their old apartment: if you want to *be* something, you have to *do* it. She'd found the advice easy in theory and terribly difficult in practice; a fact that explained why most people's ambitions never made the long, dangerous journey from dream to reality. But if she wanted to *be* a powerful Painter of the military arts, she would have to *do* it.

And so she set about to paint.

Gideon had of course taught her to always keep painting supplies on her. She'd painted paints and brushes and canvases on the very canvases she kept rolled up in her uniform's thigh-holsters. After finding a room within the newly refurbished Castle Under to call her studio, she retrieved her supplies, drawing them from their canvas. However she soon realized she didn't have an easel.

But for a Painter, anything one required was but a stroke away.

Bella propped a fresh canvas on a chair, then got to work painting an easel. At first she had every intention of painting a standard wooden one, but the Flow struck her almost immediately, and she found herself pulled in an entirely different direction. At first she resisted this – she had things to do, after all – but at length she recognized the wisdom of relaxing into the Flow and seeing where it took her.

That was the essence of magic, after all.

She painted a skeleton's hand…and then another, and another. Dozens of levitating hands, all of which came together to form a suit of bony armor on a mannequin…one that represented Bella, of course. Some of the hands formed a helm with bony palms cupping her temples. Other formed a bony breastplate, and bracers, and leg armor, and so on. The hands of her long-dead ancestors, brought to un-life by powerful magic…and devoted to protecting Bella in any way they could.

But that couldn't be all.

Gideon had taught her the importance of painting something that could solve *many* problems, not just one or two. So, as Bella stared at her painting, she tried to do just that.

There was a knock at the door.

Bella blinked, torn from the Flow. She felt an immediate flash of irritation.

"What?" she snapped.

The door opened, and Grandpa poked his head through.

"Ah, sorry," he stated. "Didn't mean to interrupt your Flow."

Bella relaxed, giving an apologetic smile.

"Sorry," she replied. "Didn't mean to snap." Grandpa came in, eyeing the painting, then Bella.

"I understand completely," he reassured. "There is no greater enemy to the creator than interruptions. And after that meeting, both of our tempers are a bit short."

Bella had to smile at that. It was most certainly true…like most things Grandpa said.

"I wanted to see how you were doing," Grandpa told her. "I know you've been through quite a lot."

"Yeah," she admitted. She turned back to the painting. "But if I focus on the past, I'll neglect the present…and the future."

"Hmm," Grandpa murmured, stepping up to her side. "That's something I would say." He eyed the painting. "What's this?" he inquired.

"I was going to paint an easel, and this came out instead," Bella answered.

"Hmm," Grandpa murmured, rubbing his beard. "You've come so far since that terrible orchid you painted back in the apartment. Do you remember it?"

Bella made a face.

"It *was* terrible," he stated. "But this…"

Bella studied the painting. Her use of color was – unlike the first painting she'd painted, of the orchid on her windowsill – exactly as she'd intended. The lighting, the shadows. The way she made the various parts of the painting draw the eye, first to this, then to that. Telling a story just the way she'd wanted to tell it.

She'd come a long, long way since that first painting. In tiny steps, so that she hadn't even realized how much she'd grown.

"Imagine what I'll be able to do a few years from now," she said. Grandpa smiled, putting an arm around her shoulders.

"I can't wait to see it," he replied.

Bella studied her painting, tapping her chin with the handle of her paintbrush.

"It's missing something," she told Grandpa. "I want it to do more."

"Like what?"

"Well, I told Dad a while ago that I wanted to make my own Conclave," she answered. "But I never got around to doing it. I can't help thinking that it's in here somewhere," she added, gesturing at the canvas.

"Maybe so," Grandpa replied. "A Conclave is a home, and home is wherever your heart says it is."

They both went silent, staring at the painting.

"Well, I'll leave you to it," Grandpa decided, giving her a peck on the cheek. "The other artists think they'll be safe hiding away forever, like they assumed they could do in Havenwood."

"No place is safe," Bella replied. That much she'd learned.

"I agree," Grandpa concurred. "And so they write their futures. It's nearly impossible to save people who won't lift a finger to save themselves."

And with that, he left Bella's makeshift studio, and she returned her focus to her painting, getting back to work.

Home is where the heart is.

She frowned, putting a hand to the amulet hanging just above her own heart.

Home is where my *heart is*, she thought.

So her Conclave had to be wherever her heart was. But her heart was inside her, so that didn't make any sense.

Unless…

She dabbed her paintbrush in black paint, then continued painting.

The dark and the light were each parts of her. Her Mom and her Dad, good and…not as good. Life and death.

Death…the Plane of Death.

She closed her eyes, a vision of the huge column in the center of the Root of the World, a column of carved corpses rising up to support the living. Bella imagined the hands of her ancestors rising from the earth, a hundred skeletal hands coming to un-life to protect her. And for each of her ancestors' bony white hands, there was the shadow it cast. And perhaps if these hands came together to form a doorway…

She felt a burst of excitement, and felt the Flow run through her, guiding her hand.

Bella painted the hands coming together on another part of the canvas, quite literally joining hands to form the perimeter of a large oval. One that bordered an inky black circular portal into a world of its own, much like Gideon's disc served as a portal to his Conclave.

She paused then, tapping her chin again with the handle of her brush. Her first impulse was to paint a house like Gideon's Conclave, but it didn't feel right. She needed something different.

Something *her.*

Bella frowned, then had a flash of inspiration. Grandpa had once told her not to paint things like the orchid on her windowsill…things outside of her. She'd immediately pictured herself painting things *inside* of her instead…her internal organs.

"Hmm," she murmured. "Weird, but we'll try it."

She went with the Flow, continuing to paint. Of course, she couldn't paint her own insides…livers and guts and stuff hardly made for a suitable Conclave. So what would?

Something to do with light and dark…

Bella stared at the perfect ring of hands forming that inky black portal. It looked almost like a pupil, surrounded by a white iris made of interlocking hands. And a pupil was darkness that let in the light. The darkness *seeing* the light.

Inspiration struck again.

Bella made the hands a portal leading through the pupil of a huge eyeball, one filled with air instead of whatever fluids normally existed in eyeballs. The inside of the eyeball formed the main chamber of her Conclave, a ray of light passing through the pupil to shine on the back wall. This, she imagined, was the great eye of her collective ancestors, watching her from beyond the grave. And through it, she could watch the goings-on in the outside world when in her Conclave. And as it always had its eye on her, it could of course guide the many skeletal hands that she'd painted.

"What else?" she asked herself when she'd finished.

She recalled the huge skeleton-chair that had brought her to the Plane of Death back in Petrusa's office over a month ago. The hands of course could form more than just armor and a portal; she painted them flying through the pupil of the giant eye, forming a skeletal chair made of finger bones and wrist bones.

"The easel," she realized.

She finished the painting by making the hands form a bony easel within the eyeball-Conclave, then stepped back from her work, studying it intently. She broke out into a smile.

"Ooo, I *like* you," she declared.

She had the sudden urge to sign the painting, and resisted it, knowing full well that it would behoove her to give herself some time away from it. After all, once she signed it, it would be finished. Sleeping on it would put some distance between herself and her work; the first draft was seldom the best, after all.

But then she thought of Gideon, and realized that she didn't have the luxury to waste any more time.

She heard scratching at the door, and walked up to it, pulling it open. Myko stepped into the makeshift studio, giving Bella a wet wolf-kiss on the nose. She laughed, wrapping her arms around his big neck and giving him a hug.

"Hey Myko," she greeted. "How's Gideon?"

Myko nodded his head once, then *wuffed.*

"Still alive?" she pressed. Myko nodded again. "Good," she stated. "We need to go find him. Can you feel where he is?" Another nod. Bella smiled, feeling relieved. If Myko could sense Dad's location, the Familiar would serve as a sort of compass for them. It would be like the Misty Marsh way back when...Myko, leading them through an unfamiliar place. Pointing the way to freedom.

She let go of Myko, then turned to face her painting. There was no time to get precious about the details...she needed to sign it now. And then she needed to paint more weapons to face off against the Pentad.

Lots more.

Bella stepped up to the canvas, grabbing her brush. She paused then, realizing she hadn't named the many ancestral hands.

"Hmm," she murmured. "What should I call it?"

"Are you asking me?" Cain inquired from his usual location at her hip. Bella flinched.

"Geez Cain, you scared me!" she blurted out.

"Ha, ha!" he chuckled. "Terribly sorry," he added, for politeness's sake.

"Sure," she told him. "What should I call it?"

"Well, I've noticed that your father loves using Latin for his paintings," Cain stated. "And I happen to know a fair bit of the language myself."

"Okay…"

"Hand is minibus, I believe," Cain stated. Bella made a face.

"Ew."

"How about Manus?" he proposed.

"Huh," Bella replied, eyeing her painting. "Manus. That's pretty good actually."

"I heartily agree," Cain replied.

"Manus it is then," she decided. "Alright, here goes."

And then she signed her name in white paint on the bottom-right corner of the painting.

A slight breeze ruffled her hair from behind as the painting came alive…and she felt a sudden chill as it did so. For she had just painted her Conclave, something that every notable Painter had.

She suddenly wished Mom and Dad were here to see it. To witness their daughter becoming more and more of a Painter. Gideon would have been so proud…and Mom…

Bella took a deep breath in, reaching up to touch the heart-shaped amulet at her chest. She felt as if her own heart were being squeezed, and blinked back sudden tears.

"Are you alright?" Cain asked.

"No," Bella answered.

But there was no time to indulge her emotions, she knew. Things couldn't be right until she had Mom and Dad back. And to save them, she needed to focus.

So she reached into the canvas, getting to work drawing the many hands of Manus out of it.

* * *

Castle Under was massive – even larger than Castle Havenwood – and built like a fortress, with enough dormitories in the eastern wing to house all of Havenwood's artists and more. Grandpa had scored one of the larger suites on the upper floors, and seeing as he was both the oldest and the most respected artist in the group, no one begrudged him this luxury. His suite had three bedrooms, an office, a bathroom, and walk-in closet, and when Bella stepped into the suite, she found Grandpa sitting at his desk in the office. Which was hardly surprising.

"Hey Grandpa," she greeted. He looked up from the notebook he was busy writing in, his eyes lighting up.

"Ah, hello sweetheart," he replied. "Just doing my part," he said, gesturing at his notebook. Bella didn't bother to ask what he was writing. Grandpa never told anyone about his work, firmly believing that he could only tell his stories one way…and that if he did it with his mouth, he'd lose the will to do it with his pen. "How's the painting?"

Instead of answering, she turned, gesturing for Manus to enter the room. Dozens upon dozens of skeletal hands flew through the doorway, stopping to levitate all around her.

"Grandpa, meet Manus," she introduced. "Manus, this is Grandpa."

The hands waved at him, and one even flew over to shake his hand.

"Ah, hello," Grandpa replied, shaking it back with a smile. "Always nice to meet a helping hand."

Bella lifted her hand, then closed it into a fist.

The hands flew right at her, attaching to her head and body. Within seconds, she was wearing them…as a suit of bony armor.

"Oh my," Grandpa murmured.

"Badass, huh?" Bella asked. Grandpa smiled.

"Quite."

"Attack me," she requested. Grandpa frowned.

"Pardon?"

"Try to hit me over the head," she clarified, making a bopping motion with one hand. Grandpa hesitated, then stood up from his seat, half-heartedly swinging his fist overhead to bop her. One of the hands making up her helmet shot upward, grabbing Grandpa's wrist and stopping him in mid-strike.

"Oh!" he exclaimed. The hand released him, re-forming Bella's helmet. "I can see where that would come in handy."

"Come *on* Grandpa," Bella complained.

"I'm a Writer," he reminded her. "I play with words with plays on words."

Bella rolled her eyes.

"I'll try to get a grip before you give me a knuckle sandwich," he promised. Bella put her hands on her hips, giving him a look.

"Really?" she complained. Grandpa chuckled. "*Any*way," she continued, "…we really should get going soon. Myko says Dad is okay, but we can't afford to waste any more time."

"I agree," he replied. "I wish I could go with you, but a Writer isn't much use in battle, I'm afraid."

"I know," she said. "It's okay. I have Simon."

"And you have me," a voice called out from the doorway. They both turned, spotting Kanja stepping into the suite. She smiled at them. "I have a few ideas that might help."

"Thanks," Bella replied.

"It's my pleasure," the woman stated. Then she gave an apologetic look. "I tried to convince the other artists to change their minds, but they won't."

"It's okay," Bella replied. "We'll do what we can with who – and what – we have."

"People are marvelous creatures," Grandpa mused. "But only one-on-one. The minute they form a group, they lose themselves to it. And in doing so, they're transformed into something terribly disappointing."

"Not always," Bella pointed out.

"True," he conceded. "A few can yet resist the pull of the mob."

"That's what art is for," Bella recited. "To find the self we've lost trying to fit in with others."

"Ha!" Grandpa exclaimed, his eyes brightening. "You do listen to me."

"I remember everything you say," she reminded him.

"Don't I know it," he agreed.

"What are *you* up to?" she asked him, glancing at his desk.

"Thinking of the future," he answered. "Unfortunately there isn't much a Writer can do in the moment," he admitted. "Actors and Musicians can make art instantly, Sculptors and Painters in as little as an hour. But my art takes a longer course."

Bella nodded.

"Now go on, save your world," Grandpa told her.

"My world?"

"The people you love *are* your world," he reminded her with a twinkle in his eye. Bella smiled, knowing Grandpa was right as usual. There was no place in the world that would be home without him…or Gideon. Or Mom. "Now go on," he urged.

"Yes Grandpa," Bella replied. Grandpa stood up, and they embraced. Bella rested the side of her head against his chest, hearing the *lub-dub* of his heart beating against her ear.

"I love you sweetheart," he murmured.

"Love you Grandpa."

She pulled away, then took a deep breath in, turning to Kanja.

"Can you sculpt on the road?" Bella asked.

"I can," Kanja answered. "As long as I can use one of your canvases to store my supplies."

"Of course," Bella agreed.

"Well then," Kanja stated. "Let's go save your father."

Chapter 24

It was common knowledge that the shortest distance between two points was a straight line. But the magic of the Underground made it quite possible to use the *uncommon* knowledge of its existence to one's advantage. So Bella, Simon, and Kanja made their way out of Castle Under, down Mount Inversus, and across the lake back to the door to the Underground. Myko and Goo and Cain came with them, of course. But the rest of the artists remained behind, seduced by the seeming safety and ease of doing nothing.

So it was that Bella found herself clad in her Manus bone-armor, walking through the Underground's purple-hued tunnels with Myko and Goo in tow. Myko paused before each of the magical doors, sensing which one would take them closest to Gideon. And after nearly two hours of studying door after door, they finally found one.

Myko stopped before it, pawing at the door, then glancing at Bella with his soulful silver eyes.

"This must be it," Bella announced, glancing at Simon. "We should prepare before we go through it."

"Agreed," Kanja replied. "We don't really know where Gideon is, so we have no idea where this door will take us. Wherever it is, the Pentad's defenses are sure to be formidable."

"I have an idea," Simon offered.

Everyone turned to him.

"Have either of you heard of Anywhere?" he asked. Both Kanja and Bella shook their heads. "It's a…special place. He explained it to them quickly, that it was a place created by all of the magical paintings in the world…and that they could travel within it. And furthermore, that while they *were* in Anywhere, time didn't pass in the real world.

"Interesting," Kanja murmured. "So we can locate Gideon's paintings in Anywhere, and see where they are in the real world?"

"And look out of the frames of the paintings near wherever he is to determine what the Pentad's defenses are," Simon explained. Bella frowned.

"I still don't get it," she admitted. "How exactly does Anywhere work?"

"It's better experienced than explained," Simon reassured.

"Let's try it," Kanja decided.

"Agreed," Bella concurred.

They all followed Simon through the tunnels of the Underground, walking for what seemed like miles. Through fork after fork in the tunnels he led them, with quiet confidence. Bella found herself having to trust that Simon knew what he was doing. It helped that she knew that Myko could lead them back to Gideon's door if needed.

Eventually they turned left down another fork in the tunnels, then came to a dead-end…and a door quite unlike the others. For it was larger, with an ornate stone doorframe surrounding it. And, also unlike the other doors, it had a golden keyhole just above the knob.

Bella spotted a rust-colored bloodstain on the ground near the door, and beside it, something else.

Two bodies, both decomposed. One in a drab gray military uniform, and the other…

She froze, glancing at Simon. He stared at this second body, swallowing visibly.

"He wanted to die here," he explained.

Bella nodded, trying not to stare at the corpse. It was mostly decomposed, clad in a dirty white suit. She didn't have to ask who it was, of course. A sword lay atop its chest, one with a glowing silver blade. Looking at it made the hairs on the nape of her neck stand on-end. For it was the same blade that had killed her mother, in Blackthorne so long ago.

She lifted her gaze to Simon.

"You okay?" she asked. Simon hesitated, his face even paler than usual.

"No," he answered.

Everyone went silent for a while, as a sign of respect. For while the Collector had been Bella's enemy, he'd also been a human being. And Simon had cared for him.

At length Simon lifted his gaze, turning to Bella.

"We used Anywhere to plan our attack on Havenwood," he admitted apologetically. "I didn't want to, but…"

Bella put a hand on his shoulder.

"I know," she reassured him. "Miss Savage used you."

"Only because I wasn't strong enough to be myself," Simon replied. But the way he said it was matter-of-fact, not to beat himself up. "I am now," he continued. "I never need to be anything but me, ever again."

He took a deep breath in, then faced the door, reciting the following verses:

"Painted places stuck in time,
One world they share,
For a single person's frame of mind
A place called Anywhere."

There was a *click*.

Simon twisted the knob, pulling the door open. He was about to step through when he hesitated, glancing back at the sword on the Collector's corpse. He knelt down, picking it up and gazing at it, its glow illuminating his pale features.

"It can cut through anything," he explained, giving Bella an apologetic look. "We may need it."

Bella nodded her consent.

"Can I store it in Goo?" he asked. She nodded again. It made sense, after all. The sword's blade wouldn't harm Goo, and he could merely keep it in his flesh until it was needed. She retrieved a rolled-up painting from her thigh-holster.

"Apertus," she incanted. The painting unrolled itself, and she reached into it, drawing Goo out a bit. Simon plunged the sword into Goo, and Bella returned the blob to the canvas, rolling it up with a word and putting it back in her thigh-holster.

Simon stepped through the doorway then, vanishing into its purple light. Bella glanced at Kanja, who gestured for Bella to go through. So Bella took a deep breath in, and did just that.

And found herself in a strange place indeed.

For she had stepped onto a sandy beach, the ocean a few yards away. But it was no ordinary beach; the sand looked for all the world like it had been painted, the ocean made of rough brushstrokes. And the waves did not move at all. Rather, they were stuck in time.

And that wasn't all.

For ahead – past the ocean – the scenery abruptly changed, to a colorful, grassy meadow. And to the left, a dark forest…and to the right, a snowy field.

And behind her…

She gasped.

For there, suspended in the air behind her, beyond the purple doorway back to the Underground, was a huge wooden frame, like a window. But it framed utter blackness.

Kanja and Myko stepped through the doorway, followed by Goo.

"What an unusual place," Cain proclaimed.

"Wow," Kanja murmured, looking around. Then she spotted the framed blackness behind them. "So this is a painting we're in?" she asked Simon.

"Yes," he confirmed.

"And that's the painting's frame," Kanja reasoned. "I thought it was supposed to look out into the real world."

"It does," Simon replied. "It's a painting in Havenwood. I think it's buried under debris. Rolled-up paintings do this too," he added. But with those, there's no frame around the window looking out."

"Oh," Kanja murmured.

"And these places," Bella piped in, gesturing at the forest, the meadow, and the snowy field around them. "They're other paintings?"

"Right," Simon confirmed. "The paintings closest to this one in the real world."

"So what if a painting in the real world is moved?" Bella pressed.

"Then its relationship to the paintings around it changes here," Simon answered.

"Huh."

"That's fascinating," Kanja stated. "Who made this place?"

"Percy," Simon revealed.

"So how are we going to find Gideon's paintings?" Bella inquired.

"Would you recognize them if you saw them?" Simon asked. She nodded. "Then we find them by looking," he explained.

"That's it?" she pressed. "We just pick a direction and go?"

He nodded.

"That could take forever!" she complained. He smiled.

"In Anywhere," he replied, "…we have all the time we need."

* * *

As it turned out, they needed less time than they'd expected.

For Myko, through his powerful bond with Gideon, was able to sense the Painter…even in another Plane of existence, which was something Bella had found quite difficult with Nemesis. Whether it was because their bond was stronger, Bella didn't know. But Myko made it quite clear they should follow him, and follow him they did.

In this way, they traversed the many painted places in the world those paintings shared, in that magical world called Anywhere.

They ended their journey in a painting instantly familiar. In fact, it was one of the first paintings Bella had seen of Gideon's.

It was of a moonlit hilltop, various objects littering the ground. A sword and two spears, as well as a few paintbrushes of various sizes, a palette, an easel, and jars of paint set out in neat rows. And a bronze fire pit sat to the right, a fire in mid-crackle within. Dark clouds hung in the sky to one side of a gigantic silver moon.

It was, Bella realized, the painting Gideon had kept Myko in.

In the middle of this scene, suspended in mid-air like the other paintings, was a rectangular portal to the outside world. But it was utterly black, and had no frame.

"It's rolled up," Bella realized, remembering what Simon had said. She turned to him. "How are we going to find out where he is?"

"By going to nearby paintings," Simon answered, gesturing at the various scenes in the distance all around them.

"Let's split up and go in different directions," Kanja proposed. "Then we'll come back here and debrief."

They all agreed, and split up to different scenes. Bella crossed over into a painting of a riverside in autumn, half-expecting the dense bed of brown leaves to crunch beneath her feet as she walked. But of course they didn't; she could affect nothing within the painting, and nothing could affect her. Finding the unframed portal within, she saw more blackness. Another rolled-up painting.

She looked around, spotting a forest in the distance. One with a small silver bell in the center. She walked to it, crossing into the painting. It was quite odd, for ripples extended outward from the bell, distorting everything around it…including a few nearby green goblin-like creatures, who clutched at bleeding ears, their faces screwed into grimaces.

Bella's eyes widened.

I remember that bell!

It was the same bell Gideon had painted for their battle with Miss Savage, the one he'd used against her.

Bella spotted the painting's frame ahead, and ran up to it. Instead of being utterly black, it looked out over something rather spectacular.

There was a man in the foreground, one standing on a wide golden-bricked street and wearing black and gold armor. Clearly a soldier, but of high rank. He was pointing to the left…and in the foreground were two huge-appearing fingers. It appeared that they belonged to somebody carrying the painting from behind…and that the soldier was directing whoever was holding the painting on where to bring it.

A moment frozen in time.

Bella marveled at the extraordinary appearance of it all. She could see everything in perfect, crisp detail. Which – after hours of being in painted landscapes – was rather startling to behold.

And what was beyond the soldier was even more startling: a breathtaking view of an enormous city.

The wide golden street the soldier was standing on extended all the way back to the horizon, flanked by tall, elegant skyscrapers that looked rather like lipstick containers, their roofs angled like lipstick-tops jutting out. They were metallic, and silver, gold, red, and white in color. Smaller buildings were scattered amongst them in city blocks organized in concentric rings outward from the foreground. And in the distance, a wide green lawn extending as far as the eye could see, with a bright blue sky above the horizon. A single bird-like creature flew high above, a dark silhouette near the sun.

"Guys!" Bella shouted, staring at the painting. "Guys, I found it!"

It wasn't long before Simon, Kanja, Goo, and Myko had reached her side. Kanja's eyes widened when she saw the scene.

"That's Centrum," she revealed. "I've seen it described in drawings and paintings. Gideon must be in the capitol!"

"I assume that's bad?" Bella asked. Kanja nodded grimly.

"It's the most well-defended city in the kingdom," she confirmed. "And if he's in Centrum, I guarantee you they're keeping him in Tartarus."

"Tartarus? What's that?"

"A prison," Kanja answered. "It's the highest-security prison in the kingdom. If anyone's ever escaped from there, I haven't heard about it."

"Oh," Bella mumbled. "Wonderful."

She felt Simon's hand on her shoulder.

"We have Anywhere," he reassured. "And we have the Gemini."

"Will that be enough?" Bella pressed. Simon patted his chest – or rather, his suit jacket.

"With Redeemer, it will be," he answered.

"Are you sure?"

"We can use Anywhere to study their defenses," Simon pointed out. "We'll take our time. Studying the locations of statues, the content of paintings. Every painting in every Painter's uniform will be available to us. Every weapon, every defense."

"He's right," Kanja realized. "That could give us quite the advantage."

"We'll eat and sleep here, so time doesn't pass in the real world," Simon strategized. "We'll draw a large map of Centrum as seen through Anywhere's frames, with the positions of every guard, every Painter, every statue."

"And if we leave Anywhere, then come back, we can figure out their patrol patterns," Bella realized. She felt a burst of hope, and broke out into a smile. "This might work!"

"It just might," Kanja agreed. "So let's *get* to work."

* * *

What seemed like days later – it was impossible to tell the passage of time in Anywhere – Bella, Simon, and Kanja had completed their task, creating a large map of Centrum. Not only that, but Bella and Simon created a list of weapons and defenses that the Pentad had painted…and could potentially use against them in the upcoming battle. Most, Bella found, were rather uninspired compared to what she was accustomed to. Indeed, compared to Gideon and Simon's works, the paintings of Centrum were rather…mundane.

"That is what happens when the government controls art," Kanja noted darkly as they all congregated around the map, which Simon had set on the ground. "To control art is to kill it."

Simon nodded, staring down at the map intently. He hadn't said much of anything since they'd started their mission, Bella found. He was easily the quietest person she'd ever met. She found herself wondering what he was thinking…but not having the courage to ask.

"Okay," she stated. "So it looks like Centrum is surrounded by this field of grass. We have two choices," she proposed. "We can either go into the city from Anywhere through one of these paintings, or we can come in from the outside."

"They'd have to be paintings brought into the city," Simon pointed out. "Paintings painted *in* the city won't be able to serve as portals into Centrum…at least if it has the same magic protecting it as Havenwood and Blackthorne did."

"Right," Bella agreed. "We can use one of Gideon's paintings then."

Simon nodded.

"Coming from the outside may be safer," Kanja theorized. "But coming out of a painting directly into the heart of the city would offer the element of surprise."

"But if we come from outside, they may see us coming," Bella noted.

"Not if we do a magic trick," Simon spoke up.

They both turned to him.

"I can send my Gemini through different paintings throughout the city," he stated. "They'll occupy the Pentad's attention while we approach from the outside and make our way to Gideon."

"Huh," Bella murmured. Her expression brightened. "That might work!"

"I agree," Kanja said. "It is a good plan. This way, your Gemini will appear near Gideon's things, so they can easily retrieve them."

"Some of the Gemini will stay with us to serve as bodyguards," Simon continued.

"Right, good idea," Bella told him.

"I'll show one of the Gemini this map," he stated. "What one knows, all will know."

"So our army will know the strategic positions of all of the Pentad's defenses, as well as their potential magic," Kanja concluded, gazing at Simon with newfound appreciation. "You are truly brilliant, Simon."

Simon gave a little smile, inclining his head at her.

"Okay," Bella decided. "Looks like we have a plan." She stretched her arms out to the sides, stifling a yawn. "So…how do we get back to the Underground, exactly?"

Simon cleared his throat, reciting the now-familiar verses:

"Painted places stuck in time,

One world they share,
For a single person's frame of mind
A place called Anywhere."

Bella heard a *click*…and then a portion of the painting in front of them swung open like a door, revealing a familiar underground tunnel, cast in a purple glow.

"Wow," Bella murmured. Simon gestured for her to step through, and she did so, emerging into the Underground. Kanja went after, followed by Myko, Goo, and finally Simon, who propped the door to Anywhere open. He reached into his pants pocket, retrieving a mirrored fragment.

"Come to me," he murmured.

Moments later, Bella spotted glittering, purple-hued figures sprinting up the tunnel toward them. It was the Gemini, she realized; they filled the tunnel, the nearest ones skidding to a halt before Simon.

"They already know the plan," he stated, showing the fragment he'd been carrying. "Go in and stand at the ready," he ordered, nodding at the Gemini. "Attack the Pentad on my command."

Most of them streamed through the doorway, while the rest stayed in the tunnel with them.

"Mirror," he commanded.

The closest Gemini transformed, its facets rearranging so that its chest and abdomen formed a rectangular mirror. Simon turned to Bella and the rest.

"Come," he prompted. And with that, he stepped *through* the mirror, vanishing from sight. Bella glanced at Kanja, then followed Simon, putting a hand through the mirror – just to make sure she wouldn't smash her face against its surface – then stepping through. Kanja, Myko, and Goo followed behind them, as did the Gemini. Bella found herself in the Plane of Reflection, in an Underground that was a mirror image of the one they'd come from. She flashed Simon a smile.

"You're really creative," she told him. He smiled back – an expression she wasn't used to seeing on him.

"Thank you."

"Okay," she stated. "So we're in the Plane of Reflection, and we can use the Gemini to go back to the real world any time we want."

"Yes," Simon agreed. "The Pentad may have less security in this plane."

"Very clever," Kanja murmured.

"Goal number one is to not get caught," Bella reasoned. "If any one of us is captured, they'll try to use that to get the rest of us to surrender."

"I agree," Kanja replied. "We must form a pact now…that we will not surrender ourselves to save each other."

Bella hesitated, glancing at Simon, who nodded. She nodded as well, reluctantly.

"We have to assume that Gideon is in that prison," She reasoned. "Which means we'll have to break into it."

"I'm sure the Pentad has anticipated that someone might try to go through the Plane of Reflection to jailbreak a prisoner from Tartarus," Kanja warned.

"Probably," Bella agreed. "Which means we need to bypass their security measures."

"Of which we haven't a clue," Kanja piped in. "Not in Tartarus, anyway." Simon nodded; there hadn't been any paintings in the prison to spy through, after all.

Bella sighed, mulling it over. Then she had an idea.

"The prison will be dark at nighttime, right?" she asked. "Prisoners have to go to sleep. I can have Luna infiltrate the prison to find Gideon."

"Who?" Simon asked.

"My dark half," she answered. She explained Luna and Lux to him, and what she could do with each.

"The Gemini are mirrors," Simon pointed out. "Lux could use them to reflect off of."

"Right," Bella agreed. But how that would be useful, she wasn't quite sure. "Either way, Luna can become one with shadows. So if she goes to the prison at nighttime, then she can become all the darkness in the prison itself…and she'll be able to sense where Gideon is immediately."

"And go right to him," Kanja concluded. "Nice."

"But that doesn't help me get him out," Bella realized with a frown. "It just lets Luna in."

"So we need something Luna can use to free Gideon from his cell, and the prison," Simon reasoned.

"Preferably without getting caught," Kanja agreed. "The problem is, prisons are designed to stop people from warping out through a portal. So we can't get him out that way."

"Maybe if Luna can bring Gideon his stuff?" Bella proposed. "I'm sure Gideon could think of a way out if he had a canvas and a paintbrush."

"The Gemini can retrieve his belongings, or Luna could just give him one of her canvases," Kanja pointed out.

"A larger distraction might help," Simon reasoned. They both turned to face him. "The Gemini can form an unlimited army," he continued. "I can have them go to every major city in the Pentad, through the Underground. They can attack all of them from all sides, simultaneously. While storming Tartarus and overwhelming the guards."

"There's no guarantee your Gemini can win against the Pentad's defenses," Kanja warned.

"They don't need to win," Simon explained. "They just need to occupy the Pentad's forces. If they have to coordinate the defenses of all of their cities at once, they'll pay less attention to what's happening in Centrum."

"While we go in and rescue Gideon," Bella concluded. She smiled, shaking her head at Simon in wonder. "That's a great idea."

"We still need a way to protect Gideon while we extract him," Kanja stated. "Perhaps that's where I come in."

"What are you thinking?" Bella asked.

"I can sculpt something to carry Gideon in and protect him while we escape," she proposed. "He'll be the most vulnerable of us without his belongings…and we have to assume we won't be able to retrieve them in time."

"Okay," Bella replied. "Then I guess we have the beginnings of a plan."

Everyone nodded.

"First thing's first," she stated. "We have to figure out where this door leads us." She turned to Myko. "How many miles do you think Gideon is from this door?"

Myko paused, then pawed Bella's hand five times.

"Five miles?" she pressed. Myko *wuffed.* "Okay then," she decided. "That should be far enough away not to alert the authorities. Let's go."

She pulled the door open…or at least tried to. It was stuck. She pulled harder, but still it wouldn't move. Myko nudged her from behind, and she took a step back, letting him try. He bit down on the doorknob, twisting it, then pulling backward.

It didn't budge.

Myko growled, his ears flattening on his head. He yanked hard once, then again…and then a third time. There was a terrible ripping sound, and then the door opened inward. To Bella's surprise, the other side of the door was covered in a thick carpet of short, bright green grass.

"Huh," Bella mumbled, staring at the verdant surface. She eyed the purple glowing portal of the doorway suspiciously. "Grass usually grows on the ground…which means this door must be lying on the ground too."

"Like the one to Miss Savage's mountain," Simon said. "The one that opened up into the bed of a stream."

"Ah," Bella muttered, remembering how she'd been soaked by that very door. "Right." Which meant that if she stepped through it, she'd fall right back into the Underground. So she got down on her hands and knees near the doorway, plunging her hands through and feeling around. The unmistakable prickling of grass greeted her fingers; she grabbed on, then pulled herself through the doorway as if she were doing a pull-up.

Her head passed through, and she blinked against sudden, brilliant blue brightness.

Pulling herself all the way through the doorway, she squinted against the light, waiting for her eyes to adjust.

And when they did, her jaw dropped.

* * *

The land a few miles outside of Centrum, the capitol city of the Pentad, was a massive, utterly flat, perfectly manicured lawn. One that extended for miles and miles in all directions, bordered by a forest far in the distance. The grass was so green that it seemed artificial, and had been trimmed to the length of a fingernail. As Bella stepped out onto that lawn, she found herself staring not at it, or at the massive expanse of bright blue sky above. Rather she found herself staring at something utterly unexpected.

A huge silver dome in the distance, its perfectly smooth surface reflecting the sky and land around it like a massive curved mirror. Five sky-bridges extended from the dome at regular intervals, floating over a hundred feet above the ground without any supporting columns…and continuing on above the forest miles away.

Myko, Goo, Simon, and Kanja came through the portal behind Bella, and Kanja stopped at Bella's side.

"What is *that*?" Bella asked, gesturing at the dome.

"I think that's Centrum," Kanja replied.

"That wasn't there in the paintings," Bella complained. There'd been the city, then the lawn beyond it…but no mirrored dome.

"Perhaps it is one-sided," Kanja proposed.

"An entire city under a dome?" Bella asked, hardly believing it.

"A clever solution," Kanja said. "The dome is very likely a mirror into the Plane of Reflection. Any attack on the dome will just pass through into that plane."

"And anyone who tries to get in will just pass through too," Bella realized. "So…how are *we* going to get in?"

"Good question," Kanja replied.

"We could dig under," Simon offered.

"Unless the dome is a sphere," Bella stated. "That's what I would have made. Half of it underground, so if anyone tries to dig through, they'll just end up right back in the Plane of Reflection."

Simon nodded. It was clear that he would have made it that way too.

"What are those bridges?" Bella pressed.

"Roads to the five major cities of the Pentad," Kanja guessed. "Each road must serve as an entrance into the capitol."

"Hmm," Bella murmured. The door to the Underground closed spontaneously, and suddenly Bella felt terribly exposed. For they were standing in the middle of a lawn extending for miles in all directions.

"We need to get out of the open," Bella warned.

"Should we go back to the Underground?" Kanja asked.

"No," Bella answered. "I've got a better idea."

She extended a hand, then made an "O" with her thumb and index finger.

Manus's many hands flew off of her, then held hands to form an oval ring in mid-air before her, one surrounding a black portal.

"Come on," she urged. And with that, she stepped through the portal into her Conclave for the very first time.

* * *

The first law of magic was, as Gideon had taught, the Law of Unintended Consequences. For magic was a wild thing, guided by art to do its thing…but possessed of a mind of its own. And, as Bella discovered upon entering her Conclave, the first law of magic had reared its head in several unexpected ways.

For she was not herself, but light.

A particle of pure light shooting downward in a sea of identical particles, extending for as far as she could see. But at the same time, she was a vibration, a soundless *hum.* This duality of being, one thing and another at once, was both startling and familiar.

Suddenly Bella slammed into something below…a floor of some kind. A dark circle, soft yet firm, illuminated by a ray of light shining from far above. She was in the center of the circle, and as she struck the floor, her true form was seen by it, and she transformed back into herself.

Bella paused, then stepped out of the dark circle…and out of the ray of light.

Then she took stock of where she was.

In a giant eyeball, that was clear. But instead of the pupil of the eye being to one side, it was at the ceiling, a good thirty feet up. A giant lens hung below the pupil, the ray of light passing from the pupil into the lens, which concentrated the ray into a straight beam of light a few feet in diameter that shot all the way down to the floor. It struck a dark circle on the floor, and beyond that circle, the floor was a reddish-yellow color. Huge blood vessels pulsed as they crawled up the curved walls all around Bella like vines on a brick wall.

And to one side on the gently curving floor, Bella saw a kind of circular yellow mound, like a large bean chair, but big enough to be a bed. She knew from school that it was the eye's optic nerve.

Something flashed within the ray of light from above, shooting downward through the lens and striking the dark circle on the floor in front of Bella. It morphed instantly into Kanja, who stepped out of the light and came to Bella's side. Goo, Myko, and Simon did the same.

Suddenly Manus's dozens of skeletal hands shot through the pupil, forming an iris floating around it like a big ring-like chandelier. Then the giant iris constricted, and the beam of light narrowed to about a foot in diameter. It was enough to cast the eyeball-Conclave in a pleasant orange-red light.

"Interesting," Kanja murmured, looking around. "Not what I was expecting."

“Me neither,” Bella confessed. She went to the bean-bag-chair-like optic nerve, sitting down on it. It was firm, but not uncomfortably so.

“Is the portal visible from outside?” Simon asked.

“No,” Bella answered. “At least I don’t think so,” she added. “If Manus’s hands are in here, then they can’t be out there to form the portal in the first place,” she reasoned.

Simon nodded.

“Alright, so we need to figure out a way into Centrum,” Bella stated. “And Kanja, will this be enough room to sculpt in?”

“Yes,” Kanja answered.

“Do you have an easel?” Bella asked Simon. He nodded, unbuttoning his suit jacket to reveal a folded-up canvas. “Then I guess we should get to work,” she decided. “Myko, is Gideon still okay?”

Myko nodded.

Bella smiled, relieved at that. But even though her father was okay now, there was no telling how much time he had left. Which meant that they needed to find a way into Centrum…and fast.

She looked up at the Manus-iris high above, extending a hand, then pointing at a section of the floor. Some of the hands broke away from the iris, coming together to form a bony easel where she’d pointed.

“All right,” she stated, cracking her knuckles and pulling a canvas from her thigh-holster. “Let’s do this.”

Chapter 25

Gideon sat cross-legged in his prison cell, facing the corner as he usually did. He heard footsteps approaching, then going away, from one of the many prison guards doing their required rounds. Every five minutes like clockwork. Far more precise and tireless than a human could be.

They had to be statues.

He stared down at the stumps of his wrists. It reminded him of the sacrifice he'd made to work for the Collector a decade ago, to have his right hand amputated. He'd seen it as a fitting punishment for letting his wife die, and for creating the Collector in the first place. Bella's forgiveness – and ending the Collector's tyranny – had made him accept his hand back.

And now, though his hands were gone, he felt whole.

Gideon closed his eyes, taking a deep breath in, then letting it out. His body was imprisoned, but his mind was not. And while his body had no hands, his mind was another story.

First he checked on Myko, who was far, far away. He could tell that his Familiar was with Bella, and that things were generally okay. There was a shift, and he suddenly felt Myko much closer. In fact, the wolf was only a few miles away now.

He took the Underground, Gideon realized. Which meant that the Underground had to have a door that led to the land just outside of Centrum.

Which meant that Bella was coming for him…and that she was in grave danger. For as clever as she was, the Pentad was far more powerful than she could fathom.

He shifted his concentration, to one of his magical gloves.

He'd sent the glove to grab his cane and fly high into the air right before Craven had captured him. To fly away from Craven and anyone else that might try to trap his prized weapon. He could still feel it – and control it –

as if it were his own hand, because it had been painted to be. Like a second skin, it was a part of him, connected to his mind.

And he could feel it not too far away from where Myko was. On the outskirts of the forest before the great lawn surrounding Centrum. He could even feel the cool hardness of the shaft of his cane in its grip, and could sense the trees around it. Not quite sight, but something like it. A just *knowing*, without knowing how.

And because it had been painted to *be* him…a part of his body…he could control it from any distance, even between planes of existence. It could not get into Centrum, not with the mirrored dome protecting it. But if Bella could somehow find a way in, he might yet have a chance at getting out of this mess.

A profoundly useful creation, his gloves. One that had gotten him out of countless predicaments…including, on a few occasions, being captured and imprisoned by the enemy.

Of course, a couple of decades ago, he never would have expected that his enemy would be the Pentad.

Opening his eyes, he stared at the corner of his cell, grinding his teeth. He'd been loyal to the Pentad and Queen Eldora for centuries. He'd given everything he had to them…and Xander, his son, had died because Gideon had been away on yet another mission for the kingdom instead of being allowed to spend time with his son on Xander's birthday.

But that, he knew now, was the power of organizations. Whether private or governmental, organizations tended toward growth. And – everything being relative – the larger they got, the smaller people seemed to them. People became a means to an end, rather than being an end in and of themselves. So instead of the organization serving the people, the converse became true. And the rules that defined the organization – which also grew and multiplied – became more tyrannical as the people became smaller and smaller.

Until the organization meant everything, its rules absolute. And the people meant next to nothing at all.

The sound of footsteps echoed through the prison, marking five more minutes. Statues marking time as well as any clock. The Pentad's statue-guards had been made to be this way, of course. Obedient to the letter of the law. Precise, uncompromising. They could work harder than any human, without rest, and could not be bribed or reasoned with. They were the perfect instruments of the Pentad, ensuring that its people were kept in line.

The footsteps faded away, and Gideon sighed, staring at the wall. Gray stone, the color of cruelty. And with the unique, magical property that nothing could stick to it. Not blood, or paint, or anything else a clever Painter might try to use to turn it into a canvas.

There could be no art here. Musicians had their mouths painted off. Sculptors and Painters lost their hands. Writers had nothing to write on. And

Actors…well, they were the hardest to contain, for their art was performed upon themselves.

But creativity defied containment. And the more creative Gideon was, the more powerful his magic would be.

The Pentad would find him guilty, and make a spectacular example out of him. He would be transformed into a symbol, a terrible warning to all other artists who dared to go rogue.

Or at least they would try.

For it was widely believed that Gideon Myles was the greatest Painter alive…and when the time came, he would be more than happy to remind them why.

* * *

Bella's Conclave proved an excellent studio for Bella, Simon, and Kanja. It was quiet, for one, and free of distractions. And within it, the Flow seemed to grab Bella effortlessly, guiding her brush to paint one scene after the next. As was typical, most of her paintings came to nothing. But each brought her a flash of inspiration, a fresh idea that she could use in her next work.

So this went, each artist losing themselves in their work, working together but separately.

In time, Bella took a break, finding herself eyeing Kanja. The woman was standing next to a huge block of gray stone that Simon had painted for her, then drawn out with Goo's help. She had a ladder and a bunch of tools, also painted by Simon, and was busy chipping away at the sides and top of the stone with a hammer and chisel.

"Do you mind if I watch?" Bella asked her.

"Feel free."

Bella did so, observing as Kanja banged her hammer on the chisel, chipping away at the boulder. Dust flew back with each blow, which explained why Kanja was wearing a transparent face shield – also painted by Simon.

"This is granite," Kanja explained as she worked. "It's really hard to work with, but it's more durable than marble, especially outdoors."

"Huh," Bella murmured.

"Luckily Simon painted these tools to work on granite really well," Kanja continued. "This would've taken four times as long with my old tools."

"What are you making?" Bella asked.

"Well, I'm not really *making* anything," Kanja corrected. "See, there are two basic kinds of sculpting: additive and subtractive. Things like modeling using clay, or casting, or assembling pieces together to form a sculpture are additive. You add stuff together until you get the finished product."

"Okay," Bella replied.

"Carving, on the other hand, is subtractive," Kanja explained. "I'm not making a sculpture…I'm revealing it."

"So you're cutting it out of the stone?"

"That's right," Kanja confirmed. "It's like…it's like I'm excavating something. Something trapped within the stone. And with every tap of my hammer, I'm revealing parts of it."

"How does that work with the Flow?" Bella inquired.

"Well, I have a general idea of what the sculpture will be, but it reveals itself to me as I go. All the details and such. As if I'm discovering it bit-by-bit, as bits of the stone around it are carved away."

"Art is excavation," Bella recited, remembering Grandpa's lesson. Kanja smiled.

"In carving, yes," she agreed.

"Do you mold statues too?" Bella asked.

"Sure," Kanja answered. "But mostly I like to carve. The magic for me is in the reveal."

"That's really cool," Bella told her, admiring the woman as she worked. She watched for a while, then returned to her own work. Or rather, getting a fresh canvas to work on. She sighed, staring at its blank surface…and finding herself thinking about what her mom had told her, back at the Guild of Necromancers a month ago.

You need to incorporate curses into your arsenal.

And Bella hadn't done that. None of her magic used curses…and as Mom had told her, curses are what people feared the most about Necromancers. And since Bella hated killing, they were a way to deal with enemies without necessarily killing them. Mom's best curse was the one she'd used on the Collector, and Miss Savage. The one that ensured that anyone who tried to kill her would end up killing themselves…and in doing so, would bring her back to life.

So what curse could Bella create?

She didn't want to kill people, or give them diseases. Or age them. That was all a bit too dark for her. Too cruel. But was it possible to curse someone with kindness?

Curse with kindness…

"Oh!" she blurted out.

And then the Flow struck her like a bolt of lightning…and she got to work.

She painted a dark cavern, with a hole in the ceiling from which a single ray of pale white light descended. This illuminated a wooden table in the center of the cavern, upon which a flask of blood-red liquid stood. It was half-full, and to the left of the table she painted a woman. Not a human woman, of course, but a monstrous orc-like creature, for painting humans was forbidden. A bit of red liquid stained the orc's lips, indicating that it had drunk of the potion…and it had its back to the potion.

To the right of the table, Bella painted another orc, a male this time. A soldier clad in rusted armor, thrusting a spear across the table into the back of the female orc's shoulder. Then she painted a ghostly spear thrusting into the back of *his* shoulder.

That done, Bella focused on both of the orcs' expressions. She made them identical, twisted in pain. Then she painted a soft pink glow around each of their chests, where their hearts were.

From there, Bella continued to paint, adding detail after detail. Time passed, although how much Bella couldn't say. But when at last she finished, she found that a considerable amount of time must have passed, for Kanja's sculpture had come along quite far, and Bella was starving.

She went back to Kanja's side, admiring the Sculptor's work. For the woman had chipped away at her granite boulder to reveal something quite extraordinary.

A monstrous creature of mouths.

Its body was shaped like a giant sphere, with innumerable mouths of various sizes and shapes carved into it. Some looked like human mouths, others more animal in nature. Even its eyes were embedded in large mouths, the upper and lower teeth forming the eyelids. And below these eyes was a huge, gaping maw with sharp teeth, from which a dozen long, forked tongues protruded. Indeed, the smaller mouths also had long tongues visible inside of them. There were no arms or legs, just mouths all the way around. At least as far as Bella could tell; for the creature's lower half was still stuck in stone.

"Wow," Bella breathed, staring at the monstrosity. Kanja grinned at her.

"You like it?"

"I *do*," Bella confirmed. It reminded her a bit of Petrusa's grotesque sculptures in the Plane of Death. "What does it do?"

"You'll see," Kanja promised. "I don't want to spoil the surprise."

A black spot appeared on the top of the thing, spreading downward across its exposed surface. As it did so, the creature came to life, its little mouths opening and closing, pink tongues snaking in and out. Its eyes moved, focusing bright pink irises right on Bella.

"Oh!" Bella gasped.

The creature struggled to free itself from its rocky prison, and Kanja patted it gently.

"It's okay Rodo," she soothed. "Just a bit longer."

The creature relaxed visibly…and promptly turned back to stone.

"It's alive?" Bella blurted out. "But it's not finished!"

"Carvings don't come alive when they're finished," Kanja explained. "The magic of carving is in freeing the sculpture from the stone, or wood, or whatever substance its trapped in. As I finish parts of the sculpture, those parts come alive."

"Wow."

"When Rodo's free, I'll show you what he can do," Kanja promised.

"Rodo?" Bella asked.

"That's his name."

Bella nodded, studying Rodo for a bit longer. Then she realized she hadn't heard much from Simon for the last…well, however long it'd been since they went into the Conclave. He'd chosen a spot to work on the opposite end of the giant eyeball-chamber, making it clear that he preferred to not be bothered. She walked up to him, eyeing his canvas. To her surprise, it was blank…and there were no other canvases around him. He just stood there, staring at the canvas.

"Hey," she greeted. "You okay?"

He blinked, as if snapped out of a trance, turning to look at her.

"Yes," he answered.

"What are you up to?"

"Thinking," he replied. She waited, and he turned back to the canvas. "Introspection, then expression."

"Huh?"

"Something Percy always tells me," Simon explained. Bella frowned, eyeing the blank canvas.

"My grandpa told me the opposite," she replied. "That introspection came during expression."

Simon gave her a look she couldn't read.

"What?" she asked.

"Nothing," he mumbled.

"Want to see what I painted?" she asked. He nodded, and she led him to her painting. He studied it for a while, as still as a statue. Then he turned to look at her.

"Empathy?" he guessed.

Bella broke out into a surprised smile.

"That's right," she confirmed. "It's a potion that I'll drink. Once I do, it'll make anyone that attacks me feel the pain they cause me."

"Like the Collector's suit."

"Sort of," Bella said. "But it won't hurt them. It'll just let them know how I feel. I think…" She swallowed past a sudden lump in her throat. "I think if people just understood the pain their actions caused others, most wouldn't want to hurt people anymore. I think people do bad things to other people when they don't *see* them as people."

Simon nodded.

"This way, I'm forcing my enemies to empathize with me," she continued. "They can't treat me like a thing anymore. They have to see me as a person, like them."

"Like I did with you," Simon murmured.

"And me with you," Bella added, wrapping an arm around his shoulders. She felt him stiffen, then relax. He lowered his gaze.

"I'm sorry I hurt you," he apologized.

"It's okay," she replied, giving him a squeeze. "I hurt you too, when I hurt the Collector. And Gideon hurt the Collector when he tried to protect the Collector by lying to him about being his real son." She paused, gritting her teeth. "And I…hurt Gideon," she confessed. "I broke a promise, and that's why he's gone."

Simon lifted his gaze to meet hers.

"I felt like I failed the Collector," he confessed. "I should've been able to save him, but he didn't care about that. All he wanted was for me to do what I felt was right. He wanted me to have a better life than he had." He gave a rare smile. "And now I do."

She smiled back reluctantly.

"You're telling me to forgive myself," she accused.

"*I* did."

Bella sighed, gazing at her painting. She realized with sudden clarity that she had empathy for just about everyone.

Everyone but herself.

She took a deep breath in, blinking away tears. She cleared her throat.

"Guess I should draw it out," she mumbled.

She reached into the canvas…and her fingertips bumped against its surface. Her cheeks grew warm, and she grimaced.

"Gotta sign it, duh," she muttered.

Retrieving a fine paintbrush, she did just that, feeling the familiar breeze from behind as the canvas came alive. She reached into the canvas, and this time her hand plunged through, allowing her to retrieve the flask of crimson fluid. She drew it out, staring at it.

"Bottom's up," she proclaimed…and drank it down in one gulp.

It was, she found, bittersweet.

Bella felt the thick fluid flow down to her belly, and it burned there a bit, as if she'd swallowed hot tea. The sensation faded, and Bella felt normal again.

Simon gave her a questioning look.

"I don't feel any different," she admitted. "We can test it though. Hit me," she requested. Simon frowned.

"What?"

"Hit me," she repeated, pointing to her shoulder. "Punch it."

Simon hesitated.

"No," he replied.

"It's okay," she reassured. "I can take it."

Still he hesitated.

"Hey, if you kill me, I'll just come back," she told him with a smile. "Every time I die, I heal."

He smiled back reluctantly, then cocked his fist back.

"Ready?" he asked. She nodded. He punched her in the shoulder…hard enough to knock her backward. She stumbled, then caught her balance, her shoulder smarting. Simon's eyes widened, and he touched his own shoulder.

"Nice right hook," Bella grumbled. "You feel anything?"

"I did," he admitted. "But not just the pain. The moment I hit you, I…was you."

She raised an eyebrow.

"I was you, for a split-second, being hit by me," he explained. "It was…strange." He frowned. "I can still feel you…the echo of your pain. But it's slipping away."

"Huh," she replied. "Well I guess it worked then."

"It doesn't stop people from attacking you once," he pointed out.

"That's okay," she replied with a smile. "It takes more than one hit to kill me for good." She sighed, turning back to her bone-easel. "Guess I better get back to work."

He went back to his side of the Conclave, and Bella got a fresh canvas to put on her bone-easel. But as she took the finished canvas off, she paused, staring at the skeletal hands that made up the easel.

They made her think of Nemesis.

She turned away, grabbing the new canvas and propping it on the easel. But the thought of their last conversation echoed in her mind. The terrible things she'd said.

I never liked you.

She swallowed past a lump in her throat.

I wish I'd never painted you.

She'd been angry at her Familiar. Bella had been ashamed of what she'd done…and that shame had made her blame Nemesis instead of herself.

You did this Bella. Not me.

She took a shuddering breath in.

You.

Bella closed her eyes, tears trickling down her cheeks. She wished she could take it back, or at least apologize. But it was too late. She'd told Nemesis she never wanted to see her again…and at the time, she'd meant it. A flash of anger had ruined their friendship.

You ruined it, she accused herself. *Just like you ruined Havenwood.*

She felt an all-too-familiar heartache, and sighed, wiping away her tears with the back of her hand…

…and then felt herself burst *out* of herself, as if she were a spirit hovering behind her body…with her ghostly fist plunged into her body's back. Gripping its heart.

Bella gasped, her thoughts shattered. In an instant, she returned to her body, clutching at her chest. She blinked rapidly, stumbling backward from the easel.

"Bella?" Kanja asked from behind. "What's wrong?"

"I don't know," she admitted. Kanja walked up to her side, as did Simon. "I'm fine," she reassured. "I just…felt something weird is all."

"You sure?" Kanja pressed.

"I am," Bella replied with the best smile she could muster. "Okay," she added, turning back to her canvas. "Let's get back to work."

Everyone did, and Bella grabbed a paintbrush, staring at the blankness of her canvas. Her mind felt identical, utterly blank. Before she could fall into the despair of staring at the canvas for hours, she dipped her brush in black paint, then slashed at the canvas.

Ruin it, Grandpa had taught her.

She felt a spark of inspiration then, staring at the angry black gash on the canvas. For the empty canvas was perfection, so much so that many Painters were intimidated by it. The empty page could only be ruined by marking it. The art would never be enough to match that perfection.

But that was wrong, of course. The canvas was the *opposite* of perfect. It was nothing, mere space. A vacuum waiting to be filled. *Wanting* to be filled.

And as with the canvas, so with her. For her soul had been like that blank canvas once…until her broken promise had ruined it. An angry black gash on the canvas of her soul.

I'm sorry Nemesis.

Now it was her job to build from that. For as Grandpa and her mother had told her, love was something you gave. So she would have to give it to her art if she wanted a chance at healing her heart.

Chapter 26

Gideon stepped into the Locus Legis, General Craven's resting place. A large hexagonal chamber, half-black, half-white, it represented the home of Law itself. Innocent and guilty, good and evil. Right and wrong.

And in the center of the chamber was a pedestal of crimson and gold. Gold on the white half, red on the black. For the law exacted a price of wealth or blood, and sometimes both. And the personification of the law stood upon that pedestal, General Craven himself.

The living statue faced the shimmering portal at the opposite end of the Locus Legis, the portal to the queen's chambers. In his state of suspended animation, Craven was a statue of pure Invictium, a most unusual metal. For as well as being virtually indestructible, it was as transparent as glass. Gideon could see right through the man, the general's gold and red armor seeming to float in midair.

The guards escorting Gideon prodded him from behind, guiding him toward the shimmering portal beyond the pedestal. A portal that would take him to the Heart of the Pentad, a fitting name for the home of Queen Eldora. For she was its heart, and always had been. She had bled for the kingdom, sacrificed everything for it.

Even herself.

Gideon reached the portal, and he stepped through it, knowing that the guards would not follow. The Queen had no fear of Gideon, or anyone else for that matter…and besides, if she herself could not deal with a threat to her person, her guards wouldn't be able to either.

He found himself at the bottom of the gilded staircase leading upward and forward, the red walls pulsing like a great artery. Up he went, until at last he'd made it to the Heart itself. To his relief, Eldora was not seated on her throne in the Apex Cor, the apex of the heart. Rather, he found her standing beside the huge globe levitating at the far right of the Heart, holding a golden monocle to one eye to study it.

The world, under the queen's watchful eye.

Gideon stopped at a respectful distance from the queen, gazing up at the globe. He knew little about it, other than that it appeared to allow her to surveil her kingdom.

Eldora ignored him for some time, gazing up at her world. Giving the illusion that she hadn't noticed him, which of course could not be true. The queen's awareness was legendary…and terrifying.

At length, she lowered her monocle, turning to gaze at him with her unusual crimson irises. She wore the only uniform he'd ever seen her wear, her blood-red robe. And as she transfixed him with her gaze, he found his breath catching in his throat. As it always had, ever since the day he'd met her so many centuries ago.

She came toward him, seeming to glide over the floor, and stopped a few feet away. Gideon held her gaze, the merest hint of her sweet scent scattering his thoughts. Eldora stood there, utterly still as she pinned him in place with her eyes, not even seeming to breathe.

Not so much as blinking.

"I'm going to miss this," she murmured at last, shattering the silence.

Gideon swallowed.

"So this is it," he deduced. She nodded.

"It is."

"How will it end?" he asked. Still she didn't blink.

"Decapitation," she answered. "By Temper, the Familiar whose Painter you murdered."

Gideon sighed, an image of Yero coming to his mind's eye. They'd been friends once. Good friends. And despite that, it'd come to this.

Loyalty to the organization trumping loyalty to friends. The group destroying the individual for straying too far from its boundaries.

"I see," Gideon murmured, lowering his gaze. She lifted one pale hand, touching the underside of his chin and gently lifting his gaze back to her. He took a deep breath in, digesting this. "When?" he pressed.

"Tomorrow."

She withdrew her hand, then turned away from him, exposing her pale back and shoulders. So slender and fragile-looking. Vulnerable. And that, Gideon knew, was intentional. This was not her turning her back on him metaphorically. No, Eldora was communicating vulnerability to him, and it was for good reason.

Not for the first time, he wondered what she truly was. And whether she was an artist or not. She gave no indication of whether she was or wasn't, but the way she communicated…every graceful movement a conversation, a story…

"Do you fear me, Gideon?" she inquired, her back still to him.

He considered this.

"No," he answered.

She turned her head so that he could see its profile.

"But I've chosen to execute you."

"Not because you want to," he pointed out. "Who you are and what you do aren't always in agreement."

She gave the subtlest smile.

"And who am I?" she pressed, still with her back to him.

"I don't know," he admitted. "But I know the struggle."

She turned to face him.

"Do you, Gideon?" she asked, arching an eyebrow.

"I know that you *do* struggle," he clarified.

"As do you," she replied.

"As do I."

She turned away from him, taking a few steps toward her throne, then pausing.

"You betrayed the Pentad for a woman."

"Yes," he admitted.

"Was it worth it?" she pressed.

Gideon hesitated. He pictured Lucia as he'd last seen her, so fearsome and confident on the battlefield. And Bella, the daughter he'd been so eager and terrified to rescue from Blackthorne.

"Without question," he answered at last.

"She must have been something," Eldora mused. Her tone was almost wistful. Gideon nodded.

"She was."

"Was she worth losing eternity?" Eldora inquired.

Gideon grimaced, knowing what she was asking him. For as the Pentad's greatest Painter, he would surely have been granted immortality as long as he'd remained loyal to the throne. Indeed, he'd enjoyed over four hundred years of life as a reward for his loyalty, and the unique value he offered the Pentad.

He could very well have enjoyed four thousand.

Gideon shrugged.

"I'll never know," he answered at last.

Eldora considered this response silently, as still as Craven had been on his pedestal in the Locus Legis. Indeed, if she was breathing, he couldn't see it. Her eyes were unblinking, boring through his, her crimson irises contrasting sharply with her deathly pale skin.

"Neither will I," she murmured.

She put a hand on his shoulder then, sliding her fingertips up to the side of his neck. They were cool and soft, sending a shiver through him…and making goosebumps rise on his arms. She leaned in then, until her lips were a hair's breadth from his ear. Closer than she'd ever been to him.

Her scent grew stronger, overwhelming his senses. He found himself unable to think, his thoughts flittering away like leaves in a sudden wind. Only his feelings remained, unburdened by logic or judgement. Uninhibited.

Free.

In that moment, he felt something that both terrified and intrigued him. A feeling he'd denied for longer than he could remember…but that, in that moment, he could deny no more. He pulled his head away a little, turning so their eyes met.

And kissed her.

Her lips were cold and soft and sweet, and to his surprise she did not pull away. He felt her react, kissing him back…and Gideon lost himself in it.

Then she pulled away, and Gideon immediately regretted not doing so first.

He backed away from her, lowering his gaze to the floor in shame and horror. If he had been capable of speech at that moment, he would have apologized.

Still, he felt her eyes on him.

"You and I are different, Gideon," Eldora stated gently. "Who you are and what you do are in agreement." He lifted his gaze, and saw her staring at him sadly. "But I chose I a different path."

His lips trembled, his vision blurring.

"Then you'll never have peace," he replied.

"Never," she agreed.

She turned away from him then, seeming to glide across the floor toward the Apex Cor…and her throne. Gideon felt his heart sink as she sat down upon it, resting her slender arms on the gold and crimson armrests.

And as she did so, her expression hardened, her cold eyes staring across the Heart of the Pentad at him.

"Leave me," she commanded. Her voice, once soft and flowing like her simple robe, was now sharp and powerful, filling the chamber. Gideon's limbs immediately obeyed, and he found himself turning away from her before he was even aware of having done so. He had the sudden, mad urge to defy her, to turn around and face her.

But his body would not obey him.

Gideon swallowed past a lump in his throat, feeling her eyes on his back as he strode toward the exit of the Heart, making his way to the gilded staircase. The blood-red walls of the cylindrical stairwell pulsed rapidly, matching the beating of his heart.

Gold and crimson, wealth and blood. For Queen Eldora's power was in equal measures from the riches she held and the blood she'd shed.

Gideon spotted the shimmering portal to the Locus Legis far below, and made his way slowly toward it, knowing that each step was one step closer to his fate. For the law exacted a price of wealth or blood, and sometimes both.

But in his case, blood would suffice.

* * *

General Craven sensed Queen Eldora's summons through his magical helm, and it woke him from Torpor, forcing him to feel again.

He emerged from the waters of his unconscious mind, feeling his flesh revitalize in a steady wave from the top of his head all the way to the bottoms of his feet. And as always, he found himself facing the portal to the Heart of the Pentad, staring at its shimmering surface. A figure emerged from that portal, stepping into the Locus Legis.

Gideon.

Craven stood there on his pedestal, using every bit of his will to keep his expression neutral. He knew at once what the queen demanded of him, and stepped down from his perch to stand before Gideon. It was not lost on him that this put them on equal footing, though Craven stood several feet taller than the Painter.

He stared at Gideon, trying to reclaim the sense of power he'd once had over the Painter. He'd defeated the man in the end, after all. Distracted as Gideon had been, it'd still been a victory. Indeed, he may have defeated the man anyway.

But then again, maybe not.

Craven turned to the guards at the entrance to the Locus Legis, opposite the portal to the Heart of the Pentad.

"Return the prisoner to Tartarus," he commanded.

"Follow," one of the guards ordered, gesturing at Gideon. The Painter just stood there, eyeing Craven.

"What time is the trial?" Gideon asked.

"At sunrise," Craven answered.

"And the execution?"

"Thereafter," Craven replied.

"Follow!" the guard repeated.

"One more question," Gideon assured them. "Where will the execution be?"

"It will begin in the mall before the entrance to the Palatium," Craven revealed. The mall was the great lawn before the palace, bisected by a wide gold and red road that led to the entrance to the Palatium. Much of the aristocracy – and a select group of the common folk – would attend the execution. For it was as much a function of communicating a message as it was exacting a rightful sentence.

That no man was above the law.

"Where will it end?" Gideon pressed.

"At the Edge of Eternity," Craven revealed.

He watched as Gideon processed this, his face turning pale. The Painter swallowed visibly, clearly rattled. For the Edge of Eternity was a cliff in Tartarus, overlooking the bowels of Hell. Anyone who died there – by virtue of having died within Hell itself – would find their soul forever trapped there, subject to an eternity of torture.

A fate far worse than death.

Few criminals ever suffered such a sentence, and death at the Edge of Eternity could only be ordered by Queen Eldora herself. She was sending her own message to Gideon…and to every artist in the Pentad. A warning of what happened to those who painted without a license, and used their power to betray her.

Craven waited for Gideon to say something more, but the Painter did not.

Instead, Gideon merely inclined his head in thanks, then walked around the pedestal upon which Craven stood, reaching the guards at the other end of the chamber. Craven watched them escort Gideon out of the Locus Legis, struck with the sudden urge to go back in time. To battle with Gideon again, no interruptions, no distractions.

Just the two of them, in a battle to the death.

For only then would Craven know the truth. Only then would he know if Gideon was truly capable of winning against him.

But this could never happen. Gideon would die tomorrow, executed by Temper. And Craven would spend the rest of his existence never knowing the truth.

He felt Queen Eldora beckoning him again through his helmet, and he turned back toward the shimmering portal to her chamber, striding up to it and passing through. Up the golden stairs to the Heart of the Pentad he went, and when he reached the top, he saw the queen sitting on her throne. But as soon as he stepped into the Heart, she stood, seeming to glide toward him. She stopped a yard away, staring up at him.

He waited.

"You are to attend the execution tomorrow," she informed him. He blinked.

"Why?"

She arched an eyebrow at him.

"That," she murmured, "…is a question I rarely hear from you."

He stood there, not knowing what to say.

"Because I want you there," she answered at last. "You will represent me."

He inclined his head.

"Yes my Queen."

He hesitated then, remembering his earlier urge.

"Why have Temper execute him?" he asked.

"To honor Yero," she explained.

"It is only a Familiar," he pointed out.

"Then you are only a statue," she retorted calmly.

"I…" he began, then stopped himself. Her eyes narrowed ever-so-slightly.

"Yes?"

"I request a battle," he stated. Her eyebrows rose. "Gideon and I. He in possession of his full strength, and me with mine."

"And why do you make this request?" she inquired.

"I…did not best him fairly," Craven confessed. He felt a chill run through him, and a sense of sudden danger. But he found himself utterly unable to stop. "He was distracted when I defeated him."

"Is distraction not an acceptable tactic?"

"It is," he conceded.

"This has been bothering you," she realized. She tilted her head to the side, eyeing him. "Do you question your abilities, Craven?"

He stood there, unable to speak. Her eyes bore into his, and he had the sudden feeling that she was staring not at him, but *into* him. That she could read his thoughts.

Perhaps she could.

He cleared his throat, finding his voice at last.

"I am insufficient," he declared, staring down at his right hand. He knew even as he said it that he was committing himself to annihilation. "I cannot be your right hand."

Queen Eldora stared at him for a long moment…then burst out laughing.

Craven jerked his gaze up to hers, stunned by her reaction. Still she laughed, a melodic sound he'd never heard before. It filled the chamber, then died away gradually. She smiled up at him, her eyes moist.

"Oh Craven," she murmured, stepping forward and putting a hand on his. "Why would you say such a thing?"

"I am vulnerable," he confessed, his lower lip quivering. "Gideon injured me. I fear he could destroy me."

"And what's wrong with being vulnerable?" she inquired.

"Your right hand should not be weak," he explained. "The law is absolute. It cannot be stopped."

"The law is made, as you were," Queen Eldora countered. "You were made to be *nearly* invulnerable, Craven. Magic does not approve of unchecked power."

"But the law…"

"Is checked by compassion," she interrupted. "You can't feel compassion without vulnerability."

He stood there, not knowing what to say.

"Have you never felt vulnerable before, Craven?" she inquired.

He shook his head.

"Well now you have," she told him.

"I request a battle with Gideon," he stated. "I…"

"Your request is denied," she interjected, slipping her hand away from his. His jawline rippled.

"I want…"

"You want to feel invulnerable again," she accused. "I won't let you."

"I am Craven," he declared. "You say that I am your right hand. But how can I be your right hand if I can be stopped?"

She smiled, holding up her right hand. Pale, slender, with fingernails that were long and translucent, and shimmered in the light.

"Can I be stopped, Craven?" she asked.

Craven stared at her, at a loss for words. He cleared his throat nervously.

"You are the queen," he replied. As if that were answer enough.

"And?"

"You have never been stopped," he stated. She sighed, turning away from him, exposing her back. In that moment she seemed vulnerable, even frail. And for the first time in his existence, Craven wondered what would happen if he grabbed her. If he wrapped a hand around her neck and squeezed.

He imagined her bones snapping, a horrible gurgling coming from her throat. And then the light fading from her eyes.

Craven recoiled in horror, taking a step back.

"True," she murmured. "I have not."

She stood there, her back to him, while he did everything he could to stop himself from trembling. That he could have imagined such a thing – laying his hands on the queen! – was unthinkable. He'd never once questioned her absolute power, over him and over her kingdom. She was older than he, by most accounts *far* older, and there were ancient tales of when she'd ventured outside of this chamber long, long ago.

Of the things she'd done to those who'd dared move against her.

"I am Queen Eldora," she proclaimed, raising her arms up to the sides. "Ruler of the Pentad." She turned then, looking at him sidelong. "But is that all I am?"

He barely heard her, still struggling with his horrible vision. She returned to him, gliding over the floor without seeming to take a step…and reached up, putting a hand on his again.

"Your hand is soft," she observed. "But with a thought, you can become the hardest substance in existence." She smiled. "I can be soft, but when I sit on that throne…"

She turned to gaze at it with a look he couldn't read.

"We have two sides to ourselves, Craven," she murmured. "We have to be true to each." She turned back to face him. "You have to make peace with who *you* are."

He swallowed.

"I had peace," he confessed.

"That peace was ignorance," she told him. "The peace of a child, Craven." She broke out into a proud smile. "My little boy is growing up."

Craven's expression darkened.

"I mean that in the fondest of ways," she reassured him. "And I look forward to getting to know the man you'll become."

With that, she turned back to face the throne with a heavy sigh.

"The day is almost done," she mused. "And tomorrow must come." She turned back to him, her eyes moist. "And who I am must yield to who I must be."

"I don't understand."

"The hard cleaves the soft," she explained without explaining.

And then she glided across the floor back to her throne, turning to face him and sitting upon it.

"Go," she commanded, her tone ice-cold. It sent a chill through him, this sudden change. "You will preside over Gideon's execution by Temper."

"Yes my queen," he replied, bowing stiffly.

Then he turned away from her, exiting the Heart of the Pentad and making his way back to the Locus Legis…and Torpor, his only respite from the torture of his mind.

Chapter 27

Hours passed in Bella's Conclave, and the ray of light shining through the bony iris in the center of the ceiling gradually dimmed, the iris opening wide to compensate for it. The lens beneath the eye contracted, going from relatively flat to more spherical, focusing the light into a tighter beam. This kept the Conclave adequately illuminated.

It was, Bella supposed, an indication of the time. Day had transitioned to night…and Kanja eventually finished her sculpture. Simon, Kanja, and Bella stood around it, and Bella marveled at the sheer level of detail the Sculptor had managed to put into it.

Rodo was a spherical creature of mouths standing nearly seven feet tall. In addition to the two eye-mouths Bella had seen Kanja carve earlier, Rodo had many other bright-pink eyes around his body, so that no matter how his body rolled, he could still see everything around him. And rolling was exactly how the sculpture got around…by using his many mouths to grip the floor and propel himself along, with a little boost from each of his countless tongues. But perhaps the most interesting part was that Rodo's interior didn't move at all. It stayed still regardless of how he rotated, so that anyone kept inside wouldn't bounce around madly inside of him whenever he moved.

"Okay, so how is Rodo going to help Gideon?" Bella asked.

"Show her, Rodo," Kanja requested. Rodo grinned with his biggest mouth, then opened it impossibly wide, showing a huge throat. One that could easily fit a human or two inside of it. "Gideon can crawl in Rodo," Kanja explained. "Rodo's skin is very tough and thick, and as strong as granite. It'll be like Gideon's wearing foot-thick granite armor everywhere he goes."

"Nice," Bella murmured. She turned to Simon. "And how are we going to get into Centrum through that dome?"

"Floppy," he answered. She frowned.

"What?"

"Floppy Disc," he clarified. "Your blood-painting."

They'd shown each other their paintings earlier, to get a handle on what their team's combat capabilities would be. Although Simon had declined to explain the nature of his new Familiar, his white suit Redeemer. One of those paintings was the one Bella had painted using her own blood while escaping from Petrusa's men with her mother. A dark disc that, when applied to any surface, made a hole through it.

"Oh," she replied, taken aback. "Wouldn't it just pass through the mirror?"

"Try it," Simon prompted. He retrieved a shard of a Gemini from his pocket, bringing it to his lips. "Come, one of you," he ordered.

Bella looked upward to the part of Manus forming the iris of the Conclave. She raised a hand, making an "OK" sign. The iris broke apart, flying upward through the pupil and vanishing from sight. A moment later, a flash of light shot downward onto the dark circle in the center of the Conclave, and one of the Gemini stepped out of the light and up to Bella. The many hands of Manus came back through the pupil then, re-forming the iris.

The Gemini transformed, making a mirror of its belly and chest.

Bella reached into her chest-painting, withdrawing Floppy Disc and placing it on the mirror. But instead of going through into the Plane of Reflection, it stuck there…and made a hole right through the Gemini.

"Oh!" Bella exclaimed. She smiled at Simon. "You were right!"

"That's our way in," Simon said. "The Gemini can go through first, and create a diversion. Then we go in and save Gideon."

"And I have to die so I can turn into Lux and Luna," Bella added. "If we go in at night, Luna can go anywhere there isn't light."

"But then the Gemini won't be able to multiply," Simon pointed out.

"Oh," Bella stated. "Right." Mom had used that very fact to defeat the Gemini when they'd attacked Havenwood a month ago. "Well, Luna can travel in the light if she wears a cloak," she realized. "What would *really* be useful is a painted cloak that would come to her whenever she needed it."

"Good idea," Simon replied.

"Funny thing is," Bella continued, "…whenever I die, Lux and Luna appear, but Cain and my Painter's uniform vanish. I can't do anything with paintings or the Flow when I'm them. But when I come back to life, all my stuff reappears where I am."

Simon frowned, considering this.

"Luna's cloak needs to be able to follow her when she becomes one with the shadows too," Bella reasoned. "That way it'll still be on her when she comes out."

"I could paint that," he offered. She paused, then shook her head.

"I should do it," she countered. "But thanks," she added, smiling at him. She felt a sudden affection for him, and stepped up to Simon, giving him a hug. He hugged her back, and at length she pulled away from him. "Thank you for everything, Simon."

"You're welcome."

"Okay," Bella said. "I think we have a plan. Anything I'm missing?"

Everyone glanced at each other, then shook their heads.

"Alright then," Bella decided. "I'll paint Luna's cloak, then we'll go."

"First we should get a quick nap," Kanja interjected. "We've all been up for a while, and I've been up for way too long. It was night-time when I jumped into the painting in the vault back in Havenwood."

Bella nodded reluctantly. The Pentad wouldn't pull any punches with them, so they needed to be at their best. A little rest would give them their best chance at successfully completing their mission.

"Alright," she decided.

And with that, everyone – except for Goo and Cain, of course – went to sleep.

* * *

When Bella awoke, the ray of light shining down from the ceiling of her Conclave was quite dim, barely illuminating the giant eyeball. She was laying on her magical cape, which kept her levitating comfortably a few feet from the floor. She sat up, spotting everyone else still sleeping. Except for Simon, that was. He was standing at the other end of the Conclave, whispering something into a small mirrored shard he held in his right hand. She thought about asking him what he was doing, but decided she wouldn't distract him.

She had a job to do, after all. She had to paint.

Bella went to her bone-easel, setting a fresh canvas upon it. Mixing her paints, she first covered the canvas in total black. The magical paint dried rapidly, allowing her to almost immediately paint atop it. She started to paint a pretty standard-looking cloak, but found herself pausing while doing so, a familiar feeling coming over her. A kind of resistance, an I-don't-want-to-do-it feeling.

At first she assumed it was laziness, and forged on. But as she'd often found, laziness was not a lack of desire to work, but a sign that what she was doing wasn't working.

So she stopped, putting the canvas aside and getting a new one.

This time she let her imagination wander free, without trying to control it so tightly. She dipped her brush in grays and blacks, letting each stroke happen as it desired. And in this way, she found herself quite naturally relaxing *into* painting.

Which was when the Flow struck.

Luna was shadow, and could only exist *in* shadow. So instead of wearing a cloak, the shadows themselves could cloak her. Bella painted a black glove, one with a long sleeve that would nearly reach her elbow. Then she painted it grabbing onto a shadow on the wall, pulling it free as if the shadow were made of cloth. This she painted wrapping around a shadowy figure – representing Luna of course – to make a kind of ninja costume. Complete with a hood and mask that completely covered her face.

She paused then, staring at the shadowy figure's hands.

Bella painted a second shadow, cast by a thin wooden stick plunged into the earth beside the shadowy figure. Then she repainted the figure's right hand, so that it was grasping not the stick, but the shadow *cast* by the stick.

And wielding it as a shadow-weapon.

Then, satisfied that she was on to something, Bella put the canvas aside and repainted the painting. Again and again, canvas after canvas, each time thinking of new details to put into her work. Perfecting it as she'd been taught, until she found herself unable to think of anything else to add or change.

Shadowfinger, she called it.

She signed the painting then, feeling a subtle breeze ruffle her hair from behind when she did so. Reaching into the painting, she drew the glove out.

It was long and silky-black, and extraordinarily soft to the touch. She resisted the urge to put it on, knowing that only Luna could wield it. Turning away from her canvas, she saw Kanja in the process of waking up, and Simon still talking to his shard. She hesitated, then walked up to him.

"Hey," she greeted. He glanced up from his shard.

"Hey."

"I finished the painting," she said, holding Shadowfinger out to him. He frowned at it.

"That's it?" he asked. "Where's the rest of the uniform?"

"You'll see," she promised with a smile. "I can't use it though. I need you to give it to Luna so I can test it and make sure it works."

Simon frowned.

"How do I…?"

"Usually Nemesis kills me to free Luna," she explained. "But I guess you'll have to do it."

He grimaced.

"I don't think I can," he admitted.

"What about the Gemini?" she asked. He hesitated, then nodded reluctantly.

"The Gemini can," he conceded. One of the Gemini walked up behind her, standing there motionlessly.

"Hold on a sec," she requested, reaching into her chest-painting and withdrawing Floppy Disc. She handed it and Shadowfinger to Simon. "Okay," she stated, turning to face the mirrored soldier. "Make it quick."

"Do it," Simon ordered…and then the Gemini slashed at Bella's neck, decapitating her.

And as her body was split into two parts, so it was that she was separated into Lux and Luna, the darkness and the light.

Lux shot into the ray of light in the center of the Conclave, while Luna was shoved right through Rodo's mouth into the darkness of his throat. Simon regarded this with amazement, then went up to Rodo's partially open mouth, offering Shadowfinger to Luna.

"Thanks," Luna said, grabbing the glove and slipping it on her left hand. It was oh-so-silky smooth, and her hand and forearm tingled as it gripped her tightly. "Mmm," she murmured, breaking out into a smile. "I *likey*."

She reached out to the shadows inside Rodo's mouth then, pinching them as if they were cloth. The shadow came right off Rodo, then sucked up Luna's arm, spreading across her chest and the rest of her body until it formed the ninja-like uniform she'd painted earlier.

It covered her body completely…cloaking her in shadow.

Luna stepped out of Rodo's mouth, and to her delight, she had no problem existing within the light.

"Let's go," she heard Lux say. "Wake up Kanja," Lux added, kneeling down and gently shaking Kanja's shoulder. Kanja woke up, taking a moment to realize what was going on. "We're going now," Lux told her.

"Okay," Kanja replied. "I'll come with you, at least till you go into the dome."

"Hold your horses, dearest sister," Luna chided. "One of us is going to have to carry a light outside…unless you want to travel a few thousand miles to the nearest daylight."

"Oh," Lux replied. "Right. Well, Bella has a will-o-wisp," Lux remembered. "We'll need to recombine to get it."

Luna sighed, rolling her eyes.

"Fine," she grumbled…and gave in to the urge to meld with her sister, becoming Bella once again.

Bella reached into her right forearm-painting then, retrieving a glowing wisp of golden light. It floated around her, attracted to her mother's amulet, just as Bella had painted it to be. She'd forgotten all about the wisp, which she'd painted as a light source before the attack on the Collector. She'd never needed to use it…until now.

"There's a problem," she realized. "The wisp is attracted to my mom's amulet, which means if I'm split into Lux and Luna, neither of them will be wearing it."

"Then let me hold on to it," Simon offered. "That way, when you split, you won't lose it."

"And you can give it to Lux," Bella reasoned. "Nice."

She did just that, taking off her necklace with the heart-shaped ruby amulet and handing it to Simon. Then she braced herself for another fatal blow from the Gemini…which came an instant later. Bella split, becoming Luna and Lux again…and Simon handed the amulet to Lux.

The will-o-wisp floated right up to her, its glow meager compared to her incredible brightness. Like the moon compared to the sun. But Lux, despite being so bright, emitted no visible light to her surroundings, whereas the wisp did. It begged the question of how anyone could see Lux if she didn't cast any light on her surroundings…but such was magic, Luna supposed.

Lux reached up, making an "OK" sign…and shot upward through the ray of light, passing into the pupil high above.

"My turn," Luna said, striding into the ray of light. To her relief, she could do so without any problem at all, her shadow-uniform protecting her completely from its repelling power. She felt herself shoot upward to the ceiling, passing through the pupil…

…and then she was stepping out into the night air, onto the miles-wide lawn of Centrum.

The moon shone brightly in the sky, countless stars twinkling from high above. And the great big silver dome surrounding the Pentad's capitol city gleamed in the darkness, its surface lit on all sides by millions of magical floating lights that swarmed around it like fireflies. It made sense, of course; mirrors required light to reflect, and if the dome's surface were *not* lit – either by the sun or these magical lights – then it would no longer function as a portal into the Plane of Reflection.

Bella glanced back, seeing Manus's portal there behind her. Simon, then Kanja stepped through it, and then Goo and Myko and finally Rodo, who rolled to a stop before them. Lux came through next, the will-o-wisp providing an island of light for her to exist within the sea of darkness.

"All right," Luna stated. "Everyone ready?"

Myko *wuffed*, and Goo jiggled. Rodo rocked back and forth, and Simon and Kanja nodded.

"I am ready as I'll ever be!" Cain proclaimed with his customary exuberance. Even the Gemini were ready, the door to the Underground opening up in the lawn nearby, Gemini pouring through it. Simon reached into his pocket, pulling out the Gemini shard and putting it to his lips.

"All forces, attack the Pentad," he commanded.

Luna broke out into a smile, feeling a thrill run through her. The thought of every major city in the Pentad under siege – all at once – was intensely exciting.

"Alright then," she declared. "Let's kick some ass."

Then something huge shot out of the front of the mirrored dome, flying right at them. A dragon over a hundred feet tall, covered in sapphire-blue scales, its glowing turquoise eyes glaring at them. It slammed into the earth before them, sending dirt and grass flying into the air. Then it spread its wings wide, opening its huge maw.

And *roared.*

* * *

"Gemini, attack!" Simon commanded.

The mirrored soldiers swarmed the dragon, who whipped its long tail at them. Dozens of the Gemini shattered with the impact, and the tail would've struck Luna had she not melded with the darkness of the lawn. She reappeared a few dozen feet away from the battle, watching as the blue dragon massacred the Gemini swarming out of the Underground.

But the Gemini merely re-formed, leaping at the huge beast with abandon.

The dragon leapt upward, beating its wings to fly above the them, then arched its neck backward, opening its maw. A blue light blasted from it, striking the Gemini in a sweeping arc.

Freezing them instantly in a sheet of ice ten feet thick.

More Gemini appeared through the door to the Underground, sprinting around their trapped comrades. The dragon stayed airborne, hovering a good fifty feet above the ground…and well out of reach of the mirrored soldiers. Moments later, they too were frozen by its bright blue beam, embedded in huge boulders of ice…as was Goo. Myko tried to moon-dash away, but he was frozen in mid-dash before he could. And Simon…

Well, he'd somehow managed to get behind the dragon, well out of the way of its icy breath.

Luna eyed the dragon, reaching into her chest-painting for her explosive sphere-weapon…and felt her hand *thump* against her chest. For she wasn't wearing her Painter's uniform; Bella was.

"Damn," she muttered. For she'd completely forgotten to give herself a weapon…which meant that, in combat, she was useless.

But Lux, on the other hand…

Bella's brighter half ran right into one of the Gemini, and promptly ricocheted off its mirrored surface, flying up toward the dragon's head, the will-o-wisp following close behind.

The dragon jerked away from Lux's incredible light, and she slammed into its left eye. Lux clung on to its upper eye-ridge for dear life as the dragon roared, squeezing its eye shut against her brightness and whipping its head back and forth. Her grip slipped, and she fell into the swarm of Gemini below…and promptly reflected off of them. She flew right back at the dragon, smacking it under the chin.

Then she fell *again,* hitting the Gemini…and ping-ponging up and down as a ray of light, hitting the dragon over and over.

Eventually the dragon managed to bat Lux away with one clawed hand, sending her flying backward onto the lawn. But during the distraction, the dragon had lost most of its altitude…and was now close enough to the ground for the Gemini to attack!

The glittering soldiers leapt at the enemy's legs and tail, grabbing ahold and climbing up to its body. The dragon flew upward, thrashing its limbs, and most of the Gemini fell off, shattering on the ice below. The dragon blasted them with its blue beam, and the Gemini were instantly frozen.

And all Lux could do was watch. For, without weapons, neither she nor Luna could be of much help.

"Sister!" Lux cried.

Luna appeared a few yards away, rising from the shadows.

"You thinking what I'm thinking?" Luna asked. Lux nodded.

"We need Bella," Lux replied.

They stepped into each other, their bodies merging to become one…and Bella felt herself become herself once again. She reached for Cain, and his spinal column shot out to form a cane.

"We need to take that thing down," Bella told him.

"Right-o!" Cain agreed heartily. Then he paused. "I've been *itching* to beat a dragon to death, but I was hoping it would be a certain smaller one."

"You're right," she realized, feeling rather foolish. The thing was far too big, and its scales were almost certainly impervious to attacks from regular weapons. She could use her explosive sphere, however…the one Gideon had given her long ago. She reached into her chest-painting to retrieve it…then hesitated. That thing had powerful armor. Even if the explosive struck it, there was no guarantee it would do much damage. But if there was some way to get *around* the armor…

Suddenly she had an idea.

"Simon!" she shouted…and spotted him standing behind the ice-dragon, who was still a good fifty feet in the air, and shaking off the remaining Gemini that clung stubbornly to it. She ran up to him, thankful that the dragon was momentarily distracted. "Can I have Floppy?"

He handed the black disc to her, and she shoved it in her chest-painting.

"Okay," she stated. "Kill me."

Simon blinked.

"Have one of the Gemini kill me," she corrected. "I have an idea."

He nodded, and a moment later, Bella heard footsteps rushing at her from behind. She steeled herself, closing her eyes…and felt a horrible pain in her neck as the Gemini's blade separated her head from her shoulders…and the darkness from the light.

Luna melded instantly into the shadows, re-appearing far enough away from Lux's brilliant silhouette to avoid the urge to reunite with her. Then she gazed up at the dragon. It'd shaken off the last of the Gemini, and was turning its glowing turquoise eyes on Lux and Simon. Lux leapt at the Gemini who'd killed Bella, reflecting off of it like a beam of light…and flying right at the dragon.

And at the same time, Luna melded into the shadows again…including those on the dragon's back. For the darkness was everywhere, not just on the ground. And with a thought, she emerged from those shadows, appearing on the ice-dragon's spine.

Just as Lux smashed into her.

They melded, re-forming Bella once again.

The dragon roared, thrashing in mid-air, and Bella dropped to her belly on its back, holding on for dear life.

"I hope you know what you're doing!" Cain cried.

Bella grit her teeth, feeling powerful, rhythmic gusts of wind as the dragon beat its wings, rising higher and higher into the air. The ground was a good hundred feet below them now…and falling away quickly. A drop that would surely kill her.

Not that she was particularly worried about that.

No, she was more worried about Simon and the others…and their mission. If they didn't defeat this dragon, they'd have no hope of getting into Centrum to save Gideon.

At length the ice-dragon stopped its thrashing, focusing on flying higher into the air. Bella took the opportunity to release her death-grip on its back, reaching into her chest-painting to retrieve Floppy. She placed the disc on its back…and saw a large hole appear in its flesh. Directly below, there was a pale yellow, slowly churning chamber with some fluid sloshing around at the bottom. A sour smell assaulted her nostrils, confirming what she was looking at.

Its stomach.

Bella smiled grimly, knowing that Floppy always created a hole that led to the nearest empty space beyond it. The air in the dragon's gut was just that. She reached into her chest-painting again, drawing out the explosive sphere…

…and the dragon rolled in mid-air, tossing her right off its back!

Bella cried out as she plummeted toward the earth, her gut flip-flopping as she fell. The lawn rushed up to meet her, and she struck it with bone-shattering force.

And *split.*

Luna and Lux stumbled backward from each other, both standing where Bella had been a split-second ago. There was a large dent in the grass there…and though they immediately rushed forward to embrace each other, they could not meld together.

"We have to wait for her to heal," Lux realized.

Luna nodded, looking upward. The ice-dragon was diving back down toward them, its great big mouth opening wide.

Luna shoved Lux backward, then melded with the shadows…right as the ice-dragon's deadly blue beam shot downward at them. Safely within the shadows, Luna could not be frozen. But Lux…

She was instantly trapped in a thick boulder of ice.

Damn it, Luna swore to herself. Without Lux, she couldn't become Bella again; and without a weapon, she was helpless.

Unless…

She remembered the explosive sphere then. Bella had drawn it out, which meant it must have fallen along with them. Luna emerged from the shadows, searching the ice trapping Lux for it, but it wasn't there. Which meant it was somewhere on the lawn.

Somewhere close.

The ice-dragon slammed into the ground nearby, the ground quaking with the impact. Wind blasted Luna, forcing her to stumble backward…and the dragon swiped at her with its huge tail.

Luna melded with the shadows again, reappearing behind it.

The dragon growled, scanning the area in front of it for Luna.

"Looking for this?" Simon asked from behind. Luna whirled around, and saw him standing there, the explosive in his hand.

"How did you…?" she began, then cut herself off. It didn't really matter, after all. She grabbed the black sphere, giving him a lopsided grin. "Thanks," she told him, turning back toward the dragon.

Who leapt into the air, flying upward once again.

"Can't outrun me," Luna muttered, melding with the shadows. She stepped out onto the dragon's back as before…and realized she wasn't carrying the sphere anymore. Apparently she couldn't carry things while traveling through the shadows.

Damn it!

She vanished, then reappeared next to Simon, picking the sphere up from the lawn. Then she gazed upward grimly, watching as the dragon gained altitude, its glowing turquoise eyes staring down at them.

"Well that didn't work," she said. "We need to ground that thing. Or we're screwed."

And then a ray of blood-red light shot outward at the ice-dragon's left wing, enveloping it in a deep red glow.

The wing changed, the webbing between its fingers thinning and becoming translucent, its arm-muscles atrophying until they were sinewy straps. The dragon tried to flap its weakened wing, but could only do so feebly.

And so it tumbled downward through the night sky, plummeting right toward Luna and Simon. Or rather, just Luna, as Simon had already starting sprinting away.

Luna became one with the shadows, just as the dragon slammed into the earth above her.

Turf blasted upward from the impact, flying high into the air all around the fallen dragon, then raining down over it. The dragon – still alive – had landed on its weakened wing, crushing it horribly beneath its body. It roared in pain, struggling to rise to all fours.

"Now!" Luna heard Simon shout.

Luna sprinted up to the dragon, but it was getting up too quickly. Gemini rushed to attack it, but the dragon stopped them with a blast of its icy breath attack. Luna cursed, winding up and throwing the sphere at the dragon's back…

…then melded with the shadows, reappearing on the dragon's back and catching the sphere.

"Ha!" Luna cried, rushing up to the hole in the dragon's back and throwing the sphere into it. She peeled Floppy Disc off then, jumping off the dragon and tumbling to the ground. Leaping to her feet, she turned around, pointing her finger at the dragon…and then lowering her finger to the lawn. It was the motion Gideon had taught her, one that would activate the sphere.

Luna melded into the shadows…just as the dragon *exploded.*

Hunks of gore flew outward from the dragon, scattering across the giant lawn.

And then, the ice-dragon left literally in pieces, the battle was done.

Luna emerged from the shadows, putting her hands on her hips and smiling grimly at her work.

"Boom!" she exclaimed. "Take that, mother-"

Something landed before her, and her breath caught in her throat.

For it was a dragon – as tall as she was – with inky-black scales and glowing red eyes. Clad in black metal armor, it had wings whose webbing was painted on their outer surface, and the color of canvas on their inner surface. The dragon stared right at Luna, a smirk curling its lips.

"Hey sugar," Nemesis greeted in a deep, sultry voice. "Apology accepted."

Chapter 28

As a being of darkness, Luna had no problem recovering from Nemesis's return, or the grisly scene of the dead ice-dragon. Together – and with the help of the Gemini – they freed their fellows from the ice. Goo thawed gradually, none the worse for wear. And Myko, having been caught mid-moon-dash, merely finished his dash, which of course healed him instantly. The will-o-wisp was just fine, but Lux, however, was not so lucky. Encased in ice for as long as she had been, she was most certainly dead.

But Bella had painted Lux and Luna such that, if one died and the other did not, one could revive the other by merely being there for them. And so Luna held Lux's cold, bright hand, and within moments Lux returned to life. She melded happily with her sister…and Bella found herself kneeling where they both had been, Nemesis, Simon, Myko, and Goo at her side. She turned to Nemesis with a lump in her throat.

"Nemesis," she began, her voice cracking. "I'm…"

"I know," her Familiar interrupted.

"But I…"

"I feel everything you feel, remember?" Nemesis interjected. "Like I said, apology accepted."

Bella leaned in, embracing Nemesis, and her dragon hugged her back, wrapping her wings around her. They held each other for a long moment, each feeling their love for each other. It was enough to make Bella cry, and cry she did. Great, awful sobs, so that she was glad for Nemesis's wings shielding her from prying eyes.

After a long moment, they separated, and Bella dried her wet cheeks with her sleeve.

"Thanks," she told Nemesis. "For everything."

"You were getting your asses kicked," Nemesis replied. "Much as I enjoyed watching that, I *do* need to keep you around."

"Ha ha," Bella grumbled. But still, she found herself smiling. "*God* I'm glad to see you."

"Glad to be seen," the Familiar replied. Then she turned to Simon. "Back with the enemy, eh?"

"He's a friend now," Bella countered.

"Uh huh," Nemesis replied. "You just like keeping the bad boys around. Can't say I blame you. They're a *hell* of a lot more fun."

Bella blushed, glancing at Simon.

"It's not like that," she replied hastily.

"Mmm hmm."

"*Any*way," Bella stated, "…we were just about to go into Centrum to save Gideon."

"I know," Nemesis replied. "I've been following you. Spying on you, actually."

"Really?"

"Yep," Nemesis confirmed. "You humans never look up."

"I'm surprised I didn't feel you," Bella admitted.

"You pissed me off so much I shut you out," Nemesis explained. "At least at first. After that, your shame shut *me* out."

"Huh," Bella murmured. She hadn't realized that anger and shame could shut them off from each other, but it made sense. The two emotions often shut regular people off from each other…and from their feelings of love for one another.

"What's that hideous…thing?" Nemesis asked, turning to face Rodo. The living statue – freed from the ice – opened its big mouth…and Kanja stepped out of it. The Sculptor was shivering uncontrollably, and terribly out of breath.

"Oh my god!" Bella gasped, rushing to her side. "Are you okay?"

"Y-y-yes," Kanja answered, hugging her arms to her chest, her teeth chattering. "I c-crawled into R-rodo b-b-b…"

"Before the ice beam hit you?" Bella asked. Kanja nodded.

"Almost r-ran out of air," she admitted.

"I'm so sorry," Bella apologized. "I…"

"She forgot about you," Nemesis pointed out bluntly. "Damn, that's cold."

Bella glared at the dragon.

"Did I say I missed you?" she grumbled.

"With tears in your eyes," Nemesis confirmed with a toothy grin. Bella rolled her eyes.

"Missed is past-tense you know," she quipped.

"Hey, what's that?" Nemesis asked, pointing a clawed finger behind them. Bella turned, spotting the portal to her Conclave a dozen yards away. Manus's bony hands-ring surrounded the portal's inky-blackness; she'd completely forgotten to have Manus re-form into her bone-armor.

"Oh," she blurted out.

"Manus might have come in handy," Simon said. Nemesis looked taken aback.

"Did goth-boy just tell a joke?" she asked. "Damn, you've come a long way kid."

"Not intentional," Simon admitted.

"You're right," Bella said. She made a hand-gesture, and Manus's hands flew back to her, forming her bone armor. At the same time, the portal to her Conclave vanished. "I forgot all about Manus." She grimaced, kicking herself mentally. "I need to do better if I'm going to save Gid…"

She had the sudden feeling that she was outside of her own body, kicking herself in the belly with a ghostly foot. As soon as the feeling came, it left her…and she gasped, doubling over and clutching her belly.

"What's wrong?" Kanja asked, putting a hand on Bella's shoulder.

"Are you okay?" Simon added.

"I'm…okay," Bella answered, straightening up. "Man, that was weird."

"Sure was," Nemesis agreed. Bella turned to her.

"You felt it?"

"I did," the dragon confirmed. "What the hell was that?"

"I…don't know," Bella confessed. "I was just thinking about how I'd failed to use Manus, and…I kicked myself."

Eyebrows went up all around.

"I mean *mentally* kicked myself," Bella clarified. "But then I felt like I was outside of my body, like a spirit…and that I was *literally* kicking myself."

Simon frowned.

"That's the same feeling I got when I punched you in the shoulder," he recalled. "Right after you drank that potion."

"What potion?" Nemesis demanded.

Bella explained the potion she'd painted, and Kanja's eyes widened.

"I think the potion is doing the same thing to you that it does to others," the Sculptor realized. "When other people hurt you, they feel like they're hurting themselves. They're putting themselves in your shoes."

"Right…" Bella replied.

"So when *you* hurt yourself…even emotionally…it feels like you're *literally* hurting yourself."

Bella's eyes widened, and she put a hand to her mouth.

"Oh!" she exclaimed. "I think that's it!"

"Well it's annoying, so quit it," Nemesis ordered.

"Aren't *I* supposed to be your master?"

"You're my creator," Nemesis retorted. "Totally different."

Bella sighed, giving her Familiar a withering look.

"Missed you so much," she grumbled.

"Anyway, I'm here," Nemesis declared, spreading her wings out for a bit, then folding them on her back. "So now we can save your daddy."

Bella smiled.

"Thanks," she replied. She leaned in again, embracing Nemesis by wrapping her arms around the dragon's lower neck. Nemesis hugged her back.

"You're welcome girl."

Bella buried her face in Nemesis's chest-armor, feeling another wave of shame come over her. For all the terrible things she'd told the dragon. She had the sudden sensation of being outside of her body again, punching herself in the back over and over.

Quit beating yourself up, Nemesis chided.

"I'm sorry," Bella blurted out. The admission brought on a fresh wave of tears. "I'm so sorry."

"I know," Nemesis murmured.

They held each other for a long while, until Bella could cry no more. Still, she held on to Nemesis, her dragon. The companion she'd wanted since she was a girl, who she'd drawn thousands of times over. Her dragon, strong and fierce, with a mind of its own. Like her mother.

"I love you," Bella whispered, clutching on to Nemesis's long neck.

"Love you too."

Bella took a deep breath in, then disengaged from her Familiar, wiping her tears from her face.

"You shouldn't," she countered, lowering her gaze. "You were right. This is all my fault." She took a deep breath in. "I broke my promise, and it got Dad hurt. And…"

She stopped, the sensation of herself beating herself coming to her again. It was so jarring – and made it so obvious what she was doing, hurting herself emotionally – that it forced her to stop. Still, she forged on with the thought.

"And I got the White Dragon killed. And all the artists. And…"

She swallowed past a lump in her throat, shaking her head wordlessly.

"Maybe," Nemesis replied.

"No, I did," Bella insisted. "I distracted Gideon. He was beating Craven until I came down."

"True."

"And now he's gone. And…"

Her voice cracked, and she stopped, unable to continue.

"We'll get him back," Nemesis promised. "I've got a plan."

Bella frowned, jerking her gaze up to meet Nemesis's. She dared to hope.

"Really? You do?"

"I wouldn't lie to you," Nemesis pointed out. "Too much work."

"What's the plan?" Kanja piped in.

"Well, you're a Necromancer, right?" Nemesis told Bella. "Petrusa should help you then. She promised to protect you."

"Already tried that," Bella muttered, shaking her head grimly. "She refused to lift a finger for me…or Mom."

"Damn," Nemesis swore. "Bitch is *cold*."

"Tell me about it."

"What about the Dragonkin?" Nemesis pressed. "They can help."

"No," Bella replied. "They've suffered enough. I won't let them destroy themselves by going against the Pentad."

"Well damn," Nemesis grumbled, crossing her arms over her chest. "There goes my plan."

"It's okay," Bella reassured. "We have a plan." She summarized it quickly for Nemesis, who glanced at Rodo when it was done.

"So Mouthball here is gonna save Gideon by just…rolling out of the capitol?"

"Right."

"Then what?" she pressed. "The Pentad's going to chase us all across the country for this stunt. We'll be wanted fugitives for the rest of our lives."

"We already are," Kanja pointed out.

"Granted," Nemesis conceded. "Guess we don't have a choice. Alright. So we use that hole-thing to get in, the Gemini wreak havoc, Bella kills herself, Luna, Myko, and Mouthball get Gideon, and Simon…?"

"I direct the Gemini," Simon answered.

"Right," Nemesis stated. "So what do *I* do?"

"You can be our eyes in the sky," Bella offered. "We'll need to have advance warnings about where the Pentad's forces are."

"I can do that."

"Alright," Bella stated. "We have a plan."

"What about that dragon?" Nemesis asked, gesturing at the remains of the blue dragon they'd battled. "If it knew about us, the Pentad might."

"I don't think so," Kanja replied. "I think it was the bird-thing we saw circling overhead in Anywhere, when we looked out over Centrum. Probably just a scout that was checking out what we were."

Myko barked suddenly, making everyone jump a little. The giant wolf was staring at something in the distance, in the opposite direction of Centrum. Bella followed his gaze, peering into the darkness, but couldn't see anything.

"What is it boy?" she asked.

Myko's body stiffened…but his eyes were bright, his tongue lolling out of his mouth. A moment later, something appeared out of the darkness. Something utterly unexpected.

A disembodied hand holding a very familiar cane.

It levitated up to them, stopping before Myko, who *wuffed* at it.

"What the…" Nemesis began.

And then Bella saw that the hand wasn't a hand at all. It was Gideon's magical glove, holding his cane. Her eyes widened.

"Oh!" she blurted out, her heart soaring. "It's Gideon's glove!"

And if Gideon's glove was still active, that meant the Painter was controlling it from within his prison…which meant he was still alive. Not only that, it meant that they were on the right track. It could lead them straight to Gideon himself, and when it did, Gideon would have his trusty weapon again!

"Wasn't expecting that," Nemesis admitted.

"We could use a helping hand," Kanja stated. Bella gave the woman a look.

"You and Grandpa with the puns," she grumbled. Kanja gave a rueful smile.

"I've been spending a lot of time with him," she explained apologetically.

"Alright, we ready to do this thing?" Nemesis interjected.

"Wait, I don't think Floppy Disc is going to be big enough to fit Rodo through," Bella realized. "I'll have to go back with Simon and paint a canvas that'll be big enough to fit him in. After that, I think I'll be ready. And you guys?"

Kanja and Simon nodded. Myko *wuffed*, and Goo jiggled stiffly, still a bit cold from being flash-frozen. Cain's eye-sockets glowed brightly.

"Ready as I'll ever be!" the skull exclaimed.

Bella smiled, patting his skull affectionately. Then she took a deep breath in, facing the mirrored dome of Centrum. Millions of lights swarmed around it, reflecting brilliantly against the darkness of the night sky. She squared her shoulders, clenching her fists at her sides.

"All right guys," she declared. "Gideon's counting on us. We can do this!"

Chapter 29

The sun was just starting to peek above the horizon in the distance, the mirrored dome of Centrum shimmering with the fading magical lights swarming around it, drawn to its surface like moths to a flame. As Bella, Simon, Goo, Myko, Nemesis, and Gideon's magical glove – and an army of Gemini – drew closer to that dome, the magical firefly-lights danced around them as well. They were, Bella found, utterly without mass, and could pass through her flesh with ease. Which of course meant that they could not be brushed away, or affected by wind. An excellent property, for they could not be pulled away from their duty of illuminating the massive dome.

And massive it was.

For with the utter flatness of the great lawn extending for miles all around Centrum, it'd been impossible for Bella to know how far away she'd been from the dome, or have any sense of perspective or scale to compare the dome with. But up close it was utterly gigantic, easily a thousand feet tall or more, and many miles in diameter.

Large enough to fit a city in.

At long last, they reached the dome, close enough to touch it. High above, the nearest sky-bridge entered the dome, leading to a mirrored door.

"Okay," Bella stated. "Guess this is it. So we send the Gemini in, let them wreak havoc, and have Myko lead us to Gideon. Once we get Gideon, we put him in Rodo, then escape and meet back in the Underground. Then we can go back to Castle Under and meet up with Grandpa and Kanja," she continued. The Sculptor – being of little use in battle – had left through the Underground to go back to Castle Under. "Any questions?"

No one had any.

Myko whined, and Bella glanced at the wolf, surprised to hear the sound. For Myko rarely whined…or made much in the way of noise at all.

"What's wrong?" she asked.

Myko turned to Gideon's animated glove, still clutching his magical cane. He whined again, turning back to Bella.

"Is it Gideon?" she asked.

Myko *wuffed.*

"Is he in trouble?" she pressed.

Another *wuff.*

"We need to hurry," she stated, her heart pounding in her chest. The thought of Gideon being hurt – or worse – made her feel sick to her stomach.

"Is Gideon in the Plane of Reflection or in the original world?" Simon asked Myko. Myko shook his head at the former and *wuffed* at the latter. "We should go back to the original world then," Simon said. "Myko will be able to sense Gideon's location better if they're in the same plane."

Bella nodded, and they all stepped into the mirrored dome…and found themselves back in the original world. Bella pulled Floppy Disc out of her chest-painting, then placed it on the mirrored wall before them. And to her relief, it didn't pass through into the Plane of Reflection, but rather created a hole in the dome, revealing a dark tunnel beyond. Gideon's glove – still carrying his cane – zoomed through the hole immediately, then stopped just beyond it, staying to one side.

"Simon, the Gemini," Bella prompted. Simon inclined his head, turning to the nearest mirrored soldier.

"Attack," he ordered, pointing at the hole.

The Gemini sprinted at it, leaping through one-by-one in a continuous stream. Thousands upon thousands of them, pouring into Centrum. With the sun already starting to rise, it wouldn't be long before the capitol was well-lit…enough so that the Gemini could continue multiplying. They could form an army of millions…an army that even the Pentad would struggle to defeat. Not for the first time, Bella found herself in awe of Simon's creativity. Such a simple concept, but in practice, absolutely devastating.

The more creative you are, the more powerful your magic will be.

Bella took a deep breath in, vowing in that moment to hone her craft, so that she might one day match Simon's ability.

Focus, she told herself. She felt jittery, the urge to shove past the Gemini and go through Floppy Disc into Centrum nearly overwhelming. Gideon was there, after all, and he was in trouble.

And the longer they waited…

"Myko, I'll ride you," Bella stated, putting a hand on the wolf's neck. Myko would know exactly where Gideon was, and that meant he could bring Bella there quicker than anyone else.

Myko *wuffed*, lowering himself so that Bella could vault up onto his back. Then he stood, and she gripped his silver collar tightly. It reminded her suddenly of the first time she'd rode him, way back at Blackthorne. She smiled at the memory; it wasn't so long ago, but at the same time, it felt like an eternity.

"Goo, you go alongside us and neutralize any soldiers that try to fight us," Bella ordered. Goo jiggled agreeably, of course.

"And I shall be forever at your side, at the ready!" Cain declared with gusto.

"Thank you Cain," she replied. Then she waited as the Gemini continued to stream into the capitol; it was going to be a while until they were all through. She glanced at Simon, suddenly concerned. With no Painter uniform and no weapons – other than the Gemini – he seemed terribly unprepared.

"Are you going to be okay…like that?" she asked him. He gave her a questioning look. "Without weapons, I mean."

"I don't need them," he assured her.

"But what if you're attacked?" she pressed.

"I'll be alright," he promised.

"Are you sure?"

"Yes," he answered, giving her what was supposed to be a reassuring smile. Bella smiled back weakly, turning to watch the Gemini streaming through Floppy Disc. Eventually Simon stopped them. "We'll leave the rest out here," he said. "They'll help us escape back into the Underground afterward."

"But what if the Pentad sees us going into the Underground?" Bella asked. "Then they'd be able to use it to hunt us down."

"If that's a risk, we'll have to escape into the forest instead," Simon replied.

"Right," Bella replied. She took a deep breath, facing Floppy Disc. "Okay, let's go. Goo, want to go first?"

Goo jiggled, then oozed up to Floppy, sliding on through into Centrum. Nemesis followed, and Simon went next, and then it was Bella and Myko's turn.

"Here goes," she muttered to herself…and flattened herself against Myko's back as he stepped through into the capitol.

* * *

Simon stepped through the great dome surrounding Centrum, finding himself standing at the end of a long subterranean tunnel that extended forward into the darkness, ankle-deep in rippling water. Or rather, sewage. Its mud-brown surface was still agitated by the passage of the Gemini, who were already out of sight. But Goo was there, as was Nemesis. The magic glove carrying Gideon's cane floated to one side, apparently waiting for them. Simon glanced back, seeing a dead-end wall behind him, and Myko stepping through the magical hole with Bella on his back.

"Oh," she blurted out, wrinkling her nose at the sludge as Myko stepped into it. For the stink of the tunnel was atrocious, and made it instantly clear where they'd ended up.

"Well, it's not as bad as the Festering Wood," Bella grumbled, retrieving Floppy Disc and putting it back into her chest-painting. Simon smiled. She was right, of course. After his many trips through the Festering Wood, this was nothing. He turned forward then, studying the tunnel. Its ceiling was ten feet up, with rectangular grates every forty feet or so. Dim beams of light cascaded down from the grates at a sharp angle, lighting on the surface of the muck below.

Bella maneuvered Myko up beside him, and he put a finger to his lips. Then he strode forward, leading them down the tunnel. Gideon's glove followed beside Myko, matching pace with the giant wolf.

Simon felt no fear as he walked. Only the gentle presence of Redeemer in his mind, surrounding his consciousness like a warm, cozy blanket.

You can do this, she whispered silently.

He smiled to himself, continuing down the sewer tunnel. It curved rightward, and he followed it, finding another long, straight tunnel ahead. The walls were ornate for a sewer, with drainage pipes pouring sewage out of the carved mouths of lions and other such exotic creatures. The spattering of that drainage reverberated throughout the tunnel.

Onward he went, reaching another turn in the sewer, this time to the left. Past this, there was another long stretch of tunnel, as far as the eye could see.

Sun is up, he noted, the rays passing through the sewer grates overhead clearly brightening. And one of these grates had been opened by the Gemini. For he heard muffled screams echoing in the distance from the surface, undoubtedly the work of his Gemini. He'd told them to go on ahead and wreak havoc in the city to provide a diversion. They'd probably stood on each other's shoulders to get up to the grate, then pulled it free and climbed over each other to the surface.

He'd ordered them to spare innocent civilians. Women. Children. And only to incapacitate, not kill those who fought back. Even the Pentad's soldiers. He could not have more unnecessary deaths on his conscience. No…he *would* not have any more. For Miss Savage – even the Collector – murder had often been the first resort.

For him, it was the last.

That was the difference between himself and the Pentad. The Pentad used its overwhelming power to kill or imprison anyone that disobeyed it. *He* would become powerful enough to not need to.

Don't be a victim like I was, the Collector had implored him. *Be a hero.*

And that meant Simon had to be true to himself…no matter what.

A tap on his shoulder snapped him out of his reverie. Glancing back, he saw Bella astride Myko, leaning in to whisper in Simon's ear.

"Shouldn't Goo go first?" she asked.

He shook his head.

Bella glanced back at Nemesis, who shrugged, and Simon continued forward, ignoring them.

Then one of the stone lion's heads came to life, bursting out of the rightmost wall and smashing into him!

Simon flew to the left, careening into the opposite wall and ricocheting off. He fell onto his back in the shallow water, just as the stone lion – a statue come to life – pounced on top of him.

"Simon!" Bella screamed.

He tried to shove it off of him, but the lion weighed a ton. It opened its maw, lunging at his head…and brought his head all the way into its mouth.

Simon grabbed its upper and lower jaws blindly, pulling them open frantically.

But it was no use.

The lion slammed its powerful jaws shut, and Simon screamed as its dagger-like teeth sank into his neck, crushing his throat with a horrible *crunch.*

The sound blasted through his brain, impossibly loud.

Hot blood welled up in the back of Simon's throat, spilling into his lungs. He choked on it, hearing a horrible *crack* as his spine snapped.

His body went limp, utterly dead. As if it wasn't even there.

And then the lion tore Simon's head off.

Chapter 30

Gideon woke to the sound of footsteps coming down the hallway toward his cell, identical to those he'd heard like clockwork since he'd been imprisoned in Tartarus. The never-ending patrol pattern of his statue-guards, perfectly designed for their role. It was no wonder the Pentad employed statues in almost every role that required such efficiency...and why its businesses tried every method possible to get their human counterparts to behave like them.

But this was impossible, of course. Humans were not statues. They were inefficient by design, naturally suspicious of being controlled. So messy and unreliable in comparison to statues. But what made them messy made them magical.

And what made them magical made them powerful.

Gideon laid on his hot stone cot, staring up at the uneven obsidian ceiling. He heard the footsteps of his guards getting louder as they approached. He waited for them to come and pass as they always did, but instead they stopped...right before his cell.

Gideon sighed, struck by a bittersweet feeling. For he knew that no matter what happened today, this was very likely the last time he'd ever see Centrum, the great capitol of the kingdom he'd spent most of his life serving. And that, whether he lived or died today, last night had been the last time he'd ever see Queen Eldora.

He recalled their kiss, surprised that he felt only a little guilt over it. He'd been under her spell, but that was hardly an excuse. Her power had merely unmasked his feelings for her. Gideon had always had a crush on Eldora, ever since he'd first laid eyes on her. But he knew there was no future in such feelings...and that having them did not in any way reduce his love for Lucia.

It was pure physical attraction, nothing more. And if he lived through this – and if Lucia came back to life – he would immediately confess his mistake.

"Get up," a harsh voice ordered from just beyond his cell door.

Gideon obeyed, sitting up and swinging his legs over the side of the stone slab. The backs of his knees were slick with sweat from the constant heat, and there were little red bumps all over his skin. Prickly heat, an itchy, painful rash from constant sweat. Lava and fire were discomfort enough, but it was the little ways that Hell tortured him that made it special.

He saw two prison guards standing before his cell; one of them unlocked the door, swinging it open.

"Come forward."

Again, he obeyed, stepping out of his cell and stopping before the guards. They had no fear of him, of course. Without hands, he was harmless...or so they assumed.

"You have hereby been summoned to stand trial at the High Court in the Palatium," the guard declared. The guard turned, striding down the hallway, and the other one prodded Gideon.

"Follow him," he ordered.

Gideon followed the first guard, and the other guard followed behind him. Down the long hallway they went. A hallway devoid of color, save for Gideon's red prison uniform. All prisoners wore red, of course. The color of blood...the price he was to pay. For the colors of the Pentad were red and gold, blood and money.

And in his case, Queen Eldora demanded blood.

Violence was true power, after all. The threat of violence was enough to pacify most. A few armed soldiers could hold back a crowd of hundreds, or even thousands, though if that crowd were to fight back, it would surely triumph.

The crowd, of course, almost never did.

Gideon followed the guard in front of him, turning rightward down another corridor. But his movements were automatic, his mind far away. For he felt not only Myko's presence nearby – mere miles away – but also his magical glove. Both in Centrum, within the mirrored dome that protected it.

He smiled to himself, knowing that Bella must have found a way through Centrum's first defense.

Clever girl, he thought.

He could also sense them coming toward him. Slowly but surely. He grimaced, knowing that this would complicate things. As proud and touched as he was that his daughter had come for him, he also knew that she'd put herself in terrible danger.

It was a familiar feeling, the same fear he'd experienced when Bella had decided to sign the contract with Petrusa. A feeling of loss, and a loss of control. For while he'd been with Bella, he could protect her. But when she'd gone off to become a Necromancer, to follow in her mother's footsteps...

Bella was, he realized, becoming a woman. And that meant he had to let her make her own decisions. Thus far she'd surprised him at every turn, proving resourceful beyond his wildest expectations. He'd tried to stop her from battling the Collector, and yet she'd been the one to defeat the man. He'd tried to protect her from Petrusa, but Bella had emerged stronger than ever. He'd been terrified to let her fight Miss Savage and Simon, yet she'd won the day even then.

You underestimate her, he chided himself. No, he'd failed to *trust* her. He hadn't been there for Xander, and Xander had died because of it. So he'd tried desperately to make up for it by protecting Bella from anything that might harm her. But if he never let her take risks, never let her make her own decisions…

He *had* to trust her. To let go, and surrender control so that she could truly live.

And that, he knew as he followed the guard through the hallways of Tartarus, was the endgame of parenthood. The great letting go. Developing trust that Bella would be okay. That she would be able to solve her own problems.

That she didn't need him anymore.

Bittersweet, that revelation.

But Gideon knew better than most that the greatest magic required a certain letting go. A trust that things would turn out alright. He started each painting with that trust, that each brushstroke would bring him closer to the finished product. And that it would be worthy of his effort.

Bella, like a painting, was no different. And despite his trepidation, he realized with sudden clarity that he did trust her.

So it was that Gideon Myles made his way through the hallways of Tartarus, a prisoner only in the minds of those who thought him imprisoned. For he was, for the first time in a very long time, utterly free.

What happened next would happen, because of his best efforts…and despite them.

* * *

Gideon was escorted to the foot of the great stairway that led forward and upward, out of Hell and into Centrum. He followed his guard up the stairs, suffering the heat from the flames flickering behind the pitted walls on either side. At length, he reached the top of the stairs, effectively regurgitated into the cavernous throat of the obsidian demon's head. He strode across its forked tongue, passing beneath its fangs to emerge into the dim light beyond. For the sun had only just peeked over the horizon far in the distance, casting its rays across the city of Centrum.

The guard ahead of him led Gideon through the gate beyond, signaling for him to stop as the gate closed. There, standing before Gideon, was

General Craven, a red-uniformed courier beside him. The wide golden street leading to the entrance to the Palatium in the distance gleamed in the light of the rising sun. Guards lined the street on either side, blocking a crowd of citizens from stepping on to the street. A crowd that would continue to grow, for the citizens of the Pentad were eager to witness the drama of the kingdom's greatest Painter falling from grace.

Holding his head high, he ignored them all, keeping his eyes glued on Craven.

The mob, waiting for spectacle. Demanding blood, as mobs inevitably did. They wanted to see him defeated, repentant. They wanted him to internalize the verdict they'd bestowed upon him.

Guilty.

They would have to live with disappointment…a common feeling after the carriage of "justice." For no amount of blood and gold could bring lasting happiness or peace. Living according to one's nature was the only way to achieve that…and by following one's conscience.

Gideon knew it…and he knew that Eldora did too. Which was why he had already found peace…and she never would.

"Come prisoner," Craven growled, staring down at Gideon. Nearly four feet taller, he towered over the humans around him. Gideon gazed up at the living statue calmly, noting a subtle ripple at Craven's jawline.

Interesting.

Craven turned, striding down the wide road toward the Palatium in the distance. Gideon followed, a half-dozen guards and Craven's courier trailing behind him. Toward the Palatium they went, to Gideon's morning trial. The High Court was within the palace, and convened only for the most important of trials. The five highest-ranking lords and ladies in the Pentad served as its judges.

And given that they served the queen, they were hardly impartial.

Ahead, an orchestra stood on either side of the wide street, musicians with instruments at the ready. As he passed them by, the guards allowed them onto the street, and the musicians fell in behind him, and began to play. Drums *thumped* in a grim marching rhythm, wind and string instruments joining in soon after.

Gideon felt his footsteps matching the beat, his heart pounding in his chest. A bolt of fear struck him, and he did his best to ignore it, knowing that it was the magic of the music. Far inferior to that of Miss Savage, a wild creature of enormous power. Which was unsurprising; the Pentad rigorously controlled what the musicians could play, and the Flow merely trickled to those so constrained.

Creativity was what happened when one *gave up* control. When one relaxed, letting the Flow take over…and seeing what magic sprung forth from it. It was about letting go, not focusing. It was about flexibility, not rigidity.

And thus most of the artists the Pentad trained were mediocre at best. Like plants in tiny pots, whose roots had never been allowed to spread out and grow. Stunted, constrained.

If it hadn't been for Thaddeus, Gideon might have ended up the same.

He smiled as he followed Craven down the street toward the great mall in front of the Palatium, the great crimson tower silhouetted by the sun rising behind the palace. The stares and jeers of the crowd faded from his awareness. He pictured Thaddeus's mansion in Centrum, the one Gideon had gone to when he was a little boy. A poor boy from the country, wide-eyed at the riches and wonders of the capitol city. That had been four hundred and fifty-four years ago, when Gideon had been eight.

And unlike the riches around Thaddeus, the man – old even then – had been just the same as he was the last time Gideon had seen him. As if magic itself had decided to come down to earth to live for a while.

Four and a half centuries, Gideon had lived One day leading on to the next, a life longer than he would have ever dreamed of as a child.

And today, very soon, his life might end.

They reached the wide golden stairs that led up to the mall, and Craven ascended them, his metallic boots *clanging* with each step. Gideon walked behind the general, ignoring the eyes of the crowd as he walked, until at last he and Craven stepped into the entrance to the great palace. A huge stone archway leading to a wide tunnel into the base of the tower, white stone statues of armored soldiers crossing swords overhead. Beyond which were a pair of golden double-doors guarded by twin statues of fierce-looking female warriors wielding long spears.

The doors opened before Craven, and the general strode through.

Gideon followed behind, knowing full well that the statues guarding the tunnel and the door were alive. That they were aware of him, and would strike in an instant to kill him if provoked. The entire city was filled with similar statues, every one of them a work of art…and a deadly guardian of the Pentad. The most fearsome guardian of all was not a statue, however. It was the gift Gideon had given Craven, who had in turn given it to the queen.

He pictured the golden snake eating its own tail, clinging tightly to Eldora's finger.

Extinctio.

Not for the first time, he regretted having parted with it. He himself had little use for a creation capable of so much destruction, but in the wrong hands…

He only hoped Eldora possessed the restraint to refrain from using it.

Craven led Gideon through the grand foyer of the palace, a large room with a domed white and gold ceiling. A huge golden chandelier hung from it, one that had been carved to look like it was made entirely of small golden scarabs. Scarabs that, Gideon knew, would come to life if an intruder managed to enter the palace, devouring whoever dared violate the sanctity of the Palatium.

Something that, in his lifetime, had never happened.

Craven turned left down a long hallway that curved gently to the right, reaching double-doors of black and white. The entrance to the High Court. He stopped before them, taking a deep breath in, then letting it out.

It's a game, he told himself. *A sham.*

There would be no justice here. Merely state-sponsored violence. They had to make an example of him, so that the Pentad's control over their artists would not be questioned. So that other artists did not dare make the same "error" that Gideon had made.

None of it matters, he reminded himself.

And then the double-doors opened.

"Enter the High Court, prisoner," Craven commanded. "Receive your judgement."

Gideon squared his shoulders, knowing that his inner calm would soon be tested. That this trial would be designed to destroy his reputation and smear him as a great villain. To execute a man required dehumanizing him first. One could not murder an ordinary man.

They had to turn him into a monster first.

Chapter 31

"Shouldn't Goo go first?"

Simon blinked, seeing Bella standing behind him, having leaned in to whisper in his ear. Nemesis was right behind her, and Goo and Myko behind them.

He paused, then nodded.

"Good idea," he replied.

His suit sent him not words, but merely a reassuring feeling, as it did every time he it gave him a second chance. For Redeemer's power was such that anything he did – or failed to do – that caused his friends or himself to suffer a horrible fate created an opportunity for a second chance. A chance at redeeming himself by doing something different.

A chance at stopping another dark tower from forming in his Memory Lane.

Simon spotted the lion's head carved in the wall of the tunnel to his right. If he died again within the same time frame as the first time, he would lose his second chance, and there would be no other. He would be dead for good…and his friends might join him. Such was the limitation of Redeemer, that she could only offer second chances.

It would have to suffice.

Goo surged forward…and Simon saw color spread across the lion-statue's face, its eyes going from stony gray to bright green. Those eyes blinked, then turned to focus not on Goo, but on *him.*

Simon threw himself backward, just as the living statue burst out of the wall, flying right at him.

The beast missed Simon by inches, the breeze of its passage whipping through his hair.

"Myko!" he heard Bella cry.

A beam of silver light shot right at the lion, even as the lion slid through the sewage into the opposite wall, slamming face-first into it. Myko collided with the living statue, shoving it backward.

And Nemesis flew overhead, landing right on the lion and clawing it with her talons.

The lion roared, scrambling to its feet and swiping at Nemesis with one big paw. Nemesis flew to the side, tumbling into the shallow water with a splash.

The lion turned to Simon, leaping right at him!

Gideon's glove zipped between them, tapping the lion with its cane…and stopping it instantly. Goo surged between them, plunging the lion into his gelatinous flesh.

"Get back!" Bella urged, grabbing Simon's shoulder and pulling him back from the lion. But there was no need; Goo engulfed the living statue like an amoeba. And while at first it thrashed madly within its green gooey prison, soon it went limp…and then shifted back to its statue-form, suspended within Goo.

"Whew," Bella said. "That was close. You okay?"

"I am," Simon answered.

"You sure?" she pressed, eyeing his suit. It was – despite the splashing of sewage – perfectly clean.

"Let's go," he prompted, continuing forward. Bella splashed up to walk at his side. "We should have Goo carry us. If any more of those things attack, he can protect us."

Goo obliged, wrapping around them and lifting them off the ground, holding them waist-deep atop himself. Their heads were, as a result, only a couple of feet below the ceiling. Simon saw Bella's face relax as fine black mist came out of her, sucking into Goo. A useful power, to be able to absorb negative emotions.

But Simon felt no different within Goo than he had previously, and no black mist came from him.

He thought back to Percy, when the ancient artist had brought him to Memory Lane. How Simon's black tower had dominated his view for so much of his life.

All along, all he'd needed to do was turn away from it…and face the light.

This is my second chance, he knew. The chance Percy had revealed to him. A life basking in the light instead of sulking in the darkness. A life spent building a great lighthouse so tall and bright that its glorious light would shine on every memory thereafter.

He felt Redeemer squeeze his torso reassuringly, her pure white glow banishing the darkness around her. She always squeezed him when he'd passed the critical period after she'd worked her magic. When enough time had passed for her give another second chance.

Wherever you go, I'll be with you, Redeemer assured him. *You'll always have a second chance with me.*

* * *

Bella's heart hammered in her chest, the near-miss with Simon and the lion still affecting her. But as soon as Goo wrapped around her, lifting her up in his cool embrace, her heart slowed. Her stress and anxiety left her, even her concern for Gideon fading away.

Until she felt nothing but utter calmness. Tranquility.

Peace.

Within Goo, nothing mattered. It was a glorious feeling, like a great weight lifted from her shoulders. So she found herself perfectly content to have him carry her and the others through the sewers. She turned to glance at Simon, who was eyeing the statues on the rightmost wall. The ones like the lion, with water pouring from their mouths into the sewer.

He blinked rapidly, as if surprised.

"Stop," he ordered.

Goo halted.

Simon pointed to the right wall, at a carving of a huge spider on it. It was like the others, but with no water pouring from it.

"Goo, you know what to do," Bella stated, patting Goo's surface. And Goo did. He reached green tentacles toward the spider…just as it changed color, jumping from the wall at them.

Bella watched serenely as the spider was stopped – and engulfed – by Goo's translucent flesh, transforming back to its statue-form as it asphyxiated. And, absorbing its anger and fear, Goo became ever-larger, able to fill the entire width of the tunnel.

"Continue," Simon prompted.

Goo flowed forward, but at the same time, he spread out enough that his sides touched the tunnel walls. Which, Bella realized, was quite brilliant. For whichever of the carvings was a living statue, they could not transform and attack without immediately being sucked up into Goo. As a result, Goo could travel much faster, without any fear of ambush.

So they zoomed down the sewer tunnel with considerable speed, rounding another corner, then coming to a fork in the sewers. Myko guided them rightward, then rightward at another fork. And then leftward.

Then Myko whined from behind Bella, and she turned to see him looking upward at one of the sewer grates.

"Stop Goo," she ordered. Goo did so, and Bella looked up through the grate. She couldn't see anything other than blue sky, of course. "Should we go up here?" she asked Myko.

Myko *wuffed.*

Goo contracted his body, becoming taller in the process, and lifted them all up to the ceiling. He extended a tendril through one of the gaps in the grate, wrapping around it and pushing it upward and to the side. He lifted Bella up out of the sewer then, and onto the surface of Centrum.

A wide city street greeted her, made of gold-colored bricks. White paved sidewalks flanked the street on either side, and beyond those rose tall, stately buildings at least eight stories high. These were shaped somewhat like lipstick containers, with angular roofs. And each building was colored either red, gold, silver, or white. High above, Bella could see the brightening blue sky, without any indication of the mirrored dome she knew surrounded the city. The street was utterly packed with Gemini…and no one else.

But more than a few puddles of blood stained the golden street.

Bella grimaced, missing the peace that Goo offered. But not caring about anything – having complete and utter peace, regardless of what was happening – seemed suddenly terrible indeed. More terrible than feeling fear or anger or disappointment. She realized with sudden clarity that her negative emotions were her body talking to her. And that she'd been desperately ignoring its message. Just to feel comfortable. To feel safe…at the price of not feeling anything at all.

She'd been using Goo to run from her pain. But she couldn't outrun something that was inside of her.

Bella took a deep breath in, lifting her gaze to the Gemini. They were actively multiplying, even as Myko rose from the sewers, then Simon, and finally Nemesis. Goo was next, oozing up onto the street. The statues inside of him were gone, however; he'd deposited them in the sewer.

"Should we ride Goo?" Simon asked.

"Not me," Bella answered. "I'll ride Myko, and you can ride Goo if you want. Nemesis, fly high and provide surveillance. If bad guys are coming for us, we'll need advance warning."

"You got it girl," Nemesis replied.

"Oh," Bella added before Nemesis leapt up to fly away. "And when the time comes, I'll need you to kill me."

Nemesis smirked, her red eyes flashing.

"It'd be my pleasure."

"Um…thanks?" Bella grumbled.

Nemesis cackled, then leapt up into the air, flying away. Cain the cane's green eye-sockets flashed at Bella's hip.

"I don't believe I like that dragon terribly much," he confessed.

"She's hard to like," Bella agreed. "But worth the effort. Most of the time." She turned to Myko then, who lowered himself to the street. "Okay Myko," she prompted, vaulting up onto his back and holding on to his collar. "Lead the way."

Myko broke out into the wolf equivalent of a sprint, bounding down the street. The Gemini army charged at either side, and Goo carried Simon from behind. In this way, they made it quickly to an intersection, and Myko turned right down a much wider street. One that led all the way to the heart of the city.

Bella gawked.

From this vantage point, she could see down the wide road, which led to a massive tower in the center of the city, miles away. An enormous red metallic tower, surrounded by a circle of five shorter golden towers. Perhaps a half-mile from these towers was a huge black stone demon's head surrounded by a tall fence. And on this street, and on the streets running perpendicular to it, were thousands upon thousands of Gemini. Glittering soldiers battling men in red and gold armor, and statues, some of them actively stepping down from their pedestals along the sidewalks and before building entrances to join the fray.

As Bella watched, a line of bat-like gargoyles crouching on rooftops a few blocks away came alive, twisting their heads around to face her with red, glowing eyes. Then they stood, spreading their wings and leaping off the rooftops, flying right toward her!

"Myko!" Bella cried, yanking back on his collar.

He leapt straight up into the air, twisting around to face away from the gargoyles, then shot away as a beam of pure silver light, pulling Bella with him. Her belly flip-flopped as she accelerated, shooting mere yards over the army of Gemini. The mirrored soldiers parted beneath them, and Myko rematerialized, landing on the street.

Behind them, the gargoyles swooped down after Bella…and then Goo sent a big wall of green flesh upward to intercept them. They struck him, then stuck like flypaper, falling headlong into the bulk of his body. Simon had luckily already managed to change position within Goo, one of the gargoyles smashing into where he'd been moments before.

The gargoyles thrashed madly as Goo enveloped them, their struggles slowing, then stopping as they ran out of air. They turned back into statues, suspended within Bella's ever-growing creation. He was as long as an 18-wheeler now, and as wide as a small house.

Beyond Goo, the war raged on, all the way to the center of the city. Gemini everywhere, battling armies of ground soldiers. Thousands of men riding flying horses blanketed the sky like a massive swarm of birds, similar to the ones she'd seen back at Havenwood.

Bella stared at them, then lowered her gaze to the building in the center of the city. The crimson tower surrounded by a circle of five shorter golden towers.

"Is that it?" she asked Myko. "Is that where Gideon is?"

He *wuffed.*

A bright light shot outward from near the tower, arcing through the air toward the Gemini. It split into a dozen lights, then slammed into the Gemini a few hundred feet from Bella, exploding on impact. Thousands of the mirrored soldiers shattered instantly, their shards flying in all directions.

Painters are coming, she heard Nemesis warn through their bond. *Lots of them.*

More magical missiles arced toward the Gemini, but this time there were *dozens* of them. And these split into over a hundred lights in midair, falling to the Gemini army in the streets and exploding. The missiles demolished the Gemini, but had no effect on the Pentad's soldiers, or its buildings.

But even as the Gemini re-formed, a massive army of gold and red-armored soldiers were amassing between them and the center of the city. Between Bella and Gideon.

Bella stared at the massive army, and at the Pentad's swarms of aerial defenses. Her resolve wavered.

There's too many of them, she realized.

Snap out of it, Nemesis ordered, swooping down to land at her side. She put a clawed hand on Bella's shoulder. "Come on girl, stay with us."

Bella swallowed, shaking her head mutely.

"We can do this," Nemesis insisted. "What would Gideon say?"

"The more creative I am, the more powerful my magic will be," Bella recited.

"Right," Nemesis agreed. "You're the third-best Painter I've ever met, you know." Bella gave her a look.

"You only *know* three Painters," she retorted.

"What about those Havenwood hacks?"

Bella couldn't help but smile.

"Granted."

"You're the granddaughter of Thaddeus Birch, the greatest Writer in the world," Nemesis declared. "Daughter of Gideon Myles, the greatest Painter. Daughter of Lucia, assassin-Necromancer...and one *hell* of a badass bitch," she added with a smile.

"Also granted," Bella conceded with a smile of her own.

"You can do this," Nemesis insisted. "You're kinda badass yourself. Problem is, you don't know it yet...and neither do they," she added, turning to gesture at the Pentad's army in the distance.

Bella took a deep breath in, letting it out slowly. Then she squared her shoulders.

"Not yet," she replied. "But they're about to."

Chapter 32

The High Court was a large room, ornate beyond description. It boasted dark wood-paneled walls with rich, elegant carvings, and golden statues that stood before them on opulent pedestals. There was a domed ceiling of the same rich wood, designed to carry sound throughout the court. Rows upon rows of benches faced a raised floor where the five Justices of the High Court sat in gilded chairs behind great wooden desks, facing the audience of aristocrats who'd come to witness the trial.

And the audience packed the courtroom, such that the benches were completely full. All of them standing at attention, watching him.

To Gideon's practiced eye, it was all art. Art that told a story of wealth and power, of the grave importance of this place. The judges' position, higher than that of anyone else in the courtroom, conveyed their superiority. As if they were gods glaring down at the mere mortals before them. The grand domed ceiling served to make the prisoner – and the audience – seem small in comparison. Made them feel as if the entire process was larger than any one of them. Even its acoustics, designed to magnify the voices of the judges, conveyed their power.

For in the animal kingdom, those who were the loudest held the most power, and struck fear into their fellows.

A wide path extended from the double-doors at the entrance of the court, leading to two desks placed before the raised floor upon which the judges presided, one to the right, one to the left.

Gideon Myles calmly strode down the path, not so fast as to seem nervous or rushed, but not so slow as to seem cocky.

He felt the eyes of the audience upon him, following him as he made his way toward the front of the courtroom. He ignored their gazes, continuing forward. This too was intentional. As the prisoner, he came into the courtroom last, so that every eye could see him. So that he could serve as a spectacle, a man under display. Every movement scrutinized, every eye judging him even before the judges did.

Few would believe that an innocent man could walk down this path. That such great men and women, presiding in this great and important room, could possibly be capable of making a mistake. Indeed, in his red prison uniform, the costume of a guilty man, few would see him as anything but.

It was art, all of it. A story told without words. And people, Gideon knew all too well, thought in stories. Not in facts or figures, not with reason. The story was everything.

Stories were *power.*

At length Gideon made his way to the two desks. A guard stood between them, gesturing for Gideon to stand before the rightmost desk.

He obeyed, facing the judges.

They were three men and two women, Lords and Ladies of the Pentad. The highest-ranking aristocrats from each of the five major cities. It was rare for them to be called into Centrum for such a trial, so important were their usual duties. And even rarer for the High Court to judge the actions of a single criminal. For they typically presided over cases of far greater import.

In this instance, Queen Eldora had made an exception.

The mere fact that his case was being judged in the High Court was a message. There would be no chance of appeal. Their judgement was final. If they deemed him guilty, his execution was assured. They were judge, jury, and executioner.

It's a sham, he reminded himself, feeling the room and its story having their effect on him. Even knowing the illusion did not stop him from being swayed by it. Such was the power of stories, even without the Flow. They exerted tremendous influence, even in the absence of magic.

The Lord in the center of the five was Lord Merkel, the eldest son of the late Lord Merkel who'd been murdered by Miss Savage. Merkel banged his gavel on his desk, and the courtroom went utterly silent.

"We are here today to render judgement on the case of defendant Gideon Myles, former Royal Painter of Centrum, former member of our armed forces, and bounty-hunter for Queen Eldora's Rogue Artist Retrieval division."

He looked down at a paper on his desk with a fierce frown.

"Gideon Myles, you are hereby accused of two counts of treason against queen and kingdom, three counts of aiding and abetting a criminal, one count of illegally mentoring an artist, ten counts of painting without a license, and one count of murder of an artist."

Lord Merkel looked up from his paper, glaring down at Gideon.

"How do you plead?" the man demanded.

Gideon paused. To answer "guilty" would be honest, but it would speed his trial along. He sensed his magical glove within the city now, still miles away.

He needed to stall.

"Not guilty," he answered.

Lord Merkel regarded him with clear disdain.

"We have already received testimony from General Craven," he stated, leaning back in his chair. "His word, of course, is absolute. It is in his nature to be utterly without deceit, wouldn't you agree?"

Gideon said nothing.

"Your murder of Painter Yero, a decorated member of our armed forces…and formerly your friend, or so we thought…is irrefutable," Lord Merkel declared. "The sentence for this alone is death by execution. And yet you plead innocent of this crime?"

Again, Gideon said nothing.

"Clearly you are not only guilty of the crimes you have been accused of," Lord Merkel stated, "…but you are also guilty of lying under oath to the High Court of the Pentad."

Gideon resisted the urge to roll his eyes. He'd never taken an oath, after all. An oversight by the Lords…but it hardly mattered. This was all theatre, of course. A show for the crowd. Any artist would have seen through the veil. But the people…they were so often blind to the mechanisms of manipulation.

"The High Court has reviewed the evidence against you, Gideon Myles," Lord Merkel declared. "Your testimony only confirms our judgement upon you."

Merkel stood then, and the other judges stood as well.

"Lord Trenton, your verdict?"

Lord Trenton glared down at Gideon.

"Guilty," he answered.

The Lady beside him stood.

"Guilty," she replied.

Lord Merkel stood then.

"Guilty," he stated.

The other two judges stood, each delivering a guilty verdict.

"The judgement of the High Court is unanimous," Lord Merkel declared, his voice booming over the crowd. "Gideon Myles, you have been found guilty of murder, treason, and aiding and abetting a criminal. You have been found guilty of painting without a license," he added. "Therefore, it is the duty of the court to sentence you to execution."

There were excited whispers amongst the crowd.

"Given the severity of your crimes," Lord Merkel continued, "…we have decided that your execution will be performed at the Edge of Eternity."

There was a collective gasp amongst the crowd, followed by hushed murmuring. The sentence was the harshest that could be given. A fate far worse than death.

"May you burn in Hell for eternity," Lord Merkel declared.

He banged his gavel on his desk, the sound reverberating throughout the courtroom.

"Court dismissed," he stated. "General Craven, escort the prisoner to Tartarus to await his execution."

"Yes Lord Merkel," Craven replied from the back of the courtroom. He stomped forward, each footstep making the floor tremble, until he reached Gideon. "Come prisoner," he ordered.

Gideon complied, following Craven out of the courtroom. He felt the eyes of the crowd upon him as he made his way out of the room and back into the hallway, and ignored them. Craven led him through the foyer and out of the Palatium, emerging from the tunnel beyond onto the wide golden street leading back to Tartarus. The crowd of people standing on the lawn on either side of the street had grown considerably, thousands upon thousands of citizens standing before two lines of guards holding them at bay.

And as they spotted Gideon emerging from the Palatium, the crowd stirred, talking excitedly amongst themselves.

Gideon ignored them as he walked out onto the great mall before the palace, his eyes not on the people, but on what stood – or rather levitated – ahead. An inky-black blade over six feet long levitating point-down before him, with a golden hilt and crossguard.

Gideon felt a sudden chill in the air as he approached, the all-too-familiar sensation of Temper's aura. A coldness even more pronounced than normal, the icy-cold sensation of utter hatred.

Of death.

But without Yero, Temper could not mirror his master's emotions. His fire, which had burned so brightly in the past, was forever quenched.

"Temper," he stated, inclining his head as he stopped a few yards from the blade.

The Familiar did not move.

"Yero was a good friend," Gideon offered. "He murdered my wife, and threatened my family. I did what I had to do, and I regret having to do so."

Still nothing.

Gideon took a deep breath in, hardly expecting the sword to give him any quarter. To kill a Familiar's Painter…to forever sever the bond between them…was devastating. For perhaps the first time in Temper's existence, he was alone. For a Familiar, that was unimaginable torture.

He could hardly blame the sword. If Gideon were murdered, he would expect Myko to feel no different.

Craven positioned himself beside Temper, staring stonily down at Gideon.

"Face the citizens of the Pentad," he ordered, his deep voice booming over the crowd. "Face those you have been accused of betraying."

Gideon complied, looking beyond Temper, to the two lines of people flanking the wide golden street. A crowd stretching back for nearly half a mile, all the way to the obsidian demon's head at the entrance to Tartarus.

"Gideon Myles, you have been found guilty of painting without a license," Craven declared. "Guilty of aiding a wanted criminal." He paused. "Guilty of treason…and murder."

Gideon felt the air grow even cooler, Temper's aura pulsing behind him.

The crowd *roared.*

"The High Court has rendered judgement upon you," Craven continued. "You will be executed at the Edge of Eternity, doomed to burn in Hell forever."

There was a collective gasp among the crowd, followed by a rousing cheer. The mob, delighting in the suffering of another.

It was as Thaddeus had often told him. People were at their best one-on-one, but in groups, they were often thoughtless and cruel. The magnetism of the collective aligned all in the same emotional direction, and individuals became mere parts of a whole. A fact those in power constantly exploited. For the mob did not invite dissent.

They began to chant.

"Burn in Hell! Burn in Hell!"

Craven turned back to Gideon.

"Follow, prisoner," he commanded. "Face justice at the Edge of Eternity."

Craven strode forward, and Gideon followed behind, stepping down from the mall onto the gilded road. People screamed at him as he passed by, their faces red and filled with hate. Citizens who'd once adored him, who'd lauded him. The same citizens he'd spent most of his life defending.

He'd risked his life for them, time and time again. And at the mere suggestion of guilt, they'd turned on him. A single accusation had erased four centuries of goodwill.

He strode after Craven, his eyes glued to the living statue's giant back. Not for the first time, he felt disgust for his fellow man.

For the mob, there was no redemption. Once someone was branded as evil, they were doomed. And Hell – an eternity of suffering, a punishment out of proportion to any possible crime – could not be just. It was, after all, a place where redemption was impossible. Without redemption, failure was fatal.

We're not worth saving, he thought.

Then he forced himself to think of Thaddeus. Of Bella. Of his wife. *Some* people were worth saving. Those who were a bit more thoughtful. Who dug a bit deeper. Who listened, and took the time to really know someone. People who saw the humanity in others.

And who valued love and forgiveness over hatred. Redemption over judgement.

The shouting and jeering of the crowd faded from his consciousness as he made his way to Tartarus. He lifted his gaze to the morning sky, marveling at the white, puffy clouds against a sea of infinite blue. It was beautiful. It was art, the universe painting a masterpiece on a canvas of itself.

Perhaps the last painting he would ever see.

Then he collided with Craven's back, stumbling backward in surprise. The general had stopped in his tracks, and was staring off into the distance, his right fist clenched at his side. Gideon followed Craven's gaze, looking past the demon's head of Tartarus, all the way to the outskirts of the city miles away.

There, far in the distance, was an army of glittering soldiers.

Charging right toward the center of the city.

Chapter 33

"Okay," Bella stated, eyeing the Pentad's massive army as it marched from the center of the city toward them. "We need a plan."

"Probably should've thought of one *before* you charged in to the most heavily-protected city in the world," Nemesis grumbled. Bella put a hand on her hip, shooting her Familiar a glare.

"What happened to being supportive?" she asked.

"Tried it," Nemesis replied. "Didn't like it."

"God I hate you," Bella muttered. Still, she smiled. "But I love you more."

"Good enough."

"So anyway, it's too risky for us to try to go through that army," Bella stated. "So we need to get around it."

"The sewers may get you closer," Simon pointed out.

"And I can use Floppy Disc to get through any walls," Bella reasoned. "But probably not into the tower itself. They'll have magic that'll stop Floppy from working."

"I'll stay above ground," Simon offered. They both turned to him.

"Why?" Bella asked.

"A distraction," Simon answered. "I can command the Gemini, but I need eyes on them to do it. I'll keep the Pentad busy while you take the sewers to get closer to Gideon."

"But I can't leave you alone," Bella protested. She gestured down the street at the advancing army. "They'll come for you. Painters, statues, soldiers…"

"I'll be fine," he reassured.

"Simon…"

"Trust me," he insisted. "I can do this."

"What if we need your help?" she pressed. He smiled.

"I'll know."

Bella hesitated, staring at him for a long moment. Then she nodded reluctantly.

"All right," she agreed. "But take Goo with you. He can protect you."

Simon nodded back.

"All right," she declared. "Goo, are you okay with that?"

Goo's surface wobbled in the affirmative.

"Okay," Bella said. "Myko, you, me, and Nemesis will go back into the sewers. We'll take a few Gemini with us as bodyguards, and to make the mirrors if we need to switch to the Plane of Reflection. We'll get as close as we can to Gideon, then come to the surface, appear wherever he is, grab him, and then go back to the sewers to escape the way we came."

Everyone nodded, and Myko *wuffed.*

"Any questions?" Bella asked.

No one had any.

She turned to Simon, leaning in and giving him a hug.

"Take care of yourself, okay?" she pleaded.

"I'll take care of *everyone* I love," he promised.

She smiled, brushing a few curly strands of hair from her face. Then she pulled away, facing the open sewer grate nearby.

"I'm a badass," she reminded herself.

"Yeah, no one who's a badass *says* they're a badass," Nemesis pointed out. "Gotta get other people to say it."

"You're the one who said I was," Bella retorted.

"Moment of weakness."

Bella rolled her eyes.

"Just fly me down there," she grumbled. Nemesis complied, leaping up and unfurling her wings. She grabbed Bella's shoulders with her hind-claws, lifting Bella up and then folding her wings to fall through the open sewer grate. Then she spread her wings again, slowing their fall to the sewage below…a bit. Bella landed on her feet with a splash, foul fluid flying everywhere.

"Ugh," Bella muttered, wiping a few drops of questionable gunk from her cheek. "Thanks a lot."

She looked up, seeing Myko looking down at them from above. She and Nemesis moved to the side, and Myko leapt down a moment later, landing nearby with another splash. Bella mounted the big wolf, waiting until a few of the Gemini hopped down to join them. The Gemini, she noted, flipped the facets on their legs around, so that the black side showed…and the sewage water didn't pass into the Plane of Reflection…or vice-versa.

"Okay Myko, lead the way," she prompted.

The Gemini moved to flank them on either side, and Myko trotted down the sewer tunnel, each splash of his paws echoing off the walls. Bella eyed those walls as they traveled, particularly the various carved animal heads protruding from them. Most had water flowing from their mouths, meaning they were unlikely to be living statues. But she spotted one without that flowing water ahead and to the right.

It changed to a jet-black color before her eyes…and leapt right at them!

"Watch out!" she cried

The Gemini burst toward it without fear, shattering in mid-stride to transform into a large mirror. The spider went right into it…and vanished from sight.

The Gemini shattered again, re-forming into individual soldiers.

"Well, that worked," Nemesis remarked.

"On reflection, yes it did," Bella agreed. Nemesis groaned, and Cain chuckled at her side. Myko continued to lead them forward, the Gemini following alongside. Eventually they came to a fork in the tunnel, and Myko immediately chose the rightward path. Down this next tunnel they went, encountering more of the living statue-guardians. And each time those statues came to life, the Gemini sent them right into the Plane of Reflection.

Onward they went, down one tunnel and another, encountering more forks in the maze-like tunnels. And each time, Myko led them confidently, choosing each path without hesitation…until they reached a dead-end.

"Oh," Bella said, staring at the wall.

"Looks like Mutt screwed up," Nemesis mused, clearly enjoying this development. Bella ignored her Familiar, glancing back the way they'd come, then looking down at Myko.

"Are you sure this is the right way?" she asked him.

Myko *wuffed*, trotting up to the wall and pawing it. He glanced back at Bella, his silver eyes gleaming.

"Is there something beyond the wall?" she asked. Another *wuff*. Bella reached into her chest-painting, drawing out Floppy Disc. Then she walked up to the wall, putting the disc on it. A hole appeared there, leading into yet another long sewer tunnel.

Myko turned to Nemesis, his tongue lolling out of his mouth. His eyes were *definitely* twinkling.

"Whatever," Nemesis grumbled, pushing past them and crawling through the hole. The Gemini followed after her, then Myko, then Bella. When she was through, she peeled Floppy Disc from the wall, stuffing it back in her chest-painting and re-mounting Myko. Onward they went…until they reached a second obstacle: a wall of vertical bars. Larger hunks of nasty sewage-sludge were heaped up against it, only the smaller chunks and water able to pass.

Myko stopped before it, looking back at Nemesis.

"Don't look at me, Mutt," the dragon told him. "I ain't fitting through that."

"We'll have to use Floppy again," Bella stated, dismounting from Myko. She walked up to the bars, withdrawing Floppy Disc and placing him on them. But nothing happened.

"Well drat," Cain piped up. "It appears the contraption only works on uninterrupted surfaces."

"No sh…" Nemesis began, but Bella shot her a glare.

"We'll have to find another way," she reasoned. She walked up to the side wall, putting Floppy on it…and saw what looked like a dark basement beyond. Myko peered into it, then shook his head and snorted as if he'd smelled something bad. "Guess not," Bella said, peeling Floppy off and turning back to the bars. "Hmm."

She gazed beyond the bars, at the shadowy tunnel beyond. There were fewer sewer grates on the ceiling, only the occasional beams of light passing down, barely illuminating the tunnel beyond.

Then she had an idea.

"Nemesis," she prompted, turning to her Familiar. "I need your help."

"Go on."

"Can you kill me?" she asked. Nemesis broke out into a big grin.

"After what you said earlier? With *pleasure*."

Bella put her hands on her hips.

"Don't make it too painful," she warned. Nemesis's smile faded.

"Spoilsport," she grumbled.

Then the dragon whipped her tail up to coil around Bella's neck, and squeezed.

Bella grimaced, feeling pressure building rapidly in her face.

God I hate this part, she grumbled silently.

"Shhh," Nemesis chided, putting a clawed finger to Bella's lips. "Let me enjoy this."

Bella rolled her eyes, even as her vision blackened. She felt the world starting to fade away, and reached the moment where her body took over, desperate to live. She reached up, pulling frantically at Nemesis's tail around her throat, trying to pry it free.

And then the world faded away, and there was nothing.

* * *

Luna felt herself split from Lux, her brighter half able to stand in the light of the will-o-wisp, still attracted to Mom's amulet around Lux's neck. Luna resisted the immediate urge to return to her sister, melting into the shadows, then rising from them just beyond the bars. She turned around, smirking at Nemesis and Myko.

"*God* that was easy," she quipped.

Gideon's glove zipped between the bars, still holding his cane. It pointed one finger up and forward. Luna frowned, glancing at Myko.

"Is Gideon's glove pointing to where he is?" she asked.

Myko *wuffed.*

"So he can sense where the glove is, and himself in relation to it," Luna deduced. "Now *that's* going to come in handy."

"The puns," Nemesis groaned.

"Come here," Luna told the glove, gesturing for it to come to her hand. Which did so, flying into her grasp. She reached out with her own magical black glove, pulling a bit of shadow from the ground and wrapping it around the glove as if putting it in a makeshift sack along with Gideon's cane. "Okay, gonna try something," she stated. And then she stepped into the shadow on the wall…and re-emerged a moment later. The cane – and Gideon's glove – were still in the shadow-sack.

She broke out into a satisfied smile.

"Now *that's* what I'm talking about," she stated. She waved Nemesis and Myko – and Lux – away. "You guys go back and play with Simon. I'll do the *real* work."

"You know what?" Nemesis replied. "Kinda hate you."

"Aww, kinda don't care," Luna replied with a wink…and sank into the shadows on the floor.

She felt herself immediately expand, *becoming* the shadows within the vast sewer network. Not all of it, of course, but a good quarter-mile in every direction. She did the psychic equivalent of frowning – for at the moment, she had no mouth – and focused on spreading herself out farther.

To her delight, she did. Only a few yards further, but hey, progress was progress.

She stepped out of the shadows where the tunnel she'd been in forked, then pulled Gideon's glove out of the shadow-sack. On a whim, she put it on her right hand. The glove flexed her fingers, and at first she resisted; but then she relaxed, allowing it to move her. It pointed at the leftmost fork, and at more of an upward angle than before.

"Getting closer," she noted.

Luna stuffed her gloved hand into the sack, then merged into the shadows again, reappearing further down the leftmost tunnel. She repeated the pointing process, and found that the glove was making her point nearly straight up. Merging one more time, she reappeared a hundred or so feet away…and his glove pointed straight up.

"This is it, huh?" she whispered to the glove.

The glove made a fist, nodding at her.

Then it pointed at her shadow-sack, and she opened the sack, allowing the glove to grab Gideon's cane. It held it at the ready, as if she were holding it herself. Strange, to have the glove control her, but if Gideon were truly controlling it, and could fight as well as he normally did…

"Alright Gid," she murmured, looking up. There were no sewer grates overhead, but there were some pipes spilling water into the sewer from the walls. She melted into shadow, extending herself through and up the pipes. One of them led to a series of toilets aboveground, in a bathroom within one of the towers, she had to assume.

Unfortunately, it was well-lit, because she couldn't extend *into* the bathroom itself. Either that or the toilet seats were down.

Definitely not a men's bathroom, then.

"Thought they used canvases as toilets," she mused, remembering what Gideon had told her when Bella had first traveled to Havenwood. "Guess they don't trust lowly people to have live canvases in their homes, huh Gid?"

The glove did not reply.

"Go up that pipe," she ordered it, pointing to the proper one on the wall. "Open the lid and turn off the lights in the bathroom."

The glove shot off her hand, vanishing into the pipe. A minute later, it returned, dripping with water. She hoped.

"Okay, meet you up there," she stated…and melted into the shadows again. She felt herself extend beyond the pipe and into the bathroom, and stepped out of the shadows there, a satisfied smile on her lips.

Boom, she thought.

Gideon's glove was there, floating above some smashed lighting fixtures. It flew up to her right hand, but she yanked her hand away from it.

"Shake off first," she ordered.

It did so, shaking water off itself like a dog, then flew onto her hand. She handed it the cane, then stepped out of the bathroom. There was a short hallway beyond, and beyond that, a large lobby of what resembled a fancy hotel. Big windows looked out onto the city streets, the sun beaming through them. And statues of knights in heroic poses stood on pedestals placed at regular intervals throughout the lobby.

Luna ignored them, her gaze drawn to the large windows. Or rather, what could be seen beyond them.

She saw a large lawn split in two by a wide golden street running parallel to the building. She was, she realized, on the first floor of the one of the five golden towers she'd seen earlier, the ones encircling the taller red tower in the center of the city. The lawn was packed with people, all of them rushing like a crazed mob toward the five golden towers. Hundreds of them reached her building, storming through the entrance and rushing into the lobby. The moment the first of them spilled into the building, the statues on the pedestals came to life, color spreading across their surface.

She ducked back into the hallway just as the statues stepped down from their pedestals, facing the crowd.

"They're coming!" one of the men in the crowd cried at them. "Help us!"

The statues stomped toward the entrance, pushing their way outside. They flanked the entrance, ushering people in.

Crap, she thought. Now she had to get through the statues to get out.

And then Gideon's glove shot off her hand, flying over the crowd and right out the door!

"Hey!" Luna blurted out, watching as the glove zipped over the lawn beyond, zooming toward the golden street with cane in hand.

Two of the statues must have heard her, and turned to eye her suspiciously. They strode toward her, unsheathing their swords.

"Great," she muttered. "Just great."

Chapter 34

General Craven was a seasoned veteran of more wars than most people had ever heard of, much less been in. A thousand years of near-constant warfare had taught him many things. One such lesson was to expect the unexpected. The other was to always have a plan in case the unexpected happened.

So upon spotting the army of faceted soldiers miles away from the city center, somehow having made their way past the dome into the outskirts of Centrum, Craven felt no fear. He did not hesitate.

He just *did.*

For in addition to allowing Queen Eldora to summon him, his helmet allowed him to contact every other living statue in the city, as well as the human guards. And the city's aerial defenses, including the Fire Drake, sister to the great Frost Drake that guarded the land around Centrum's dome. And the Sky Cavalry, a contingent of human soldiers riding winged horses.

With a thought, Craven mobilized them all.

He looked down at Gideon then, standing quite still behind him, the criminal's eyes also on the approaching army of odd soldiers. Gideon did not look surprised, a fact that came as no surprise to Craven.

"Bring the prisoner to Tartarus," he ordered the guards nearby. "Temper, if the prisoner attempts to resist, remove his feet."

The air turned chilly, Temper's aura providing confirmation of the order. Craven turned to Aldo, the courier in a blood-red uniform that had accompanied him. "Return to the Palatium and inform Queen Eldora that Centrum is under attack," he ordered. "Tell her: 'Ecce populus venit de speculo ad recipiendum Gideon. Nos postulo vos mea regina.'"

The courier bowed, then broke out into a sprint back to the palace.

"Go," he commanded Gideon's guards. "I will coordinate the city's defenses and defend the queen."

* * *

Gideon stared at the army of mirrored soldiers in the distance, the same soldiers that had attacked Havenwood and nearly destroyed it. Though his eyes were on the approaching army, his mind was elsewhere…with his glove, ahead and underground, in the sewer tunnels below the city with Luna. And it was approaching rapidly.

He sensed it *shift*, darting closer…and then he felt it within one of the golden towers to his left.

"Move!" one of the guards behind him ordered, shoving him down the street toward Tartarus. He felt the air grow colder, and knew without turning that Temper had drawn up closer behind him. Gideon obeyed, striding slowly toward the obsidian demon's head in the distance, even as the crowd on either side of the street panicked as they spotted the invading army.

"Into the towers!" the guards flanking the streets ordered the people. "Go!"

There were screams, and the crowd surged toward the towers around the Palatium.

"Don't run!" another guard shouted. "Stay calm!"

But the crowd had become a mob, and the mob rushed to safety, pushing and shoving their way toward the five golden towers. Some fell, and were trampled underfoot by those behind them.

Gideon ignored the chaos, feeling his magical glove gripping his cane. It was in the Tower of Sculpture, behind and to his right. A mere hundred yards away, with Luna.

He felt Temper's presence behind him, mere feet away. And his guards. Eight of them, each a living statue. Nine versus one…impossible odds for just about anyone.

But not for Gideon Myles.

Myko, he called out. *It's time.*

And then he called out to his magical glove, summoning it.

His glove shot out of the Tower of Sculpture, zooming over the lawn and the heads of the mob. Gideon extended his right wrist-stump to the side, ignoring the startled looks the movement earned from his guards.

His glove flew right onto his stump…and he spun around, whipping his cane at Temper just as the blade dipped down to slash at his ankles.

The weapons struck with a *clang*, Gideon's cane instantly absorbing Temper's momentum, freezing the Familiar in place for a split-second. Gideon swung his cane at the nearest guard's temple, the impact sending it stumbling to the side…and into another guard. They both tumbled to the street, even as the other six guards drew their swords from their scabbards.

Temper recovered, slashing at Gideon's neck, and Gideon blocked, stopping the blade in its tracks. He batted Temper away, sending the blade whirling backward…and spun to block just as one of the guards thrust their sword at his belly.

A streak of silver light smashed into the guard's side, sending him flying into the line of guards by the roadside.

Myko materialized, skidding to a halt before Gideon, his eyes bright, his tongue lolling from his mouth in a big canine smile.

Love you too, Gideon told his Familiar. *Let's get my stuff.*

He vaulted onto Myko's back, leaning over and hooking his left forearm under the wolf's collar. They lurched forward and upward as Myko dissolved into pure silver light, bursting away from the guards surrounding them. He sailed over the golden street toward Tartarus…

…and felt something smash into his left shoulder, sending him flying off Myko's back!

The gut-wrenching sensation of free-fall gripped him, and he cried out, the lawn rising rapidly to meet him. Myko completed his moon-dash, then dashed again, streaking right to him. The wolf rematerialized right as he reached Gideon, clamping down on the back of Gideon's red prison uniform with his jaws.

They both fell toward the earth…and Myko moon-dashed right before they struck, nearly tearing Gideon's shirt off. Gideon grit his teeth as the lawn became a blur a mere yard below him…and then fell to the ground as Myko let him go.

He tumbled to the grass with a grunt, rolling a few yards before coming to a stop on his back.

Gideon got to his feet as more than a dozen guards rushed to surround him and Myko…and as General Craven stomped up between them. Craven's right gauntlet – the thing that had knocked Gideon off Myko – flew back onto Craven's hand, and Craven glared down at Gideon.

"Yield!" he commanded.

Gideon hesitated, spotting Temper zooming up to the ring of guards to stop beside Craven. He leaned on Myko, matching Craven's gaze calmly.

"Why?" he replied. "So you can execute me in Tartarus?" He shook his head. "I'd rather die here."

"You must die in Tartarus," Craven retorted. "Justice demands it."

"If you think revenge is justice," Gideon countered, "…you're no better than the Collector."

"Executing the law is justice," Craven shot back.

"Protecting my family is righteous."

"You knew the law and you broke it," Craven insisted.

"I dared to know my own power instead of letting you control it," Gideon argued.

"The people cannot be trusted with their power."

"They are the *only* ones who can be trusted with it," Gideon retorted.

Craven's jawline rippled, and he pointed his gauntleted hand at Gideon.

"Seize him!" he commanded.

***

Simon waited for Bella, Nemesis, Myko, and a few of the Gemini to descend through the open sewer grate, then lifted his gaze to Goo. The blob had grown considerably since he'd first seen it, back in Castle Under in the Collector's office.

"Take me," he requested.

Goo extended a large tentacle out, wrapping it around Simon's waist and pulling Simon into himself. Simon felt Goo's flesh flow in a kind of current, pulling him upward and forward until he was immersed waist-deep at the very top of the blob. Simon looked down at the nearby Gemini, awaiting his command...and the massive army of Gemini ahead, battling the Pentad's forces.

And though he was once again laying siege to a kingdom, he felt none of the guilt and shame that had plagued him when Miss Savage had commanded him to do so. He wasn't doing this for revenge. He had no desire to kill. His mission was merely to save a friend.

It was *his* decision. *His* desire.

The Collector's dying words came to him.

Don't be a victim like I was. Be a hero.

He reached into his breast pocket, pulling out the small shard from one of his Gemini and bringing it to his lips.

"Surge," he commanded.

The Gemini army surged forward around him...and ahead, it broke into an all-out charge, streaming around the soldiers it'd been fighting instead of engaging with them. Many were shattered by the Pentad's forces, but came back together rapidly, continuing the charge. Toward the center of the city...and the great crimson tower there.

"Forward Goo," he commanded, putting a hand on the blob's translucent green skin. "Absorb every soldier you can. Kill no one."

Goo's surface rippled under his hand, and the blob moved forward down the wide street, the Gemini parting around him. He sent out a half-dozen tendrils to the Pentad's soldiers, trapping them and sucking them into himself much as he had done to Simon. Black mist escaped their bodies, representing their negative emotions. Goo absorbed all of it.

And as he did so, he grew.

Goo flowed faster forward through the street, the sea of ever-multiplying Gemini parting before him. A literal army of the Pentad's soldiers had congregated in the streets closer to the middle of the city, holding back the mass of Gemini charging at them.

"Mirror push," Simon ordered into his shard.

The Gemini at the front lines complied, transforming into mirrors with their black backings facing Simon. The Gemini standing behind these mirrors grabbed onto them, using them like greatshields…and shoved them at the Pentad's soldiers.

The enemy soldiers vanished within, banished to the Plane of Reflection.

Simon watched as the Gemini holding the mirrors charged forward, row after row of enemy soldiers vanishing into the alternate plane. And, packed together as they were, there was no escaping the assault. The soldiers' weapons could not damage the mirrors, merely passing through into the Plane of Reflection.

In this way, the Gemini army defeated the soldiers blocking their way, without killing a single one of them.

"Sea of mirrors," he ordered, using the catchphrases he'd trained the Gemini on earlier, while Bella had been painting and Kanja had been sculpting in the eyeball-Conclave.

The Gemini behind the front lines shattered into millions of pieces, falling to the street. Then they reorganized, covering every inch of the city streets, every sidewalk. Connecting to form a gigantic mirrored surface.

So that anywhere the Pentad's soldiers walked became a portal into the Plane of Reflection.

The front lines of the Gemini army continued the charge forward, while the enemy soldiers they'd left behind fell into the sea of reflection. These soldiers bobbed up and down between planes of existence, unable to move. Trapped in an ocean of mirrors.

Even the street ahead of Goo became a mirror. But as Goo approached, the shards of that mirror flipped onto their black backsides, forming a solid floor for Goo to travel on. And as soon as Goo passed, these shards flipped back behind him, reforming the mirrored surface.

In this way, Goo made his way quickly down the street, following the Gemini army as they made their way gradually to the center of the city. And every enemy soldier that Goo passed, he sucked up into himself, growing larger and larger. Dozens, then hundreds of soldiers, until he was five stories tall. Then ten, and so wide that he brushed up against the buildings flanking the street.

And still he grew, sending dozens of tendrils out at a time, plucking soldiers from the ocean of mirrors and swallowing them whole. He extracted their anger, their hate…and then deposited them back onto the mirrored streets to bob up and down helplessly.

Simon watched as Goo grew bigger and stronger, neutralizing the enemy without a single casualty. He had to smile, knowing that Bella would be proud of her creation. It was so *her*, to wage war gently. To be kind even to those who were unkind to her.

He suddenly wished she could see this, so that he could share this feeling with her.

The larger Goo got, the faster he moved, eventually making it right behind the front lines of the Gemini. The Pentad's ground forces didn't stand a chance.

But their aerial defenses were another story.

Soldiers on winged horses flew in the air above the Gemini, circling overhead and shooting explosive arrows down at Simon's army. These of course merely passed through the Gemini's mirrored facets, exploding in the Plane of Reflection instead. So the flying archers quickly changed tactics, aiming for the street ahead of the Gemini army.

Their arrows rained on the street, exploding on impact.

The Gemini on the front lines shattered, shockwaves spreading out from the explosions and sending their fragments flying backward into Goo. Goo sent a wall of his flesh upward to shield Simon just in time, shards and pieces of rubble from the street pelting it. Simon's ears rang as blast after blast assaulted his eardrums, and he covered them with his hands, gritting his teeth.

Then one of the arrows flew right into Goo, plunging not two feet in front of Simon. He stared at it, a black shaft with a sharp arrowhead that pulsed bright red.

And exploded, tearing him apart instantly.

* * *

Simon blinked, finding himself immersed up to his waist in Goo.

He looked up, spotting the winged soldiers flying over the rooftops of the buildings flanking the street, their bows in hand. They went into a circling pattern, then sent a rain of arrows into the Gemini army ahead of Goo.

The arrows plunged right through the Gemini, harmlessly as before.

He put a hand on Goo's surface.

"They're going to shoot arrows into you," he warned. "Toss them out as soon as they do." He paused. "Aim near them, but try not to hurt them. Just make them think twice before shooting again."

Goo's surface rippled under his hand.

Sure enough, the winged soldiers switched tactics as before, sending a rain of arrows onto the street ahead of the Gemini army. They exploded on impact, shockwaves spreading outward and shattering the Gemini. Goo sent a wall of his flesh upward to shield Simon, and shards and rubble pelted it, leaving Simon intact.

Then an arrow plunged right into Goo, not two feet in front of Simon.

Goo immediately sent a tentacle shooting straight upward, the arrow at its tip. He flung the arrow into the sky at the flying cavalry, and it exploded below them with an ear-splitting *boom.* A blast of wind struck Simon…and the winged steeds above as well, sending them scattering. A few lost control, falling through the air and slamming into the rooftops…and a few plummeted toward the street.

"Catch them," Simon spoke into his shard.

A few of the Gemini burst forward, throwing themselves on the street and forming a large mirror there. The soldiers fell into it, vanishing from sight. They of course were hurtling upward in the Plane of Reflection…and would fall again. Moments later, burst out of the mirrors, flying upward in *this* plane, but only half as high as they'd originally fallen. After a few more passes through the mirror, they were bobbing gently….and Goo sent tendrils out to grab them, bringing them into himself. They protruded from his body, some near Simon, but in moments were utterly relaxed, the will to fight drained from them.

Then Goo expelled them behind his massive body, onto the mirrored streets to bob up and down helplessly.

The huge obsidian demon's head near the center of the city was little more than a mile away now. But Simon soon saw that the way forward was about to get far more difficult. For ahead of them were not only more soldiers, but men and women clad in Painter uniforms.

Dozens of them.

Simon heard the beat of drums from ahead, and the shrill sound of violins piercing the air. If it hadn't been for Goo's calming power, he supposed the music would have affected him. Yet again, Bella's creation – so simple in design – had proven surprisingly useful.

And Goo was just getting started.

He sent more and more tendrils out, plucking enemy soldiers from the street ahead and absorbing their negativity, then tossing them into the mirror-ocean. Goo sent more tendrils upward, snatching some of the flying cavalry right out of the air for a similar fate.

Then it was the Painters' turn.

Most of them stayed close to the red tower in the center of the city, but Simon saw two of them break from the ranks, sprinting down the wide street ahead toward him. A tall, very thin middle-aged man with long white hair and a smooth-shaven face, and a shorter, well-built woman with brown hair in a pixie-cut. The man reached up into the air with one hand, then pulled that hand downward.

Something huge descended rapidly from the heavens, plunging downward to stop just below the rooftops of the tall buildings on either side. A massive spider, its body six stories long, and covered with thick plates of glistening black armor. It was hanging on a thick gossamer rope of silk…and as Simon watched, it shot out more webbing, rapidly creating a thick net between the buildings a hundred feet before the advancing Gemini.

"Cut it down," Simon ordered the Gemini through his shard. He felt Redeemer squeeze him, letting him know his suit had recharged, allowing him another second chance if he needed it.

The Gemini charged toward the spider's web, reaching it and slashing at it with their sword-arms. But the webbing proved impervious to their attacks…and what's more, incredibly sticky. The Gemini sword-arms got stuck, and despite the Gemini struggling to free themselves, there was no getting un-stuck.

And the more the mirrored soldiers struggled, the more enmeshed in the web they became.

The white-haired Painter gestured at the spider, who shot web out of its rear, then rolled, the webbing spiraling around its thorax. It shot a second web down at the Painter, who grabbed the rope-like web, and the spider swung him up…right onto its back.

The Painter wrapped the web-rope around his waist, then tied it to the webbing spiraled around the spider's thorax…creating a kind of seatbelt holding him securely to his Familiar.

"Goo, grab that spider," Simon ordered.

Goo shot thick tentacles at the spider, but the spider shot webbing at these in rapid-fire, tying them up and attaching them to its larger web. But Goo, being gooey, merely oozed his tentacles through the gaps in the sticky threads, the webbing unable to hold him for long. He sent the tentacles at the spider, who jumped to the right with shocking speed, landing and sticking to the side of a building.

The female Painter rushed at Goo, reaching into her chest-painting and throwing a huge fireball through the webbing at Goo. The webbing burst into flames, and the fireball slammed into Goo, blackening a small amount of his flesh.

At the same time, the spider sent more webs out, leaping from building-side to building-side, weaving a massive web to cover Goo completely.

The webbing fell over Simon, and he tried to shove it aside. But the thick, sticky threads – each as big around as his pinky – held fast to him.

Then the female Painter threw another fireball at Goo, striking him with similar effect. Except this time, it ignited the webbing covering Goo. The flames spread all over Goo's surface…racing all the way up to the top.

Toward Simon.

Simon thrashed against the sticky webs, but it was pointless. The flames engulfed the mesh of webbing covering him, the heat sudden and overwhelming. Even inside Goo, he felt fear threaten to overwhelm him.

"Goo!" he screamed.

Goo reacted instantly, and Simon felt himself being pulled downward into the blob. Goo covered the burning webbing atop Simon with his own flesh, the green goo blackening as the fire seared it. Simon took a deep breath in, but it was hardly necessary. For Goo left a long straw-like tube to the outside world above Simon, creating a hollow chamber inside of himself for Simon to be safe within. That chamber sank downward until it was all the way in the center of Goo's massive body, perfectly protected from the spider's burning web. And everything else that might harm Simon, for that matter.

But as a consequence, Simon couldn't see what was going on through Goo's massive bulk of green flesh.

A moment's thought brought a solution; Simon spun around, facing back the way they'd come, then held up his mirrored shard, using it as a rear-view mirror. And since Goo didn't exist in the Plane of Reflection, it allowed Simon a perfect view of the street beyond.

But of course, he couldn't see the spider or the Painters either, because they were in the original world.

Unless….

He spotted the mirrored street formed by his Gemini through the reflection in his shard. And through the reflection of the reflection, he could see the spider!

Simon smiled, feeling rather proud of himself. Even Redeemer gave him a little squeeze of encouragement.

Nice work, she told him.

Thanks, he replied.

Through the double-reflection, he saw the spider leap away from Goo's reaching tentacles again and again, shooting more webs to try to bind Goo up. But neither had any success at trapping the other…and ahead, Simon spotted the female Painter standing beside the white-haired man. And beside her, what could only be her Familiar.

A monkey.

It was no ordinary monkey, however. It was taller than her, a good six feet in height. And its fists were huge, and were made of golden metal. It leapt into the air – thirty feet high! – and grabbed onto a tendril of the spider's web above, swinging toward the front lines of the Gemini. It landed before them, smashing one fist into the street just before the mirrored soldiers.

The street *rippled*, a shockwave bursting outward from the impact.

Gemini exploded as the shockwave struck them, the windows of nearby buildings shattering instantly. Goo's surface wobbled violently as the force smashed into him, and while Simon was insulated from the blast, the Gemini around and behind him were not. They shattered, exploding backward violently.

Then they reformed, rushing back at the monkey and the spider…and the two Painters.

"Get the woman," Simon ordered his Gemini.

The mirrored soldiers found a few gaps in the large net of webbing between them and the Painters, and leapt through them, charging at the two. The woman reached into her chest-painting to fling another fireball at them, but the flames did nothing to the Gemini, merely passing into the Plane of Reflection.

However, as one of the Gemini lunged at her, transforming into a large mirror and colliding with her, so did she.

"Target the monkey," Simon ordered.

The Gemini charged at the monkey, who leapt upward three stories high, grabbing onto the spider's web and climbing up it. It clearly knew which of the spider's strands were sticky and which were not, navigating the web expertly. And even as the monkey climbed, the giant spider aided it, shooting more and more strands between the buildings on either side to allow the monkey to swing high above the Gemini army…and even above Goo.

It swung directly over Goo…and then dropped down, its fists glowing red-hot!

Goo intercepted the monkey with one tentacle, but the monkey thrust one big fist downward to strike it. The tentacle exploded, another shockwave rippling through Goo's entire body. The monkey fell right on top of Goo, its red-hot fists burning right through Goo's flesh, charring it instantly.

And as his green flesh blackened, it shrank and separated…and the monkey plunged right *through* Goo…plummeting right toward Simon. Simon didn't even have time to scream before it reached the cavern within Goo.

Smashing him in the face with its fiery fist.

Chapter 35

Gideon leaned against Myko's side, his stump hooked under the great silver wolf's collar as he locked gazes with General Craven. The dozen or so guards forming a circle around Gideon and Myko held their weapons at the ready, swords and axes and spears gleaming in the sunlight.

"Seize him!" Craven commanded.

Up, Gideon thought.

Myko dissolved into a beam of silver light, shooting straight up into the sky…and pulled Gideon along for the ride. Gideon's guts lurched as the ground fell away, and he ignored the sensation, swinging onto Myko's back with practiced ease. He saw Craven's magical gauntlet shoot up after them with formidable speed.

But he was already swinging his cane, having anticipated the attack. For while Craven had many fine qualities, creativity was not one of them.

Gideon's cane intercepted the gauntlet, smashing into it…and stopping it instantly.

Myko's moon-dash ended, and Gideon's stomach flip-flopped again as they decelerated, reaching the peak of their flight over a hundred feet above the earth. He scanned the city, spotting the Gemini army still over a mile away…and a truly massive green blob towering behind it, over half as tall as the buildings on either side.

He broke out into a smile, feeling a flash of pride for his daughter. Goo, the small blob Bella had painted in protest of his having killed the soldiers in Devil's Pass, now a fearsome juggernaut facing the Pentad's army.

"Let's get out of here Myko," he told his Familiar.

But even as Gideon said it, Craven flew upward toward his magic gauntlet, reconnecting with it in mid-air, then shooting it outward again at them. It struck Myko in the chest.

Hard.

Myko burst upward, spinning in a backflip with the force of the blow. Gideon's stump slipped free from Myko's collar, and he was flung from the wolf's back.

His stomach shot up into his throat as he plummeted helplessly toward the earth.

Myko!

The wolf moon-dashed after him, but Craven zoomed upward to his gauntlet again, grabbing Myko in mid-air and holding onto him as he dashed to Gideon's aid. They both reached Gideon, and Craven threw Myko to the side, grabbing Gideon by the waist.

Myko moon-dashed again at Craven. But the general lifted his shield to intercept, and Myko ricocheted off.

The ground rose up to meet Gideon with deadly speed, even as Craven held him around the waist with a vise-like grip.

Craven shot his gauntlet forward right before they struck, and used its magic to pull himself toward it. This stopped their fall abruptly, a mere ten feet above the ground. They reached his gauntlet, then fell to the grass with a *thump*.

Or rather Craven did, his feet striking the earth. He bent his knees, absorbing the impact easily…and lowered Gideon to the ground.

Myko moon-dashed at the general again, but again Craven lifted Aganon to intercept, blocking the wolf's attack with a *clang*. Gideon tried to swing his cane at Craven, but Craven shoved him to the side, sending him tumbling to the grass.

Then Craven stomped toward him, and knelt down, extending one hand to grab Gideon by the throat.

Gideon willed his magical glove to shoot off his stump…and whack Craven across the temple with its cane.

Craven's head snapped to the side, and he stumbled, barely managing to keep his balance. He righted himself, pointing his gauntlet at Gideon and shooting it at him. Gideon's cane intercepted, stopping the gauntlet in mid-air with a *whack*, then hitting it again. The gauntlet flew right at Craven, smacking him in the forehead.

All while Myko moon-dashed to Gideon's side.

Gideon got to his feet and vaulted onto his Familiar's back, hooking his stump under Myko's silver collar once again. Craven tried to charge at them, but Gideon's glove flew at the general, smacking him in the forehead with Gideon's cane. The general froze in place for a split-second…and Myko moon-dashed up and away.

Again Craven lifted his gauntleted hand to aim at them, but Gideon's glove struck his gauntlet just as it started to fly off, making it veer to one side. Gideon willed it to strike the general again and again with rapid-fire blows, every other hit freezing the living statue in place for a moment.

And Craven, the invincible juggernaut feared world-wide, could do nothing to stop it.

Or so Gideon thought.

Craven managed to get Aganon in front of him, and the shield glowed with a ferocious golden light. A massive shield of pure energy extended from Aganon…blocking Gideon's glove from getting anywhere near Craven.

Myko finished their moon-dash, and Gideon recalled his magical glove, which flew back onto his right stump. He felt Myko prodding him psychically.

"Okay boy," he told the wolf.

Myko twisted in mid-air, then moon-dashed again, this time toward the nearest of the Golden Towers, the Tower of Sculpture. Gideon didn't need to ask Myko what the wolf was doing, for they were of one mind. Luna had brought his magical glove to that Golden Tower right before he'd recalled it to himself, after all.

Bella's dark half had saved him…and now it was time to get her, and get out.

* * *

Luna cursed as the statue-guards at the entrance to the lobby of the golden tower spotted her. She ducked back down the hallway she'd come from, waiting for a few seconds. Then she peered around the corner, looking past the crowd of people still spilling into the lobby.

Two of the statue-guards were pushing through the crowd, their swords gleaming in the sunlight streaming through the windows.

Coming right for her.

Luna swore again, backing into the hallway. She had two options: stay and fight, or run. Gideon was still out there somewhere – she could only assume his glove had gone to him – and he might need help. But with no weapon to defend herself with, she'd be hard-pressed to get past these guards.

Their heavy footsteps *clunk, clunked* toward her, audible even over the panicked voices of the crowd filling the lobby.

Luna glanced down the hallway at the door leading back to the bathroom, then hesitated. If she fought them, the statues would probably murder her.

But if she *didn't*, and Gideon was in trouble…

She looked around quickly, searching for shadow to step into. But there was none in the hallway, nor any shadows dark enough in the lobby beyond for her to melt into. And she had no weapon whatsoever, other than her hands and feet. Which, against a living statue with a sword, would be of no use at all.

The two guards turned the corner suddenly, stomping into the hallway…and their eyes went right to her.

"Stop!" one of them commanded in a deep voice.

Luna cursed under her breath, freezing in place. They were only a few yards away, their swords gleaming.

"Don't move," the other ordered.

"You first," she shot back.

"On your knees," he commanded. "Hands behind your head!"

She considered this.

"No," she decided.

"Do it!"

"Make me," she retorted…and immediately regretted the outburst. Because they were clearly prepared to do just that.

They charged.

The closest guard thrust his sword at her belly, and Luna dodged to the side just in time, the blade's cruel tip missing her by mere inches. She shoved the guard's shoulder, but she might as well have tried pushing a…well, a statue. She stumbled backward, her back striking the wall behind her.

Just as the other guard reached her, slashing at her throat!

Luna gasped, ducking down and to the side, and the deadly blade whizzed an inch above her head, the wind of its passage ruffling her hair.

The second guard followed up with a thrust, and Luna scrambled away, backpedaling as quickly as she could. But she was too slow; the tip of the blade struck her in the chest, cutting right through her uniform and burying itself into her breastbone.

Luna cried out, the impact shoving her backward violently. She fell right on her ass, the guard's blade pulling free from her chest. She clutched at her wound, gritting her teeth at the awful pain.

God *damn* that hurt!

Still the guard advanced, charging at her. He lifted his blade up above his head, bringing it right down on her. She cried out, throwing her arms up above her head to block…

And felt a powerful force slam into her chest, shoving her backward across the floor!

Luna slid all the way down the hall, the guard's blade striking the floor where she'd been a mere fraction of a second ago. Her back slammed into the wall at the start of the hallway, air blasting from her lungs at the impact. She gasped, clutching at her still-aching chest…and felt the force shoving her vanish.

She blinked, looking down at her hands…then lifting them from her chest. The force shoving her backward resumed…and it was suddenly clear what was going on.

There was a hole in her shadow-uniform where the guard had penetrated it…exposing her inky-black skin to the light. And that light had shoved her backward.

Huh.

She lifted her gaze, finding herself a good twenty feet from the guards. Who had recovered, she realized.

And were charging after her.

"Wonderful," Luna grumbled, rising unsteadily to her feet. The pain from the stab wound to her chest burned something awful, but when she covered it with her hand – bringing it into shadow – the pain lessened. She knew her wound was healing, because *all* of her wounds healed in shadow.

The shadow nurtured her. It *was* her.

And it appeared that the light, which repelled her, was her best defense.

She smirked at the two guards as they stomped toward her, swords at the ready. Having no idea what she was. She was the shadow, dammit. The darkness.

They didn't stand a chance.

The first guard reached her, thrusting his sword at her chest.

Luna dodged to the left, but instead of pushing him, she grabbed his wrist, turning to face the dead-end wall of the hallway…and lifted her other hand from her chest.

The light shoved her backward violently, sending her flying down the hallway in the opposite direction…and yanked the guard along with her.

A moment later, she covered the hole in her uniform.

The light-force stopped instantly, and she landed flat on her back, sliding backward across the slick floor. She let go of the statue, watching as he careened all the way into the lobby, crashing into the crowd of people there and sending them tumbling to the ground. His sword fell from his hands with a clatter…and Luna rolled onto her belly, scrambling toward it. She picked it up, flinging it at the other guard – who was still standing at the opposite end of the hallway, near the bathroom – and watched as it struck him hilt-first in the face.

His head snapped backward, and he stumbled into the wall behind him, dazed.

Luna fantasized for a split-second about messing him up…and then remembered Gideon.

She turned, bolting toward the lobby exit and leaping over the fallen people there. The people still standing parted frantically, giving her a clear path to the doorway. But two more statue-guards were standing at the doorway, blocking the way.

"Halt!" they both commanded in unison.

Luna skid to a stop…then turned around, facing away from them.

She pulled the slit in her uniform open wide, and felt the sunlight kick her in the chest.

She burst backward, flying right through the entranceway and into the two guards. The impact blasted the air from her lungs, pain shooting through her spine. She knocked them clean over, sailing right out of the tower and careening over the lawn beyond. The grass was a blur below her as she continued to pick up speed.

Crap!

She put a hand over the tear in her uniform, and the acceleration stopped.

Luna fell onto the grass, the world spinning madly around her as she tumbled backward. At length she came to a stop, flopping onto her back on the lawn. The bright blue sky greeted her, and she stared up at it, gasping for air.

Her right shoulder was on *fire.*

She tried to get up, but pain shot through her injured shoulder, a tingling sensation traveling down the front of her arm. Looking at it, she could tell that it had been dislocated by her tumble on the grass.

And that the guards she'd bowled over were rising to their feet near the entrance to the golden tower, a good two hundred feet away.

They turned, spotting her…and charged toward her.

Lux!

She groaned, trying to get to her feet, but her right shoulder spasmed horribly. The pain was so bad it literally took her breath away, freezing her in place. She could only watch as the soldiers rushed toward her.

Lux!

Luna knew that her sister was coming, for even though they were split – two consciousnesses now instead of one – she still had the ability to feel her sister's presence. And she felt that presence zooming toward her, moving impossibly fast.

She rolled onto her left side, wincing at fresh spasms in her right shoulder, and tried to prop herself up to a seated position. The guards were a hundred feet away now, and closing in fast.

Fifty.

Luna grimaced, watching as they drew their swords, the long silver blades shimmering in the light of the sun.

Come on sister!

Her shoulder *clunked* back into place suddenly, in a jolt of pure agony. She screamed, falling onto her back on the grass…just as the first of the guards reached her.

He skid to a stop before her, then lifted his sword high above his head.

And swung it right down on hers.

Chapter 36

Simon blinked.

He found himself suspended in the hollow chamber within Goo, a small tunnel in the chamber ceiling running through Goo and leading straight up to the surface. The Gemini were charging the monkey-Familiar with the glowing red fists, who leapt upward three stories high, grabbing onto the spider's web and climbing up it rapidly. The giant spider aided the monkey, shooting more and more strands between the buildings on either side to allow the monkey to swing high above the Gemini army…and Goo.

"Gemini, come to me!" he shouted into his shard.

His heart leapt in his throat as the monkey finished its swing, now directly above Simon, visible through the vertical tunnel above Simon's head. It dropped down, its fists burning red-hot, and punched downward with both of them.

Goo swung a tentacle at the monkey, but the monkey smashed it with one fist, making the tentacle explode. Then the monkey punched downward with both fists, falling toward Goo's gelatinous body.

Its fists slammed into Goo's flesh, burning right through it as if it weren't even there.

"Mirror!" Simon cried.

And then the monkey plunged through the ceiling of the chamber, swinging its fist at Simon's head!

A Gemini burst through the side-wall into the chamber, shattering in mid-air and transforming into a large mirror. It struck the monkey in mid-fall, right before its fist struck Simon's face.

The monkey vanished, sent into the Plane of Reflection.

The Gemini shattered again, reforming into a mirrored soldier before striking the opposite wall of the gelatinous chamber. Goo sucked it in, passing it all the way through to the outside of his body.

And Simon stared where it'd been moments before, his heart pounding in his chest.

He wiped sweat from his brow, taking a deep, shuddering breath. For if the monkey had succeeded in killing him so soon after he'd gotten his second chance, that would've been it.

The end.

You need to be more careful, he told himself.

We will be, Redeemer promised. *You can do this.*

He nodded, but for the first time since they'd come into Centrum, he wondered if he could.

Simon focused.

"Goo, bring me up top," he requested. Goo complied, and the floor of the gelatinous cavern rose up, collapsing until it'd closed altogether. He continued to rise through the tunnel above, emerging from it to stand immersed waist-deep atop his host. The giant spider was still before them, and had spun a big web all around Goo and the Gemini army, trapping the mirrored soldiers.

Or so the spider thought.

"Goo, gather the Gemini. Absorb them into yourself, then go over that webbing."

The Gemini turned, running straight into Goo's huge body. They were immediately absorbed, and Goo rose up, elongating his body until he was over ten stories tall. He latched onto one of the buildings then, a towering structure twice his height.

And, using his sticky flesh, he climbed right up it.

The spider leapt to intercept Goo, but Goo sent dozens of tentacles toward the thing. The spider had to leap away, its webbing useless to stop Goo's flesh.

But the white-haired Painter riding the giant spider proved anything but useless.

The man reached into his chest-painting, pulling out a small white ball. He tossed this high above Goo and Simon, and it exploded right over Simon's head. Webbing shot out in all directions, thick ropes of it slamming into the sides of the buildings all around it. And into Goo, burying a few feet into his body…including one rope that plunged a few yards away from Simon.

Then, from those ropes, hundreds of other smaller webs shot out from their sides, and more threads shot out from *their* sides, until a massive network of thick webbed mesh had filled the area.

A split-second later, the ropes shot back into the sphere, yanking everything around it into itself. Windows and chunks of stone from the buildings, huge hunks of Goo, and hundreds of Gemini flew into the white ball in the center of the network, slamming together with lethal force.

Simon could only stare as a huge chunk of Goo ahead of him was torn right off, sucked into the white sphere. He'd barely avoided getting sucked in with it.

But he had no time to feel relieved.

For the white sphere seemed to eat everything it'd pulled into itself, growing considerably larger in the process. It shot out more web-ropes, plunging them into the buildings and Goo in slightly different places…and as before, more and more ropes and threads shot out of the sides of these. They too pulled into the sphere, ripping more chunks out of Goo and pulling them into the ever-growing white sphere.

Then it repeated the process, shooting more thick ropes outward. One of them whizzed by Simon's head, plunging into Goo's flesh inches from Simon. Goo reacted instantly, shoving Simon outward in a massive tentacle and lowering him toward the street far below.

The ropes sucked inward with terrible speed, yanking more chunks of Goo into itself. It also tore off the base of Goo's tentacle, which promptly fell – with Simon still stuck in it – to the street over a hundred feet below.

Simon's heart leapt into his throat, the golden street zooming toward him with deadly speed.

He held his breath as he felt himself get sucked all the way into the tentacle, which morphed into a huge ball of goo around him, easily twenty feet in diameter.

One that struck the street with bone-shattering force.

The sphere flattened with the impact, Simon decelerating to a full stop so rapidly his breath blasted from his lungs. A moment later, he felt himself rise up to the surface of the green flesh, to sweet, sweet air. He sucked it in greedily, his body feeling numb.

But to his surprise, he was utterly intact.

He looked upward, spotting Goo's huge body stuck to the side of the building nearest him, the white sphere going through its cycle over and over again, pulling more and more pieces of Goo – and the surrounding buildings – into itself. The Painter who'd thrown it sat astride his giant spider, watching with grim satisfaction.

Then a ray of pure red light enveloped the spider and the white-haired Painter, and their flesh seemed to shrink.

The Painter's face sunk, his muscles wasting away. And the spider's thorax crumpled, its legs thinning. A few even broke off, and the spider fell from its web, plummeting toward the street.

The two slammed into the golden pavement with a gruesome splatter, never to rise again.

Simon stared at them, then spotted the silhouette of a dragon diving toward him. A dragon clad in midnight-black armor, with blood-red eyes and black scales…and wings painted on the outside.

It landed beside him, folding its wings on its back.

"Hey," Nemesis greeted. "Looked like you were getting your ass kicked."

"Uh huh," was all Simon could manage. He felt Redeemer squeeze him, letting him know she'd recharged, and let out a breath he hadn't realized he'd been holding. That'd been close; if Goo and Nemesis hadn't acted so quickly, he would've been dead.

Permanently.

Nemesis glanced at what remained of the spider and the Painter, a smirk on her lips.

"Can't say they didn't stick the landing," she quipped.

Simon ignored the comment, looking upward. Goo was busy crawling down the side of the building, almost a quarter of his massive body torn away by the magical white web-sphere. He dropped to the street beside Simon, the ground quaking with the impact. Wind blasted outward when Goo struck, the shockwave striking Simon and Nemesis and shoving them backward a few steps. Simon covered his ears, grimacing at the sudden pain there.

"Damn Snot," Nemesis blurted out, eyeing the giant blob. "You been working out?"

Goo didn't ripple, which was as close to pointedly ignoring the dragon as the blob could manage.

"Well, seeing as you can't even handle a spider and a monkey, I'm gonna have to keep helping you," Nemesis decided. "Come on, let's finish this."

* * *

Luna watched helplessly as the first of the guards charging toward her reached her, skidding to a stop in the grass before her. He lifted his sword up high above his head, the cruel edge of his weapon gleaming in the sunlight. He swung it down at her head, seeming to move in slow-motion.

And then there was light.

Luna felt her sister reunite with her, the light enveloping her even as she merged with it. And in a split-second, she was not Luna, and Lux was not Lux. She was one again.

She was Bella.

The sword descended toward Bella's head, threatening to split her skull in two. But Manus, her magical bone-armor, had other ideas.

Bony hands shot outward from her head and chest, grabbing the sword just before it struck her. Manus tore the weapon from the statue's hands, swinging it at the guard's…and lopping off its head.

More guards rushed up to Bella, and she scrambled to her feet, facing them.

"Stay back!" she warned.

They ignored her.

Dozens more of Manus's hands left her body, flying out at the statue-guards and grabbing their weapons. Manus tore them from the guards, then hacked away at them with their own swords and axes, felling them in seconds. All of the guards turned rapidly to stone, their heads separated – however temporarily – from their shoulders.

Then Manus's hands zoomed back to Bella, re-forming her bone-armor.

"Wow," Bella blurted out, admiring her handiwork. Easily thirty of the statue-guards lay on the lawn before her. "Damn."

One of Manus's skeletal hands on her forearm detached, giving her a thumb's up.

Bella smiled, feeling a burst of affection for Manus.

"Good work," she told him. "All right, let's find Gideon."

The skeletal hand twisted, pointing left. At a streak of silver light shooting down toward them. At first she felt a burst of fear, thinking it was another enemy. But it most certainly was not.

Myko!

The great silver wolf materialized a few feet above the lawn, landing with a *thump* before her. And there, riding on Myko's back, was none other than Gideon Myles...alive and well!

"Daddy!" Bella cried.

"Bella!" Gideon exclaimed, breaking out into a huge smile. He leapt from Myko's back, rushing up to Bella and embracing her. She hugged him back...and then frowned, realizing that his left hand was missing.

"What happened to your hand?" she asked.

"They painted them off," he explained. "Both of them."

"We need to get you out of here," she told him. "Come on!"

She grabbed his upper arm, turning away from the center of the city and back toward the approaching Gemini army...and froze. For a huge black sword was flying toward them, leading a small army of enemy soldiers...and a man who stood head and shoulders above them all, clutching an all-too-familiar golden shield.

Bella's blood went cold, a vision of Castle Havenwood crumbling under the awful power of that shield coming to her. Of her home being destroyed in a matter of minutes.

"Stop where you are!" General Craven commanded, his voice booming over the heads of his soldiers. At the same time, Temper flew right up to Gideon and Bella, coming to a halt before them. It levitated there, point-down.

The air turned ice-cold under Temper's aura, giving Bella goosebumps.

Craven and his guards reached them soon after, stopping just behind Temper. The general towered over Bella and Gideon, easily three feet taller than they were. He lifted his right hand, pointing his gauntleted finger at Gideon.

"Stand down," he ordered. "There is no escape. The army you've brought to save you will be destroyed. You cannot win."

Gideon put an arm around Bella's waist, eyeing Craven calmly.

"Telling me is one thing," he admonished, lifting his cane to a defensive position. "Showing me may be quite another."

Craven glared down at him…then shifted his finger, pointing it at Bella.

His gauntlet shot out at her, its fingers opening as it struck her in the throat. Those fingers closed…and the gauntlet yanked her backward, reconnecting with Craven's hand. Manus tried to stop the gauntlet, but it was too powerful; Manus's bony fingers had no hope of prying the gauntlet free from Bella.

"Bella!" Gideon cried.

Manus's many hands leapt off Bella's body, pummeling Craven, but he ignored the blows, utterly unfazed by them. But as he squeezed her throat harder, his eyes narrowed.

"What magic is this?" he demanded.

Bella realized that Craven had to be feeling the effects of her empathy potion; that as the first person who'd hurt her since she'd tested it out with Simon, Craven must be feeling what *she* was feeling.

And unfortunately, was utterly unfazed.

Gideon whipped his cane at Craven, who blocked with his massive shield. Temper slashed at Gideon's right forearm at the same time, and Myko leapt to intercept, grabbing Temper's hilt in his jaws. Then Myko used Temper as if wielding him, moon-dashing past Craven and slashing at the soldiers behind him.

Temper cut right through a dozen of the soldiers' necks, decapitating them.

Myko finished his moon-dash, kicking off the chest of the guard in front of him, then moon-dashing back at Craven. He struck the nape of Craven's neck with Temper's deadly blade…but it bounced off with a *clang*, knocking Temper from Myko's jaws.

The dark blade whirled in the air, landing on the grass. And while Craven's flesh was unharmed, the terrible blow left a small chip in Temper's fine edge. The Familiar lay there for a moment, stunned…and then floated upward, flying rather unsteadily to the relative safety of Craven's side.

Meanwhile, Bella gasped for air, clutching at Craven's gauntlet. Cain stirred at her hip.

"Bella, use me!" he cried.

She reached down, grabbing Cain. His spine shot out from the base of his skull, and she swung it at Craven. It struck him on the chest, bouncing off harmlessly.

Craven ignored her, facing Gideon.

"Surrender," he ordered. "Or I bring your daughter to Tartarus and execute her."

"You can't do that," Gideon retorted. "She's had no trial!"

"She has led an army to attack us," Craven argued. "We are at war, and the laws of combat dictate that I can."

Gideon's jawline rippled.

"Let her go," he ordered.

"Choose," Craven shot back. He squeezed Bella's throat a little harder, and she grimaced, feeling pressure building in her head. "Surrender, or your daughter will burn in Hell for eternity."

"If you hurt her…" Gideon warned.

"Very well," Craven stated…and turned, walking toward a golden street in the distance, dragging Bella with him. A street that led to a huge, black sculpted demon's head surrounded by a tall wrought-iron fence. His remaining guards stayed with Gideon, blocking Gideon's way.

"Gideon!" Bella croaked, barely able to force the words out.

"Stop!" Gideon shouted, leaping at Craven and smashing his cane on the general's back. It stopped him for a moment…but he merely continued forward. Craven's guards tried charging Gideon, but Myko kept them at bay, moon-dashing into them and throwing them backward while Gideon whacked them with his cane.

And Bella could only watch, helpless to do anything.

She reached into her chest-painting, searching for something – anything – to attack Craven with. But there was nothing there that fit the bill. She reached down for the rolled-up canvases in her thigh-holsters, grabbing one and pulling it out.

"A…pertus," she croaked.

It unrolled, then unfolded several times, revealing a giant canvas. The one with Rodo in it. Bella tried to throw it in front of Craven, to trap him within it, but the living statue merely batted it away. The painting fell to the side on the grass, painted-side up…and Craven yanked the other rolled-up canvases from her thigh-holsters, tossing them aside as well. Leaving Bella nothing left that would hurt him, much less kill him.

"If…you kill me," she gasped at Craven, "…you'll feel…what I…feel."

Craven ignored her, stomping toward the obsidian demon's head. And there was nothing she – or Gideon – could do to stop him.

Unless…

Unless she could kill herself.

When Craven had grabbed her neck back in Havenwood, Nemesis had killed her, making her split into Lux and Luna. And while Luna had been trapped, Lux had gone free, as it'd been night-time.

But she had nothing she could use to do it.

Nemesis, she called out silently. *Kill me!*

Little busy, Nemesis answered.

I don't have time, she pressed.

Can't get there, Nemesis pressed. *There's a literal army in the way.*

All the while, Craven dragged Bella closer to the huge sculpted head. A giant demon's head, its mouth gaping wide, like the mouth of the Water Dragon cave.

A memory came to her then, of her standing in the darkness of the Water Dragon tunnel, squinting at the light beyond the cave. A place where dark met light…and where she'd tried to split herself into Lux and Luna without dying.

She looked down at her hands, remembering how they'd started to separate into blackness and light. Before she'd given up.

Okay, she told herself. *I can do this.*

Do what? Nemesis asked.

Cut myself in half, Bella answered.

She focused then, concentrating on her hands. Her eyebrows furrowed, her jaw clenching. Focusing on the two sides of herself, she willed them to come apart, like two pieces of Velcro. Again, she saw her hand become outlined in bright light on one side, inky black on the other.

Come on…

She tried harder, pushing herself to her mental limit. But as hard as she tried, as much as she visualized ripping herself in half, she couldn't do it. The two sides of herself – good and evil, light and shadow, love and hate – would not separate.

Bella clenched her fists until her knuckles turned white, but still she couldn't do it. She gave up, cursing herself.

She'd failed. Again. Only in the utter surrender of death could she separate the two sides of herself.

Surrender.

She blinked, realization dawning on her.

Death *was* surrender. A letting go of her *self*. There was no forcing involved. It was utter relaxation…allowing the two sides of herself to go free. And only in that utter release could she see herself for who she truly was: two sides of the same coin, the heroine and the villain. The better and the worse, for better or worse.

Like feeling the Flow, knowledge of herself meant letting go of herself first.

So Bella surrendered. Utterly. Her hands unclenched, her brow relaxing. She stopped forcing and instead focused within, at the beings within her. The beings that *were* her.

Go free, she told them. *Be yourselves instead of me.*

And in that moment, so much like the last seconds before death, Bella felt her *self* fade away. And the twin sisters of her soul came apart with ease.

Lux found herself still trapped in Craven's grasp, as was Luna. But Luna tore part of her ninja uniform off, tossing its shadow-fabric to the ground. To her surprise, it formed a true shadow there, with nothing at all casting it…and Luna was shoved by the sun into that shadow, merging with it. *Becoming* it.

General Craven's eyes widened, and he froze in his tracks.

Then a most curious thing happened.

For Temper, still at Craven's side, began to glow with a strange white light.

It started at Temper's hilt, crawling up his crossguard to continue up both sides of his blade. Then it shot forward, plunging right into Lux's chest.

Or rather, the heart-shaped amulet there, hanging from her neck.

Temper's blade went from gleaming to faded, and then cracks spread outward from the chip in its edge. The Familiar froze in shock, then burst away from Lux frantically, but by then it was too late.

Temper crumbled, falling to dust on the grass.

And at the same time, the heart-shaped ruby in the center of Lux's amulet began to pulse with a steady crimson glow.

Chapter 37

Lucia stood on the grassy plains before Yero, watching as he donned his magical golden mask for the second time. His entire body turned to gold, the bleeding from the gaping wound she'd made in his belly stopping immediately. His mouth opened impossibly wide, so large that it could swallow her whole.

She activated the abilities Animus gave her, transforming into mist and bursting backward away from the Painter as quickly as she could.

But she wasn't quick enough.

For Yero's mouth created a powerful vortex, a howling wind that threatened to suck her into it. She'd heard of Yero's golden mask from Gideon, of course. From the tales he'd told her about his former co-worker and friend.

And she knew that, should she fall into that gaping maw, she would be trapped…and sent to the Pentad, where she would face certain doom.

Lucia felt that vacuum pull her toward him, and fought against the terrible force, willing herself to fly away faster. But it was too great to resist. If she'd gotten just a few yards further away from him, she might've had a chance.

But she hadn't.

Dozens of flaming daggers summoned by the fiery Temper whirled around her, plunging through her mist-body harmlessly over and over again. If she remained in her mist-form, they couldn't harm her…but she'd be sucked into Yero. If she transformed back to her real body, she might be able to get away…but the swords would cut her to ribbons.

Crap!

Lucia focused, acknowledging the terrible truth. That she would not escape this time. A sudden calm came over her, as she accepted her fate. As she accepted what was to be.

She *pulled* herself into her true form, slamming the palm of her hand into the skull at her left breast.

Its eyes glowed black, and black tendrils as thick as fingers shot out of her boots and legs, her uniform coming alive to obey her will. Those tendrils sank deep into the earth, pinning her to the ground so completely that Yero's great maw could not consume her.

Just as dozens of flaming daggers plunged into her body…and Temper's fiery blade sliced through her neck.

* * *

Lucia blinked.

She found herself standing on charred grass in the middle of the battlefield, as she'd been an instant ago. But Yero was gone. And the giant mushroom cloud of dust from Gideon's meteorite was also gone.

She tried to move, but her legs were rooted to the ground. Pressing the small skull at her left chest fixed that, making the root-like tendrils her uniform had sent into the earth suck back into her suit. A suit that, painted to *be* her – much as Gideon's gloves were – resurrected when she did.

Turning in a slow circle, she spotted the massive body of the White Dragon laying on the blasted, charred grass a quarter-mile away, its wings severed…and its head.

It lay there, motionless. It's eyes open but lifeless.

Dead.

She stared at it, then lifted one hand, running it over her scalp. Her hair – lost when she'd been murdered by the Collector and her body had decomposed – had just started growing in again. But now it was gone, burned off by Temper's burning daggers.

Which meant she'd died. Again.

She turned all the way around, spotting Dragon's Peak in the distance. A good portion of the mushroom forest around it was charred, mushrooms burned down to black stumps. What's more, the entire mushroom forest was surrounded by a massive army of Gemini, the mirrored soldiers that the kid Simon had used to storm Havenwood with that Miss Savage bitch.

Lucia ignored them, looking beyond, to the mountain itself. Her gaze drew up it, past the shattered downtown buildings and the streaks of blackened rock. All the way up to the very top. To Castle Havenwood.

But it was gone.

Lucia's breath caught in her throat, and she stared at Dragon's Peak in disbelief.

"Well shit," she swore.

She lowered her gaze, putting a hand to her chest to feel her heart-shaped amulet. It was gone, of course. She'd given it to Bella…which meant that she'd died, and that Temper had just been killed by her little spitfire of a daughter.

She felt a surge of hope.

Lucia transformed into her mist-form, zooming upward and forward toward the top of the mountain. The mushroom forest and the crystal-clear water of Lake Fenestra passed beneath her, and she quickly reached the cliff's edge at the top of the Everstream. She hesitated – nearly continuing onward to the mouth of the Water Dragon cave – but went upward instead, reaching the top of the mountain.

It was, to her surprise, absolutely *teeming* with Dragonkin.

The dragon-like people were hard at work, clearing the rubble of Castle Havenwood. Some were already starting to rebuild, laying the foundations of a new castle. A few of the Dragonkin spotted her as she descended toward them, transitioning back to her human form. They needed no introduction, of course. All of the Dragonkin knew of the daughter of Thaddeus Birch, the Creator.

"Hey," she greeted. "Where's Gideon and Bella?"

"Daughter of the Creator!" one of them exclaimed, a woman wearing the standard blue and white armor of the Dragonkin militia. "We feared that you had perished!"

"Popped that cherry a while ago."

"The Pentad hath succeeded in destroying Havenwood," the Dragonkin woman declared grimly. "They…"

"Got that. Where's Gideon and Bella?"

"Gideon Myles has been taken prisoner by the Pentad," she answered. "Bella Birch hath delivered the Creator to safety, and has allied with the Painter called Simon to retrieve your husband from the clutches of the enemy."

Well, that explained the Gemini.

"Where is Thaddeus?" Lucia pressed.

"In the Castle Under, which our scouts hath informed us has been miraculously restored to its former glory," the Dragonkin woman answered.

"And Bella?"

"We know not," the Dragonkin admitted.

"Yeah, well I know who will," Lucia replied. "Thanks," she added.

And then she dissolved into mist, flying off the edge of the mountain and descending back to the cliffside where the Everstream flowed. She zoomed toward the mouth of the Water Dragon cave. Down into the belly of the mountain, toward her mansion…and the magical black coffin that would lead her to the Plane of Death.

To Petrusa.

* * *

Lucia stood before Petrusa, Queen of the Dead, on the great rocky platform midway up the massive column that served as the Root of the World. Constructed entirely out of statues of corpses, the Root of the World symbolized the central tenant of the Dark Circle…and of the Plane of Death itself.

For all life was possible only through death, each living organism supported by the deaths of countless others. This was the way of the universe, that the living could only remain so at the expense of the living. And that from the dead, life inevitably bloomed.

A fact that normally gave Lucia comfort, knowing that even in death, she would serve her purpose. But her daughter had chosen a different path. A path where death meant only the splitting of her psyche. And where true death – the death of Lux and Luna – would result in annihilation.

And so in life, Bella would serve life. But in true death, she could serve no one.

"No," Petrusa stated, crossing her arms over her chest. The Queen of the Dead was dressed, as usual, in her badass bone-armor. Armor even more awesome than Lucia's.

"No?" Lucia retorted incredulously. "She's an initiate of the guild. You're contractually obligated to help her!"

"I'm contractually obligated to *protect* her," Petrusa clarified. "In case of her being attacked. But in addition to attempting to save Gideon, it seems your daughter has decided to start a war with the Pentad."

"What?"

"She's allied herself with Simon, and at this very moment, they've simultaneously attacked all five major cities in the kingdom, as well as Centrum itself," Petrusa revealed. Lucia frowned, processing this.

"Oh," she replied. "Damn. Girl's got balls."

"She is her mother's daughter," Petrusa agreed.

"Bella's not the vindictive type," Lucia said. "Why attack the whole kingdom?"

"I suspect to distract them from her attempt to save your husband."

"Clever girl," Lucia murmured, feeling a flash of pride. "So she's in Centrum?"

"Yes," Petrusa answered.

"So help her get Gideon," Lucia prompted. "Get in, get out. She'd call off the attacks, and that'll be that."

"No."

"Why not?" Lucia pressed. "You have a lot to lose from this war," she pointed out. "Those Gemini are a pain in the ass to deal with, and an attack on the Twin Spires can't be good for business."

"War *is* good for business," Petrusa retorted. "As long as we win. And we *will* win."

"So you're not going to help your own?"

"Attacking the Pentad was not a sanctioned action," Petrusa reasoned. "The Dark Circle cannot intervene in every war its members – and potential members – initiate."

"Granted."

"And Bella is not yet a Necromancer," Petrusa continued. "She has yet to pass her Test. Therefore, our support of her will remain limited until such time as she *does* pass her Test."

"Her contract says she has to undergo a three-year internship before she can take her Test!" Lucia complained.

"Her contract specifies that she will be enrolled in a three-year internship that can *prepare* her for her Test," Petrusa corrected. "If she passes it sooner, all the more impressive."

"So you're just gonna sit this one out?" Lucia asked.

"If I didn't, it wouldn't count."

Lucia crossed her arms over her chest, glaring at Petrusa.

"Well aren't you a cold-hearted bitch," she grumbled. Petrusa only smiled.

"That," she replied, "…is something we have in common."

"Yeah, well *I'm* not sitting on my ass waiting for my family to be slaughtered," Lucia retorted.

"I expected nothing less."

"Wonderful," Lucia muttered. "Thanks for the help."

She turned away from Petrusa, looking out over the edge of the rock platform. The city of Arx Mortus lay far below, a city of shadows. The dead milled about on the streets, slaving away in death as they had in life. All for their queen, a woman that – despite being alive – often seemed as dead inside as her subjects.

"If you do attack the Pentad," Petrusa called out after her, "…and your daughter fails, I will not protect you."

"They're going to kill my husband!" Lucia snapped, whirling around to glare at the woman.

"Then I suggest you don't fail," Petrusa replied evenly. Lucia jabbed a finger at her.

"*You're* the one who taught me that we were family," she accused. "That the Dark Circle cared for their own!"

"I also taught you your first lesson," Petrusa countered evenly.

Lucia grimaced, lowering her hand to her side. She felt her anger dissipate, knowing that Petrusa was right. The first lesson the woman had taught her was the same lesson that Lucia had taught Bella not long ago. It was the very nature of the Test to become a full Necromancer. A member of the Dark Circle.

"Learn to solve my own damn problems," she recited.

Petrusa smiled, gesturing at the city beyond the edge of the cliff…and at the cemetery far in the distance, that served as the main entrance – and exit – of the Plane of Death.

"You're still a bitch," Lucia muttered.

"Naturally," Petrusa agreed. "I'm a Necromancer."

With a thought, Lucia dissolved into mist, flying off the edge of the platform and zooming over Arx Mortus toward the cemetery in the distance. There was, she knew, a coffin within that would take her to the Underground…and then to the land bordering Centrum.

And when she got there, heaven help whoever was stupid enough to get in her way.

Chapter 38

Gideon watched as Temper crumbled to dust, the white light that'd surrounded the living blade drawn into the amulet around Lux's brilliant neck. Lucia's amulet, possessed of the power to trade Lucia's soul with whoever was foolish enough to kill her.

It was Temper who had killed Lucia, decapitating her before she could be trapped by Yero. And so, at the moment of her death, they'd traded souls, and Temper had murdered his own spirit. Kept alive only by possessing Lucia's soul, Temper had managed to continue existing.

But now Lucia's heart had come to claim what was hers.

The amulet pulsed with a ruby-red light, and Gideon knew with sudden elation that his wife was once again whole.

General Craven's eyes widened as he beheld this spectacle. Luna kicked off the reflective inner surface of Aganon, bursting backward as the being of light that she was. For not even Craven's powerful grip could hold onto pure light.

Lux shot away from the living statue, colliding with Luna to form Bella once again.

"Back!" Gideon told her, leaping between her and Craven. He held his cane before him, even as Myko kept Craven's guards at bay. Though the guards managed to score a few strikes with their swords and spears, Myko merely moon-dashed to heal instantly, crashing into them in the process and sending them flying backward onto the lawn.

Craven recovered, turning to glare at Gideon, his right hand clenched into a fist.

"What have you done?" he demanded.

"You're asking the wrong person," Gideon replied. Craven glanced at Bella, then returned his gaze to Gideon. And while Craven's guards continued to attack them – what remained, anyway – Manus joined the fight, his many hands shooting off Bella and grabbing the guards' weapons, decapitating them.

In mere seconds, they were all neutralized. Leaving Bella and Gideon alone with Craven. Manus returned to her, re-forming her bone armor.

"Very nice," Gideon murmured, eyeing Bella's newest creation with approval.

"Certainly has come in handy," Bella replied with a wink. Gideon chuckled at the pun…as did Cain.

"It makes me laugh every time," the cane mused, shaking his skull-head.

"You leave me no choice," Craven declared. "I will call on the armies of Centrum to destroy you where you stand. Even you and your army cannot succeed against the full might of the Pentad."

"Perhaps not," Gideon conceded. "But I can certainly handle *you.*"

Craven's expression hardened.

"You forget the outcome of our last battle," he growled.

"I seem to remember being a bit distracted," Gideon shot back. "And to be honest, I was going easy on you, for Eldora's sake."

"*Queen* Eldora," Craven snapped.

"Had I been trying," Gideon continued, "…you wouldn't be standing here right now. You'd be dead."

Craven said nothing, but his expression said everything.

"In fact, I'd wager I can take you again," Gideon mused, his magic glove flying off his hand and floating beside him. He displayed his forearm-stumps for Craven. "With my hands tied behind my back, so to speak."

"You cannot defeat me," Craven retorted. "I am the right hand of the queen!"

"Don't tell me," Gideon replied. "Show me."

Craven hesitated, gazing down the street, past the entrance to Tartarus. The Gemini army was a half-mile away now, battling the countless soldiers and Painters of the Pentad. But towering over them all was a truly massive green blob, standing taller than even the tallest buildings around it. Well over a hundred feet tall, and as wide as three city blocks, it was clearly Goo.

And Goo was *decimating* the enemy.

For he was sending hundreds of tentacles outward from his body, pulling in Centrum's soldiers dozens at a time. And their Painters, and the Painters' Familiars. He flowed around the buildings, coming toward them slowly but surely.

Craven turned back to Gideon.

"Very well," he said.

* * *

Craven stood before Gideon, gripping Aganon tightly. He settled into a fighting stance, waiting for the Painter to attack.

"Hardly a fair fight considering I don't have my uniform or my paintings," Gideon told him. "Mind if I borrow my daughter's boots and cape?"

Craven paused, considering this. Gideon *was* significantly handicapped. With no uniform and no hands, even if Craven defeated Gideon, he would always wonder if things might have turned out differently if the Painter had possessed his full powers.

"It is permissible," Craven decided.

He watched as Bella removed her boots and her cape, handing them to Gideon. The Painter put them on, then faced Craven.

"I want you to know that my admiration of you has not changed, old friend," Gideon stated. "Regardless of our differences – and the outcome of our battle – I regard you warmly."

"You were a man of honor," Craven conceded. "I take no pleasure in your fate."

"Shall we?" Gideon asked. Craven inclined his head.

"For the Pentad," Craven declared, lifting his shield in the air in salute.

"For my family," Gideon replied, lifting his cane.

"Let it begin," Craven declared.

And then he lifted his right hand, shooting his gauntlet at Gideon.

Gideon whipped his cane at the gauntlet, stopping it instantly in mid-air, then whacked it again, before it even had a chance to fall. It flew right at Craven's face, striking his forehead with a *clang*.

Craven barely felt it.

He recalled the gauntlet with a thought, and it flew back onto his hand. Gideon was already leaping at him, swinging his cane at Craven's chest.

Craven blocked with Aganon, and felt it freeze in his hands for a split-second. Gideon's cane ricocheted off, and Gideon used the momentum of that ricochet to spin around and *whack* Craven's shield to the side.

It barely moved.

Craven lunged forward, ramming his shield into Gideon. But Gideon merely tapped it with his cane, stopping the shield instantly. But as Craven was still moving forward, he slammed into his own shield.

It was like hitting a brick wall.

He stumbled backward, and Gideon *whacked* his shield, shoving it backward right as Craven was off-balance. Craven fell, landing on his back with a *thump*.

Craven grunted, aiming Aganon at Gideon and gripping the shield tightly. With a thought, he activated it, summoning the God Ray.

Aganon's golden metal glowed impossibly bright, brighter than the sun.

Gideon tapped the shield right before it discharged, dodging out of the way just as the God Ray shot outward from the shield.

Craven tried to turn the shield to aim at Gideon, but having just been tapped by the Painter's cane, its momentum had been momentarily halted. The beam discharged…leaving Gideon unharmed.

Rolling onto his side, Craven got to his feet, facing the Painter. He inclined his head reluctantly.

"Well done," he conceded.

Gideon smiled, inclining his head in response.

Craven shot his gauntlet at Gideon then, purposefully missing a few inches to the left. It sailed past Gideon's head, continuing onward over the gilded street…and Craven recalled it, stepping to the side so that the gauntlet's path back to him would make it strike Gideon in the back of the head.

But Gideon's cape activated, wrapping itself around the gauntlet and deflecting it to the side.

Gideon threw his cane at Craven's head, and Craven lifted Aganon to block. The cane struck harmlessly, bouncing off…and Gideon's glove shot out, catching the cane in mid-air and flying around Craven, whacking him in the back of the head.

He felt himself freeze momentarily, and the cane struck the back of his head again. His head snapped forward, banging against his shield. A blow that did no damage, of course.

But it was *irritating.*

The magic glove flew back onto Gideon's stump, and Craven recalled his gauntlet back to his right hand.

"You seem upset," Gideon observed, smirking at Craven.

"I am not," Craven retorted.

"Mm hmm," Gideon replied. "Sure."

Craven grit his teeth, activating Aganon again. It glowed bright gold, drawing on its stored power to release the God Ray. At the same time, he shot his gauntlet out at Gideon's head to distract the Painter.

Gideon dodged, striking the gauntlet with his cane. Then he shot his glove and cane at Craven, striking the very bottom of the shield. It rotated downward to face the ground…and Craven's feet. The glove zipped between Craven's legs then, striking him right in the butt.

Which again, didn't hurt. But it stopped him from being able to lift his shield in time before Aganon fired.

The God Ray burst out of the legendary shield, right at Craven's feet.

The lawn under him burst instantly into flames, and Craven shot upward, the God Ray launching him hundreds of feet into the air. He ended the God Ray with a thought, then – instead of recalling his gauntlet to himself – he called himself to it.

And conveniently, it happened to be at Gideon's feet.

The wind screamed in Craven's ears as he burst downward toward his gauntlet, and he held Aganon before him, activating it again. It began to glow bright gold, though not as brightly as before. Its power was limited, taking time to recharge.

Then Gideon shot his magic glove to intercept.

It flew right under Craven's shield, whacking his foot…and stopping him cold in mid-air.

Aganon, however, did not stop.

It tore free from Craven's grip, and Gideon's glove zoomed after it, dropping the cane and grabbing the shield by its handle in the back. It spun the shield around, aiming right at Craven.

Just as the God Ray fired.

The deadly beam struck Craven in a flash of blinding light and heat, bringing him to a lurching stop almost instantly. He felt himself being flung backward into the air, his body and armor getting hotter and hotter.

The pain was sudden and excruciating.

Craven screamed as the God Ray blasted him ever-upward, its assault unrelenting. The pain overwhelmed his mind, allowing for no thought. No strategy.

Only agony.

Then, at last, it was done.

The blinding light faded, and Craven felt himself decelerating. He blinked, his vision slowly returning. He saw the city of Centrum over a thousand feet below him, his armor and body glowing red-hot, like molten metal. Indeed, his armor *was* molten in spots, melting against his skin. Even his helmet had partially melted, streams of gold and red dripping down his face like sweat. Drops of liquid metal fell from his body, his powerful armor no match for Craven's ultimate weapon.

He reached the peak of his flight, and began to plummet toward the earth.

He recalled his gauntlet to himself, willing it back to his hand. It shot upward toward him, even as his flesh cooled from the wind screeching louder and louder in his ears. It reconnected with him in mid-fall, and Craven shot it out at Aganon, using it to tear the shield from Gideon's glove and bring it back to him. Then Craven activated Aganon again, holding it straight down below him.

It flashed gold, and then a massive energy shield grew from it, over a hundred feet wide.

The great expanse of lawn rose up to meet Craven, and he slammed into it with terrible force. Earth shot up around him, blasting upward into the sky. And the earth cratered beneath him, sinking a few feet.

He deactivated his shield, then stomped out of the crater, finding Gideon standing on the street over a hundred feet away, resting his weight on his cane. Craven's feet – still glowing red-hot – scorched the grass with each step, the water within the grass and earth sizzling and steaming.

Gideon eyed him as he approached. Or rather, eyed Craven's partially-melted armor.

"You *do* have live canvas under your armor," the Painter observed. "And it appears it couldn't stand up to the God Ray."

Craven looked down. His armor *was* lined with live canvas on the inside, to prevent him from being trapped in a painting. Much of that canvas had burned away, but of course the armor at his back had fared better.

"You are clever," Craven conceded. "But even my God Ray cannot defeat me."

"So it seems," Gideon agreed. Craven grimaced, finding the Painter's calmness profoundly irritating. Which he knew very well was Gideon's intent. Irritation led to losing one's temper, and that losing one's temper led to mistakes.

The Painter was not only a master of his craft, but a master of combat. No wonder that Queen Eldora had held the man in such high regard.

"You cannot generate enough force to harm me," Craven pointed out, stopping ten yards from Gideon. "You don't have the White Dragon to feed power to your cane."

"No," Gideon agreed. He pointed his stump at something over Craven's shoulder. "But I *do* have him."

Craven twisted around…and froze.

For there, not a hundred feet away, flowing around the tall buildings of downtown Centrum, was a giant green blob. Over a hundred feet tall, as wide as four city blocks now. A mass of translucent flesh that towered over the city, with an army of multifaceted soldiers swarming around it.

And atop that blob stood a figure in a bright white suit, wielding a glowing silver sword.

A mere boy.

The blob lowered the boy to the street by extending a piece of its flesh in a sort of tentacle, and the boy strode toward them, sword in-hand. The boy lowered the sword's tip to the street, and it plunged through without any resistance at all, cutting a deep rut in the golden pavement as he approached. An army of the mirror-faceted soldiers walked with him, thousands upon thousands of them.

"Goo!" Gideon shouted. "Jump!"

The blob flattened itself to the ground, drawing into itself, and then burst up into the air, sailing hundreds of feet upward…and forward.

Right toward them.

Craven lifted Aganon, mentally triggering its energy shield. A shield that spread outward over a hundred feet wide and long above Craven's head.

But not nearly big enough to stop Goo.

At the same time, Gideon whipped his magic glove up at Goo, cane in hand. It reached Goo in mid-jump, whacking the massive blob.

And stopping its momentum instantaneously.

The blob hovered in the air motionlessly for a moment, then began to fall straight down, far enough away to miss Craven and Gideon. But

Gideon's glove zoomed back to Gideon's stump, and the Painter charged at Craven, sending the magic glove and cane flying at him.

Craven lowered his shield to block, the large energy shield dissipating, and the cane struck it.

With an ear-shattering *boom*.

Craven careened backward so rapidly that the ground was a blur beneath him. Within seconds, he'd flown a quarter-mile backward, smashing through the fence around Tartarus. He slammed into the left side of the obsidian demon-head's jaw, coming to an abrupt stop.

Embedded three feet within it.

Craven grunted, trying to pry himself free of the obsidian. But he was wedged so tightly he could barely move. His shield had slipped out of his grasp, burying itself into the obsidian a few inches from his left hand, which he couldn't even budge. But he managed to pry his right hand and forearm out, bringing hunks of obsidian out with them. They fell to the street with a clatter.

He stared at Gideon through the gaping hole in the fence he'd created. The Painter had mounted Myko, and was moon-dashing toward him, approaching rapidly. But the silver wolf's light was fading, each moon-dash bringing him a shorter and shorter distance. Gideon shot his magic glove upward at the still-descending Goo, stopping the blob just before it struck the ground.

Craven tried to pry his shield-arm out, but it was thoroughly stuck. And Gideon stopped moon-dashing, landing a mere fifty feet away. Myko galloped toward Craven...and Gideon's glove flew back into his hand, returning his cane to him.

Craven lifted his right hand, pointing his gauntlet at Gideon.

And fired.

His gauntlet shot right at the Painter, zooming through the hole in the fence and flying at Gideon's head. Craven focused, willing himself to be recalled to it...knowing that in doing so, it would pull him free from the black demon's head of Tartarus.

He felt its pull, and smiled grimly...until Gideon swung his cane to intercept.

The gauntlet *exploded.*

Craven's eyes widened, the force pulling him forward vanishing instantly. His gauntlet shattered, its shrapnel striking the fence and the obsidian statue, and pelting his face and body. But he barely felt the pain of their impact. Barely felt anything at all.

Except shock.

For his gauntlet Dextro, as old as he was and nearly as legendary as Aganon, was gone.

Craven roared, straining against the three feet of rock that imprisoned him. Willing himself to be free of it. But he had no leverage to work with.

And as he struggled helplessly, Gideon dismounted, stepping through the hole in the fence and striding up to him.

Behind Gideon, the great green blob had landed, and was oozing rapidly toward them.

Gideon stopped a few feet from Craven, resting his weight on his cane.

"You have not defeated me!" Craven shouted, straining against his rocky prison. He heard the rock *crack*, and he found himself able to move his left arm forward a bit. He strained to reach for his shield, knowing that if he could just grab its handle, he could activate the God Ray and be freed.

Gideon stepped forward, *whacking* Craven between the eyes, stopping his movements momentarily.

"Yield," the Painter ordered, pointing the butt of his staff between Craven's eyes. Craven glared at him.

"You have not defeated me!" he insisted.

"I have no desire to destroy you," Gideon shot back calmly. "Yield and I will leave with my daughter."

"I will not," Craven snapped, straining for Aganon. His hand slipped a fraction of an inch closer. Gideon eyed that hand, then sighed.

"So be it," he muttered.

The boy in the white suit strode up to Gideon's side, offering the glowing silver sword to Gideon. Gideon hesitated, then gave his cane to Myko. The wolf held it between his teeth, and Gideon took the silver sword, holding it before him.

Its blade glowed bright silver.

"This was my son's," Gideon confessed, eyeing the sword wistfully. "I painted it for him. A blade that could pass through anything by transforming into something harder than whatever it touched."

"I am Invictium!" Craven declared.

"And this is magic," Gideon retorted. "The more creative we artists are, the more powerful our magic will be. And the magic in this sword," he added, gazing at its fine edge, "…is beyond anything the Pentad would have approved."

"You admit to violating the law," Craven growled.

"The law is wrong."

"The law keeps the people safe," Craven argued. "If you artists could create anything you wanted…"

"Then you would have to trust that the good natures of most would counteract the evil natures of a few," Gideon interjected. "You would have to trust people to do the right thing instead of using violence to force them to."

"Artists cannot be trusted," Craven argued. "You know this. You spent your life bringing rogue artists to justice!"

"As I – and many others – would have even if we hadn't been compelled by the queen to do so."

"You are not above the law," Craven insisted.

"You are the Law personified," Gideon retorted. His cape whipped off his body, wrapping around Craven's right hand and pulling his arm taught. "The law is not perfect."

Craven tried to pull his right hand away from the magical cape, but its grip was surprisingly strong. It forced his arm out straight, and Gideon lifted the sword up high over his head.

"And neither are you," he declared…and chopped downward with the silver sword.

The glowing blade struck Craven's wrist, the razor-sharp edge sinking an inch into his flesh.

The pain was instantaneous…and excruciating.

Craven howled, staring at the blade in disbelief. Gideon yanked it free, and Craven immediately tried to enter Torpor to heal the inch-deep gash. But Gideon swung again, striking the exact same spot…and the blade buried itself halfway through his wrist.

Torpor came to his feet first, spreading up his legs and his hips. They went numb, as if dead…and that numbness rose to his belly, toward his chest. As it did, his flesh turned utterly transparent, the true appearance of Invictium.

Gideon tore his blade free from Craven's wrist, then cried out, chopping downward with all his might. The sword struck true as before, slicing into Craven's flesh even as Torpor reached his chest and spread down his arms.

The glowing blade went right through, severing Craven's hand just before the wave of Torpor reached it.

Craven's eyes widened in horror…and then his head passed beneath the surface of his consciousness, and Torpor – the little death – claimed him.

Chapter 39

The Guardians of the Heart watched as a man in the red uniform of a courier burst into the Locus Legis, weaving around the gold and red pedestal and rushing toward the shimmering portal that led to the Heart of the Pentad. They lifted their white swords to cross each other, blocking the courier's way into the portal.

The courier skid to a halt before them, his eyes wide, pupils wider. The vessels at his temples pumped rapidly, engorged with blood. And his forehead was slick with sweat, his breath coming in short, desperate gasps.

"The enemy!" he blurted out. "They're almost at the Palatium. They're coming for the queen!"

The guardians said nothing, nor did they move.

"I need to speak with the queen," the courier insisted. "General Craven ordered me to relay a message personally!"

The guardians glanced at each other, then at the courier.

They lowered their swords.

The courier gave a relieved smile, bowing at them, then stepping into the portal. And the Guardians of the Heart resumed their silent stillness, ever-watching, ever-waiting. For their Creator had willed it so. They could not disobey her will, for her will had become theirs.

And to guard her life was to guard their own.

* * *

When Aldo, personal courier to General Craven, reached the very top of the golden staircase leading to the Heart of the Pentad, he stopped to catch his breath, bending over and resting his hands on his knees. A moment later, he continued, stepping into the huge heart-shaped chamber that served as Queen Eldora's throne room, living quarters, and meeting chamber.

He resisted the urge to gawk, having never seen it before.

And though he'd never seen Queen Eldora either, he knew her instantly when he laid eyes upon her. For she was standing before a huge levitating orb, what appeared to be a replica of the world. A slender woman with the palest skin he'd ever seen, dressed in a simple red sleeveless gown. Wide strips of red cloth extended from the back of the gown near the shoulder blades, wrapping around her arms all the way to her wrists. She had long red hair, as straight as an arrow, and was holding a small golden monocle in one hand, which she was using to peer upward at the levitating orb.

Aldo stepped closer, then hesitated, remembering himself. He lowered himself to one knee, dropping his gaze to the floor.

"My queen," he stated. "I have…"

"I know," she interjected.

Aldo's breath caught in his throat, and he stood, lifting his gaze to her. She lowered her monocle gracefully, turning to gaze at him. With blood-red irises that seemed to glow in the light of the chamber.

"General Craven wishes me to relay a message," Aldo insisted apologetically.

She just stared.

"Ecce populus venit de speculo ad recipiendum Gideon. Nos postulo vos mea regina," he recited.

"Indeed," she replied, setting the monocle on a small wooden stool nearby. She gazed up at the orb then. "The enemy approaches, and my right hand has been vanquished."

Aldo watched her. As she just stood there, utterly calm. Staring at the orb. Not even seeming to breathe.

"My queen," he began, but she lifted a hand to stop him, turning to face him with those eerie eyes.

"Do you doubt me?" she inquired.

Aldo swallowed.

"No my queen," he replied.

"Then why are you so afraid?"

He paused.

"Because I fear for you, my queen," he answered.

"You do," she agreed. She turned away for a moment, then spun to face him, extending an arm out gracefully at the same time. The cloth wrapped around her arm came free, whipping outward to his right. She grabbed it, and with a flick of her wrist, it wrapped around his neck several times, the end coming to a rest draped over his chest.

He froze, resisting the urge to take a step back. The cloth was silky-smooth, and had a sweet scent to it. Aldo's thoughts scattered, his mind suddenly unable to focus.

Queen Eldora moved toward him then, seeming to glide across the floor rather than to walk. She stopped before him, far closer than he would have found comfortable, her face a foot from his. And though she was shorter than he, Aldo felt profoundly vulnerable in her presence. He found himself trembling, and willed himself to stop. But the more he tried to control it, the worse it got.

She stared up at him with those strange eyes, her expression unreadable.

"Do you trust me?" she inquired.

"Of course," he blurted.

"Why?"

He blinked.

"You are the queen," he answered.

She stared at him a moment longer, then turned around, gliding away from him. And with another flick of her wrist, the cloth around his neck came free. She twirled her arm, the cloth snapping back to her and wrapping around her slender arm once again.

Then she stopped in the very center of the Heart of the Pentad, turning so her profile was visible to him. She gazed down at her right hand, at a golden ring on her right ring finger.

"Strange," she murmured, sliding it off her finger and holding it between her thumb and forefinger. She lifted it upward, gazing at it. "That we often create the means of our own destruction."

"My queen?" Aldo asked. She turned to regard him.

"Every good story has a villain," she explained. "And a villain is most often their own undoing."

She lowered her arm, turning to stare at the ring again. She dropped it into her palm, closing her hand around it.

"I have a choice, Aldo," she stated.

Aldo blinked, taken aback. For he had not told her his name.

"I can pretend to be vulnerable, and allow a good man to live," she told him. "Good shall triumph, and my subjects will lose confidence in me. Artists will be emboldened to defy the law, and rival kingdoms will seize the moment to attack."

She paused.

"I can seize this opportunity to show *my* strength," she continued, "…and end this myself. A good man will die, but my kingdom will remain safe. And all will be reminded of why I am worthy of the throne."

She opened her hand, displaying the ring again.

"Or I can end this story the way it began," she concluded, "…and use Gideon's gift against him. So that all artists might know what happens to those who defy the laws that I, in my wisdom, have created."

Aldo stood there, uncertain of how to respond…and of whether he should respond at all.

"Do you know why I live within this heart?" she inquired, gesturing around her.

"No my queen."

"The Pentad is a living thing," she explained. "A kingdom bound by laws, as all life is. Laws that shape it, create order from it. Without them, there would be chaos, and the organism would perish."

She paused.

"This Heart reminds me of this," she continued. "My kingdom is an organism built of many lives. And all organisms must exclude that which is not them, as a body fights infection. Though the infection is not evil, the organism must destroy it, or be destroyed. You can fight the infection, or in failing to do so, feed it."

"Yes my queen," Aldo murmured.

"This is the heart, and you," she told him, her crimson eyes flashing, "...are the blood."

Aldo stood there, transfixed by her gaze.

"So be it," she murmured. "Extinctio, Perdere inimici mei. Parce meis amicis!" she cried.

She threw the ring straight up into the air, then swung her arms so that the cloth wrapped around them unfurled. They shot outward to her sides ten feet in either direction, and she spun in a rapid, graceful circle, the long trails of cloth twirling to form a much larger circle. She flicked one as it sailed upward toward the ring, sending a wave through the ribbon that traveled all the way to the tip. And the tip of the cloth snapped like a whip just as it touched the ring, sending it bursting upward to the ceiling.

At the same time, she shifted her dance, twirling so rapidly and gracefully that she seemed to be a thing of fluid, not flesh and bone. Her pale limbs flashed in the magical light of the chamber as they spun, seeming to bend at impossible angles.

And the space around her seemed to *shift*, reality bending with her. It contorted, space and substance rippling and twirling, until the floor under Aldo's feet lurched clockwise.

He cried out, falling to the side, and watched as the queen spun faster, her body and the long crimson tails of her gown forming shapes and symbols that tore their universe apart.

The ceiling far above Queen Eldora opened like a flower, exposing the bright blue sky. Sunlight spilled into the Heart of the Pentad.

And to Aldo's horror, the queen burst into flames!

She *shrieked*, the sound tearing through Aldo's ears and into his soul. Yet still she danced, even as flames consumed her. The golden ring flew right through the opening in the ceiling, soaring up into the blue sky.

Queen Eldora stopped

The world righted itself instantly, the floor shifting back to its original position and the ceiling re-forming itself. The sunlight vanished, and the flames that had engulfed Queen Eldora a moment earlier were snuffed out. Smoke rose from her body, her pale skin charred, her face red and blistered. Her eyes were closed, the lids blackened.

But when she opened them, her crimson irises remained untouched, boring right into Aldo's soul.

He struggled to his feet, swaying a little. His heart hammered in his chest, his whole body trembling. He could only watch in horror as his queen, burnt almost beyond recognition, stared back at him.

Then she glided forward, stopping a foot before him.

Aldo grimaced, the smell of burnt flesh making him want to gag. But he stood tall, refusing to insult his queen. She smiled at him, putting a hand on his cheek. It was rough and dry, and sent a chill through him.

"You have served your purpose," she murmured, her voice as smooth and gentle as ever, in stark contrast to her mutilated body. "I give you one more."

"Yes my queen," he whispered.

"You are the blood," she reminded him.

"I am the blood," he agreed, transfixed by her gaze. Twin circles of crimson fire, glowing against the darkness of her pupils.

Exquisite, like her every movement. Like her dance.

"Give yourself to me," she murmured, wrapping her hands behind the back of his head, cradling him. She stepped closer, until their bodies touched. He moaned, unable to stop himself.

Her touch was ecstasy.

He closed his eyes, feeling her closeness. There was no heat emanating from her, and her charred flesh against his should have filled him with disgust. But he felt only rapture, a feeling that, for the first time in his life, everything was *right.*

Aldo was where he was supposed to be, with whom he was destined to be. Doing what he should do.

Queen Eldora closed her eyes, resting her lips against the side of his neck.

And as the world fell away from Aldo, his hopes and fears fading into oblivion, he felt utterly content to feel nothing at all. For though he knew with sudden clarity that this was his end, it was, like his beginning, a miracle.

Chapter 40

The depths of Torpor did not soothe Craven. Like death itself, the little death offered an absence of suffering, but also the absence of every other emotion. He was only vaguely aware of a *self*. That there was an "I."

Time passed, though if an eternity or mere seconds, he could not know.

Craven became aware of a beckoning then, a psychic prodding. Without knowing what he was doing or why, he willed himself to rise from the depths of this ocean, his vast unconscious mind. He burst through the thin veil of the surface, emerging into the light…and an awareness of his life.

Brilliant blue assaulted his eyes, and he blinked, seeing a dark shape silhouetted against it. Something close to him, merely a foot away.

It was, he realized as his vision focused, him.

Or rather, a part of him.

Craven stared, seeing his right arm extended before him. He followed it from his muscular shoulder down to his bicep, then to his forearm. Then his wrist.

His eyes widened, his breath catching in his throat.

For there, where his right hand should have been, was…nothing. A flat stump.

He gazed at it, feeling suddenly and absolutely certain that this arm was someone else's. That it wasn't his at all. But when he moved his arm, the stump moved with it.

"Myko," he heard a voice say. "Give Goo a hand, would you?"

Craven looked beyond his stump, seeing Gideon Myles standing before him. A glowing silver sword was in the Painter's right hand, and beside him, the giant wolf Myko, Gideon's cane clutched in its mouth. And beside Myko, the girl Bella.

And beyond *them*, a massive green blob.

The blob called Goo extended a small tentacle outward to Myko's side, and Myko dropped the cane, picking something up from the ground near Craven's feet and handing it to the tentacle. It was a severed hand.

His hand.

Goo sucked it into its green tentacle, bringing Craven's hand into his massive body. It vanished from sight.

Gone.

Gideon held the glowing silver sword, gazing at Craven with an icy expression.

"Promise to never come after myself or my family," the Painter ordered. Then he lifted his blade, setting it against the side of Craven's neck. "Or your head is next."

Craven stared back at the Painter, a chill running through him. For he knew without a doubt now that the Painter could – and would – make good on the threat.

Execute the law, the queen had ordered him.

He'd failed.

For he was not an invincible juggernaut. He did not deserve the honor of being the right hand of the queen. And while the law was inviolable, he had been violated, his flesh cut from him.

He was Craven, and who he was…was not enough.

"Promise me," Gideon insisted.

"Never," Craven replied.

Gideon sighed, his jawline rippling.

"Very well," the Painter muttered.

Gideon wound up then, and swung the silver sword at the side of Craven's neck. The blade cut into his flesh, sinking an inch deep before stopping. The pain was instantaneous and agonizing, unlike anything Craven had experienced.

He grunted, biting off a scream.

"Dad," Bella protested, putting a hand on Gideon's shoulder.

Gideon ignored her, pushing her backward, then jerking the blade free from Craven's neck. He wound up again, the silver blade glowing against the backdrop of Goo's hulking presence.

"Daddy!" Bella insisted.

Gideon swung again, striking in precisely the same spot as before. Craven gasped as the blade sank halfway into his thick neck, and again as Gideon jerked the blade free.

"Mr. Myles," an urgent voice interjected. It was the boy in the white suit. He grabbed Gideon's shoulder, gripping it tightly. "We need to run."

"Simon," Gideon began.

"*Now,*" Simon interrupted.

And then a golden glow appeared around Craven, surrounding his body. He found himself suddenly unable to move even his severed stump.

Gideon turned away from him, staring at something in the distance. The crimson tower of the Palatium, a quarter-mile away. The tower's peak seemed to swell, and opened suddenly like a blooming flower. A tiny golden light flew out of it, rising upward into the blue sky.

A golden light that grew rapidly, making it quite clear what it was.

A gold serpent biting its own tail, fashioned into a ring.

Craven watched as it grew ever-larger, rising above the Palatium until it was far above the tower's peak, and easily a hundred yards in diameter. The serpent-ring stopped then, hovering in the air…and began to spin. At first slowly, then faster and faster.

And in the center of the ring, the blue sky was replaced with utter blackness.

"Run!" Simon shouted.

"Kill me," Craven interjected, glaring at Gideon. The Painter ignored Craven, handing the silver sword to Simon. Then he retrieved his cane, and vaulted onto Myko's back.

"Bella, get on," he instructed, even as Myko lowered himself to the ground to let her. Bella did as she was told, climbing behind Gideon on Myko's back.

"Kill me!" Craven yelled. But still Gideon ignored him. He struggled in vain to free himself from his obsidian prison. To attack Gideon and force the man to end him.

He *deserved* to die.

But it was futile; Gideon ignored him. Treated him as if he were nothing of concern. Unworthy of consideration…cast aside like a useless relic.

"What is that thing?" Bella asked.

"Extinctio," Gideon answered grimly. "And if we don't leave right now, we're all going to die."

* * *

Bella wrapped her arms around Gideon's waist, and Myko took off, moon-dashing over the fence surrounding the obsidian head. He was almost out of moonlight, his moon-dash barely clearing the fence to the street beyond.

"Go!" Gideon cried.

Bella clung on to Gideon, twisting around to look back. High above the red tower, the serpent-ring grew ever-larger, until it was easily a hundred feet in diameter. All around them, the Gemini that had covered the streets as mirrors shattered, re-forming into their humanoid bodies. The Pentad's soldiers and Painters…many still fighting the Gemini…glowed with a golden light, identical to the one that had appeared around Craven. It froze them in place like statues.

"What's going on?" Bella asked Gideon as they charged down the street.

Then the wind came.

It started as a strong breeze that whipped through Bella's hair, threatening to shove her backward off of Myko. She pressed herself against Gideon's back, but the wind only intensified, screaming through the streets and around the buildings. And while none of the Pentad's defenders seemed affected by it, the Gemini were another story.

The mirrored soldiers around them slid backward…and then *flew* backward and upward into the air.

Bella gasped, watching as hundreds of the Gemini sailed through the sky, tumbling madly in mid-air. Toward the snake-ring rotating faster and faster above the crimson tower.

Toward the black void it had created.

The snake-ring rotated even faster, until it was a golden blur around the black circle, like the sun during an eclipse. And the Gemini – hundreds of them…*thousands* of them…were sucked toward that blackness.

They shattered when they drew close, their fragments vanishing into the dark circle.

"We must retreat!" Cain cried at her hip. "To the sewers!"

More of the Gemini flew backward and upward, nearly all of Simon's soldiers all over the city rising from the streets. They filled the sky like millions of glittering diamonds, sailing in a steady stream toward oblivion. It didn't matter where they were in Centrum; all were taken.

The wind shrieked in Bella's ears, pulling her backward. She cried out, her grip on Gideon slipping. Myko tried moon-dashing forward, but barely went twenty feet. And as the wind grew ever more powerful, Myko's gallop slowed, then stopped.

They began to slide backward.

"Dad!" Bella blurted out.

And then her hands slipped from his waist, and the wind shoved her backward, throwing her off Myko's back.

"Bella!" Gideon cried.

Bella's guts lurched as she flew upward, the street dropping out from beneath her. The world spun around her as she tumbled through the air, rising faster and faster. She spread her arms and legs out wide, and the tumbling slowed.

Gideon and Myko leapt to save her, moon-dashing toward her. But Myko was out of moonlight, and his dash ended as soon as it began.

"Bella!" Gideon screamed. He and Myko flew after her, pulled toward the black disc above the crimson tower just like Bella and the Gemini. Gideon tucked his cane in his armpit, and his magic glove shot off his stump, flying toward her. Bella reached out, and it grabbed her hand, pulling her downward. Or it tried to; the wind was growing stronger, and the glove only managed to slow her ascent, not stop it.

"It's not working!" she shouted.

The glove let go, zipping back to Gideon and grabbing his cane from his armpit. It zoomed back to Bella…and tapped her with the cane.

She stopped instantaneously.

There was no sensation of deceleration. She'd been moving one moment, and rendered utterly still the next. But a split-second later, she was yanked backward and upward again. She grabbed onto the cane reflexively.

"Goo, catch her!" Gideon cried. "Bella, hold on to the cane!"

Goo was ahead and below them, his huge body rippling violently in the screaming wind, like the surface of the ocean in a hurricane. Even he was starting to lift up from the street, his front half rising into the air. Goo sent long tentacles after Gideon and Bella, tentacles of green gelatin that rippled so violently that they started to disintegrate. Gobs of his translucent flesh tore off.

Goo sent thicker tentacles after them, and one managed to reach Myko and Gideon, wrapping around them and propelling them down toward the bulk of Goo's body.

Bella held on to Gideon's cane, his glove resisting the pull of the dark circle as best it could. Another one of Goo's tentacles reached for her, grabbing her ankles and wrapping around them. The tentacle pulled at her…and then tore free from the rest of Goo's body in the violence of the gale, flying past her.

With the tentacle letting go of her ankles suddenly, her legs swung backward, her body rotating so that the butt of Gideon's cane smacked her in the upper chest, just above her chest-painting…and discharged its stored energy.

It was like being hit by a truck.

Bella shot backward, her breath blasting from her lungs. She couldn't even scream as horrible pain radiated from her chest to her back. Her hands slipped away from the cane as she careened backward, flying rapidly away from Goo.

"Bella!" Cain cried from her hip.

Goo sent more tentacles after her, even as more of his body lifted from the street, pulled upward by the vortex like a giant piece of taffy. His body narrowed as it stretched, rippling madly in the wind.

Bella gasped for air, watching helplessly as Goo tried in vain to save her.

Then she saw something atop Goo. A boy in a pure white suit, being propelled up Goo's body toward her.

"Simon!" she croaked.

* * *

Simon blinked, taking a moment to get his bearings. He found himself watching as Gideon stood before Craven, the Collector's sword in the Painter's hand. It was déjà vu, the second time he'd seen it. He closed his eyes for a split-second, picturing Craven's head falling from his shoulders as Gideon cut all the way through the general's neck. And the horrible things that'd happened afterward.

Craven had been made to be indestructible. But his Sculptor had made it clear that if the impossible occurred, that his destroyer would join Craven in annihilation.

Along with everyone around him.

"Promise to never come after myself or my family," Gideon was commanding. The Painter set the Collector's blade against the side of Craven's neck. "Or your head is next."

Craven just glared at him with naked hatred in his eyes.

"Promise me," Gideon pressed.

"Never," Craven spat. Gideon let out a resigned sigh.

"Very well," he muttered. And then he swung the silver sword, striking Craven's neck. The blade cut an inch deep, then stopped. So incredibly strong was Craven's Invictium flesh that the magical blade – one Simon knew could cut through wood, stone, and flesh with utter ease – could not slice through in a single cut.

Craven bit off a scream, the sound sending a chill down Simon's spine.

As it had the first time.

Simon reached out, grabbing Bella's shoulder and gripping it tightly. An image of his dream came to him then, of the endless parade of men, women, and children approaching him. Of each of them picking up a sword and slashing his throat…and decapitating themselves as the Collector's suit did unto them what they would have done unto him.

"No," he blurted. Bella glanced at him, and he shook his head. "Not like this."

"Dad," Bella urged.

"Not now, Bella," Gideon scolded.

"Mr. Myles," Simon insisted. Gideon glanced at him, then back at Craven, whose face was twisted with pain. Gideon's jawline rippled, and he yanked the blade free, then wound up to strike again, swinging the sword as hard as he could…and chopping halfway through Craven's neck.

"Mr. Myles," Simon urged, rushing between Gideon and Craven. "Don't do this."

He felt Redeemer give him a squeeze.

"Simon, we don't have a choice," Gideon countered, yanking the blade free. "If we don't stop him now, he'll never stop hunting my family."

"There's always a choice," Bella interjected. Gideon glanced at her, then grimaced.

"There is," he agreed. "And I choose to protect my family. No matter what it takes."

"Then you're no better than Miss Savage," Simon argued. "And no better than him," he added, pointing at Craven. "They both do whatever it takes to get what they want. We have to be better."

"Kill me," Craven blurted out.

"Step aside Simon," Gideon ordered.

"No," Simon replied.

"Simon…"

"If you do this, we all die," Simon revealed. "It's already happened once. And unless you make a different choice than you did the last time, you won't get another chance."

Gideon just stared at him.

"My Familiar," Simon told him, gesturing at his suit. "Redeemer. It gives me a…second chance. When something bad happens to me or someone I love."

Gideon's eyes widened.

"You mean…?" he began. Simon nodded.

"I've lived this once," he confessed. "Choose differently, or it'll be the last choice you make."

Gideon swallowed visibly, then nodded.

"Alright," he decided.

And then the wind struck.

It came without warning. A wall of wind that smashed into all of them, flinging them upward and backward into the air. The world tumbled madly around Simon, and he cried out, spreading his arms and legs out wide to steady himself. Thousands of Gemini were flying in the air with him, like a sea of glittering diamonds around him. And behind him…

A giant ring of gold bordering a black hole levitating high above the peak of the Palatium.

"Bella!" he heard Gideon cry, even as the Painter tumbled in the air alongside Myko. Goo sent tentacles out to try to catch everyone, but it was too late. The tentacles rippled so violently in the wind, ever more so as everyone approached the black hole, that they tore apart. As did the Gemini, who shattered into millions of pieces, flying right into the black disc.

And vanishing.

Simon could only watch as his army was destroyed. He reached for Bella, trying in vain to grab her. To save her. But she was too far away, tumbling head-over-heels in the powerful gale.

A moment later, she passed into the black disc, vanishing from sight…and Simon joined her.

* * *

Simon blinked.

He was standing before Gideon and General Craven, and Gideon's sword was embedded halfway through Craven's neck. Gideon jerked the blade free.

"Mr. Myles," Simon called out urgently. He grabbed Gideon's shoulder, gripping it tightly. "We need to run."

"Simon..." Gideon began.

"*Now*," Simon snapped.

He turned toward the Palatium, pointing at it...just as the tower's peak swelled, then opened like the petals of a flower. A flash of gold light flew out of it, rising upward into the blue sky. It grew quickly, a golden serpent biting its own tail. Then it started to spin, and as it did so, the sky within the ring it formed grew dark...then pitch black.

"Run!" Simon shouted.

"Kill me," Craven ordered. Gideon ignored Craven, handing the silver sword to Simon. Then he retrieved his cane, and vaulted onto Myko's back.

"Bella, get on," he instructed. She did so, sitting behind him.

"Kill me!" Craven yelled.

"What is that thing?" Bella asked.

"Extinctio," Gideon answered grimly. "And if we don't leave right now, we're all going to die."

Myko did a short moon-dash over the fence, carrying Gideon and Bella with him.

"Go!" Gideon cried. Simon lifted his Gemini shard to his lips.

"Reform soldiers and get out," he ordered. The Gemini obeyed, charging down the streets away from the Palatium. A strange golden light appeared around all of the Pentad's forces, freezing them in place.

And while they stayed frozen, the blast of wind struck everyone else.

Simon managed to grab hold of the fence right as the blast struck him, grunting as it slammed into his chest and belly. His legs flew out from underneath him, the force of the wind nearly tearing his grip from the bars. Goo came to the rescue, passing a part of his body through the fence and enveloping Simon. Then Goo lifted him over the fence, propelling him atop his monstrous body.

All around the city, Gemini lifted off the streets, rising into the air like a glittering ocean. Even Myko started to slide backward...and then Bella flew from his back, hurtling into the air!

"Goo, grab her!" Simon shouted over the screaming wind. Goo sent tentacles after her...and after Myko and Gideon, who had been sucked upward after Bella.

But even as Goo did so, the front of his body lifted up from the street, rising toward the black hole. Goo stretched as it pulled on him, his body narrowing as it grew longer.

"Wrap yourself around some buildings," Simon instructed. "Find sewer grates and anchor yourself to the sewer tunnels!"

Goo did so, wrapping himself around the base of nearby buildings. But Simon knew very well that, as Goo stretched thinner, his body would be at risk for tearing apart in the wind. Indeed, the tentacles he shot at Gideon and Myko managed to grab them…but as they went for Bella, they rippled so violently they tore apart.

Simon watched as Gideon shot his magic glove after her, and it grabbed her hand, trying to save her. But even it could not stop her. Gideon summoned the glove back to him, then sent it out with his cane. It tapped Bella, stopping her instantly for a moment, just as Goo reached her with one of his tentacles. It wrapped around her leg, pulling her forward…then tore off.

She burst backward.

"Bella!" Simon yelled out. "Goo, send out thicker tentacles. Gemini, form a mirror between her and the black hole. Gemini in the sewers, get into Goo and come to me!"

He watched the Gemini react to his commands, then put a palm on Goo.

"Goo, bring me as close as you can to her," he requested. He felt Goo answer by propelling Simon forward and upward, toward the deadly spinning serpent ring, now only a quarter-mile away. If he could get her into the Plane of Reflection, she'd be safe from the serpent-ring…in fact, they *all* would be.

But if not, then it was almost certainly too late to save her this time. Redeemer still hadn't fully recharged…and if she didn't soon, this would be the last chance he'd get.

Chapter 41

The pain in Bella's chest was excruciating.

She watched as Simon zoomed toward her, riding Goo's stretched-out body. Goo's flesh rippled madly in the wind, like the surface of the ocean during a hurricane. Hunks of him tore off as they closed in on her, sucked into the vortex behind her.

"Simon!" she cried, managing to catch her breath at last. Gideon's glove shot over Simon's shoulder at her, grabbing her ankle and pulling her backward. It managed to slow her ascent, but still she was drawn toward the serpent-ring, foot by foot. Wind screamed in her ears, the city streets hundreds of feet below her now.

"Behind you!" Simon yelled over the wind.

Bella glanced back, seeing Gemini fragments coalescing into a giant mirror right behind her. She grabbed it before it could be whisked away, holding on tight. The mirror's surface wobbled slightly, the fragments barely able to hold themselves together in the gale.

Bella grit her teeth, then pulled herself through it, passing into the Plane of Reflection. Goo vanished, as did Gideon and Myko and Simon.

But to her horror, Extinctio remained. A black hole in the sky with a halo of gold, it sucked her ever-backward and upward. And as she watched, the wind shrieking in her ears and pummeling her body, thousands of Gemini approached that void. They shattered as they drew near, and their fragments vanished as they were drawn into the utter blackness.

A few Gemini ahead of her transformed, turning into another mirror. But she couldn't reach it.

Terror gripped her, panic threatening to overwhelm her.

Think!

She focused, staring at the mirror's reflective surface, then at the steadily approaching black hole. She was only a few hundred feet away from it now, and the closer she got to it, the more powerful its vacuum. Bella stared at it, the black circle against the light of the blue sky…and had a flash of inspiration.

The dark and the light!

She relaxed, and one became two.

Luna grabbed the tear in the front of her shadow-uniform, opening it wide. The sunlight slammed into her like a giant's fist, shooting her toward the dark circle behind her…and the mirror the Gemini had created for her. She grabbed onto Lux's arm as she did so, pulling her sister along with her toward the mirror.

Before they could merge, Luna passed through the mirror, returning to the original world. But as a being of light, Lux reflected *off* the mirror, tearing free from her sister's grasp and shooting downward and backward toward the street below as a particle-wave of light.

Her momentum carried her away from the gaping hole, the ground rising up to meet her. She slammed into the golden street, reflecting off its shiny surface and flying upward and away from Extinctio. She sailed away, the city falling away as she flew higher and higher. Up into the bright blue sky.

As light, the wind could not touch her. As light, she was free.

It was exhilarating.

Lux laughed, feeling herself soar through the open sky…and suddenly she saw a massive silver dome appear below her. It was the dome surrounding Centrum…a one-way mirror. And while nothing was supposed to be able to get in, apparently getting out was no problem at all.

The great lawn surrounding the city fell away, magnificent green against the reflected sky.

Lux realized suddenly that if she became corporeal, she'd fall toward the earth…and that unlike when she'd traversed the ocean after Bella had tried to commit suicide, she wouldn't be able to reflect off a non-reflective surface. But when she'd struck the cliff before the Water Dragon cave, she'd merely diffused a bit, and had been utterly unharmed.

She pulled herself together, becoming a weighty thing once again.

Lux felt gravity and wind then, her ascent slowing, then stopping. Her stomach flip-flopped as she fell toward the great lawn below, the wind's scream rising in pitch as she gained speed.

Then she smashed into the ground.

There was no pain, only a kind of *expanding*, as if she were a ray of light scattering as it struck a matte surface. Her body pulled together almost instantly, and she found herself tumbling head-over-heels on the grass. Within moments, she came to a stop, lying belly-up.

The sun shone above, as bright as she was.

Lux smiled at it, then got to her feet, turning to face the great dome of Centrum.

Come on sister, she urged. *I believe in you!*

For she was free, it was true. But without her other half, she could never be whole. There was no way back into Centrum for Lux, no way to help her sister.

All she could do now was wait.

* * *

Simon floated hundreds of feet above the city streets, embedded in Goo's ever-thinning flesh. He saw Bella vanish into the mirror…and breathed a sigh of relief.

"Okay Goo, bring me through the mirror now," he requested. "We're going home."

But a moment later, something shot out of the mirror.

At first he thought it was Bella, but then he saw it was a figure in an all-black suit. Clearly a woman.

Luna!

The mirror wobbled violently, then shattered, fragments flying toward the spinning vortex ahead. Now about a hundred yards away…and closing in steadily.

"Luna!" he shouted. "Goo, bring me closer!"

Goo did so, stretching ever-thinner. He was not even twenty feet thick now, and the thinner he stretched, the more violently he rippled in the wind.

And the more likely it became that he would tear apart, leaving Simon to fly into the abyss to his doom.

He got within thirty feet of Luna, but couldn't go any further. Goo's body was too thin ahead, pieces of his green flesh ripping off and flying past Luna into the abyss a hundred yards away.

"Come on!" he shouted at Luna.

She turned around, one hand on her chest. Goo tried to make it to her, but his flesh was pulled too thin, breaking apart before it could reach her.

"Go," she yelled back. "Goo can't reach me. Leave before he breaks apart!"

"Come with me," he insisted.

"It's okay," she reassured him with a smile. "I'm shadow. So is that thing. It can't hurt me."

"But Lux…"

"She's fine," Luna insisted. "She's in the Plane of Reflection. She got away from Centrum. Now go!"

"Luna…"

"Go," she shouted. "Before it's too late!"

Simon hesitated, glancing at the black hole. It was less than a hundred feet away now, and Goo's body was stretched to its limit. Huge hunks of Goo's flesh were breaking off even now, flying past Luna into the abyss.

"Are you sure?" he yelled back over the screaming wind. She smirked.

"Do I look sure?" she asked. Simon had to smile. "Now get the hell out of here," she insisted.

Simon nodded.

"See you soon," he called out. Then he put a hand on Goo.

"Come on Goo," he prompted. "Bring me home."

Goo retracted, propelling Simon down his giant body…and away from Luna. Simon watched as she faced Extinctio. She put a hand to her chest…and flew forward, right at the void. He lost sight of her as he continued down Goo's slightly curved body, and for that, he was thankful.

Redeemer gave him a squeeze, signaling the return of her power.

Simon felt Goo propel him faster and faster, sending him down his long body like a giant slide. The streets of Centrum rose up to greet Simon, and he spotted an open sewer grate ahead, one that Goo had plunged a tentacle into. He held his breath as Goo sucked him right down the sewer grate, depositing him into the dark sewer below with a splash.

Simon gasped as he struck the cold sewage, the smell of excrement filling his nostrils.

Gideon and Myko were already there, along with Nemesis. And as Simon watched, Goo's tentacle tore free from the tunnel, vanishing through the sewer grate above.

Simon stared through the grate, seeing Goo's entire body tearing free from the streets of Centrum, hurtling toward Extinctio.

"Goo!" he cried.

"He's gone," Gideon told him grimly. "And we will be too if we don't get out of here." He paused then. "Where's Bella?"

"Lux escaped," Simon told him. "Luna went into the shadows in Extinctio."

Gideon's face paled.

"She *what?*"

"She said she'd be fine," Simon reassured. Gideon shook his head.

"No," he whispered. His knees wobbled, and he fell to his butt in the sewage. "No no no!"

"What's wrong?" Simon asked.

And then Simon blinked.

Chapter 42

Luna went back-first right through the Gemini mirror, returning to the original world. Behind her, the mirror shattered, fragments scattering all around her like diamonds in the sun. And whereas before she'd been facing away from Extinctio, after passing through the mirror, she was facing *toward* it, the mirror right ahead of her.

The mirror warped, then shattered, its fragments flying toward the void ahead. Since she was still holding the tear in her uniform open with one hand, the sun shoved her *away* from the void now. At first Luna thought the force of the sun might overwhelm Extinctio's pull, but it only mostly counteracted it. She still found herself being pulled toward that ever-growing vortex, foot-by-foot, at an agonizing pace.

She tore her uniform, ripping the hole at her chest open wider, but the added force from the sun was still not quite enough. Inch-by-inch she drew closer to annihilation.

And around her, Gemini exploded into fragments, flying to their extinction.

I'm going to die, she realized.

She felt her sister escape Centrum, and knew that Lux would be the only part of Bella that would survive. Half of the whole, forever more. The shadow – the darkness, the evil, the violent and awful part of her – would be destroyed.

I was the lesser half.

She stared at the great instrument of her death. Blackness beyond black, the deepest shadow she'd ever seen.

Shadow!

If Extinctio was shadow, then it could not destroy a thing of shadow. Luna would be able to merge with it. To expand to become it…at least until it was inactivated.

She broke out into a smile, eyeing the slowly approaching void. She was a hundred feet away now, approaching inch-by-inch.

"Here goes nothing," she told herself.

"Luna!" a voice behind her shouted.

She turned her head, seeing Goo stretching out toward her, a mere thirty feet away. And atop him, a very familiar boy.

"Come on!" Simon shouted, gesturing for her to come to him. But it was clear that Goo couldn't get much closer to her without risking being torn apart in the process.

"Go," she yelled back. "Goo can't reach me. Leave before he breaks apart!"

"Come with me," Simon insisted.

"It's okay," she reassured. "I'm shadow. So is that thing. It can't hurt me."

"But Lux…"

"She's fine," Luna insisted. "She's in the Plane of Reflection. She got away from Centrum. Now go!"

"Luna…"

"Go," she shouted. "Before it's too late!"

"Are you sure?"

She smirked.

"Do I look sure?" she shot back. Simon smiled back reluctantly. "Now get the hell out of here," she insisted.

Then she saw Simon blink.

* * *

Simon found himself embedded in Goo's body, not a hundred feet from the abyss of Extinctio. Goo's flesh rippled madly in the shrieking wind, fragments tearing off ahead of him…and narrowly missing Luna's inky silhouette, barely visible against the darkness of the void beyond. Terror gripped him.

"No, don't do it!" he cried.

"I'm not arguing with you," Luna shot back. "Save yourself Simon."

"No," he pressed. "You don't understand…it won't work. You'll die!"

"Simon…"

"You tried it already," he insisted.

"I what?"

"My suit," he told her. "Whenever someone I love dies because of something I did or didn't do, it gives me a second chance to redeem myself."

"Like…time travel?"

"Like a do-over," Simon corrected. "It happened because you died when you went in there," he pressed. "I won't get another one."

"Goo can't reach," she told him. "Not without ripping himself apart." She shook her head sadly. "You can't save me Simon. Save yourself. Bella still has Lux. Half of her is better than none of you."

"You're wrong," he argued. "There is no Bella without you."

"She's the better half," Luna insisted.

"Without two sides, there's no coin," Simon argued. "There's good and evil in every person. And the good redeems the evil, and evil makes good heroic. The light within us…it redeems our darkness."

Luna wavered, glancing back at Extinctio.

Goo's body rippled ever more violently as they approached the vortex. They were running out of time…and Simon knew it. Goo was getting stretched so thin that he might tear apart at any moment.

Look forward to the future, he remembered Percy telling him.

Simon took a deep breath in, letting it out.

Build something that'll shine brightly when we look back at it.

The decision was instant.

"Goo, form a tube from here to the sewers," Simon instructed. Then he lifted the Gemini shard to his lips. "Line Goo's tube, black side facing inward."

Goo propelled the Doppelgangers within his body, forming a long tube within himself and bringing them into it. The Doppelgangers shattered, their fragments lining the tube to form a black inner lining. One that cast the inside of the tube in shadow.

"Go," he ordered. "While this shadow is still closer than Extinctio's.

Luna hesitated.

"What about you?" she asked.

"I'm going to build a lighthouse," he replied.

She just stared at him.

"I'll be with you," he promised with a smile. "Every time you look back, I'll be right there. The first and brightest thing you see."

"Simon…"

Goo's body stretched to the limit, and Simon looked back, seeing Goo's flesh tearing from the edges inward, not fifty feet from Simon.

"Tell Bella…tell her not to waste her time painting what was," he requested. "Tell her to paint what ought to be."

The tear in Goo's flesh worsened, spreading inward toward the inner surface of the Gemini tube.

"No," Luna told him, shaking her head. "I won't do this."

Simon sighed, putting a hand on Goo.

"Take me to her," he requested.

Goo obeyed, extending even further, even as he tried to repair the expanding tear behind Simon. It was futile; he could only postpone the inevitable.

"Simon!" Luna protested.

He reached her, grabbing her from behind and hugging her close.

"I love you," he whispered into her ear.

And then he tore the hood of her uniform off, the shadowy fabric ripping with ease.

Luna screamed, flying backward toward the nearest shadow…which was in the Gemini-tube. She vanished within, merging with its darkness.

Gone.

Goo grabbed onto Simon, desperately propelling him away from Extinctio. The tear in his flesh was near-complete, only the Gemini tube holding him together.

And as Simon watched, Goo's body began to pull free from the streets of Centrum…as he knew it had to.

He put a hand on Goo.

"Thank you Goo," Simon told him. "For everything."

Then Simon lifted his Gemini shard to his lips one last time, turning to face Extinctio.

"Protect Bella and her family," he commanded. "From now on, you take orders from her."

He gazed down at the shard…and at his right forearm. His sleeve had fallen down a bit, exposing the innumerable scars there. A memory came to him then, of sitting in his cell in the Pentad, before Miss Savage had "saved" him. Of how he'd kept the Doppelganger's shard with him always. Of how many of the scars on his wrists – and in his mind – were from it.

Simon pictured his father lying on the floor of their home, in a pool of his own blood. And the Doppelganger standing over the man, a bloody beer bottle in its hand. Just as Simon had painted it, for the very purpose it had executed.

I did that, he thought.

And for the first time, he felt no shame. No guilt. He'd stopped violence with violence, though he'd never killed anyone with his own hands. And though his father had hit him many times, Simon had done far worse to himself.

Introspection, then expression.

He smiled, facing the void calmly. He felt Redeemer give him a squeeze.

"I won't be needing that," he told her, patting his suit gently. And he knew full well that there would be no second chance this time. He had no more need for redemption.

This *was* his redemption.

Simon felt Goo's body jerk forward as it continued to tear free from the street far below…and as it slipped further down the Gemini tube, which was seconds from shattering.

He closed his eyes, picturing himself standing on his Memory Lane, facing forward. The street terminated in a dead-end, a white wall blocking his way. He lifted his gaze, following the wall as it went ever-upward. All the way to the top.

To the peak of an enormous lighthouse, shining with a light as brilliant as the sun.

He looked back in his mind's eye, gazing out at his past. And while the dark tower in the distance still stood, the light from his lighthouse ahead was so tall and bright that it shone on everything else. Every building, all the way to the very beginning.

Casting it in a brilliant, beautiful glow.

Don't be a victim like I was, he heard the Collector's voice tell him. *Be a hero.*

"I am," Simon whispered.

And in that moment, anyone who happened to have their eyes on the heavens would have seen something quite extraordinary. For against the brilliant blue sky and clouds of white, a ring of gold shined like the sun, and within it a circle of utter, devastating black. But against that utter absence shone a bright white figure standing atop an island of green, his arms spread to the sides.

In the end, there was light shining in the darkness.

It was Simon.

And it was good.

Chapter 43

Luna screamed as Simon ripped the hood of her uniform from her head, exposing it to the sun. She burst backward, now not only pushed by the sun, but also drawn by the shadows of the dark tube that the Gemini had formed within Goo. She stopped deep within it, on all fours, facing its opening. The tube rattled violently, the screaming wind threatening to tear it apart.

And in the distance ahead, she saw Simon standing atop Goo, his pristine white suit glowing brilliantly against the blackness of the void. He faced it calmly, his arms out to his sides.

"Simon!" she yelled.

The Gemini tube entrance collapsed, blocking her view…and plunging her into utter darkness.

"*Simon!*"

The tube tore around her, light peeking through cracks between the shards. She burst back further down the tube, drawn to its shadow. The tube tore free completely ahead, and she cursed, melding with the darkness. Becoming it. At once, her body grew to encompass the shadow all the way down the tube…and into the sewers far, far below.

You goddamn fool, she swore to herself.

And then she emerged from the darkness within the sewers, finding Gideon, Myko, Nemesis, and a small contingent of Gemini waiting for her there.

"Luna!" Gideon cried, rushing up to her and giving her a big bear hug. "Oh thank the gods you're okay," he added. Then he frowned, pushing her back. "Where's Lux?"

"She's fine," Luna mumbled, staring at her feet.

"Where is she?"

"She's *fine*," Luna snapped, turning away from him. She reached into shadow with Shadowfinger, her magical glove, pulling shadow from the nearest wall and reforming the hood of her uniform and repairing the hole at her chest. Slipping the hood on, she stepped into the beam of light cascading down from the open sewer grate high above. She saw a giant green blob in the sky, being slowly sucked into Extinctio.

"Goo!" she cried.

"Too late girl," Nemesis told her, slithering up to Luna and putting a clawed hand on her shoulder. "Goo's gone."

"No," Luna protested.

"He died a hero," Gideon told her. "He saved all of us, Luna. Me, Myko, and Nemesis."

Then he frowned.

"Where's Simon?" he asked with sudden alarm in his voice.

Luna grit her teeth. She knew she should feel devastated, both by Goo's death and by Simon's. But she was the darkness. She was evil, the personification of all of Bella's awful traits. As when Bella had tried to commit suicide, Luna could feel no guilt. No shame. No deep despair. And neither could Lux, for she was a thing of pure light. Of happiness and peace.

Only with each other could they form something truly human. For the darkness could only know itself by being illuminated by the light, and the light was only bright in comparison to the darkness.

"Dead," she answered at last. She turned to face Gideon, her expression grim. "He sacrificed himself to save me. To save Bella." She paused, remembering what he'd said about his suit. How he'd seen them die over and over. "He saved all of us."

The blood drained from Gideon's face.

Myko whined, nudging Gideon's shoulder…and Nemesis cleared her throat.

"Sorry to be the cold-blooded bitch here," the dragon interjected, "…but if we don't get moving, Simon will have died for nothing. The entire city is going to come looking for us. We need to get the hell out of here. Like *now*."

Gideon swallowed visibly, then nodded. He turned to Myko.

"Come on," he told his Familiar. Myko lowered himself a bit, and Gideon vaulted onto his back. "Luna, can you get us out of here?"

"I think so," Luna replied.

She melted into the shadows, expanding to encompass much of the sewers. By stepping out of the shadows at the very edge of her existence, then merging into them again, expanding to exist further down the underground tunnels, she was able to map out the sewer system in short order. Including the locations of the guardian statues, the sewer grates…and the tunnel they'd arrived into the city through.

Luna returned to the others, rising out of the floor to face them.

"Follow me," she instructed.

She led them down the sewers toward the periphery of Centrum, warning the Gemini about each of the living statues carved into the walls. The Gemini dispatched these with ease, forming mirrors to trap them in the Plane of Reflection. It wasn't long before they'd reached the tunnel they'd come into the city through; Luna led them to the dead-end stone wall there, stopping before it.

"Okay," Nemesis said. "Do you still have Floppy Disc?"

Luna frowned, patting her uniform. Then she cursed.

"What?" Nemesis asked.

"Bella has it," Luna answered. "And Lux is outside Centrum."

"Which means she can't get back in," Gideon realized.

"So no Floppy," Nemesis concluded. "Well isn't that just *spectacular.*"

"Shut up," Luna grumbled. "I need to think."

"Centrum's dome is a one-way mirror," Gideon reasoned, turning to look at the sewer grate on the ceiling behind them. "If we go aboveground, we all should be able to walk out."

"What about Extinctio?" Luna pressed.

"It only lasts for a short while," Gideon answered. "And it'll take a decade to recharge. I made it with limitations, of course," he added. "A weapon of that power requires it."

"I'll fly up to check," Nemesis offered. And with that, the dragon leapt upward, flapping her wings until she'd reached the ceiling. She grabbed the sewer grate with her claws, holding herself there and peering out.

"I don't hear any wind," she called out.

"It must be done," Gideon reasoned. "We should go now before the Pentad's forces recover. Gemini, can you boost us up?"

The Gemini did so, forming a humanoid ladder of sorts, allowing them to climb up to the sewer grate. One of the Gemini lifted the grate and set it aside, and Gideon went through. Nemesis tried flying Myko up, but apparently the wolf had just enough moonlight-power left to dash up and out of the sewers. Luna was last, melting into the shadows, then reappearing to descend from the ceiling next to the open sewer grate, grabbing the ledge and hauling herself up.

She found herself standing in the middle of a wide street, short stone buildings on either side.

Surrounded by the Pentad's soldiers.

"Wonderful," she muttered.

* * *

The mid-morning sun cast its rays at a forty-five-degree angle on the earth, striking the buildings of Centrum to cast shadows on the streets below. And coincidentally, it cast shadows of each of the soldiers surrounding Luna and her friends.

And their weapons.

Luna eyed these shadows, her lips curling into a grim smile.

"Hello my little pretties," she greeted, flexing Shadowfinger.

Then, even as Myko, Gideon, Nemesis, and the Gemini attacked, Luna got to work.

One of the soldiers thrust their spear at her, and she dodged out of the way, grabbing the spear's shadow with Shadowfinger. Like in her painting of the magical glove, the shadow-spear pulled free from the ground as a shadow-weapon. She thrust it at the soldier's face, burying it in his left eye-socket.

He shrieked…and promptly turned to stone.

"They're statues!" Luna warned, jerking her shadow-spear free. Another soldier ran after her…but his shadow preceded him. Luna sank into his shadow, moving with it as it moved. The soldier stopped, looking quite confused.

And then Luna rose up from his shadow, thrusting her spear up into his chin from below.

He too turned into stone.

"Oh this is gonna be *fun*," she exclaimed, even as more soldiers rushed at her. She merged with their shadows, then took them out one-by-one, relishing the experience. And as she worked, the Gemini sent the rest of the soldiers into the Plane of Reflection, and Gideon and Myko and Nemesis held their own, assisting the Gemini.

In moments, the soldiers were defeated.

"Painter!" Nemesis warned, pointing behind them. For there *was* a Painter rushing toward them. A woman in a standard Painter's uniform, a large monkey rushing ahead of her.

One with huge, glowing fists.

And behind her, more soldiers were rushing toward them, along with an army of soldiers riding winged horses high in the sky. Beyond them, Extinctio was shrinking above the Palatium, the golden ring slowing its spin…then stopping.

Gideon faced the approaching army, his jawline rippling.

"Normally I'd stay and fight," he stated. "But I don't have my stuff."

"Right," Nemesis replied. "Shall we run?"

"Definitely," Gideon answered.

Nemesis leapt up, grabbing Luna by the shoulders and beating her wings powerfully. They lifted off the street, and Nemesis flew up and away from the city center, toward the great expanse of lawn beyond the outskirts of the city. Gideon mounted Myko, who broke out into a gallop away from the city, while the Gemini stayed to intercept the approaching army.

The mirrored soldiers multiplied exponentially, rapidly forming a formidable fighting force. But while they could most certainly give the approaching soldiers – and perhaps the Painter – a run for their money, they were powerless to stop the Pentad's aerial forces.

The soldiers on their winged steeds flew rapidly toward Luna and Gideon, closing the distance quickly.

"Fly faster!" Luna yelled at Nemesis.

"Would if I could," the dragon snapped.

"They're catching up with us," Luna warned.

"Really?" Nemesis muttered. "Thank *god* for you, otherwise I wouldn't have noticed."

They reached the perimeter of the city…and suddenly the mirrored dome of Centrum appeared behind them, the approaching forces vanishing from sight. Below, the great expanse of lawn surrounding Centrum greeted them. But the Gemini that had been left behind on the lawn hours ago to aid in their escape were gone.

"What…" Luna began.

And then the lawn shimmered, and a massive army clad in the red and gold armor of the Pentad appeared out of thin air surrounding the dome.

Thousands upon thousands of infantry for as far as the eye could see. Archers. Painters and Musicians. Winged beasts, including a red dragon almost identical to the blue one they'd fought getting into the city. Dozens of giants similar to the forty-foot-tall ones that'd guarded Blackthorne.

All waiting for them…and blocking the way back to the Underground, wherever that was.

Gideon and Myko skid to a stop before the front lines of this army, and dozens of archers pointed their bows up at Nemesis and Luna.

"Halt!" one of the soldiers cried. "Yield or die!"

Gideon and Myko froze.

"Damn it!" Nemesis swore. Luna stared at the army with a sinking feeling. This was it, she knew.

End of the line.

"Sorry girl," Nemesis told her.

"It's okay," Luna replied. "We did our best. Bring us down," she requested.

Nemesis complied, dipping down to land at Gideon's side. Gideon dismounted, putting a hand on her shoulder.

"Thank you," he told her. "For everything."

"Dad…"

"It's over," he interjected, giving her a warm smile. "You did your best. You were amazing," he added. "But I've lived a long life. A good life. It's your turn now."

"Daddy, no," Luna protested.

"Hide in the shadows," he told her. "Find Lux and go far away from here. Somewhere the Pentad won't go."

"I'm not leaving you," Luna insisted.

"The better a story, the more powerful its magic," he lectured gently. "And you've made my story magical indeed." He put a hand on her cheek. "But every story has an end. And this is mine."

"I can't leave you," Luna argued. "All of this is Bella's fault." She shook her head. "Lux and I can handle that, but Bella won't be able to."

"Yes she will," Gideon shot back. "I did."

Luna opened her mouth to reply, then snapped it shut. There was nothing for her to say, after all. He was right.

"I've made a lot of mistakes in my life," he told her. "I wasn't there for my son, and he died. I created the Collector, and he murdered countless people. I'm responsible for your mother missing out on her daughter growing up. I'm responsible for Bella spending her childhood in hiding."

"Dad…"

"I've caused a lot of suffering," he interrupted. "But I did it with the best intentions. All I can hope is that the good I've done outweighs the bad."

He leaned in then, embracing her.

"Goodbye," he murmured in her ear. "I love you Bella. The darkness and the light."

Then he let go, turning away from Luna and striding toward the army waiting for him, Myko at his side.

* * *

Gideon strode toward the front line of the Pentad's army, his hand on Myko's big head. He felt a burst of affection come from the wolf, and smiled, scratching his Familiar behind one big ear.

"Dad!" he heard Luna call out after him.

He kept walking.

"Guess this is it old boy," he mused. Myko didn't reply, but the emotions the wolf sent through their bond were reply enough. After centuries of being together, their journey was complete at last. The end of an epic adventure. A life truly lived.

Gideon felt no fear as he stopped before the armored soldiers. Only a profound sense of peace.

It would all be over soon.

"Drop the cane!" one of the soldiers ordered.

Gideon complied, tossing it aside.

"On your knees!", the soldier barked. "Hands behind your head!"

Again, Gideon complied.

Okay Myko, he prompted silently. *You know what to do.*

Myko whined.

It'll be a kindness, he soothed the wolf. *Make it quick.*

Again, Myko whined, his whole body trembling.

Do it!

Myko lunged at Gideon's throat, clamping his jaws around Gideon's neck.

And then the sky went black, daylight plunged into night.

Myko let go of Gideon's throat, his fur glowing silver in the sudden moonlight. And from the heavens, a great mist plunged toward them, slamming into the ground beside Gideon.

It coalesced, forming the body of a woman. A beautiful woman in black leather, studded with silver skulls and spikes. Skin nearly as dark as the night, her short hair missing in patches. She wore a pair of midnight-black sunglasses that hid her eyes completely.

She smirked at him.

"Gotta say, seeing you kneel all helpless before these jokers…not very attractive," she quipped. "I thought the second-best Painter in the world would've been a little more, you know, dominant."

Gideon broke out into a huge smile, even as Lucia grabbed him under one armpit, lifting him bodily to his feet.

"Hey love," was all he could say.

"Hey yourself," she replied. Then she turned to the line of guards. "Okay, I'm gonna give you idiots one chance to surrender. Any takers?"

"On your knees!" the soldier who'd ordered Gideon snapped. "Both of you!"

"Not for you, sweetheart," Lucia retorted.

"Honey, you know I love you," Gideon stated, putting a hand on her shoulder. "But even you can't beat an entire army."

"Pfftt," Lucia replied. "Watch and learn, darling."

Then she recited the following:

"When day becomes night,
A dread paradox,
The dead shall answer
The call of Nox."

The moon turned blood-red…and an army of undead rose from the great lawn. Skeletal soldiers burst from the ground between the soldiers, attacking them viciously…and even the corpse of the ice dragon they'd fought earlier came to un-life amidst the army.

Lucia arched an eyebrow at Gideon.

"Impressed?" she inquired.

"I mean it's not *bad*," Gideon replied.

"Mmm hmm."

Then the Pentad's soldiers charged at them!

Lucia dissolved into thick mist, surrounding Gideon, Luna, Myko, and Nemesis. And any soldier who got close was instantly smashed by fists and feet of magical mist, hurtling backward into their fellows. At the same time, the army of undead attacked the enemy, providing a formidable distraction indeed.

Gideon shot his magic glove at his cane, retrieving it. Then he vaulted onto Myko's back, hooking his left stump under it.

"Luna, use the shadows to escape. Nemesis, stay with Lucia," he ordered. Then he lowered himself to Myko's back. "Go boy!" he cried.

Myko glowed bright silver, then shot forward and upward as a beam of moonlight, flying over the enemy soldiers!

He twisted around to look back, and saw Luna melt into the shadows. Lucia rose into the air, carrying Nemesis in a cloud of mist. Enemy archers shot flaming arrows at them, but Lucia's mist-form repelled them, leaving Nemesis unharmed.

Myko's moon-dash ended, and he dashed again, then again, zipping through the air with incredible speed. The wind howled in Gideon's ears as they flew ever-upward and forward, now hundreds of feet above the Pentad's forces. Even with the blood-red moon of Nox, Myko was able to recharge his power, and endlessly moon-dash to safety.

They sailed right past the army, toward the tree line a few miles away.

"Down!" he ordered. "Stay low and go dark!"

For in the darkness of the sudden night, they would be all-but-invisible to the soldiers. And Myko could charge up his moonlight stores for when they inevitably passed the influence of Luna's magical sunglasses and emerged into daylight.

Myko complied, shooting forward and downward until he'd landed on the lawn. He galloped away from the enemy, and Gideon glanced back, seeing Lucia's mist-form following far behind them. More arrows shot at her, and the Fire Drake – the massive dragon-like creature that, along with her brother the late Ice Drake, defended Centrum's lands – took to the air. It went after Lucia, opening its great maw to breath fire.

Gideon whipped his magic glove off, sending it and his cane flying backward at the drake. It smashed into the drake's nose, stopping the creature instantly in mid-air. The drake dropped toward the ground, then recovered, flapping its wings to regain altitude.

Then it breathed a jet of fire at Lucia…right as Gideon's cane whacked it in the eye.

The Fire Drake's head snapped to the side as every bit of the momentum of its entire body – concentrated on a single point – struck it. Its eyeball burst, and its fiery breath shot downward and to the side, setting a huge swathe of the Pentad's soldiers aflame. Screams pierced the night, black smoke rising into the air behind Lucia as she escaped the Fire Drake, managing to pass beyond the army's ranks.

Gideon summoned his glove, and it flew right back onto his stump. He felt a burst of pride from Myko, and smiled.

"It *was* impressive, wasn't it?" he mused.

They raced across the lawn, the tree line of the forest only a mile away now. Behind them the Pentad's ground forces were mostly preoccupied with Nox's undead army. But the aerial forces…and a few dozen Painters…were not so easily distracted.

They'd been waiting outside of Centrum, of course. Waiting just in case Gideon managed to escape.

Craven.

The general had been in countless battles, and despite his supreme confidence in his own abilities, Craven always planned for the worst-case scenario. He'd commanded the Pentad's statue-guards to defend the city itself…and posted most of the Painters and more powerful defenses *outside* of Centrum

Just in case he'd failed.

Well done, General Craven, Gideon thought. But it was a grim one. For while he could certainly run from mere infantry – and even the injured Fire Drake – a few dozen Painters would not be so easily escaped.

He glanced back, seeing the Painters – with Familiars of every imaginable kind – breaking past the ranks of the army, rushing after him.

Go Myko go!

Myko moon-dashed forward, the grass beneath them a blur as they shot toward the forest. He spotted Luna appearing out of the shadows ahead, a dark silhouette against Myko's silver glow. She gave him a thumb's up, then vanished into shadow again.

Behind him, the enraged Fire Drake was gaining on them…as were many of the Painters, a few riding on winged Familiars. Magical arrows arced through the air toward them, automatically targeting Gideon and Myko.

Myko moon-dashed in a zig-zag pattern to avoid them, and Gideon flattened his body against the wolf to make himself a smaller target. He felt Bella's cape unclasp from around his neck, whipping around to bat one of the arrows away. Another struck Myko's hindquarter, burying itself to its fletching in his flesh.

Myko *yelped*, then moon-dashed again, healing instantly.

"Come on boy!" Gideon urged. The forest was only a few hundred feet away now, and the trees would provide cover against the arrows. Unless the Fire Drake was clever enough to set the forest on fire, forcing Myko, Lucia, and Nemesis to fly above it.

Another arrow slammed into Myko's hindquarter…and then Gideon felt his cape whirl around to deflect another. A third managed to get through, piercing all the way through his left shoulder.

He bit back a scream, blood staining his red prison uniform. An arrowhead stuck out of his shoulder, but this one was different than the ones that'd struck Myko. It pulsed with a red light.

Gideon grabbed the arrow, snapping its head off and chucking it to the side.

It *exploded.*

Gideon's cape applied pressure to the wound to staunch the bleeding, while Myko moon-dashed one more time…and then stopped, skidding to a halt right before the tree line.

For there, floating inches above the forest floor amongst the trees, was a giant skull.

"What…?" he blurted out.

The skull's mouth gaped open impossibly wide, a shimmering blue portal appearing within. And from that portal stepped a woman.

A very familiar woman.

She was tall and slender, with skin as pale as death, and long, perfectly straight black hair. Clad in a multilayered suit of armor composed of intricately interconnected bones, she was imposing…and strikingly beautiful. For she was possessed of perfect arched eyebrows and high cheekbones, and sky-blue eyes

Eyes that were staring back at him.

"Hello Gideon," she greeted.

"Petrusa!" he blurted out.

"Now now," she admonished. "Don't use my name in public. Queen of the Dead will do."

"What are you…"

"Doing here?" she interjected. "I heard that my latest apprentice just passed her Test almost three years early," she answered. "Congratulations are in order, don't you think?"

He stared at her mutely, then glanced back at the approaching army.

"Um…this might be a bad time," he confessed. She smirked, shifting her gaze to Luna, who rose from the shadows beside Gideon.

"Ah, there she is," Petrusa stated, inclining her head at Luna. "Half of her, anyway. Congratulations. You've passed your Test."

"What?" Luna blurted out.

"You've earned the right to join the Dark Circle," Petrusa proclaimed. "You are now a member of the Guild of Necromancers."

Luna glanced at Gideon incredulously.

"Really?" she blurted out. "Um…kinda have the whole frickin' Pentad coming after us at the moment. In case you didn't notice."

"I noticed," she replied evenly. "As an apprentice, you were afforded minimal protection," she explained. "Now that you're a Necromancer, however…"

Lucia reached them then, coalescing back into her human form. Nemesis stood beside her, looking as shocked as Gideon had been.

"Hey boss," Lucia greeted.

"Calypso," Petrusa replied. The giant skull's mouth opened again, displaying its shimmering blue portal. A black coffin floated out of it, lowering itself to the forest floor. Its lid swung open.

"Care for a ride?" Petrusa inquired. Lucia smirked.

"Thought you'd never ask."

"Ladies first," Gideon offered. Lucia leaned in to give him a kiss.

"What a *gentleman*," she murmured, reaching down and giving his butt a squeeze. She got in the coffin then, closing the lid. A moment later, the lid opened again…and the coffin was empty.

"You're next," Gideon told Luna.

Luna did the same, the coffin's lid closing, then re-opening a moment later, empty once again.

"You are Bella's Familiar," she told Nemesis, "I will grant you access to the Plane of Death. Go on," she prompted…and the coffin's lid reopened.

Nemesis got in, folding her wings in front of her. The lid closed., and Petrusa turned to Gideon and Myko. The great wolf whined, glancing behind them. More magic arrows arced toward them, and the Fire Drake, Painters, and the rest of the army were charging toward them, only a quarter-mile away now…and closing in fast.

"We need to hurry," Gideon warned, turning back to Petrusa. She arched an eyebrow at him…and then promptly stepped forward out of the forest, walking calmly toward the Pentad's approaching forces. She waited for them then.

The Fire Drake was unfortunate enough to reach her first.

It dove right at her, its wings spread wide and its great maw open, fire building within. Petrusa stopped, just standing there as it hurtled toward her.

The giant floating skull flew up from behind her, intercepting the Fire Drake. Its eyes glowed brighter and brighter blue, a blue-green aura appearing around it.

Then, just before the Fire Drake would have slammed into the skull, that aura shot outward in all directions, in a shockwave that sent the winged monstrosity hurtling backward. It slammed into the lawn, rolling to a stop in front of the approaching Painters and their Familiars…and the thousands of infantry behind them.

"Surrender!" one of the Painters commanded as they approached. The woman with the monkey Familiar. "On the ground or you're dead!"

"I am Queen of the Dead," Petrusa replied evenly. "And those of you who don't run for your little lives now will become my subjects."

No one ran.

"Very well," Petrusa decided.

The floating skull opened its jaws wider, and huge bones flew out of the shimmering blue portal within. Vertebrae to form a huge spine, then ribs, arm bones, a pelvis, and then leg bones. They connected to the skull and each other with blue-green energy at the joints…forming a complete skeleton.

A very *large* skeleton.

Its eye-sockets flashed brightly, and a brown mist burst out of its mouth, flowing over the approaching army. Everywhere the mist touched, the grass turned yellow, then brown, then crumpled and turned black. The soil seemed to liquify, decomposing before Gideon's very eyes.

And those who had the misfortune to be standing in the now-liquified muck watched in horror as their clothes decomposed…and then their feet and legs. The mist fell over the Fire Drake, and its flesh putrefied rapidly, sliding right off her bones.

It was then that the Pentad's forces came to the realization that perhaps the Queen of the Dead was *not* the type of person that would be wise to cross.

So it was that, a bit later than they should have, those that still could turned and ran.

Petrusa watched them go, then strode back to Gideon, stopping before the still-closed coffin.

"That was…" Gideon began, staring past her at the rapidly decomposing remains of those unlucky enough to have been affected by the giant skull's mist.

"A message," she replied. "Perhaps Queen Eldora will think twice before attacking my Necromancers – or their families – again."

"Much appreciated."

Petrusa turned to eye the coffin.

"You are not a member of the Dark Circle, nor of the Guild of the Golden Coin," she noted. "I already allowed you entrance into the Plane of Death twice. As it stands, our laws demand that you be barred from entering again, unless it's your corpse that's doing the entering."

"I would prefer that not be the case," Gideon replied wryly.

"You do however have significant talents," she pointed out. "And are currently unemployed."

"Perhaps we can come to a business arrangement?" Gideon inquired.

"Indeed," Petrusa agreed. "It would solve the…complications of having several family members in the Dark Circle, while being outside of it yourself."

"What do you propose?"

"I wish to create a new role for you," she proposed. "As a bounty hunter for the Guild of the Golden Coin."

"Go on."

"Your job would be to hunt down men and women of…undesirable character, and ferry them to the Plane of Death."

"That would require them dying first, no?"

"Part of the job," she replied. "As is ensuring that they arrive in the Plane of Death in whatever specific degree of decomposition I demand."

"You want me to do my wife's job," he realized.

"Oh no," Petrusa retorted. "Your wife's job is *far* more important. But yes, you would technically be an assassin. And you could work together, if your wife approves. She would of course outrank you considerably."

"And if I don't want to kill them?"

"Then there would be no reason for you to travel to the Plane of Death," she concluded.

Gideon grimaced, eyeing the coffin.

"I've had enough of death," he confessed. He returned his gaze to Petrusa. "Bella was right. She and Simon found a way to fight an entire army without killing."

"I see," Petrusa replied. She paused for a moment. "Then I propose an alternative arrangement. Your job will be to retrieve targets I wish to preserve completely. People without any decay whatsoever. You will bring them – alive – to the Plane of Death."

"And then?" he asked. She smiled.

"Then *we* will kill them," she answered. "And already being within the Plane of Death upon their death, they will be perfectly preserved…and retain the entirety of their memories."

"Hmm."

"It will be like they never died at all," she pointed out.

Gideon hesitated.

"I won't go after anyone I find it unethical to target," he warned.

"Fair enough."

He hesitated, then nodded.

"We have ourselves a deal," he decided, extending a hand. She shook it.

"We'll consider this a verbal contract," she told him. "I will have a written contract drafted shortly. Your employment will be renewed every seven years at the discretion of both parties."

"That's fair."

"Then it is decided," she proclaimed. The giant skeleton by her side disassembled in the reverse of how it'd come together, each of its bones flying back into its portal-mouth. A moment later, it was merely a floating skull again. Petrusa reached into it, pulling out a large black duffel bag. She handed it to Gideon.

"What's this?" he inquired.

"Your things," Petrusa answered. "The Gemini extracted them, but were driven into this forest by that army. I…acquired them."

"You've been busy," he observed. She smirked.

"I always am."

"Thank you," he told her.

"No need," she replied. "You'll be a more effective employee with them."

"Indeed."

The coffin lid opened then, and Petrusa gestured at it.

"Go on," she prompted.

"Myko first," Gideon requested. Petrusa gestured at the duffel bag, and Gideon opened it, retrieving a rolled-up canvas. "Apertus," he incanted…and the canvas unrolled itself. Myko jumped into it, and Gideon rolled it back up, putting it in his duffel bag, then got into the coffin, lying down and placing the bag atop his chest and belly. The lid closed…and he felt a sudden sensation that he was rotating to the left.

And when the lid opened, Gideon found himself no longer in the forest surrounding the great lawn of Centrum, but in the Plane of Death…with his family all around him, safe at last.

Chapter 44

The Plane of Death, it turned out, served merely as a stepping stone in the family trip back to Castle Under…and to Grandpa. They all appeared within the underground tomb at the entrance to Petrusa's vast undead kingdom, the one with row after row of coffins. Each of which led to coffins scattered throughout the living world. But instead of leading them to one of these, Mom gestured for them to go up the stone steps in the opposite direction, toward the stone archway with the huge ivory skull in the center.

"Where are we going?" Luna asked. "I thought we were headed to Castle Under."

"We are," Mom answered. "Have to reunite you with your sister first. Petrusa found her and brought her here for safekeeping."

"Ah."

"I still can't believe that Castle Under is standing again," Gideon admitted. "How did that happen?"

"It's a long story," Luna answered. "I'll tell you all about it later."

Mom led Gideon, Luna, and Nemesis up the stone steps to the great archway with the skull-carving. It came to life as it had many times before, going from ivory to black. Blood started oozing from its eye-sockets.

"WELCOME, CALYPSO," its voice boomed, a light within its eye-sockets growing brighter.

"Hey Death," Lucia greeted. Calypso, Luna remembered, was Mom's code name in the Guild of Necromancers…also known as the Dark Circle.

"WELCOME, SHADE OF BELLA," Death greeted, turning to Luna. "WELCOME, GIDEON MYLES. YOU MAY PROCEED."

"Thank you," Gideon replied, inclining his head respectfully.

The huge skull shifted back to its original state, the light within its sockets fading. Mom brought them to a wooden door beyond the archway, which opened up into a familiar graveyard. She continued to lead the way, bringing them out of the graveyard and up a small hill. At the top, there was a magnificent view of Arx Mortus, capitol city of the Plane of Death.

"Never get used to it," Nemesis mused.

"It *is* pretty," Luna agreed.

"It's alright," Gideon conceded. "If you like that sort of thing. Which you all do," he added.

"We *are* pretty weird, aren't we?" Luna mused.

"*Oh* yeah," Mom agreed.

"Thank god for that," Luna stated, putting an arm around Mom's shoulders as they walked. "Hate to be normal."

"Wonder what it's like," Mom said. She glanced at Gideon, who was walking on her other side. He gave her a look.

"Don't look at me," he grumbled, holding his injured shoulder gingerly.

"I mean, you *are* pretty vanilla," Luna pointed out. "Kinda like Lux."

"Some would say boring," Mom added.

"Really?" Gideon retorted, raising his eyebrows. "I'm a four-hundred-year-old bounty hunter with a giant wolf and a magical cane that smashes dragons."

"He does have a point," Nemesis conceded.

"Yeah, but do you have daggers that make people allergic to their own blood?" Mom inquired. "Or a mist-form that makes people's bodies turn inside-out?"

Gideon blinked.

"A what?" he asked. "Do you actually have that?"

Mom eyes twinkled.

"Oh baby, you haven't even *begun* to see what I have," she told him, petting him on the head. "You'd be amazed at what the world's best Painter is capable of."

"Second-best," Gideon corrected.

"Mmmhmm. Keep telling yourself that."

"As I recall, you had a bit of trouble with Yero and Temper," Gideon reminded her. "I seem to remember you losing your head over it."

"You were about to lose yours," Mom shot back. "I like prison red on you," she told him, eyeing his uniform. "It says: 'I'm a little bitch,' but you know, with flair."

"To be fair, Bella distracted me," Gideon pointed out. Luna's eyes widened, and she glared at him.

"Wow Dad," she muttered. "Low blow. If I were Bella, that would've made me feel really bad."

"Better grab a handkerchief," Mom warned. "Because you will be soon."

Sure enough, Luna could feel Lux somewhere in the distance, within the vast city of Arx Mortus. At length one of the three gates in the great wall surrounding the city opened, and Luna saw her sister's impossibly bright body shining in the gloom like a miniature sun. Lux made her way toward them, slowly but surely.

"Guess my shoulder'll have to do," Mom quipped.

"Mine's out of commission," Gideon noted, gesturing at the wound in his shoulder from the magical arrow. He chuckled, and Mom did too. Or rather, she cackled, as one might expect a Necromancer would do. Then Nemesis joined in, making two cacklers. Hardly surprising, given that the dragon was technically Bella's repressed memories of her mother.

The only one who wasn't laughing, of course, was Luna.

"Ha ha," she grumbled. And then she sank into the shadows, feeling her body expand to encompass the shadows cast over the bleak terrain. She emerged a few yards in front of her sister, who skid to a stop before her.

"Hey!" Lux greeted with a radiant smile…and they came together, intertwining to become one.

Then Bella was whole again.

And while the two sides of her, when separate, had experiences that were rather flat and lifeless, the darkness and the light together created countless shades of gray. Their memories – particularly Luna's – came to Bella not just as Luna had experienced them, but as Bella would have felt about them.

And one vision above all came to her then…light shining against the darkness, Simon's suit silhouetted by the black void of Extinctio.

"Simon!" she gasped, putting her hands to her mouth. Her eyes widened in horror.

"I'm sorry Bella," Gideon apologized.

"We have to save him," Bella insisted, turning to him. "You made Extinctio. There has to be some way to…"

"There's no way," Gideon interjected grimly. "He's gone."

"Gideon, you have to…"

"When someone goes in, they don't come out," Gideon insisted. "They go extinct, Bella. They're destroyed."

Bella stared at him, tears welling in her eyes and trickling down her cheeks. She shook her head at him.

"Why?" was all she could manage.

"Why what?"

"Why would you give them that thing?" she demanded. For Gideon had given Extinctio to Craven of his own free will, back when they'd visited Craven in the military camp after escaping Devil's Pass.

"To save you," Gideon answered.

"To save me?" she pressed. "You didn't need to give it to them. You could've just left!"

"At the time, it seemed like the best way to placate them," Gideon explained. "Craven wanted me arrested. I wanted to avoid fighting them."

"You beat Craven!" she retorted. "You could've beaten him then!"

"I couldn't risk that with you there," he pointed out. "I would have been distracted by trying to protect you."

Bella felt a chill run through her.

"You mean like I distracted you with Craven," she stated.

"Bella…"

"No, I get it," she muttered, wiping the tears from her cheeks. She lowered her gaze to the floor. "If I hadn't distracted you, you would've beaten Craven. You never would've been captured, and Simon would still be alive right now. And Goo," she added.

"Bella you can't think like that," Gideon insisted.

"But it's *true*," she shot back miserably. She had a sudden feeling that she was outside of herself, kicking herself in the belly. Bella blinked, the sensation fading as quickly as it'd come. Her empathy potion in action…forcing her to realize what she was doing to herself.

"Pumpkin…" Mom began, but Gideon held up a hand to stop her.

"I've got this," he reassured. Then he put a stump on Bella's shoulder. "Bella, I did what I felt was right in the moment, when I gave Extinctio to Craven. I had no way of knowing it would be used against me, or that it would kill Simon and Goo."

"I know," Bella mumbled.

"I did what I thought was right when I answered the Pentad's call the day that Xander died," he continued. "And when your mother insisted that I stay in Havenwood while you two went to visit Thaddeus, your mother thought *that* was the right thing to do."

"It's true," Mom agreed.

"She had no idea the Collector would attack you," Gideon explained. "If she'd known that he'd kill her – that she'd miss out on you growing up – she never would've asked me to stay behind."

Bella glanced up at Mom, who gave her a sad smile.

"The thing is, our actions are like pebbles thrown in a pond," Gideon stated. "They send ripples outward into the future…and we can never know what the result will be. We can only do what feels right in the moment, and deal with the consequences."

Bella nodded, wiping away more tears. Gideon smiled at her, lifting her chin so that her gaze met his.

"Remember the first law of magic?" he inquired. She flashed a rueful smile.

"The Law of Unintended Consequences," she recited.

"It's not just for magic," Gideon revealed.

Bella sighed.

"Well I hate it," she muttered. Gideon chuckled.

"This won't be the last time you experience it," he warned. "Goodness knows how many terrible things your mother and I have done with the best of intentions."

"Speak for yourself," Mom retorted, crossing her arms over her chest and smirking at him. "Most of the terrible things I've done were *entirely* intentional."

"And that's why I love your mother," Nemesis quipped.

Everyone chuckled despite themselves, and Bella sighed again, wrapping her arms around Gideon and giving him a hug.

"Thanks Dad."

"You're welcome," he replied.

Just then, Cain stirred at Bella's hip.

"Terribly sorry," he began, "…didn't want to interrupt your conversation. Seemed important. But um…what'd I miss?"

Everyone stared at him, then burst out laughing. For of course Cain – having vanished into who-knew-where when Bella split into Luna and Lux – had absolutely no idea what had happened.

"I'll fill you in," Bella promised, patting his skull.

"In the meantime, I think it's time we got back to Castle Under," Mom told Bella. "Your grandfather's got to be worried sick."

"Alright," Bella agreed. "Let's go."

"Terribly sorry," Gideon interjected, mimicking Cain's voice. "But would someone please paint the hole in my damn shoulder first?"

* * *

After painting the damn hole in Gideon's shoulder – but not giving him back his hands, at least not yet – Mom led the family back to the graveyard and the underground tomb, to a coffin that would take them to a place close to the Underground. An unfamiliar forest, dark and foreboding. But they didn't have to hike through it for long, for Mom found an illusory rock wall on a random cliffside, stepping through into a small cave. A door to the Underground was there.

So they opened it, stepping into the Underground and making their way to a familiar destination: the shore of the lake surrounding Mount Inversus, atop which stood the fortress that was Castle Under.

Mom flew over the lake and up the mountain as a dense mist, Myko moon-dashed Gideon – after he put on his Painter's uniform and top hat and such from Petrusa's duffel bag – and Nemesis flew Bella. They reached the top, landing before the entrance.

"Remarkable!" Gideon breathed, staring up at the castle. "It's as if it were never demolished!"

"Turns out the guy who built it was a friend of Simon's," Bella explained. "An artist named Percy. He said architecture was an art form. He just told it to rebuild itself and it did."

Gideon frowned at her.

"That's not true," he countered. "There are only five artistic disciplines. Perhaps he meant architecture was a form of sculpture?"

"No," Bella replied. "He was pretty clear."

"Hmm," Gideon murmured, clearly unconvinced. "I would very much like to meet this man."

"So I guess I'll meet you two inside," Mom declared, opening the door and stepping through. She slammed the door behind her for good measure. Bella arched an eyebrow at Gideon.

"We should feed her," he noted.

"Quickly," Bella agreed. For Mom's black moods when hungry were legendary, and one simply did not treat the moods of assassin-Necromancer-Painters lightly.

They went into the castle, but Mom was already gone, having undoubtedly used her mist-form to fly to the castle's dormitories where Grandpa's suite was. Bella led Gideon, Myko, and Nemesis through a maze of corridors and more than a few staircases until they reached Grandpa's door. It was already open…and Grandpa was within, seated as usual at his writing desk, talking with Mom. And, it turned out, Kanja.

"Hey!" Kanja blurted out, spotting Bella before Grandpa did. She hurried to embrace her. "I just heard that you made it! Oh, I'm so glad you're okay."

"Thanks," Bella replied. Kanja disengaged, embracing Gideon in turn.

"You have a marvelous daughter," she told him. Gideon smiled.

"Don't I know it," he agreed.

"She takes after me," Lucia piped in. Gideon rolled his eyes…but Bella ignored both of them. For Grandpa's face had lit up instantly upon seeing her, and he shot up from his chair, rushing up to her and giving her a big bear hug.

"Sweetheart!" he cried, lifting her up and twirling her around.

"Grandpa!" Bella gushed, hugging him back. He set her down, beaming at her from behind his golden eyeglasses.

"My Bella," he breathed, holding her at arms' length and shaking his head in wonderment. His brown eyes twinkled…and grew a bit moist. "I was worried sick I'd never see you again!"

"Thanks for the vote of confidence," Nemesis quipped. Grandpa, of course, had the good sense to ignore her.

"I'm so proud of you," he told Bella.

"I had a lot of help," Bella countered. Then her lower lip quivered, and she dropped her gaze to her feet. "Simon, he…didn't make it."

"Oh no," Grandpa blurted out. "I'm so sorry Bella," he said, hugging her close and rubbing her back. "I know how much he meant to you."

She buried her face in his shoulder, his comfy sweater absorbing her tears. But she was too exhausted to cry much. It'd been a long, long day…and she'd barely slept the night before. Suddenly she wanted nothing more than to be in her bed, to snuggle under warm covers and nuzzle into her pillow. To let the whole day just fade away into sleep.

"I'm sorry Bella," Kanja offered from behind, putting a hand on Bella's shoulder. "He was a good person."

Bella pulled away from Grandpa then, wiping away the last of her tears.

"He was," she agreed.

Grandpa gave her a sad smile, running a hand through her long curly hair.

"You're the one who gave him the permission to be," he told her.

"To be what?"

"Good," he clarified. Bella gave him a look.

"I don't know about *that*," she mumbled.

"I do," Grandpa replied with a wink. "He's the one who told me, before you left the castle."

Bella blinked, feeling a chill run through her.

"Really?" she asked.

"Really," Grandpa answered. "He told me to tell you, in case he…you know."

Bella nodded, feeling a fresh wave of tears coming. Grandpa embraced her again, and she closed her eyes for a bit, letting the tears trickle down her cheeks.

"There there," Grandpa soothed. "It'll be alright sweetheart."

"No," she muttered miserably. "It won't."

"It won't be the same," Grandpa conceded. "But every wave has its crest and its trough. And the deepest, darkest part of the trough is where the crest begins."

She sighed, pulling away from him.

"You always did have a way with words," she told him. He smiled.

"And you have a way with hearts," he replied. "I daresay yours is the greater power."

Bella smiled despite herself.

"I love you Grandpa."

"And I love you," he replied. Then he cleared his throat, putting his hands on his hips. "Well now, seeing as how we have the family back together, I'd say it's high time we went back home."

"Home?" Bella asked. "We are home."

Grandpa gave her a sour look.

"This place? Gah!" he exclaimed. "Dark! Dull! Depressing!"

"Delightful," Lucia added.

"It won't do," Grandpa proclaimed. "Not for me, and not for the brighter part of you," he added, gesturing at Bella.

"Grandpa, there's no other place for us to go," Bella pointed out. "This is the safest place for us right now."

"Poppycock!" Grandpa exclaimed, crossing his arms over his chest rather imperiously. "I squirreled you away in that dreadful book for ten years in the name of safety. I'd rather live dangerously than die safely!"

"Thaddeus…" Gideon began, but Grandpa cut him off with a gesture and a glare.

"Come with me everyone," he commanded, marching right out of the suite.

"Where are you…" Bella began. He whirled around, gazing down at her with a gleam in his eye.

"Trust me Bella," he insisted. "That's all I ask."

Bella hesitated…then sighed.

"Okay Grandpa," she decided.

"Promise?" he pressed with a wink. She nodded, knowing that it was precisely the exchange they'd had long ago, back in the old apartment. When he'd asked her to trust him about his seemingly paranoid delusions. All of which, naturally, had proven true.

"I promise."

He smiled, clearly relieved. For they both knew it was exceedingly rare for Bella to make a promise, as she made them only when absolutely certain she could keep them.

"Do try to keep up," he stated. Then he turned about, guiding them out of the dormitories, toward only *he* knew what.

Chapter 45

So it was that Bella found herself following Grandpa out of Castle Under, across the great lake, into the Underground…and to a familiar door therein, bringing them to rolling hills a good twenty miles away from the place where this particular story had begun.

Havenwood.

And though everyone offered their various proclamations as to why it was a terrible idea to go back to this ruined place, Grandpa would have none of it. He merely continued onward, remarkably spry since being given his fresh coat of paint. And everyone, loving him and wishing to protect him even from himself, was forced to follow to do just that.

As they approached Dragon's Peak, Bella spotted a literal army of Dragonkin flying around it…along with something else. What appeared to be a vast moat before the mushroom forest that surrounded the base of the mountain. A lake whose surface was utterly, perfectly smooth, reflecting the brilliant blue late afternoon sky high above.

Grandpa led them right up to it, stopping at its shore. Everyone stopped beside him.

"What is this?" Gideon asked.

"I don't rightly know," Grandpa confessed.

Bella frowned, then knelt down, dipping her fingers in the water. But to her surprise, they went right into it…without any feeling of wetness at all. Her frown deepened, and she stood, staring at it for a while.

Then she had a hunch.

"Show me what you are," she requested.

The lake *shattered.*

Billions of glittering fragments shot up from the surface, coalescing into an enormous number of Gemini. Millions of them, surrounding Dragon's Peak. They all turned as one to face Bella, then knelt before her.

Everyone gasped.

The Gemini closest to her pulled a piece of itself free, a small mirrored shard. He offered it to her.

A chill went down her spine, and she swallowed past a sudden lump in her throat.

Simon did this.

The thought that he'd given her this last gift…a gift beyond the grave…filled her with emotion, and she stood there, overwhelmed by the gesture. Blinking away years, she accepted the shard.

"Thank you," she told the Gemini.

Every one of them stood, awaiting her command.

"Can we get through?" she asked.

The vast army parted before her, forming a long path into Havenwood.

Bella felt a hand on her shoulder, and saw Gideon smiling at her. She smiled back, giving him a silent nod.

"Okay Grandpa," she prompted. "Lead the way."

Grandpa did just that, leading them through the great sea of mirrored soldiers, glittering like so many diamonds in the sun. Eventually they made it to the mushroom forest. Bella was surprised to discover that, amongst the burnt, broken stalks, cute little baby mushrooms were emerging from the charred soil.

"The Dark Circle," Bella murmured. From death, life.

Like with Simon.

"Now you're getting it," Mom observed.

But instead of going through the mushroom forest toward Dragon's Peak, Grandpa took them around the perimeter of the healing forest. Eventually, Bella spotted something ahead.

The White Dragon.

It was lying there where it'd been the last time she'd seen it, its enormous head separated from its long neck, its wings amputated. An absolutely enormous number of flies were covering it like a second skin, the sound of their buzzing so loud it was practically deafening. And the smell…

It was gag-inducingly *awful.*

"Ugh," Bella blurted out, pinching her nose and gagging a bit as they approached. She stopped. "That's close enough for me," she announced.

"No no," Grandpa declared, forging onward despite the stench. Flies buzzed all around him in a dense cloud. "Come on, I want to show you something."

"Seen enough," Bella replied, staying right where she was. Grandpa stopped, glancing at Gideon.

"Can you remove these flies?" he inquired.

"Of course," Gideon replied. "Gather around me," he requested. Everyone did so, and Gideon retrieved his magical lantern from his chest-painting, holding it out. "Eruptus!" he incanted.

An explosion of light shot outward in all directions, sparing them of course. The shockwave rippled across the landscape, doing nothing to the White Dragon…but blasting the flies right off of its head, which was closest to them.

"Ah," Grandpa declared, beaming a smile at the dragon. "That's better."

He led them forward then, all the way up to the White Dragon's corpse, stopping at the head. It was resting on its side, and Grandpa stepped up to its huge nose, resting a palm on the thick white armored plates covering it. The dragon's scales and natural armor had not decomposed at all, of course.

Grandpa studied the dragon with a wistful look in his eyes. Bella immediately felt a pang of guilt.

"Sorry Grandpa," she told him.

"I'm not," he replied, smiling at the dragon. "He did what I created him to do."

"But Havenwood is destroyed," she protested.

"And my family lives," Grandpa pointed out. "Home is where you are, Bella. Home is family, whoever you wish them to be."

"I know," Bella said. "But I still feel terrible."

"I understand," he replied. Then he sighed. "I wrote The Magic of Havenwood for your mother, as a place that would protect her from the Pentad. I think I felt awful that I'd failed to protect her mother, and was desperate to make it up to her."

Mom put a hand on Grandpa's shoulder, and he patted it, gazing sadly at her.

"I also wrote it because on the day your mother was murdered, Lucia, I lost you…and you lost yourself. Your innocence, your joy. All of the light and color in you was taken out."

Mom lowered her gaze, uncharacteristically subdued.

"So I wrote The Magic of Havenwood," he continued, gesturing at Dragon's Peak in the distance. "A place where light and color abounded, where the innocence of childhood could thrive, protected from the dark forces of the world. But also a place that would hold and protect the darkness that you'd become. The fascination with death that your mother's murder bestowed upon you."

"My mansion," Mom realized.

"That's right," Grandpa confirmed with a smile. "I spent so much time when you were young trying to protect you from that darkness. From the consequences of my failure to protect us. I should have let you explore it. I should have let you have it and process it and accept it instead of trying desperately to drive it from you. That's why I drove you away."

"I was also a little bitch," Mom admitted. Grandpa chuckled.

"That too," he agreed. "In any case, Havenwood was my answer. My gift to you, and to those who wished to live in peace and innocence, protected from the Pentad, Epirus…anyone who would try to threaten them with violence and control."

"That turned out great," Mom grumbled. "All those useless artists, refusing to lift a finger to help themselves. Expecting us to do everything."

"True," Grandpa admitted with a sigh. "And that is also my failure. That in trying to protect people from darkness, they develop no defenses against it themselves." He shook his head ruefully. "As a Writer, I should have known better. Without undertaking their Hero's Journey, the dependent are doomed to remain so."

"Mine was becoming a Necromancer," Mom stated.

"A badass assassin-Necromancer-Painter," Nemesis corrected.

"Damn right," Mom agreed.

"And I tried to save you from that," Grandpa confessed. "I should have supported you."

"You're making up for it," she replied with a smirk. "Got a ways to go though."

Grandpa nodded, turning to gaze at the body of the fallen White Dragon. He went silent for a while, and had such a philosophical expression that no one dared interrupt it. At long last, he stirred.

"Stories are funny things," he mused, sliding his fingertips down the White Dragon's armored nose. A single scale was many times his size. "There's no magic to a story by itself," he continued. "Only when a reader reads it."

He turned to Bella.

"Do you know what that means?" he asked. She shook her head. "It means that books are the only magical art that requires others to create," he explained. "The Writer only creates part of the story…the reader fills in the rest."

"Huh," Bella murmured. She hadn't thought of it that way.

"And *that* means that everyone who reads these books has magic," Grandpa reasoned. "The power to create all of this," he added, gesturing at the White Dragon, then Dragon's Peak. "Using the magic of their imaginations. After all, I didn't make this real," he added. "My readers did."

He smiled to himself.

"Reading proves that everyone has magic," he mused. "Perhaps our imaginations are a magical art in and of themselves. Magical parts of our souls that only each person themselves can experience…unless they have the power to express it."

"Introspection, then expression," Bella recited, feeling a little chill run through her. Grandpa frowned.

"Hmm?" he asked.

"Something Simon told me once."

"Hmm," Gideon replied, rubbing his chin thoughtfully.

"Grandpa," Bella protested, still holding her nose against the stench of decay. "Can we please have this conversation somewhere else?"

"I think not," Grandpa replied evenly. "I have a point to get to."

"Can you get to it a little faster?" she pressed.

"Oh very well then," he grumbled. He eyed the White Dragon, then turned to regard Bella with a mischievous gleam in his eyes. "Bella, do you remember our old apartment, back in that awful book?"

"The Chronicles of Collins Dansworth," Bella recalled, giving him a rather disgusted look. And not just because of the stench.

"Indeed," Grandpa agreed. "We used to have a ritual, you and I. Something you always did to go home. Do you remember what it was?"

"Of course," Bella answered. She'd done it every day for nearly a decade, after all. "How could I forget? Thirteen knocks, wait thirty-three seconds, then seven more knocks."

"Correct," Grandpa replied. Mom frowned.

"Seven for when I first felt the Flow," she realized. "Thirteen is when my mother died…and I started as an apprentice under Gideon."

"And twenty years before being under me made *her*," Gideon quipped, waggling his eyebrows at Bella.

"At the age of thirty-three," Mom concluded.

"So gross," Bella muttered, lowering her face to her hands and only half-pretending to gag.

"Also correct," Grandpa confirmed. "And a bit too much information," he added with a grimace. Gideon chuckled. "In any case, it's no accident that the code started with death and ended with life," Grandpa revealed.

"Why?" Bella asked.

"Because it helped remind me that every beginning has an end…and every end a new beginning."

Bella smiled despite herself.

"There you go, being all mysterious again," she mused.

"I'm a writer," he replied matter-of-factly. "It's what we do."

He turned to the White Dragon then, his expression turning grave.

"I knew when I wrote 'The Magic of Havenwood' that the Pentad would one day decide to destroy it," he confessed. "Tyrants cannot tolerate a place free from tyranny. If people saw that they could be trusted to govern themselves, they wouldn't need tyrants anymore."

Bella glanced at Gideon, seeing him nodding in agreement.

"Every beginning has an end, and every end a new beginning," Grandpa repeated. And then he recited the following, his powerful voice booming:

"A dragon circle,
White and good,
Will *this* day rise
For Havenwood!"

Goosebumps rose on Bella's arms…and then it happened.

The White Dragon's head moved.

It rolled slowly, tilting away from them. Grandpa hurried backward, and everyone else followed suit, putting a considerable distance between themselves and the rolling giant. And at the same time as it rolled, the head slid backward, making a huge gouge in the earth as it did so. Backward it went, sliding toward its neck…until it reconnected.

"Oh my…!" Bella gasped.

The flesh there knitted together, and then the White Dragon's enormous wings lifted from the blasted plains from far away. They went right to the stumps they'd been severed from, fusing there.

Then, before Bella's very eyes, the White Dragon's eyes opened, and it drew in a great, deep breath.

"Grandpa!" Bella cried, grabbing his arm and bursting out in joyous laughter. She gazed at the dragon in sheer wonder, feeling as if she were floating on air.

And then, whole once more through the magic of Havenwood, the great White Dragon did indeed rise. And as it did, so too was the dragon's magic that Havenwood could not fall whilst it was alive. Thus, before the eyes of Bella and all her family, the White Dragon lifted itself so that its great head loomed over the peak of Dragon's Peak, its eyes on the remains of the castle it was sworn to protect.

Its eyes flashed with the light of twin suns, and in that moment, Havenwood's end ushered in a new beginning. For the great white castle, through the power of its guardian, rose as well.

Like a phoenix rising from the ashes, Castle Havenwood was resurrected. And as Bella beheld it, she felt as if a great light had been shone on the darkness in her soul.

She thought back to Simon then…and his white suit Redeemer.

Whenever someone I love dies because of something I did or didn't do, it gives me a second chance to redeem myself.

Bella smiled, feeling a warmth around her, almost as if Simon himself was there, embracing her.

"My second chance," she murmured. The White Dragon was *her* redeemer. And if Simon could find redemption after all of the terrible things he'd been forced to do, then so could she.

Tears welled up in her eyes, the vision of Castle Havenwood blurring. For she understood then what Simon had really done. That what he'd felt might've felt a little like this.

She felt eyes upon her, and turned to see Gideon staring at her with a concerned look on his face.

"Are you okay?" he asked.

"Yes," she answered. "And no."

"What's wrong?"

"I screwed up," she answered. "And Simon's dead because of it."

"Maybe," Gideon replied.

"Gideon!" Mom chided.

"Maybe," he insisted. "And if so, it's not okay. It never will be. But a wise person once told me that it doesn't *have* to be okay," he continued with a wink. "That if you make a mistake – even a big one – that you can still come back from it."

Bella leaned her head against his shoulder, tears dripping down her cheeks.

"Everyone is the main character of their own story," Gideon recited. "And the story we tell ourselves *about* ourselves guides everything we do." He gazed down at her. "It was true for me. True for Simon…and it's true for you."

"Now you sound like Grandpa," Bella said, but not without a smile.

"I learned from the best," Gideon replied with a wink. Bella sighed, turning to embrace him.

"Love you Dad."

"You don't have to tell me," he replied, giving her a squeeze. "You've already shown me."

They held each other then, Bella, Mom, Dad, and Grandpa, Myko and Nemesis ever-faithful at their sides. Watching as the White Dragon lowered itself in a great circle around the kingdom of Havenwood, closing its eyes to rest. For its duty was done, and it would wait patiently until it was needed again.

So, past their ring of Gemini, ever-watchful, and within the dragon circle, white and good, Bella and her family circled up the spiraling street to near the top of Dragon's Peak, then circled down the great spiraling tunnel of the Water Dragon cave. To the underground mansion they went, their home in the heart of Havenwood…and a gateway to a second home for Bella and Mom, within the Dark Circle.

Chapter 46

Craven stood within the Heart of the Pentad, his gaze fixed on Queen Eldora. She was seated on a small stool in the middle of the chamber, facing away at a three-quarter's angle. Her long hair fell over her back, contrasting with her blood-red gown. And with her arms, so pale as to be almost utterly white. Her skin was slightly translucent, blue veins forming a web beneath her flesh.

He found himself staring, wondering how fragile that flesh was.

For the queen had always been, to him, someone of enormous power. Not only by virtue of the throne she sat upon, but a *personal* strength.

But now he found himself glancing down at the stump of his right wrist, at the jagged end where his hand had been hacked off. Then at her slender shoulders and neck. A neck that he could fit his hand around easily.

Again, he imagined himself squeezing it, her bones crumpling under his grasp.

"You wanted to see me, Craven?"

He blinked, lifting his gaze. She'd turned her head, and was staring at him with her crimson eyes. He felt immediate shame at his daydream…and a sudden pang of fear.

What if she could read his mind?

He had the sudden urge to hide his stump behind his back so that she couldn't see it. And though she was not looking at his mutilated limb, he knew that she must be judging it. And him.

"I…" he began. He sank to one knee then, bowing his head before her. "I wish to tender my resignation, Queen Eldora."

She gazed at him for a long while.

"Declined," she replied at last.

His brow furrowed.

"But…" he began. She stood in one fluid motion, so graceful and with such ease that it was like poetry. Not a single wasted movement, beautiful to behold.

No one moved like her, he realized. No one.

She glided forward, the edges of her crimson gown sliding across the floor, then stopped before him, gazing down at him.

"Get back on your feet," she ordered.

He obeyed, standing nearly twice as tall as she was. She was so small compared to him, a little bird of a thing. And yet she looked up at him, only a foot away, utterly at ease.

"Then have me destroyed," he requested. He lifted his stump, displaying it to her. "I am vulnerable," he added, his eyes drawn to the golden ring on her right ring finger. A serpent biting its own tail. "It can be done."

"Of course it can," she agreed.

"Then order it," he insisted.

"No."

"Why?" he demanded. The word came out far harsher than he'd meant it to, and his jaw snapped shut with a *click*. A fresh burst of fear struck him; he'd never spoken so brashly to the queen.

Suddenly he wanted to *force* her to destroy him. To give her no choice.

"Why do you want to be destroyed?" she shot back. Her tone, however, was implacably calm. Serene, even.

His jawline rippled.

"I failed you," he answered. "I failed the Pentad. I am insufficient."

"You did fail," she agreed.

"And now the enemy has escaped, and made fools of us all," he argued. "My failure will embolden our enemies and any artists who wish to follow in Gideon's footsteps."

"It will," she agreed.

"I cannot be trusted," he insisted. "I am too weak to be the right hand of the queen!"

She just looked up at him, her eyes unblinking. Utterly still, moving not a muscle.

"Anyone who sees me will know my failure," he pressed, displaying his stump again. "They will know the truth!"

"They will."

"Then let me resign!" he insisted. "Make another to replace me!"

"No."

"*Why*?" he snapped. And instantly regretted it. He took a step back, staring at her mutely. If he'd had blood, it would have drained from his face.

Yet still she merely stared at him.

"Why?" he repeated, more civilly this time. She lifted a hand, touching his stump gently with her fingertips. He resisted the urge to pull away.

"You tried," she answered. Then she smiled. "You did your best."

"And I failed."

"If I executed everyone who failed, I wouldn't have anyone left to govern," she reasoned.

"But I was made *not* to fail," he insisted.

"You were made to be strong," she countered, stroking his stump gently. "You were made to be dependable. You were made to believe in me."

She paused, eyeing him.

"Do you still believe in me, Craven?" she asked.

He froze.

Almost immediately, he tried to speak. To come up with an answer. But the words stuck in his throat. He recalled his previous vision, of him snapping her neck with one hand, and a chill ran down his spine.

It was too late to recover from this. She *knew*.

"I…I'm sorry," was all he could say.

She nodded.

"I know you are," she replied. "It's all right, Craven. You don't believe in yourself anymore. And you are my right hand, are you not?"

Craven hesitated.

"I was," he answered.

"You *are*," she insisted. "Until I tell you you're not."

He inclined his head.

"Yes, my queen."

"You've failed, and you've found your vulnerability," Eldora told him. "It's about time, really."

He gave her a questioning look.

"This is the beginning of your journey," she explained. "You'll live with your vulnerability and your failure. You'll learn from it. You'll learn about yourself." She smiled. "And I look forward to discovering who you really are."

"I am insufficient," he insisted.

"You are the same you you've always been," she corrected. "Nothing has changed except your self-perception. Yet now that you know your true self, you believe that who you are is no longer enough."

"It is not."

"Yet it was for a thousand years," she pointed out. "How is it that in your ignorance, you were sufficient, yet with wisdom, you are not?"

Craven swallowed, though he had no need of the bodily function.

"I'm ashamed of who I am," he confessed. "I'm ashamed of how I've spoken to you."

"Good," she replied. "You should be."

"A general should not speak to his queen this way," he insisted. She arched an eyebrow, gesturing at her throne at the far end of the Heart.

"Am I sitting on my throne?" she inquired.

He shook his head.

"I'll never punish you for doing your best," Eldora stated, "...and I'll never punish your loyalty. Give me these, and I will always have need of you."

Craven bowed his head, feeling a surge of emotion.

"Yes my queen," he murmured.

"That is all," she stated, withdrawing her hand from his stump. He lifted his gaze, staring at her, then at his ruined limb.

"A prosthesis," he requested. "May one be built for me?"

"No."

"But the public..." he began.

"Will believe what it believes," she interjected. "Do I look worried about what they believe?"

He paused.

"No."

"I assure you, if your injury emboldens my enemies, let them come for me," Eldora stated, her tone still gentle. "If I must, I will show them what I am capable of."

He nodded, struck with the sudden urge to ask her what she *was* capable of. For Eldora was a great mystery. Few ever got to meet her, and no one – not even he – truly *knew* her. Indeed, though he was a thousand years old, she'd been ancient even at his creation. Far older than all of the Lords, even Lord Merkel, who'd called her cousin.

But he did not ask. He could not.

"Go now," she requested. "Rest up, Craven. I will call for you soon enough."

"To apprehend Gideon?" he asked. She smiled.

"No," she replied.

"Every day he is free is a failure of justice," he pointed out. "Every day he lives is *my* failure."

"Yet you are my right hand, so the failure is mine," Eldora replied. "And I am content to live with it."

"But I must redeem myself," he insisted.

"Not in that way."

"It is the *only* way," he pressed.

"Find another."

He grimaced, his jawline rippling.

"I cannot."

"You haven't tried," she retorted. "Now go."

Craven hesitated, then bowed, more deeply than he normally did. Then he turned about, striding back to the gilded staircase leading forward and downward, back to the Locus Legis.

"And Craven?" he heard Eldora prompt.

He stopped, turning to face her.

"The first step toward redemption," she told him, "...is believing that you're worthy of it."

Craven lowered his gaze, then turned back to the staircase. Downward he went, through the long tunnel leading out of the Heart, his boots *thumping* as he descended. At length he reached the shimmering portal leading out of the queen's chambers, emerging into the Locus Legis. His home, just below the queen.

The home of justice.

He stepped up onto the great gold and crimson pedestal, turning to face the portal. His eyes always on the queen, even in Torpor. For she was the woman for whom he'd been created, carved out of a single block of Invictium. Nearly invincible. And though his right hand was no longer with him, he was still the right hand of the queen.

Fallible. Vulnerable. Filled with doubt, not only for himself, but for the woman who commanded him.

He remembered his terrible urges, when he'd contemplated harming her. Or even killing her. Not because he hated her, but because he needed to know.

That she was stronger than he. That she was truly what she seemed to be.

She'd been right, of course. Now that he doubted himself, he doubted her. He doubted *everything*. And yet that did not disturb her. That fact – that she was not alarmed – should have reassured him. For regardless of her physical strength, her wisdom was one thing he did not doubt.

Enough, he told himself.

Craven quieted his mind, relaxing into Torpor. And like a man sinking into the depths of a lake, descending into his own subconscious, his body went to sleep. First his feet, then his legs, all the way up to his belly and chest. Then his neck, and his jaw.

And finally, his head.

For Craven, Torpor was the little death, its end a kind of rebirth. And for the first time since his first battle with Gideon, he felt a spark of hope, that he might emerge to find himself reborn. And that when he was, he would venture out into the world as if for the first time, and begin the long journey toward finding himself.

Chapter 47

It was the peculiar habit of stories to travel not in a straight line, but in a circle. And while a circle possessed no real beginning or end, it was nevertheless true that one's story tended to end at its beginning.

Thus Bella found herself plodding up the staircase from her mother's foyer to the second floor of the subterranean mansion, the overstuffed duffel bag on her back threatening to pull her backward and send her tumbling down the stairs. But she hardly minded its weight, for it was Gideon's bag, containing most of his things…and helping him carry it fed her soul. After all, she loved to do kind things for those she loved, and knew that Gideon would do – and *had* done –anything and everything he could for her.

Besides, seeing as how she had hands and he did not, it was only right for her to have offered.

She trudged along until she'd reached the second-floor landing, continuing down the hallway and depositing Gideon's bag by his room. Then she went to another door nearby. A dull brown door, in fact, one that was usually closed. Stepping up to it, she smiled to herself, feeling rather playful.

She knocked precisely thirteen times, in the rhythm she'd long since memorized.

There was no answer.

She counted to herself, reaching thirty-three, then knocked again, seven times.

"Yes?" a deep, muffled voice inquired from beyond the door.

And then she recited the following passage:

> "A dragon circle,
> White and good,

Will one day rise
For Havenwood."

The door swung open, and Grandpa was there beyond it, peering down at her suspiciously.

"Did anyone follow you?" he demanded. She sighed, rolling her eyes as if she'd heard it a thousand times. Which she had, but not recently.

"I'm alone Grandpa," she replied with mock weariness. He broke out into a big smile, chuckling, then stepping forward to give her a hug.

"You've still got your sense of humor," he noted. "Brings back memories, doesn't it?"

"Yes Grandpa," Bella answered, smiling back. She gazed at him, feeling utterly happy in that moment. For while once Grandpa's back was bent with age, his beard and hair drained of color and his clothes ratty and worn, now everything about him was bursting with life.

"It wasn't all bad, was it," he mused. "Living in that dreadful apartment."

"It wasn't dreadful to me," Bella countered. "It had you in it, so it was my favorite place to be."

"Oho!" he exclaimed. "You've inherited my penchant for rhyming I see!"

Bella gave him a look; after all, he'd rhymed *her* rhyme. She had a suspicion that he didn't quite do it on purpose, however.

"Dinner's ready?" he inquired, rubbing his hands together rather hopefully, a gleam in his eyes. For he liked nothing better than having his meals with Bella. To feed his belly, but at the same time, his soul.

"It will be when you help me make it," she replied with a wink. He laughed.

"Lead the way, chef Bella!" he exclaimed, gesturing for her to do so. And do so she did, going down to her mother's kitchen. She grabbed a painting from the pantry – one she'd painted herself before her most recent adventure, and had planned on using the night Craven attacked – and propped it on the counter, pulling ingredients from it as they were needed. Grandpa, of course, could not retrieve anything from paintings, as that was the talent of Painters. But he could chop onions and such, and hand things to Bella when needed. So he did.

Together, they made Grandpa's favorite meal: chicken and bell-peppers with roasted garlic and caramelized onion. It was simple and delicious…but Bella knew full well that it wasn't merely its flavor that endeared it to Grandpa so. For as he'd taught her, meals – like any other art form – told a story.

And this particular meal told the story of the two of them, the best of friends, sitting at the tiny old table in their apartment night after night. A story of her love for him, and her desire to nourish him. So often when eating it, in all those years spent lost in a book, they hadn't said a word to each other. But her preparing the meal – and him devouring it – had itself said quite enough.

"Ooof," Grandpa complained, squeezing one eye shut as he diced the onion. Tears dripped down his cheeks.

"Want me to do it?" Bella asked.

"No no," he replied. "You've suffered enough for one day."

That, Bella knew, was an understatement.

"One of the numerous benefits of not having eyes," Cain noted from his perennial position at her hip. Both Bella and Grandpa chuckled. "If I had hands, I'd help," Cain added.

"Oh, Manus!" Bella exclaimed. She snapped her fingers, and a moment later, a slew of bony hands flew into the kitchen, floating at the ready. She pointed at the onions, then at Grandpa's knife, and one of the hands offered to take it from Grandpa.

"Oh," Grandpa murmured. "Why thank you."

He stepped back, and Manus diced the onions like a professional chef, making rapid work of it.

"Oh my," Grandpa exclaimed. "Isn't that handy!"

In no time at all, Manus finished, and Bella sent the floating army of hands back upstairs. She threw the onions on her pan with a satisfying sizzle, spreading them out evenly. The trial of the fire transformed the onion from something distasteful to a treat quite delightful, and it wasn't long before the meal was done. With Grandpa's help, Bella set the table, and Grandpa went eagerly to fetch everyone else. For he knew that he would not be allowed to eat until the whole family was present.

Not tonight, anyway.

Myko came first, his keen nose notifying him before Grandpa could. Then Gideon, then Nemesis. Then Kanja, and finally Mom, who once again was the last to the party, so to speak. They sat around the dining room table adjacent to the kitchen, and Bella served them each.

Then she sat down with them, smiling from ear to ear.

"Mmm, this smells *good*," Gideon exclaimed, digging in to his meal. Myko whined from his spot curled up on the floor by the table, and Bella gasped, leaping up from her chair and going back to the kitchen.

"Sorry Myko," she called out, grabbing a particularly large plate and lowering it to the floor by the great wolf's head. And though the food was steaming hot, he wolfed it down without a care. Another example of the Law of Unintended Consequences, Bella supposed. For Myko's behavior was guided by his unique magic in a way Gideon had almost certainly not anticipated. The worst part about burning one's mouth wasn't the burn itself, but the aftermath…and for Myko, the aftermath could be dashed away.

Bella sat back down to enjoy her own meal, though at a far more leisurely pace. For a while, the only sounds were the smacking of lips and the occasional compliment, followed by the inevitable lean-back, tummy rubs, and contented sighs all around.

"Well then," Grandpa declared happily. "That hit the spot!"

"Thank you Bella," Gideon offered.

"Grandpa helped," Bella replied. "He cut the onions."

"Thank you for your sacrifice," Gideon added gravely. Grandpa rolled his eyes.

"Of all the people here, my sacrifice was the least," he pointed out.

"I lost my head," Mom said.

"I lost my hands," Gideon added. "Thanks for painting them back on, darling," he told Mom. She gave him a little smile.

"I expect you to make good use of them later," she told him.

"Ugh," Bella blurted out, making a face. "Why, Mom? Just…why?"

Everyone laughed at that – except for Bella, and Mom's laugh was more of a cackle – and even Kanja joined in, eyeing Grandpa and even giving him a nudge with her elbow. Mom noticed, and eyed them suspiciously.

"You two still platonic?" she asked bluntly. Grandpa blushed, clearing his throat rather noisily. His mouth worked, but nothing came out.

"We'll be discussing that tonight," Kanja replied with a sly wink.

"Bet clay isn't the only thing that comes alive in a Sculptor's hands," Mom quipped. Bella gagged a bit, then glared at her mother.

"Really?" she exclaimed.

"Aww, my innocent little daughter," Mom mused. "You know, by the time *I* was sixteen…"

"Don't want to know," Bella interjected.

"Honestly, me neither," Gideon chimed in.

"Oho, this from the man who strayed from his marriage?" Mom exclaimed, eyeing Gideon. He froze, looking back at her with the guiltiest expression Bella had ever seen.

"I…um," he stammered.

"That little tart in the Twin Spires," Mom continued. "She held your hot little hands," she continued, arching one eyebrow. "Are you sure that's all she held?"

"Yes," Gideon insisted, looking rather relieved for some reason. Still, his face flushed spectacularly.

"Uh huh."

"Lucia…" he began.

"Kinda glad your hands got painted off," she mused, eyeing his new appendages. "At least *these* hands weren't the ones all over her."

"Lucia!" Gideon protested.

"Her name," Mom insisted, crossing her arms over her chest and eyeing him with a deadly serious expression. He eyed her suspiciously, then visibly deflated.

"You won't kill her?"

"Of course not," Mom answered. "Like I said, I just want to see what your taste in women is."

"Then look in a mirror," Gideon countered.

It was quite clear that Mom enjoyed *that* response. Still, she remained undeterred.

"Her *name*."

"Fine," he decided. "If you must know, it was Olivia. Olivia Perkins."

"Thank you," Mom told him, leaning over and giving him a peck on the cheek. She beamed a smile at him, then slid her chair back, standing up.

"Where are you going?" Grandpa inquired.

"I'm going to slit that little harlot's throat," Mom replied breezily. "I'll be back in an hour to tuck you in, pumpkin," she added, winking at Bella.

"Wash your hands after," Bella replied. "Don't want to get blood on my sheets."

"Honey!" Gideon cried in horror, bursting up from his seat and grabbing Mom's shoulders.

"Kidding," Mom said, sitting back down. Gideon sat down beside her, obviously relieved. "Still going to pay her a visit though."

"Don't scare her," Gideon warned.

"Mmmhmm."

Gideon groaned, burying his face in his hands.

"Well, it's been a long day," Mom declared, standing up from her chair again. "I'm going to turn in soon."

"Me too," Kanja agreed. The Sculptor stood as well, taking Mom's plate, and helping Bella and Grandpa clean up.

"By the way, what happened to Rodo?" Kanja asked Bella. Bella grimaced.

"Um…he didn't make it," she confessed. "I tried drawing him out from my canvas, but…"

"It's okay," Kanja reassured. "I was just curious."

Gideon rose from his chair to help them clean up, but Bella wouldn't have it.

"Then I suppose this is goodnight," he decided, leaning in to kiss her cheek. She hugged him back, kissing his cheek in turn, and then he left to go upstairs. After cleaning the dishes, everyone went upstairs, and Bella went to her bedroom, changing into her pajamas and flopping onto her bed. The instant her head struck her pillow, she felt her eyelids grow heavy. They would have closed if there hadn't been a knock on the door.

"Come in," she called out.

Grandpa stepped into the room, then got into bed beside her as per their nightly ritual, lying on top of the blanket. He gazed at her over his gold-rimmed glasses.

"Still want a story?" he asked. Bella smiled.

"Always."

With that, Grandpa spun a short tale so splendid that it brought Bella to tears, filled with peaks of ecstatic joy and valleys of danger and despair. He ended with the former rather than the latter, to Bella's relief, and after he was done, she regarded him with wonder.

"How do you *do* that?" she breathed. He chuckled.

"I think the same when I watch you and your parents paint," he confessed. "There's nothing more magical than the magic you can't do," he mused. "Without each other to be astounded by, how mundane life would be!"

Bella smiled at him.

"I love you Grandpa," she murmured, resting her head against his chest. His heart *thumped* against her ear like a clock, a *lub-dub* in lieu of a *tick-tock*.

"And I love you," he replied.

"More than anything in this world?" she inquired. He smiled.

"Or any other world, for that matter."

He kissed her forehead, then got up, walking to the door. He paused there, silhouetted against the light from the hallway, his golden glasses glinting. Then he closed the door, leaving Bella in darkness. She got comfortable in her bed, finding herself thinking about Grandpa's bedtime story. Much like the story of Simon's life, it had been short but sweet. A story filled with heartache and pain and wonder and joy. And in the end, peace.

For some reason, her mind went to "The Chronicles of Collins Dansworth," the dreadfully long and boring book she and Grandpa had been trapped in. It occurred to her that despite the formidable length of the story, compared to Simon's, there'd been far less of a story within it.

But she didn't have long to ponder this. For there came another knock on her door.

"Come in," Bella said.

Mom stepped into the room, sitting on the edge of the bed beside her, and put a hand on Bella's cheek.

"Hey pumpkin," she greeted.

"Hey you."

"Thanks for bringing me back to life," Mom offered.

"Wasn't me," Bella countered. "It was Lux."

"Half of you," Mom corrected with a smile. "By the way, now that you're an official member of the Dark Circle, you're going to need to come up with a code name."

"Like Calypso?"

"Something like that," Mom confirmed. Bella frowned, thinking it over.

"I think…I think I'll call myself Gemini," she decided. "In honor of Simon."

"Certainly fits," Mom agreed. Bella nodded.

"Hey…want to see what I learned to do?" she asked.

"Sure munchkin."

Bella focused inwardly, then relaxed, allowing the two parts of herself to separate. Lux and Luna, the twins that, together, were her. Luna melded with the shadows in the room, at least until Lux could get off the bed and go to the light by the open door.

"Hey, my necklace," Mom realized. For Lux still had it around her neck, the glowing will-o-wisp attracted to it an island of light within the darkness. "Give it," she ordered.

Lux obeyed, handing it to her. Which meant that will-o-wisp stayed with Mom, and Lux was banished to the hallway. Luna reappeared in bed, resisting Lux's draw.

"Now *you* I could get along with," Mom murmured, eyeing Luna.

"*Oh* yeah," Luna agreed with a mischievous grin.

Then she frowned, feeling something tickling the skin at her forearm. She pulled off her shadow-glove, and something crawled out from under her sleeve.

Something tiny…and green.

"What…?" Luna blurted out. She watched as it fell off her wrist, landing on her blanket. She promptly scrambled out of bed, going to the doorway and combining with Lux. Then she was Bella once again.

She turned on the light, then walked up to her bed, peering down at her blanket.

There, crawling like an inchworm atop it, was a tiny green blob.

Bella's eyes widened.

"Goo?!" she blurted out.

She reached down, probing it with her finger, and sure enough, the green glob crawled onto it. Bella lifted it close to her face, studying it intently.

"Goo, is that you?" she asked.

It raised the tiniest of proboscises, making a nodding gesture. Bella gasped, her eyes widening.

"Goo!" she cried joyously, her heart soaring. "You're alive!"

Another teeny tiny nod.

"How did you…?" she began. Then she stopped, remembering how Goo had brought Simon to Luna. How Simon had embraced her from behind, right before tearing off her uniform.

She looked down at Goo.

"Simon knew," she realized. "He knew you'd die, so he put a little bit of you on Luna, under her uniform."

Another nod.

It made complete sense, of course. Anything under Luna's shadow-uniform could travel with her when she melded with the shadows…and Simon had known that. Even in the very end, as he faced his own death, he'd thought of her.

Bella blinked back sudden tears.

Thank you, she whispered silently.

"I'm happy for you pumpkin," Mom told her, leaning in and kissing Bella's forehead. "He was a good kid, wasn't he?"

"Better than he gave himself credit for," Bella replied, lying back down on her bed. Goo started the long journey up her arm to her shoulder, resting there. She wondered how many times Simon had saved them, using his magical suit. How many times he'd been forced to watch them die. "He finally got to show the world who he really was."

"Instead of who they wanted him to be?"

"Yeah," Bella agreed. "Beauty in the darkest dark."

Mom nodded, running a hand over Bella's scalp.

"Ooo, scratches," Bella murmured, turning onto her side. Mom complied with her demands, giving her head scratches for quite a while. Until Bella's eyelids grew heavy, and threatened to close. Then Mom stood, gazing down at her daughter.

"Love you pumpkin," she murmured.

"Love you too, Mom."

With that, Mom left, closing the door behind her. Bella sighed contentedly, letting her eyes close at last…and then there were more scratches. Not on her scalp, but at the door.

"Come in Myko," she mumbled.

Sure enough, Myko nudged the door open, stepping into the room and kicking the door closed with a hind leg. He jumped up onto the bed, curling up behind Bella and draping a big paw over her, resting it on her chest. She snuggled back into him, even as he pulled her closer with his paw. It reminded her of the first time he'd held her so, way back in the Misty Marsh.

"Love you too Myko," she murmured.

Myko *wuffed.*

Then, surrounded by the great silver wolf who…

Bang!

Bella flinched, her eyes snapping open…just as her bedroom door did the same. Nemesis slithered into the room, shutting the door behind her with her tail.

"Jesus," Bella muttered, relaxing into her pillow again. "Ever hear of knocking?"

"Yeah, but I assumed it was a myth," the dragon replied. She paused, staring at Bella. "Is that…snot?" she asked, pointing at Bella's shoulder with a clawed finger.

"Yup," Bella replied. "With a capital 'S.'"

"Huh," Nemesis replied. "Thanks for saving all of our lives back there," she added, making it quite clear that the admission that Goo had done anything even remotely useful was terribly painful for her.

Goo jiggled, something Bella felt as a slight vibration on her shoulder.

"Gonna have to find some angry fruit flies for him to feed on," Nemesis quipped.

"Go to bed," Bella grumbled. Myko growled at the dragon, a deep rumbling in his chest.

"Ooo, scary," Nemesis muttered. Still, the surly dragon curled up on the floor beside the bed, resting her head under one wing.

Bella smiled, feeling quite snug in her bed, surrounded by her furry…and not so furry…friends. For while – like Simon and Gideon – she'd made terrible mistakes, causing pain and suffering to herself and others, she'd redeemed herself. And thanks to Simon and Goo and all the others, she had her second chance. To become the best version of herself by learning to forgive herself.

By having *empathy* for herself.

She remembered Grandpa's letter then, the one he'd left for her back in the apartment when she thought he'd been killed.

Love is something you give, as I gave mine to you.

Like Simon and Gideon, she'd come full circle, discovering herself through her art. Gideon through Xander, and Simon through Redeemer. Sure, there was darkness and light within her, but in reconciling these opposites instead of denying them – by giving love not just to others, but to herself – she'd healed her heart.

For it was the peculiar habit of stories to travel not in a straight line, but in a circle. And while the perimeter of a circle possessed no real beginning or end, it was nevertheless true that one's story tended to end at its beginning.

But as Bella knew full well, when it came to circles, for every end there was a new beginning. And while there was no hope for the past, for those who had the courage to find light in the darkest dark, there was always hope for the future.

Epilogue

Petrusa emerged from the foul, rotting stench of the Festering Wood, stepping onto the short green crabgrass of the wide lawn beyond. Flames from a firepit flickered in the distance, casting warm, shifting light on the small log cabin beyond. And above this was the dark veil of infinite space, countless stars twinkling there. Perhaps they were the eyes of the gods, ever-watching from their home in the cosmos. Or perhaps they were the light of God itself, peeking out of holes in that great black drapery.

She gazed at them, feeling as she always did when she came to this place. The mundanity of her world stripped away, its mysteries brought to the forefront of her attention. Crossing over into this space, she felt like a child again.

To a child, everything was mysterious…and mystery was where magic lived.

Petrusa continued forward toward the firepit, knowing full-well it'd been lit for her. She felt both giddy anticipation…and a trickle of fear.

She spotted a man seated at a chair before the firepit, his back to her. And, of course, a single empty chair placed next to him. She strode up to the empty chair, spotting a cup of tea set upon the rightmost armrest. Still steaming. She paused, then sat down, turning to look at the man seated beside her. A middle-aged man, his long red beard barely streaked with bits of gray. His bald pate reflected the light of the firepit, as did his eyes. He wore his usual gray shirt and pants, the same clothes he always wore. Indeed, everything about him was the same as it'd always been, as if no time at all had passed since the last time she'd seen him.

He was timeless. Eternal.

"Hello," she greeted, wrapping her fingers around her cup. Hot, but not so much as to burn her. The perfect temperature. As was the fire, giving just enough heat to counter the slight chill in the air. She wondered if that chill was intentional; the thought made her shift uneasily in her chair.

He said nothing, staring into the fire.

"I'm sorry," she apologized. "It's been a long time. Too long," she added. "I've been so busy that…"

She stopped herself with a grimace, knowing that she was blabbering. It was profoundly disconcerting, feeling like this. For in every other aspect of her life she was in complete control. She hated feeling this way…but he made her feel this way every time.

He stirred, taking a sip of his tea, still staring into the campfire. His eyes, she realized, were moist. His cheeks damp. She looked away, feeling embarrassed, and stared down at her cup instead. Picking it up, she sipped the hot tea.

It was bitter, she found. But with a sweet aftertaste.

She set the cup down, eyeing him. And waited.

Minutes passed, and he sipped his tea every once and a while. In the silence, Petrusa felt herself easing into the moment. Relaxing into the *now*. Her trepidation slowly faded, replaced by an inner quiet. She turned her attention away from him, gazing at the campfire. First the flames, ever-dancing. Then at their fuel, the logs in the firepit. They glowed with a beautiful red-orange light that peeked out from the crevices of their bark, little sparks flying upward into the air every once and a while.

How long had it been since she'd sat at a fire? How long since she'd sat and done nothing…nothing at all?

Petrusa felt herself melt into her chair, the rest of the world fading away. It was only her and the fire, and the tea.

"I missed this," she realized with sudden clarity. She turned, smiling at him. And put a hand on his shoulder. "I missed you."

He took a sip of his tea, then set it down, turning to gaze at her. But he didn't reply. Just looked at her, his expression utterly unreadable.

"I…" she stammered, swallowing past a sudden lump in her throat. She tried to withdraw her hand, but his hand was already on it, holding it gently but firmly to his shoulder.

"Enjoy both," he told her, breaking out into a sad smile. "While you have them."

Petrusa bit her lower lip, then nodded.

He let go of her hand, lifting his cup and taking another sip from it.

"Bittersweet," she murmured, doing the same. "Is that what seeing me feels like? Or is that what I'm feeling?" For everything he did had meaning, every taste, every scent. Every sight, every movement. Everything words in a story, strokes of color on a canvas. Every action and inaction like waves of sound – pressure and vacuum, presence and absence – from an orchestra.

Persnickity Gibbons *was* art.

"No," he answered.

She waited for him to elaborate, but he didn't.

"Are you mad at me?" she asked, feeling another burst of anxiety.

"No."

"Then what's wrong?" she pressed. He was unusually quiet, even for him. Subdued.

He sighed.

"Nothing can be wrong," he answered. "Everything is as it has to be." He paused. "I lost someone I loved," he confessed.

Petrusa blinked.

"Oh," she mumbled. "I'm sorry."

"That's what you're supposed to say, isn't it," he mused.

"I…"

"You think big," he interrupted, gazing up at the stars and gesturing at them. "You shine the light of your attention on so much!" He lowered his gaze to look at her. "But a beam of light spread so wide casts little light on any one thing, and so you remain in the dark."

She stared back at him, not quite knowing what to say.

"You and your sister," he mused with a little smile. "The bigger your lives become, the smaller everyone else's seem in comparison." He turned back to the firepit, sipping his tea. "Until they mean nothing at all."

"Grandad…" Petrusa began, but he stopped her with a gesture.

"Only an attack needs a defense," he told her.

Petrusa grimaced. He'd told her that countless times before, of course. Only an attack needs a defense, and Grandad didn't attack. Not anymore.

A lesson is not an attack, she recited. *But an attack can be a lesson.*

Her reaction – to defend her way of life – proved that she was not at peace with it.

Which, of course, was true.

She settled back into her chair, staring into the campfire along with him. Sipped her tea like him. And realized that she would be unpacking this evening for years to come, as she'd done with most of their previous meetings. Perhaps that's why she didn't visit more often; it took so long to process each meeting. She couldn't imagine spending every day with him…or imagine what that might do for her.

Or *to* her.

She felt his hand on hers then, and turned to see him smiling at her.

"I love you," he said.

Her lower lip began to quiver, and tears welled up in her eyes. She bit back a sob, desperately resisting the sudden surge of emotion, but Persnickity leaned over, embracing her.

She buried her face in his shoulder, crying uncontrollably. And after a moment, she stopped trying to control it. She let it happen, and it happened for a long, long while.

At length, it left of its own accord, and she felt peace.

Persnickity let go of her, leaning back in his chair and watching her.

"See?" he said. "You *do* have a heart."

She wiped the tears from her face, giving a bitter smile.

"It's colder than yours," she retorted. He chuckled.

"Always has been," he agreed. "That's who you are."

"I didn't ask for it."

"You didn't ask to live," he pointed out. "We are what we are. And I am me without apology."

"Yes, well, you have the warmest heart I've ever seen," she countered. "And you don't have to live with someone like *you* always making you feel…" She hesitated, searching for the right word. "Not enough."

"Why do I make you feel that way?"

"Because you're *you*," she answered, gesturing at him. "And I know I'll never be anywhere close to that."

"If you were," he replied with a twinkle in his eye, "…you wouldn't be you."

"Yes, well," Petrusa grumbled, shifting in her chair. "I also have to compare myself to my sister."

"Ah yes, that," Persnickity replied. "Funny that your body is warm and your heart is cold, and your sister's body is cold but her heart is warm."

"Funny?"

"The living ruling the dead and the dead ruling the living," he mused. Another chuckle. "And how the living struggle to truly live while they're alive!"

Petrusa considered this, remembering how she'd felt as she'd stepped out of the Festering Wood. How the world had gotten bigger. How her day-to-day had faded away, and she'd felt…like she did now. She'd spent the last near-century never allowing herself to be vulnerable. For she was Petrusa, president of the Guild of the Golden Coin, ruler of the Plane of Death.

"You and your sister lead bigger and bigger lives," Persnickity stated, "…while I make mine smaller and smaller."

"So other peoples' lives seem bigger?" Petrusa guessed. He nodded.

"To know someone, you can't be bigger than them," he explained. "And you have to be only you," he added. "No hierarchy, no title. No role to play." He pointed at her chest. "The difference between your heart and your role," he stated, "…is the source of your suffering. And your sister's."

"Our roles are important," she argued.

He just shrugged.

"They are," she insisted. "And I love my role. I'm drawn to it."

"And you suffer by having it," he replied. "Like your sister, with a heart so big she traps herself within it."

Petrusa gave a rueful smile at that.

"You always did have a way with words," she admitted.

"I have a way with everything," he replied.

That, Petrusa knew, was the truth. Not that Persnickity lied. He didn't need to. Lying was deception, a way to trick someone so you could get what you wanted. Persnickity wanted for nothing…and there was nothing anyone could give him that he couldn't give himself.

She slid her chair closer to his, until the armrests were touching, and leaned against him, wrapping an arm around his shoulders. He did the same, and she enjoyed his warmth, and the warmth of the fire.

"You're a good man, Grandad," she told him.

"Mmm," he murmured. "But if you consider everything I've chosen *not* to do, you'd think me the most god-awful villain you've ever met."

"You can't save everyone," she pointed out.

"I could do a lot more," he retorted. She frowned.

"So why don't you?"

He grabbed his cup, taking a sip of tea.

"I don't want to," he confessed. "I like people like this," he explained. "One at a time."

"Me too," she realized. "But I don't get to do it very often."

"You're a person and a role," he told her. "I gave up my role, so now I'm only a person. I'm quite simply *me.* And being simply me is the only way others will be able to be simply *them.*"

"Is that the secret?" she asked. "To being happy?"

"It's the secret to finding peace," he answered. "And to truly knowing yourself. And others, as much as one can."

"Hmm."

He eyed her with a mischievous twinkle in his eyes.

"Who knows you?" he asked. She paused, then gave him a smile.

"Only you," she answered.

"Then there it is," he concluded with a wink.

She sighed, facing the flames, which were starting to die out. Odd, that he chose to gather real wood for the fire, when he could simply make a fire that never went out. Logs that would burn without ever being consumed.

"I'd have to give up everything I've built," she realized.

"If you truly wanted to, you would," he countered.

"I don't want to," she admitted. "Peace isn't worth it."

"Yet," he added.

"Yet."

He smiled, patting the back of her hand.

"When you feel like making yourself smaller for a time, come visit," he counseled.

"Okay," she agreed.

"Will you be staying the night?" he inquired. Petrusa twisted around, looking through a window of the cabin. The bed in the makeshift loft was made, the blanket pulled back on one corner, as if inviting a guest to sleep there.

"It seems I will," she replied, turning forward again.

She took another sip of tea, which was getting cold. Bittersweet, but the sweetness more pronounced now. The sugar had settled to the bottom over time. She wondered suddenly if that too was intentional, and eyed him questioningly. But he'd turned away from her, staring into his teacup. His eyes were moist once again, like they'd been when she'd first sat down.

"What are you thinking?" she asked.

He swirled the last of his tea in his cup, staring into it silently for a long while. Then, at last, he spoke.

"I've been thinking about stories," he told her. When he didn't say more, she frowned.

"What about them?" she pressed.

"I told a friend not long ago that I like beginnings better," he explained. "So much mystery. So much potential!" He smiled then, a smile as bittersweet as his tea.

Petrusa nodded, watching him as he stared into the dying firepit, the flames having finally died out. Yet the embers still glowed with their orange-red light, lending their warmth to fight the chill of the night.

Persnickity stirred, looking down at his cup.

"But sometimes I find that the sweetest part of a story," he added, bringing the cup to his lips and drinking the last of his tea. "…is the end."

www.ingramcontent.com/pod-product-compliance
Lightning Source LLC
Chambersburg PA
CBHW030421310726
48979CB00009B/1564/J

* 9 7 8 1 9 4 8 4 9 7 0 8 4 *